"I Need A Wife."

Faith stared at him, apparently sure she hadn't heard him correctly. He couldn't blame her. As soon as the words were out, he'd decided he was crazy.

"You need *what?*"

"A wife." Stone could hear the impatience in his tone, and he forced himself to take deep, slow breaths. Calming breaths.

She spread her hands in confusion, and her smooth brow wrinkled in bewilderment. "But how can I help you with that? I doubt I know anyone who—"

"Faith." His deep voice stopped her tumbling words. "I'd like *you* to be my wife."

Her eyes widened. Her mouth formed a perfect "O" of surprise. She put a hand up and pointed at herself as if she needed confirmation that she hadn't lost her mind, and her lips soundlessly formed the word "Me?"

He nodded. "Yes. You."

Dear Reader,

Celebrate the rites of spring with six new passionate, powerful and provocative love stories from Silhouette Desire!

Reader favorite Anne Marie Winston's *Billionaire Bachelors: Stone*, our March MAN OF THE MONTH, is a classic marriage-of-convenience story, in which an overpowering attraction threatens a platonic arrangement. And don't miss the third title in Desire's glamorous in-line continuity DYNASTIES: THE CONNELLYS, *The Sheikh Takes a Bride* by Caroline Cross, as sparks fly between a sexy-as-sin sheikh and a feisty princess.

In *Wild About a Texan* by Jan Hudson, the heroine falls for a playboy millionaire with a dark secret. *Her Lone Star Protector* by Peggy Moreland continues the TEXAS CATTLEMAN'S CLUB: THE LAST BACHELOR series, as an unlikely love blossoms between a florist and a jaded private eye.

A night of passion produces major complications for a doctor and the social worker now carrying his child in *Dr. Destiny*, the final title in Kristi Gold's miniseries MARRYING AN M.D. And an ex-marine who discovers he's heir to a royal throne must choose between his kingdom and the woman he loves in Kathryn Jensen's *The Secret Prince*.

Kick back, relax and treat yourself to all six of these sexy new Desire romances!

Enjoy!

Joan Marlow Golan

Joan Marlow Golan
Senior Editor, Silhouette Desire

Please address questions and book requests to:
Silhouette Reader Service
U.S.: 3010 Walden Ave., P.O. Box 1325, Buffalo, NY 14269
Canadian: P.O. Box 609, Fort Erie, Ont. L2A 5X3

Billionaire Bachelors: Stone

ANNE MARIE WINSTON

Published by Silhouette Books
America's Publisher of Contemporary Romance

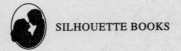

SILHOUETTE BOOKS

ISBN 0-373-76423-5

BILLIONAIRE BACHELORS: STONE

Copyright © 2002 by Anne Marie Rodgers

Visit Silhouette at www.eHarlequin.com

Printed in U.S.A.

Books by Anne Marie Winston

Silhouette Desire

Best Kept Secrets #742
Island Baby #770
Chance at a Lifetime #809
Unlikely Eden #827
Carolina on My Mind #845
Substitute Wife #863
Find Her, Keep Her #887
Rancher's Wife #936
Rancher's Baby #1031
Seducing the Proper Miss Miller #1155
*The Baby Consultant #1191
*Dedicated to Deirdre #1197
*The Bride Means Business #1204
Lovers' Reunion #1226
The Pregnant Princess #1268
Seduction, Cowboy Style #1287
Rancher's Proposition #1322
Tall, Dark & Western #1339
A Most Desirable M.D. #1371
Risqué Business #1407
Billionaire Bachelors: Ryan #1413
Billionaire Bachelors: Stone #1423

*Butler County Brides

ANNE MARIE WINSTON

RITA Award finalist and bestselling author Anne Marie Winston loves babies she can give back when they cry, animals in all shapes and sizes and just about anything that blooms. When she's not writing, she's chauffeuring children to various activities, trying *not* to eat chocolate or reading anything she can find. She will dance at the slightest provocation and weeds her gardens when she can't see the sun for the weeds anymore. You can learn more about Anne Marie's novels by visiting her Web site at www.annemariewinston.com.

To all the nurses at the Waynesboro Hospital who have shared my midnight vigils. My thanks do not begin to express my appreciation for your kindnesses.

Prologue

Smythe Corp. will be yours...on one condition." Eliza Smythe's eyes narrowed as she studied her only son.

Stone Lachlan stood with one arm negligently braced on the mantel above the marble fireplace in his mother's Park Avenue apartment in New York City. Not even the flicker of an eyelash betrayed any emotion. He wasn't about to let his mother know what her offer meant to him. Not until it was his and she couldn't take it away.

"And what might that condition be?" He lifted the crystal highball glass to his lips and drank, keeping the movement slow and lazy. Disinterested.

"You get married—"

"Married!" Stone nearly choked on the fine Scotch malt whiskey.

"And settle down," his mother added. "I want

grandchildren one of these days while I'm still young
enough to enjoy them.''

He set his glass on a nearby marble-topped table
with a snap. It took him a moment to push away the
hurtful memories of a small boy whose mother had
been too busy to bother with him. His mouth twisted
cynically. ''If you plan to devote yourself to grandchildren as totally as you did me, why are you planning to retire? It doesn't take much time to give a
nanny instructions once a week or so.''

His mother flinched. ''If it's any consolation to
you, I regret the way you were raised,'' she said, and
he could hear pain in her voice. ''If I had it to do
over...''

''If you had it to do over, you'd do exactly the
same thing,'' Stone interrupted her. The last thing he
needed was to have his mother pretending she cared.
''You'd immerse yourself in your family's company
until you'd dragged it back from the brink of bank-
ruptcy. And you'd keep on running it because you
were the only one left.''

His mother bowed her head, acknowledging the
truth of his words. ''Perhaps.'' Then she squared her
shoulders and he could see her shaking off the moment of emotion. Just as she'd shaken him off so
many times. ''So what's your decision? Do you accept my offer?''

''I'm thinking,'' he said coolly. ''You drive a hard
bargain. Why the wife?''

''It's time for you to think about heirs,'' his
mother said. ''You're nearly thirty years old. You'll
have responsibilities to both Smythe Corp. and Lachlan International and you should have children to follow in your footsteps.''

God, he wished she was kidding but he doubted his mother had ever seen the point of a joke in her entire life. A wife…? He didn't want to get married. Hadn't ever really been tempted, even. A shrink would have a field day with that sentiment, would probably pronounce him scarred by his childhood. But the truth, as Stone saw it, was simply that he didn't want to have to answer to anyone other than himself.

Where in hell was he going to get a wife, anyway? Oh, finding a woman to marry him would be easy. There were dozens of fresh young debutantes around looking for Mr. Rich and Right. The problem would be finding one he could stand for more than five minutes, one that wouldn't attempt to take him to the cleaners when the marriage ended. When the marriage ended…that was it! He'd make a temporary marriage, pay some willing woman a lump sum for the job of acting as his wife for a few weeks.

"Draw up the papers, Mother." His voice was clipped. "I'll find a wife."

"Which is why it's conditional."

That got his attention. "Conditional? What—you want final approval?" Another thought occurred to him. "Or you're giving me some time limit by which I have to tie the knot?"

Eliza shook her head. "The last thing I want you to do is rush into marriage. I'd rather you wait until you find the right woman. But at least now I know you'll be thinking about it. The condition is that once you marry, the marriage has to last for one year— with both of you living under the same roof—before the company becomes yours."

One year… His agile mind immediately saw the

fine print. He would find a bride, all right. And the minute the ink was dry on the contract with his mother, there would be a quiet annulment. A twinge of guilt pricked at his conscience but he shrugged it off. He didn't owe his mother *anything*. And it would serve her right for thinking she could manipulate his life this way.

He smiled, trying to mask his newfound satisfaction. "All right, Mother. You've got a deal. I find a bride, you give me your dearest possession."

Eliza stood, her motions jerky. "I know I haven't been much of a mother to you, Stone, but I do care. That's why I want you to start looking for a wife. Being single might seem appealing for a while, but it gets awfully lonely."

He shrugged negligently, letting the words hit him and bounce off. No way was he going to let her start tugging at his heartstrings after all this time. She was the one who had chosen to leave. "Whatever."

Eliza started for the door. "At least give it some thought." She sighed. "I never thought I'd say it, but I'm actually looking forward to having some free time."

"I never thought you'd say it, either." And he hadn't. His mother lived and breathed the company that had come to her on her father's death when she was barely twenty-five. She'd loved it far more than she had Stone or his father, as his dad had pointed out.

Smythe Corp. He'd resigned himself to waiting for years to inherit his mother's corporation. But he'd never stopped dreaming. Now he would be able to implement the plans he'd considered for years. He'd merge Smythe Corp. with Lachlan Enterprises, the company that had been his father's until his death eight years ago.

As his mother took her leave, he moved into his office, still thinking about finding the right woman to agree to what sounded like an insane idea. A temporary wife. Why not? Marriage, as far as he could tell, was a temporary institution anyway. One he had never planned to enter. But if marriage was what it took, then marriage was what his mother would get.

While he turned the problem over in his head, he thumbed through the day's mail. His hand slowed as he came to a plain brown envelope. In the envelope was the report he received quarterly, giving him updates on his ward, Faith Harrell.

Faith. She'd been a gawky twelve-year-old the first time he'd seen her. He'd been fresh out of college, and they both were reeling from the death of their two fathers in a boating accident a month earlier. He'd been absolutely stunned, he recalled, when Faith's mother had begged him to become her guardian.

A guardian...him? It sounded like something out of the last century. But he hadn't been able to refuse. Mrs. Harrell had multiple sclerosis. She feared the disease's advance. And worse, she'd been a quietly well-to-do socialite for her entire married life, pursuing genteel volunteer work and keeping her home a charming, comfortable refuge for her husband. She knew nothing of finances and the world of business. They'd been married for a long, long time before they'd had Faith and their world had revolved around her. His father would have wanted him to make sure Randall Harrell's family was taken care of.

And so Faith became his ward. He'd taken care of

her, and of her mother, in a far more tangible way
when he'd discovered the dismal state of Randall's
investments. The man had been on the brink of ruin.
Faith and her mother were practically penniless. And
so Stone had quietly directed all their bills to him
throughout the following years. He'd seen no reason
to distress the fragile widow with her situation, and
even less to burden a young girl with it. It was what
his father would have done, and it certainly wasn't
as if it imposed a financial strain on his own immense
resources.

Faith. Her name conjured up an image of a slender
schoolgirl in a neat uniform though he knew she
hadn't worn uniforms since leaving her boarding
school. It had been more than a year since he'd seen
her. She'd become a lovely young thing as she'd
grown up and she probably was even prettier now.
She would be finishing her junior year at college in
a few months. And though he hadn't seen her in person recently, he looked forward to reading the update
on her from the lawyer who had overseen the mon-
etary disbursements to Faith and her mother.

He slit the envelope absently as he returned to the
problem of where to find a temporary wife.

Five minutes later, he was rubbing the back of his
neck in frustration as he spoke to the man who provided the updates on Faith Harrell. "What do you
mean, she withdrew from school two weeks ago?"

One

A huge, hard hand clamped firmly about her wrist as Faith Harrell turned from the Carolina Herrerra display she was creating in the women's department of Saks Fifth Avenue.

"What in *hell* are you doing?" a deep, masculine voice growled.

Startled, Faith looked up. A long way up, into the furious face of Stone Lachlan. Her heart leaped, then began to tap-dance in her chest as pleasure rose so swiftly it nearly choked her. She hadn't seen Stone since he'd taken her out for lunch one day last year—he was the last person she had imagined meeting today! Her pulse had begun to race at the sound of his growling tones and she hoped he didn't feel it beneath his strong fingers.

"Hello," she said, smiling. "It's nice to see you, too."

He merely stared at her, one dark eyebrow rising. "I'm waiting for an explanation."

Stone was nearly ten years her senior. His father and hers had been best friends and she'd grown up visiting with Stone and his father occasionally, chasing the big boy who gave her piggyback rides and helped her dance by letting her stand on his feet. He'd been merely a pleasant, distant-relation sort of person until their fathers had died together in a squall off Martha's Vineyard eight years ago. Since then, Stone had been her guardian, making sure her mother's multiple sclerosis wasn't worsened by any sort of stress. Technically she supposed she still was his ward, despite the fact that she'd be twenty-one in November, just eight months away. And despite the additional fact that she was penniless and didn't need a guardian anyway.

Stone. Her stomach fluttered with nervous delight and she silently admonished herself to settle down and behave like an adult. She'd been terribly infatuated with him by the time she was a young teenager.

He'd teased her, told her jokes and tossed her in the air. And she'd been smitten with the fierce pain of unrequited love. Though she'd told herself it was just a crush and she'd outgrown him, her body's involuntary reactions to his nearness now called her a liar. *Ridiculous,* she told herself sternly. *You haven't seen the man in months. You barely know him.*

But Stone had kept tabs on her since their fathers' deaths, though his busy schedule apparently hadn't permitted him to visit often. He'd remembered her at Christmas and on her birthday, and she'd occasionally gotten postcards from wherever he happened to be in the world, quick pleasantries scrawled in a strong masculine hand. It hadn't been much, she supposed, but to a young girl at a quiet boarding school, it had been enough.

And she knew from comments he'd made in his infrequent letters that he had checked on her progress at boarding school and at college, which she'd attended for two and a half years.

Until she'd learned the truth.

The truth. Her pleasure in his appearance faded.

"I work here," she said quietly, gathering her dignity around her. She should be furious with Stone for what he'd done, but she couldn't stop herself from drinking in the sight of his large, dark-haired form, so enormous and out of place among the delicate, feminine clothing displays.

"You quit school," he said, his strong, tanned features dark with displeasure.

"I temporarily stopped taking classes," she corrected. "I hope to return part-time eventually." Then she remembered her shock and humiliation on the day she'd learned that Stone had paid for her education and every other single thing in her life since her father's death. "And in any case, I couldn't have stayed. I needed a job."

Stone went still, his fingers relaxing on her wrist although he didn't release her, and she sensed his sudden wariness. "Why do you say that?"

She shook the index finger of her free hand at him. "You know very well why, so don't pretend innocence." She surveyed him for a moment, unable to prevent the wry smile that tugged at her lips. "You'd never pull it off."

He didn't smile back. "Have lunch with me. I want to talk to you."

She thought for a moment. "About what?"

"Things," he said repressively. His blue eyes were dark and stormy and he took a moment to look at their surroundings. "You can't keep this up."

She smiled at his ill temper. "Of course I can. I'm not a millionaire, it helps to pay the rent." Then she remembered the money. "Actually, I want to talk to you, too."

"Good. Let's go." Stone started to tow her toward the escalator, but Faith stiffened her legs and resisted.

"Stone! I'm working. I can't just leave." She waved a hand toward the rear of the department. "Let me check with my supervisor and see what time I can take my lunch break."

He still held her wrist and she wondered if he could feel her pulse scramble beneath his fingers. He searched her face for a long moment before he nodded once, short and sharp. "All right. Hurry."

Faith turned and walked to the back of the store at a ladylike pace. She refused to let Stone see how much his presence unsettled her. Memories ran through her head in a steady stream.

When he'd come to visit a few months after the funeral to help her mother tell her what they had decided, he'd been grieving, but even set in unsmiling severe lines, his face had been handsome. She'd been drawn even more than ever to his steady strength and charismatic presence. He talked about the friendship their fathers had shared since their days as fraternity brothers in college but she'd known even before he started to talk that he'd feel responsible for her. He was just that kind of man.

He intended to continue to send her to a nearby private school in Massachusetts, he told her, and to make sure that her mother's care was uninterrupted and her days free of worry. And though she hadn't known it at the time, Stone had taken over the burden of those debts. At the time of his death, her father had been nearly insolvent.

"Faith!" One of the other saleswomen whispered at her as she rushed by. "Who is that gorgeous, gorgeous man standing over there? I saw you talking to him."

Faith threaded her way through the salespeople gathering in the aisle. "A family friend," she replied. Then she saw Doro, her manager. "What time will I have my break today?"

Doro's eyes were alive with the same avid curiosity dancing in the other womens' faces. "Does *he* want you to have lunch with him?"

Wordlessly Faith nodded.

"That's Stone Lachlan!" One of the other clerks rushed up, dramatically patting her chest. "Of the steel fortune Lachlans. And his mother is the CEO of Smythe Corp. Do you know how much he's worth?"

"Who cares?" asked another. "He could be penniless and I'd still follow him anywhere. What a total babe!"

"Sh-h-h." Doro hustled the others back to work. Then she turned back to Faith. "Go right now!" The manager all but took her by the shoulders and shoved her back in Stone's direction.

Faith was amused, but she understood Stone's potent appeal. Even if he hadn't been so good-looking, he exuded an aura of power that drew women irresistibly.

Quietly she gathered her purse and her long black

wool coat, still a necessity in New York City in March. Then she walked back to the front of the women's department where Stone waited. He put a hand beneath her elbow as he escorted her from the store and she shivered at the touch of his hard, warm fingers on the tender bare flesh of her neck as he helped her into her coat and gently drew her hair from beneath the collar.

He had a taxi waiting at the curb and after he'd handed her into the car, he took a seat at her side. "The Rainbow Room," he said to the driver.

Faith sat quietly, absorbing as much of the moment as she could. This could very well be the last time she ever shared a meal with him. Indeed, this could be the last time she ever saw him, she realized. He had taken her out to eat from time to time when she was younger and he'd come to visit her at school. She'd never known when he was going to show up and whisk her off for the afternoon—Lord, she'd lived for those visits. But she and Stone lived in different worlds now and it was unlikely their paths would cross.

At the restaurant, they were seated immediately. She sat quietly until Stone had ordered their meals. Then he squared his big shoulders, spearing her with an intense look. "You can't work as a shop girl."

"Why not? Millions of women do and it hasn't seemed to harm them." Faith toyed with her water glass, meeting his gaze. "Besides, I don't have a choice. You know as well as I do that I have no money."

He had the grace to look away. "You'd have been taken care of," he said gruffly.

"I know, and I appreciate that." She folded her

hands in her lap. "But I can't accept your charity. I'd like to know how much I owe you for everything you did in the past eight years—"

"I didn't ask you to pay me back." He leaned forward and she actually found herself shrinking back from the fierce scowl on his face.

"Nonetheless," she said as firmly as she could manage, given the way her stomach was quivering, "I intend to. It will take me some time, but if we draw up a schedule—"

"No."

"I beg your pardon?"

"I said no, you may not pay me back." His voice rose. "Dammit, Faith, your father would have done the same if I'd been in your shoes. I promised your mother I'd take care of you. She trusts me. Besides, it's an honor thing. I'm only doing what I know my father would have done."

"Ah, but your father didn't make risky investments that destroyed his fortune," she said, unable to prevent a hot wash of humiliation from warming her cheeks.

"He could have." Stone's chin jutted forward in a movement she recognized from the time he'd descended on the school to talk to her math teacher about giving her a failing grade on a test she'd been unable to take because she'd had pneumonia. "Besides," he said, "it's not as if it's made a big dent in my pocketbook. Last time I checked, there were a few million left."

She shook her head. "I still don't feel right about taking your money. Do you have any idea how I felt when I learned that you'd been paying my way for years?"

"How did you find out, anyway?" He ignored her question.

"In February I went to the bank to talk about my father's investments—I thought it would be good for me to start getting a handle on them since you'd no longer be responsible for me after my twenty-first birthday, which is coming up later this year. I assumed I'd take on responsibility for my mother's finances then, as well. That's when I learned that every item in my family's budget for *eight years* had been paid for by you." Despite her vow to remain calm, tears welled in her eyes. "I was appalled. Someone should have told me."

"And what good would that have done, other than to distress you needlessly?"

"I could have gotten a job right out of high school, begun to support myself."

"Faith," he said with ill-concealed impatience. "You were not quite thirteen years old when your father died. Do you really think I would have left you and your mother to struggle alone?"

"It wasn't your decision to make," she insisted with stubborn pride, swallowing the tears.

"It was," he said in a tone that brooked no opposition. "It *is*. Your mother appointed me your guardian. Besides, if you finish your education you'll be able to get a heck of a lot better job than working as a salesclerk at Saks."

"Does my mother know the truth?"

Stone shook his head. "She believes I oversee your investments and take care of the bills out of the income. Her doctors tell me stress is bad for MS patients. Why distress her needlessly?"

It made sense. And in an objective way, she admired his compassion. But it still horrified her to think of the money he'd spent.

The waiter returned then with their meal and the conversation paused until he'd set their entrées before them. They both were quiet for the next few moments.

Stone ate with deep concentration, his dark brows drawn together, obviously preoccupied with something.

She hated to be keeping him from something important but when she said as much, he replied, "You were the only thing on my agenda for today."

Really, there wasn't anything she could say in response to *that,* she thought, suppressing a smile. "Since that's the case," she finally said, "I'd really like to have an accounting of how much I owe you—"

"*Do not* ask me that one more time." Stone's deep voice vibrated with suppressed anger.

She gave up. If Stone wouldn't tell her, she could figure out a rough estimate, at least, by combining tuition fees with a living allowance. And she should be able to get a record of her mother's fees from her doctor. "I have to get back to work soon," she said in the coolest, most polite manner she could muster.

Stone's head came up; he eyed her expression. "Hell," he said. "You're already mad at me; I might as well get it all over with at once."

"I'd prefer that you don't swear in my presence." She lifted her chin. Then his words penetrated. "What do you mean?"

"You're not going back to work."

"Excuse me?" Her voice was frosty.

He hesitated. "I phrased that badly. I want you to quit work."

She stared at him. "Are you crazy? And live on what?"

He scowled. "I told you I'd take care of you."

"I can take care of myself. I won't always be a salesclerk. I'm taking night classes starting in the summer," she said. Despite her efforts to remain calm, her voice began to rise. "It's going to take longer this way but I'll finish."

"What are you studying?" His sudden capitulation wasn't expected.

She eyed him with suspicion. "Business administration and computer programming. I'd like to start my own business in Web design one of these days."

His eyebrows rose. "Ambitious."

"And necessary," she said. "Mama's getting worse. She's going to need 'round-the-clock care one of these days. I need to be able to provide the means for her to have it."

"You know I'll always take care of your mother."

"That's not the point!" She wanted to bang her head—or his—against the table in frustration.

"My father would have expected me to take care of you. *That's* the point." He calmly sat back against the banquette, unfazed by her aggravation, an elegant giant with the classic features of a Greek god, and she was struck again by how handsome he was. When they'd entered The Rainbow Room, she'd been aware of the ripple of feminine interest that his presence had attracted. She'd been ridiculously glad that she was wearing her black Donna Karan today. It might be a few years old but it was a gorgeous garment and she felt more confident simply slipping it on. Then she remembered that *his* money had paid for the dress, and her pleasure in her appearance drained away.

"I'm sure your father would be pleased that you've done your duty," she said with a note of asperity. "But we will *not* continue to accept your charity."

He grimaced. "Bullhead."

"Look who's talking." But she couldn't resist the gleam in his eye and she smiled back at him despite the gnawing feeling of humiliation that had been lodged in her belly since the day she'd found out she was essentially a pauper. "Now take me back to work. My lunch hour is almost over."

He heaved an impatient sigh. "This is against my better judgment."

She leaned forward, making her best effort to look intimidating. "Just think about how miserable I will make your life if you don't. I'm sure your judgment will improve quickly."

He shot her a quirky grin. "I'm shaking in my boots."

He didn't want to notice her.

She had been an unofficial little sister during his youth, and his responsibility since her father had died. She was ten years younger than he was. He was her guardian, for God's sake!

But as he handed her back into the car after their meal, his eye was caught by the slim length of her leg in the elegant high heels as she stepped in, by the way her simple dress hugged the taut curve of her thigh as she slid across the seat, by the soft press of pert young breasts against the fabric of the black coat as she reached for her seat belt.

He'd seen her standing in the store long before she had noticed him, her slender figure strikingly displayed in a black dress that, although it was perfectly discreet, clung to her in a way that made a man want to strip it off and slide his hands over the smooth curves beneath. Made *him* want to touch, to pull the pins out of her shining coil of pale hair and watch it slither down over her shoulders and breasts, to set his mouth to the pulse that beat just beneath the delicate skin along her white throat and taste—

Enough! *She's not for you.*

Grimly he dragged his mind back from the direction in which it wanted to stray.

He hated the idea of her wearing herself out hustling in retail for eight hours a day, and he figured he'd give it one more try. The only woman he'd ever known who really enjoyed working was his mother. Faith shouldn't be working herself into exhaustion. She should be gracing someone's home, casting her gentle influence around a man, making his life an easier place to be. He knew it was an archaic attitude and that most modern women would hit him over the head for voicing such a thought. But he'd lived a childhood without two parents because his own mother had put business before family. He *knew,* despite all the Superwoman claims of the feminist movement, that a woman couldn't do it all.

Diplomatically he only said, "Why don't you go back to school for the rest of the semester? Then this summer we can talk about you finding a job."

Her eyes grew dark and her delicate brows snapped together. "You will *not* give me money.

More money," she amended. "I'm not quitting work. I need the money. Besides, it's too late in the semester to reenroll. I've missed too much."

He looked across the car at her, seated decorously with her slender feet placed side by side, her hands folded in her lap and her back straight as a ramrod. Her hair was so fair it nearly had a silver sheen to it where the winter sun struck it, and her eyes were a pure lake-gray above the straight little nose. She had one of the most classically lovely faces he'd ever seen, and she looked far too fragile to be working so hard. The only thing that marred the picture of the perfect lady was the frown she was aiming his way. The contrast was adorable and he caught himself before he blurted out how beautiful she was in a snit.

Then he realized that beautiful or not, she was as intransigent as a mule who thought she was carrying too heavy a load. "All right," he said. "You can keep doing whatever you want. Within reason."

"Your definition of reason and mine could be quite different." Her tone was wry and her frown had relaxed. "Besides, in eight more months, you won't have any authority to tell me what to do. Why don't you start practicing now?"

He took a deep breath, refusing to snarl. He nearly told her that no matter how old she got she'd always be his responsibility, but the last thing he needed was for her to get her back up even more. Then he recalled the image of her stricken face, great gray eyes swimming with the tears she refused to give in to as she told him how she'd found out about her financial affairs, and he gentled his response to a more reasonable request. "Would you at least consider a different kind of job? Something that isn't so demanding?''

She was giving him another distinctly suspicious look. ''Maybe. But I won't quit today.''

He exhaled, a deep, exaggeratedly patient sigh. ''Of course not.''

When the taxi rolled to a stop in front of Saks, he took her elbow as she turned toward the door. ''Wait,'' he said before she could scramble out.

She turned back and looked at him, her gray eyes questioning.

''Have dinner with me tonight.''

Could her eyes get any wider? ''Dinner?''

He knew how she felt. He hadn't planned to ask her; the words had slipped out before he'd thought about them. Good Lord. ''Um, yes,'' he said, wondering if thirty was too early for the onset of senility. ''I'll pick you up. What's your address?''

She lived on the upper West Side, in a small apartment that would have been adequate for two. But he knew from the talk they had shared over lunch that she had at least two roommates from the names she'd mentioned.

''How many people do you live with?'' he asked dubiously, looking around as she unlocked the door and ushered him in.

''Three other girls,'' she answered. ''Two to each bedroom. Two of us work days and two work nights so it's rare that we're all here at the same time.''

Just then, a door opened and a girl in a black leotard and denim overalls came down the hall. Stone examined her with disbelief. She was a redhead, at least mostly. There was a blue streak boldly marching through the red near the left front side of her curly hair. She had a wide, friendly smile and green eyes that were sparkling with interest.

"Well, hey," she said. "Like, I hate to tell you, handsome, but you *so* do not fit in here."

He couldn't keep himself from returning the grin. "My Rolex gave me away?"

"Gretchen, this is Stone Lachlan," Faith said. "Stone, one of my roommates, Gretchen Vandreau."

"Pleased to meet you." Gretchen dropped a mock-curtsy, still beaming.

"You also, Miss Vandreau." He grinned again as her eyes widened.

"Are you—oh, wow, you are! *The* Lachlans." Her eyebrows shot up as she eyed Faith. "Where did you find him?"

"Actually I found her," Stone said. "Faith and I are old friends." He turned to Faith. "Are you ready?"

"Ready? Like, to go out?" Gretchen looked from one to the other with delight. "You go, girlfriend."

"It's not like *that*," she said to Gretchen.

"Depends on what *that* is," Stone inserted.

Faith turned and glared at him. "Stone—"

"Better hurry, I have reservations for eight." He felt an odd sense of panic as he gauged the mulish expression on her face. Was she having second thoughts? Was she going to back out? He had to battle the urge to simply pick her up and carry her back down to the car.

She retrieved a black cape from the small coat closet with her friend chattering along behind her. He stepped in to help her on with the garment, and they went out the door to the sound of Gretchen's enthusiastic, "Have a blast!"

He took her elbow and urged her into the elevator, conscious of a ridiculous sense of relief sweeping through him as they exited the cramped apartment. It was only that he felt it was his duty to take care of her, he assured himself. Faith didn't belong in a crowded apartment or behind a counter in a department store. Her family had intended that she be gently raised, probably with the idea that she'd marry a polite young man of the upper class one day and raise polite, well-mannered upper-class children. After all, she'd been sent to the best private schools, had learned the sometimes ridiculous rules that accompanied moving in society.

He wished the idea didn't fill him with such a sense of…unease. That was all it was. He wanted the best for her and it would be up to him to be sure any suitors were suitable.

He surveyed her covertly as they stood in the elevator, waiting for the ground floor. Her blond hair was smoothly swept back into a shining knot at the back of her head and the harsh lighting in the elevator made it gleam with silvery highlights. She was chewing on her bottom lip; he reached out and touched it with his index finger to get her to stop. Alarm bells went off in his head as a strange jolt of electric awareness shot through his body.

He stared down at her. She had her gaze fixed on the floor and he had to restrain himself from reaching for her chin and covering her lips with his own. What would she taste like?

Then he realized what he was thinking…totally

inappropriate thought to be having about a girl who was like his little sister. Again.

Little sister? Since when do you wonder how your little sister's curves would feel pressed up against you?

He almost growled aloud to banish his unruly thoughts and Faith's gray eyes flashed to his face with a wary look he thought was probably normally aimed at large predators.

"Something wrong?" he asked.

"No." Then she shook her head. "That's not true. Why are you doing this?"

He gazed calmly back at her. "Dinner, you mean?"

She nodded.

"I'm your guardian. It struck me today that I haven't done a very good job of it, either, so I thought we'd spend a little more time together. You can tell me more about your plans."

She nodded again, as if his explanation made sense.

The ride to the small, quiet Italian restaurant where he'd made reservations was a short one. As the maître d' showed them to their table, Faith caught his eye. As the man walked away, she whispered, "If this isn't a Mafia haven, I don't know what is!"

He chuckled, surprised she'd picked up on it. He'd been coming here for years—the food was reputed to be some of the best Northern Italian cuisine in the city. But the waiters, the bartender, certainly the man who appeared to be the owner greeting guests, had an air of authority, underlaid with an indefinable air of menace. "It's probably the safest place to be in Manhattan," he said.

Over dinner, he asked her questions about her interest in computers.

"I had a knack for it," she told him, "and I started helping out in the computer lab at school. It got so that the instructors were coming to me with questions about how to do things, and how to fix things they'd messed up. That led me into programming and eventually I set up the school's Web site. And once I did that, other people began to ask me to design their sites. It occurred to me that I could make a living doing something I really enjoy, so I decided on a double major in computers and business."

"You're planning to open your own company when you get your degree?"

She nodded, and her eyes shone with enthusiasm. "Eventually. I think I'd like the challenge. But I'll probably start at an established firm." She paused and her gaze grew speculative. "You had to take over Lachlan after your father passed away, and you've clearly been successful at it. You can give me some pointers."

He shrugged. Discussing business with Faith was hardly at the top of his list of things he wanted to do. "I'm sure you'll have no trouble."

Their dinners arrived and while they ate, he inquired about her mother's health.

"She isn't able to get around without using a motorized scooter now," she said, her face sobering. "She's sixty, and the disease has started to accelerate. Recently she's been having a lot of trouble with her vision. Some days are better than others. But it's only a matter of time before she needs live-in assistance or she has to go to some kind of assisted care facility. She wasn't happy that I'm working, either, but we're going to be facing some serious expenses one of these days.'' He could hear the frustration in her voice.

''She's only thinking of you,'' he said. ''She wants you to have the freedom and enjoy normal experiences for a young woman your age.''

Moments later, Faith excused herself from the table and made her way to the ladies' room. As he watched her walk across the room, he was struck again by her elegance and poise. Every man in the room watched her and he caught himself frowning at a few of them in warning.

That was ridiculous. He wasn't her keeper.

Well, in fact he supposed he was. But this wasn't the Dark Ages and she didn't need his permission to accept a suitor. Or a husband, for that matter.

He didn't like that thought. Not at all. Faith was still very young, and she fairly screamed, ''Innocent.'' She could easily be taken advantage of now that she wasn't in the somewhat protected environment of an all-girls' college. She was still his ward, though in her mind, at least, it was a mere technicality. In his, it was altogether different. He was supposed to take care of her. And he'd never forgive himself if she came to harm, even if it was only getting her heart broken by some cad. It frustrated the hell out of him that he wasn't going to be able to keep her safe.

Then the perfect solution to his frustration popped into his head. He could marry her!

Marry her? Was he insane? They were ten years apart in age, far more than that in experience. But, he decided, the kind of experience he was thinking of could play no part in a marriage with Faith. It would be strictly a platonic arrangement, he assured himself. Simply an arrangement that would help him achieve a goal and protect her at the same time. If she was married, Faith wouldn't be a target for trouble. In another year or so she'd be more worldly, and the best part was that he would be able to keep her safe during that time.

He was going to have to marry to satisfy his mother's conditions anyway. And if they married soon, as soon as possible, then he'd be only a year away from achieving the goal of which he'd dreamed for years. He would be able to merge Smythe Corp. and Lachlan Industries into one bigger and better entity.

Then he forgot about business as Faith appeared again. She walked toward him as if he'd called to her, and as she drew closer he could see her smiling at him. He smiled back, knowing that the other men in the place had to be envying him. Long and lean, she had a smooth, easy walk with a regal carriage that ensured instant attention when paired with that angelic face. He doubted she even realized it.

As she passed one of the waiters, the man flashed a white smile at her. She gave him a warm smile in return, and she had no idea that he'd turned to watch her back view as she continued on through the restaurant to their table.

And *that* was exactly why she needed his protection, Stone thought grimly. He stood as she arrived and walked around to settle her in her chair. She glanced up at him over her shoulder with the same sweet smile she'd just given the waiter, and he felt his gut clench in response. She was far too potent for her own good.

"So," he said, picking up his water and taking a healthy gulp, "while you were gone I was doing some thinking, and I have a proposition for you."

"A proposition?" Her eyes lit with interest. "Are we talking about a job here?"

"In a sense." He hesitated, then plunged ahead. "Are you serious about paying me back?"

"Yes," she said immediately.

God, he hadn't been this nervous since the first day he'd stood in front of the assembled employees of his father's company for the first time. "I could use your help with something," he said slowly.

Faith's gaze searched his expression, clearly looking for clues. "You need my help?"

He nodded. Then he took a deep breath and leaned forward. "I need a wife."

She stared at him, apparently sure she hadn't heard him correctly. He couldn't blame her. As soon as the words were out, he'd decided he was crazy. "You need *what?*"

"A wife." He could hear the embarrassment and impatience in his tone and he forced himself to take deep, slow breaths. Calming breaths.

She spread her hands in confusion and her smooth brow wrinkled in bewilderment. "But how can I help you with that? I doubt I know anyone who—"

"Faith." His deep voice stopped her tumbling words. "I'd like *you* to be my wife."

Her eyes widened. Her mouth formed a perfect O of surprise. She put a hand up and pointed to herself as if she needed confirmation that she hadn't lost her mind, and her lips soundlessly formed the word, "Me?"

He nodded, feeling an unaccustomed heat rising into his face. "Yes. You."

Two

Stone couldn't have shocked her more if he'd asked her to stand and start stripping. Faith stared at him, convinced he'd lost his mind.

"Not," he said hastily, "a *real* wife. Let me explain." He took a deep breath. He was looking down at his drink instead of at her, and she was surprised to see a dull bronze flush rising in his cheeks. "My mother is beginning to think about retirement. She's offered me her company, but before she'll turn it over she wants me to be married."

"Why would she do that?" She was completely baffled. What kind of mother would put her own child in a position like that?

"She thinks I need to settle down and give her some grandchildren." He snorted. "Although I can't imagine why. She's not exactly the most maternal person in the world."

She wondered if he heard the note of resentment and what else? Longing, perhaps, for something that hadn't been, in his voice. "Forcing you into marriage seems a little...extreme," she said carefully.

His face was grim. "My mother's a control freak. This is just one more little trick she's playing to try to arrange my life to suit herself." He bared his teeth in what she felt sure he thought was a smile. "So this time I intend to outfox her."

"What happens if you refuse to get married?"

He shrugged. "I guess she liquidates or sells. I didn't ask." He leaned forward, his eyes blazing a brilliant blue in the candlelight. "It would mean a lot to me, Faith. I want to keep Smythe Corp. a Lachlan holding."

"Why?"

He stared at her, clearly taken aback. "Why?" When she nodded, he sat back, as if to distance himself from the question. "Well, because it's a good business decision."

"But surely there are other companies out there that fit the bill. Why *this* company?"

"Because it's my heritage. My great-grandfather founded Smythe Corp. It would be a shame to see it pass out of the family."

There was something more there, she realized as she registered the tension in his posture, something she couldn't put her finger on, that underlay his stated reasons for wanting that particular company. But she had a feeling he wouldn't take kindly to being pushed any further.

"Will you do it?" he asked.

"I don't know." She chewed her lip. "It seems so dishonest—"

"Any less dishonest than trying to force me into marriage just because she's decreed it's time?" he demanded. For the first time, his control slipped and she caught a glimpse of the desperation lurking beneath his stoic facade. But he quickly controlled it, and when he spoke, his voice was calm again. "It would only be for a year," he said, "or a bit more. Strictly temporary. Strictly platonic. Except that we'd have to convince my mother that it's a real marriage. I'm not asking you to lie about anything that would hurt anyone." He stared deep into her eyes. "Think about that company, Faith. It's been in my family for three generations. If it's sold to an outsider, who knows what kind of restructuring might occur? Hundreds of people might lose their jobs."

She frowned at him. "That's emotional blackmail."

He grinned ruefully. "Did it work?"

She stared at him, her thoughts crashing over each other in chaotic patterns. "Would we live together?"

He nodded. "You'd have to move into my place for the duration. But we'd get an annulment when the time comes. And I'd expect to pay you for your time."

Pay you. She was almost ashamed of the mercenary thoughts that rushed through her head. Practical, she told herself, not mercenary. Not much. She couldn't possibly let him pay her. Not after all he'd done for her. This would be a good way to do something for him in return. Besides, if she moved in with him, she wouldn't have to keep renting her apartment.

She could go back to school, get a lot farther along in her education more quickly, if she didn't have living expenses. She only had a year and a half to go. Which meant that she'd be able to start repaying him sooner. Because regardless of what he said, she *was* going to pay back everything he'd done for her and her mother in the years since her father had died. And suddenly, that goal didn't seem so totally out of reach.

A profound relief washed over her and she closed her eyes for a moment.

"Are you all right?" He reached across the table and cupped her chin in his hand.

She swallowed, very aware of the warmth of his strong fingers on her skin. His touch sent small sizzling streamers of excitement coursing through her and she suppressed a shiver of longing. "Yes." But it came out a whisper. She cleared her throat. "But you can't pay me."

He released her chin, his brows snapping together. "Of course I'll—"

"No. I'm in your debt already."

"All right," he said promptly. "How about this: if you marry me for the time I need to get Smythe Corp., I'll consider all the debt you imagine you owe me to be paid in full."

She froze for a moment as hope blossomed. Then she realized she couldn't possibly make a deal like that. It wouldn't be fair to him. She started to shake her head, but before she could speak, Stone raised a hand.

"Hear me out. Marriage would be a sacrifice. You'd lose a year of your freedom. You'd be expected to attend social functions with me and play the part of hostess when we entertain. We'd have to convince my mother it was a real marriage for real reasons.''

She didn't ask what he meant, but she could feel a blush heating her own face now as she sat silently considering his proposal.

''It's a fair deal,'' he urged. ''An exchange of favors, if you like.''

She wasn't so sure of that. Taking care of her mother and her for eight years weighed a lot more on her scale than one measly year of marriage did. But when she met his gaze, she could see the iron determination there. If she didn't agree to this, he was liable to start in about paying her again.

And there was another factor, one that outweighed even her concerns about her finances. A moment ago, she'd seen naked panic in his eyes at the thought of losing that company. It wasn't financial, she was sure. But it was terribly important to Stone for some reason. And because she'd discerned that, she knew what her answer had to be.

''All right,'' she said hoarsely. ''It's a deal. But there are three conditions.''

He only raised one eyebrow.

''I'd like to continue with my education—''

''You don't need to finish school.'' Impatience quivered in every line of his big body. ''You'll be doing me an enormous favor with this marriage. The least I can do is settle a sum on you at the end of the year. You won't need to work at all.''

''I *want* to work,'' she insisted. ''And I want to go back to school.''

''You won't be able to work,'' he said. ''Can you imagine what the press would do with that?''

Unfortunately she could. As one of the richest men

in the country, Stone dealt with a ridiculous amount of intrusive press.

"You'd have to consider being my wife your job," he said. "But I'll pay your tuition if you insist on taking classes."

"I do," she said firmly. "I'll reenroll for the summer session."

"All right. Now what's the third thing?"

She hated that she had to ask him for help with anything, but she had no choice. And it wasn't for her. "My mother," she said quietly. "The cost of her care—"

"Is not a problem for me," he said firmly. Then he leaned forward. "In fact, if you like, we could move your mother into my home. There's an apartment on the main floor for live-in help but I've never had anyone live in. She could stay there."

It was a generous offer and a generous thought, even if he was doing it for selfish reasons. She swallowed, more tempted by the thought than she should be. It would make her life much easier in many ways. And she'd be able to see her mother every day, perhaps even help with her care

"Please," Stone said. "I'd really like you to do this, Faith."

She studied his handsome face, serious and unsmiling, his eyes intense with the force of his will and an odd feeling rippled through her. "All right," she said. Then she cleared her throat and spoke more firmly. "I'll marry you."

The next morning, Saturday, he picked her up in his silver Lexus and took her to his home so that she could see where she'd be living and check out the apartment for her mother. He'd asked her to stop working immediately, and though he could tell she didn't like it, she'd informed him when he picked her up that she was no longer employed.

"Don't think of it as unemployed," he advised. "You just switched jobs."

She was silent as he maneuvered the car through Manhattan's insanely crowded streets to the quieter area where he made his home.

He could see her chewing her lip as she had the night before and he wondered what she was thinking. Worrying, probably, about whether or not she'd made a bad decision.

As he braked for a light, he said, "Thank you. I know this isn't an easy thing for you to do." He put his hand over hers where it lay in her lap and squeezed. This time he was prepared for the sensation her soft flesh aroused. Or so he told himself. Still, the shock he'd absorbed when he'd touched her last night reverberated through him. All he'd done was place his hand beneath her chin, letting his fingers rest against the silken skin of her cheek.

He thought he'd steeled himself for the same reaction that had hit him yesterday when he'd touched her lip.

But he hadn't been prepared for the strong current of attraction that tore through him, making him want to deepen the skin-to-skin contact in a very basic way. It was as if she was a live circuit and touching her plugged him in to her special current. He mentally shook his head. What was he doing, asking the girl to live in his home? Putting temptation right under his nose probably wasn't the smartest thing he'd ever done.

Still, as he drew her from the car and took the elevator from the garage to his Fifth Avenue town house across from Central Park, he felt an immense relief. Faith had been sheltered her entire life. Who knew what kind of things might happen to a naive girl like her on her own? He'd promised his father's memory that he'd take care of Faith, and he would.

Unlocking the door, he ushered her into his home. Inside the door, Faith stopped in the large central foyer, looking around. Though she'd spent her early years in a family that wanted for little, he imagined that the place seemed luxurious compared to the seedy little apartment in which she was living. Looking at it through her eyes, he watched her as he realized he was holding his breath waiting for her reaction.

"This is lovely," she said quietly. "Simply lovely."

He smiled, relieved. Straight ahead of them, a hallway led to the back of the house while a staircase just to the right of the hall climbed graciously to a landing that led to an upper floor. To the left was a formal living room with an equally formal dining room through an archway behind it; to their right was Stone's office, with its masculine desk, lined shelves of books and office equipment that filled the surfaces of the built-in counters along one wall.

"I'm glad you like it." He stepped around her and indicated the stairs. "Would you like to see the upstairs? I'll show you your room."

She moved obediently in the direction he indicated, climbing the stairs as he followed. He took her down the hallway past an open set of double doors, pausing briefly to indicate the masculine-looking master suite done in striking shades of burgundy, black and gold. "That's my room." Turning, he pointed to the doors just opposite. "And across the hall is a guest suite. Your room will be the next one on the right. It should suit you. It belonged to my mother years ago and I've never changed it." He shook his head. "She may have her flaws but I can't fault her taste."

Leading her to her room, he pushed open both doors.

"Oh," she said on a sigh, "it's *perfect.*"

It was a charming, feminine suite decorated in soft lavenders and blues accented with pure white. Though it was slightly smaller than his, it was still spacious, with a walk-in closet, a sitting area and a large full bath. He walked past her into the bathroom. "Our rooms are connected," he told her, sliding back a large set of louvered doors to reveal his bath and bedroom beyond. "No one will have to know we don't share a room."

She couldn't look him in the eye. "All right," she said in a muffled tone.

"Faith." He waited patiently until finally, she gazed across the room at him. "This will be a good arrangement for both of us. I promise to respect your privacy."

She nodded. Her cheeks had grown pink and he knew that she understood that he was telling her, in as gentle a way as he could, that she had nothing to fear from him sexually. No, appealing as she might be, he had no intention of changing the platonic status of their relationship.

By the time they had finished the house tour, it was lunchtime. He'd decided to show her how it would be when they lived together so he took her into the kitchen and seated her on a stool at the large island while he made tuna salad, sliced tomatoes and piled the combination between two halves of a croissant with cheese. He grilled the sandwiches while he sliced up a fresh pineapple.

"I didn't expect you to know your way around a kitchen," she told him, filling two glasses with ice and water as he'd asked her to do.

He grinned. "Figured I'd have a chef on standby waiting to fulfill my every wish?"

"Something like that." She glanced up at him and smiled. "I can cook, although I'm no Julia Child. I'd be happy to do the cooking."

"Actually," he admitted, "I do have a woman who comes in Monday through Thursday unless I have to be away. Why don't we keep her for the time being until you see how much free time you're going to have?"

"I'll have free time from nine-to-five every day of the week," she said. "If there's anything I can help with, all you have to do is ask."

He couldn't imagine asking her to get involved in any of his business dealings except in a social fashion, and he had someone to clean the house, so he couldn't think of anything he'd want her to do. "You'll have studying to do as soon as the summer term starts," he said instead. "And you'll be able to spend some time with your mother."

She brightened, and he remembered her pleasure last night at the idea of spending time with her mother. It was ironic, really, that they both had been deprived of their mothers for part of their childhoods. The difference was, she looked forward to spending precious time with her mother while he went out of his way to avoid close contact with his. "That will be nice." Her light voice broke into the dark thought. "We haven't had a lot of time together since I went away to school."

Which was not long after the accident in which their fathers had died, he thought, as an awkward silence fell.

"Sometimes it doesn't seem possible that Daddy's been gone for eight years." Her voice, quiet and subdued, broke the moment.

A stab of grief sharper than any he'd allowed himself to feel in a long time pierced his heart. "I know what you mean. Sometimes I still expect mine to walk through the door."

Her gaze flew to his. "This was your childhood home?"

He nodded. "Dad and Mother lived here when they were first married. After the divorce, she moved out."

"That must have been hard," she offered. "How old were you?"

"Six. And no, it wasn't particularly hard." He willed away the memories of his youth, of the nights he'd spent crying into his pillow, wondering what he'd done to make his mother leave. Of the days he'd envied schoolmates who had had mothers who cared enough to show up for visitors' days and school plays, mothers who sat in the stands during baseball games and cheered, mothers who planned birthday parties and actually remembered cake and presents. "My mother was rarely here and when she was, she and Dad were shouting the walls down half the time."

The sympathy shining in her silvery eyes moved him more than he wanted to admit. "My childhood was just the opposite. Extremely quiet. My mother's illness was diagnosed when I was less than two years old, and my father and I did our best to keep her from getting upset about anything." She rested her elbows on the bar and crossed her arms. "In that respect, we have something in common. I went to my dad with my problems, because I couldn't go to my mother."

He smiled. "Did you know I used to go to the Mets games with your father and mine?" He shook his head. "Dad had great seats right along the third base line and we never missed a home game. Those two knew every player's stats going back to the beginning of time. And they used to argue about who the MVP was each season, who should go to the All-Star team, who ought to be traded...looking back, I think they just argued because it was fun."

Her eyes were crinkled in laughter. "I've never heard about this before." Her smile faded slightly, wobbled. "I guess you probably have a lot of memories of my father that I don't."

He hesitated, torn between lying to spare her feelings and telling her the truth. Truth won. "Yeah, I guess I do. Some of my best memories are of times I spent with my dad and yours. I'll tell you some more when we have time." He rose and took the lunch plates to the sink for the housekeeper. "This afternoon, I'd like to go pick out rings. Is that all right with you?"

Her gray eyes widened. "Rings? Is that really necessary?"

He nodded, a little disappointed that she didn't yet

seem to grasp the seriousness of his proposal. "Yes. This will be a real marriage, Faith." He almost reached for her shoulders, then stopped himself, remembering the desire that had knocked him over the last time he'd touched her. "Our reasons might be a little different from most people's but we'll be as legally wed as the next couple. So let's go get rings."

He called ahead, so that they would have some privacy while they shopped, and thirty minutes later, he handed her out of a cab in front of Tiffany & Company. Faith was a quiet presence at his side as they waited for the doors to be unlocked.

As they stepped into the cool hush of the store, a beaming saleswoman was upon them. "Welcome, Mr. Lachlan. It is Tiffany's pleasure and mine to serve you. How can we help you today?"

"Wedding rings," he said.

The woman's eyes widened as did those of the other employees ranged behind her, and he wondered how many minutes it would be until the press got wind of his marriage. He supposed he should warn Faith, though certainly she knew how ridiculously newsworthy his life was. Then he realized that they had better each tell their mothers about their plans before they read it in tomorrow's paper.

"We have a lovely selection right back here." The saleswoman had recovered quickly and was indicating that they should follow her.

Twenty minutes later, Faith was still perched on the edge of a comfortable chair, quietly staring at the array of precious stones scattered across the black velvet before her. She shook her head. "I couldn't possibly—"

From where he stood behind her, Stone said, "All

right. If you can't decide, I'll choose one." He knew she'd been going to say something ridiculous, like, "I couldn't possibly accept such an expensive ring when you've already done so much for me." It bothered him that the salespeople hovering around with their antennae primed for gossip would find rich pickings if they knew the truth about this marriage. Only, of course, because he couldn't risk having his mother find out. Of course.

He bent down to Faith and murmured in her ear. "Be careful what you say in here—it will get into the papers."

That startled her, he could tell by the way she jerked around and stared up at him, her face wearing an expression of shock. While she was still staring at him, he reached for a stunning square, brilliant-cut diamond ring with progressively smaller diamonds trailing down each side. It was set in platinum. He'd liked it the moment the woman had pulled it out of the case, and he suspected Faith liked it, too, from the way her eyes had caressed it. He lifted her left hand from her lap and immediately felt the tingling electricity that arced between them as their flesh connected. He took a deep breath and slipped the ring onto her third finger. There was just a hint of resistance at the knuckle before it slid smoothly into place and he quickly dropped her hand as if it burned. It was the same feeling he'd convinced himself he hadn't felt when he'd taken her chin in his hand, indeed when he touched her in any way.

"A perfect fit." He caught her gaze, forcing himself to behave as if nothing out of the ordinary had happened. "Do you like this one?"

"It's..." She shrugged, lifting dazed eyes to his. "It's beautiful," she whispered.

"Good." He studied the way her long, elegant fingers set off the ring, a deep satisfaction spreading through him. His ring. His wife. He was surprised at how much he liked the thought. Maybe this year wouldn't be such a trial at all, with Faith at his side. The more he thought about Faith and marriage, the better he realized his solution was. She could protest all she liked, but he would set up a trust fund for her and her mother so that once this arrangement ended she wouldn't be afraid of where her next meal would come from or how her mother's next medical bill would be paid.

He turned her hand and linked his fingers through hers. To the saleswoman, he said, "We'll take the matching wedding bands."

"Stone!"

"Faith!" he teased. "Did you think I was going to let you get away without a wedding band?"

The saleswoman had flown off in a twitter to get the proper ring sizes. He followed her across the room, catching her attention and motioning for quiet. "I'd also like the sapphire-and-diamond choker and matching earrings in the display window. But don't let my fiancée see them."

The woman's eyes got even wider. "Very good, Mr. Lachlan. And may I congratulate you on your engagement, sir."

"Thank you," he replied, resigned to the fact that tomorrow's paper would carry a mention of his upcoming wedding. His only consolation was that it would take them a day or two before they figured out who the bride-to-be was. "I'd like you to deliver the wedding rings and the sapphire set to my home. She'll wear the engagement ring."

He called his mother the moment they got back into a cab. She wasn't available so he told her assistant that he'd gotten engaged that afternoon and that he'd like her to come for dinner and meet his bride Saturday evening, and hung up.

Within thirty seconds, the cell phone rang. He chuckled as he punched the speaker button on the phone. "Hello, Mother."

"Was that a joke?" Eliza Smythe demanded.

"Not in the least." He kept his tone pleasant. "We'd like you to come to dinner tonight to make her acquaintance."

"So I don't know her?" The tone was exasperated.

"You know of her, I believe," he replied. "Faith Harrell. She's the daughter of—"

"Randall." His mother's tone was softer. "He was a good man. I was so sorry when he—good Lord!" she said suddenly. "Stone, that girl isn't even legal! Are you crazy?"

"Faith will be twenty-one this year," he said coolly.

"All right." Eliza Smythe changed tactics abruptly. "I'll come to dinner. I can't wait to meet Miss Harrell."

"She'll be Mrs. Lachlan soon," he reminded her. "Why don't we say seven o'clock? See you then."

She couldn't stop staring at the engagement ring. It was breathtaking, the central stone over three carats. He'd paid an obscene amount of money for it, she was sure, though no one on the Tiffany staff had been indiscreet enough to actually mention payment in front of her. She had noticed Stone placing a hasty phone call to his insurance agent, so at least if she left it lying in the ladies' room somewhere it would be covered.

Not that she ever intended to take it off her finger.

She was so preoccupied that when Stone opened the cab door and put a hand beneath her elbow, she looked up at him in confusion. "Where are we going now?"

"Shopping." He helped her from the car. "You probably need some things for the formal occasions we'll be going to from time to time. Next weekend, we'll attend a charity ball. That will give everyone an opportunity to hear about our marriage and gawk at you. After that, things should settle down."

A charity ball? She'd never had any experience with such things although her family had been modestly wealthy—unless you compared them to Stone, in which case they didn't even register on the personal fortune scale.

"Um, no, that would be fine," she said. "I suppose the sooner the news of this gets out, the sooner the fuss will die down."

He glanced down at her. "I'm sorry if the thought of the media unnerves you. I generally don't do much that excites them. This will make a splash but it'll fade the minute there's a scandal or someone bigger crosses their sights."

She shook her head, smiling at him pityingly. "You underestimate your appeal."

He grinned at her, so handsome and confident her heart skipped a beat. "You'll see." Then his face sobered. "I'd like to get married soon," he said.

"Well, it shouldn't take long to get things organized," she said. If the mere thought of marrying him unnerved her like this, how was she going to get through the real thing? "I'm assuming you don't want to make a fuss of this wedding so we probably could get it together in three months—"

"Faith."

She stopped.

"If I apply for the license tomorrow we could be married on Thursday or Friday."

She blinked, shook her head to clear her ears. "*Next* Friday?"

"Mmm-hmm."

"But how can we possibly...never mind." She smiled feebly. "I guess you have people who can arrange these things."

He nodded. "I do. Do you prefer a church or the courthouse?"

"Courthouse," she said hastily. Getting married in a church would feel sacrilegious, when they had no intention of honoring the vows they would be taking. A dull sense of disappointment spread through her, and she gave herself a mental shake.

"All right." As far as he was concerned, the matter appeared to be settled. "Then let's go get you a wedding dress."

"Oh, I don't need—" She felt as if she'd hopped a train only to find it racing along at top speed, skipping its regular stops.

"Yes," he said positively. "You do."

Shopping with Stone was an education. *More like a nightmare,* she thought, suppressing a smile as he fired orders at a salesperson. She tried repeatedly to tell him she didn't need all these clothes; he rolled right over her objections. She supposed she should be grateful for small mercies. At least he hadn't followed her into the dressing room or insisted she model for him.

He dragged her from one shop to the next. Neiman Marcus, Barney's, the new Celine flagship store. For day, a short black Prada, a Celine herringbone suit and a striking black-and-pink Cavalli blouse with Red Tape jeans. Everywhere they went, he was recognized sooner or later. She could tell exactly when it happened from the appraising looks that began to fly her way. For the first time, it occurred to her that marrying Stone might change her life forever. He was a public figure and without a doubt, she would become one for the duration of their marriage. But would she be able to resume her normal anonymous lifestyle after they parted?

"We'll take all three of those gowns she liked," he said, oblivious to the direction of her thoughts as he nodded at the fawning saleswomen.

"All three" included an Emanuel Ungaro seafoam-green silk mousseline wrap dress with a halter collar, no back and a slit clear up her thigh, a strapless Escada with a fitted, silver-embroidered bodice and a full, Cinderella-like skirt with tulle underlayers in silver and blue, and a classic black organza with laser-cut trim by Givenchy.

And there were shoes. Walter Steiger pumps for the day dresses. Sergio Rossi mules in black for the jeans. Silver heels from Ferretti, a pair of Jimmy Choo Swarovski crystal-and-satin slip-ons in the same soft green as one of the dresses. And for the classic black, equally classic open-toe Versace heels. All with matching bags.

It was mind-boggling, she thought, as he hustled her back into the car after the final store. When Stone made a decision, he didn't let time lapse before carrying out his plans. It might be something to remember.

It was actually a relief to see the sturdy stone facade of her soon-to-be residence appear. Stone's home overlooking Central Park was everything she'd expected the first time she'd seen it that morning. And more. Much more. Brass and glass. Modern cleverly blended with antique. Fresh flowers and thriving potted plants. Understated elegance.

At his direction, all of their recent purchases had been sent to his home since, as he pointed out, they'd simply have to move them again when she moved in. When they arrived, everything had been delivered and the housekeeper had it all piled in Faith's room.

Her room. She couldn't believe she would be living here with him, *sleeping* just one room away from him, in only a few days. Since they didn't have a lot of time, she'd brought over what she would need for this evening's dinner with his mother and planned to change there.

"I'll meet you back down here in…forty-five minutes?" Stone was consulting his watch. "That will give us a few minutes to relax before my mother arrives."

His mother. Her stomach jumped as she nodded and went to her room. She'd never met Eliza Smythe and knew only what she'd read in the news about the hard-hitting, hardworking female who had taken over Smythe Corp. after her father's unexpected death from a heart attack at a young age. She took deep breaths and tried to settle the nerves that arose at the thought of being vetted by the woman. What if his mother didn't like her?

Three

She was right on the button when she descended the steps a few minutes after he did. Stone, in the act of entering the drawing room, glanced up—and froze where he was.

Faith wore what at first glance appeared to be a simple dress in a lightweight Black Watch plaid. But a second glance at her figure in the soft brushed fabric dispelled any doubt that this was a demure dress for the classroom or office. She wore the collar open and turned up, framing a long, delicate neck and fragile collarbone, and her hair was up in a classic, shining twist. A matching fabric belt encircled her slender waist. The sleeves were three-quarter-length and tiny buttons ran from a point between her breasts to midthigh, allowing a slight glimpse of smooth, slim leg as she came down the stairs.

And as he realized that those thighs were encased

in black fishnet stockings and incredibly well-displayed in a pair of the new heels they'd just bought, his blood pressure shot straight through the roof. He'd never thought he was a leg man, but he sure wasn't having much success keeping his mind off Faith's legs. Or any of her other perfectly rounded feminine attributes, either, for that matter.

"You look very…nice," he said, and then winced at the banality.

But she smiled. "Good. I know your mother will be coming straight from the office and I thought this would work better than something that's really for evening. It's a Ralph Lauren," she added smugly. "I got it at a secondhand shop for a pittance!"

He grinned. She hadn't realized yet that cost was a concept she no longer needed to consider. "Would you like a drink?"

She hesitated. "I'm not really much of a drinker. A glass of wine, perhaps?"

"How about champagne? Since we are celebrating our engagement." He gestured for her to precede him into the drawing room, which gave him a chance to scrutinize the back view of her dress. Yeow. It was a good thing this marriage wasn't for real. He could imagine getting overly possessive at the thought of other men putting their hands on her, even in a correct public dance position.

Duh. What was he thinking about that for? Wasn't going to happen. Was. Not. Besides, he reminded himself, he shouldn't be ogling her, either. She was his ward.

The caterer he'd hired had set out an assortment of hors d'oeuvres on a table in a corner. A small flame beneath a silver chafing dish kept some crab balls warm, and around it, a selection of fruits, vegetables and a paté with crackers made an attractive display.

"Pretty," she commented, picking up a strawberry and biting into it. "I've never had champagne. Will I like it?"

"Probably, if you like wine," he said, crossing to the bar where an ice bucket contained a tall-necked French bottle. Watching the way she savored the luscious red fruit, the way her lips had closed around the morsel as her eyelids fluttered down in unconscious ecstasy, he was uncomfortably aware of the stirring pulses of arousal that threatened to turn his trousers into an article of torture. He might be her guardian but he was also a human male...with a healthy sexual appetite. And right now, he was hungry for *her*. Hastily he turned away and poured a glass of the pale golden sparkling liquid for her and one for himself.

Taking a deep breath and reaching for self-control, he came to where she stood in the middle of the room. He handed her one flute and held his aloft in a toast. "To a successful partnership."

"To a successful partnership," she repeated, lifting her gaze to his as their glasses sounded a pure chime and they each lifted them to drink. Their eyes met and held for a moment before she looked away, a warm pink blush rising in her cheeks.

He watched her over the rim of his glass as she tasted her first champagne. Her eyes widened slightly as she inhaled the fruity fragrance, and then she promptly sneezed as the bubbles tickled her nose.

"Bless you," he said, laughing, glad for the distraction. "You have to watch that."

"It's delicious," she said, taking an experimental sip. Then she slanted a flirtatious smile at him from beneath her lashes. "Is this one of the benefits of being married to a millionaire?"

He felt his whole body tighten in reaction to that teasing smile. He was sure she had no idea what that smile made a man want to do, and he forced himself to ignore the urge to reach out and pull her against him to erase it with his mouth. "This is one of the benefits of being married to a man who likes a good wine,' he said. "Listen, we need to talk a little bit before my mother arrives."

"About what?" She held her glass very correctly by the stem and he was reminded that although she didn't have a lot of money, she'd grown up in a very genteel home and a carefully selected school which had only enhanced her ladylike ways.

"My mother," he said carefully, "has to be convinced that we married for...the reasons normal couples get married."

He watched as she processed that. "You mean you want me to pretend to be in love with you," she pronounced.

"Uh, right." He'd expected some coy reaction, not such a straightforward response, and he forced himself to acknowledge that a corner of his pride might be dented just the smallest bit. She appeared completely unaffected by the idea of being in love with him. That was good, he assured himself, since that particular emotion would royally foul up their arrangement for the coming year.

"Okay."

"Okay? It might not be easy," he warned, dragging his mind back to the topic. "She's going to walk in here in a foul temper. So just follow my lead.''

''Yes, o master.'' She smiled as she took another sip of her drink.

He took her glass of champagne and set it firmly aside, guiding her to the food. ''Get yourself a bite to eat. The last thing I need is for you to be silly with drink when my mother arrives.''

''I've only had half a glass,'' she said serenely. But she allowed him to spread paté on a cracker and lift it to her mouth. She leaned forward and opened her lips, closing them around a portion of the cracker, crunching cleanly into it with straight white teeth. Her lips brushed his fingers, closed briefly over the very tip of one, and then withdrew.

And he realized immediately he'd made a monumental mistake. The sensation of her warm, slick mouth on him brought erotic images to flood his brain and his body stirred with a powerful surge of sensual intensity. Hastily he stepped back, hoping she hadn't noticed his discomfort. His fingers were wet from her lips and he almost lifted them to his own mouth before he realized what he was doing. Wiping them on a napkin, he tried desperately to fix his thoughts on something, anything other than the unconscious sensuality that his ward—his wife, soon—wore like other women wore perfume.

She chewed the bite for a time, then licked her lips. ''That's excellent!''

Watching her pink tongue delicately flick along the outer corner of her mouth, he couldn't agree more. God, she was driving him crazy.

Faith was practically a sister to him, he reminded himself sternly. This was merely a business type of arrangement from which they both would benefit. He'd fulfill his mother's wishes, in his own fashion and get Smythe Corp. Faith could finish her education, which she seemed determined to do. And it had the added benefit of making her feel as if she was paying him back, of divesting herself of the debt she imagined she owed him for the years he'd taken care of her and her mother.

Yes, it was going to be a good arrangement. And if he couldn't stop his overactive imagination from leaping straight to thoughts of what it would be like to have her writhing beneath him in a big, soft bed, at least he could keep her from knowing it.

The doorbell rang then and he glanced at his watch. His mother, ever-punctual. "Brace yourself," he warned Faith as he started for the foyer. "I'll let her in."

Faith looked up from the grape she was about to eat. "Surely she isn't that bad."

He merely raised one eyebrow.

The doorbell rang again, impatiently, and she made a shooing motion as she set down her plate. "Go! Let her in. And be nice."

Be nice. He snorted with amusement as he walked to the massive front door and twisted the knob. Like his mother had ever needed anyone to be nice to her. She'd probably steamroll them right into the pavement as she moved past.

"Good evening, Mother." He stepped aside and ushered in the petite woman whose dark hair was still the same shade as his own, with the added distinction of a few silver streaks at her temples.

"Hello." His mother whipped off her gloves and coat and thrust them unceremoniously into his arms as she stalked in. "Would you care to explain to me exactly what you think you're doing?"

"Excuse me?" He deliberately infused his tone with innocence.

Eliza made a rude noise. "Where's this woman you've talked into marrying you? And how much did you have to pay her?"

"I didn't pay her anything." That was absolutely true, so far. "My bride-to-be is in the drawing room." He indicated the archway and his mother strode forward.

As Eliza entered the drawing room, he hastily disposed of her outerwear and followed her. Faith came across the room as they appeared, her hand extended. For a moment, he couldn't take his eyes off her. She wore a welcoming smile that looked too genuine to be faked, and her slender body moved gracefully beneath the soft fabric of the fitted dress.

"Hello, Ms. Smythe," she said, her gray eyes warm. "It's a pleasure to meet you."

The older woman took her hand and Stone watched her give Faith a firmer than necessary handshake. "I wish I could say the same," she said coolly. "What did my son promise you for going through with this ridiculous charade?"

Faith's eyes widened. Shock filled them, then he could see the distress rush in. "I, uh, we—"

"Mother." He spoke sharply, diverting her attention from Faith. "You can either be courteous to my fiancée in my home or you can leave. You should have no trouble remembering the way out," he added, unable to prevent the acid edge to the words.

His mother had the grace to flush. "Please forgive my rudeness," she said to Faith, sounding like she meant it. Then she turned one gimlet eye on her son. "But I believe this hasty union was arranged for the purpose of circumventing my wishes in regard to an offer I made my son."

"How could you possibly know why I want to marry her?" he demanded. "You don't know enough about my life to be making snap judgments."

"She's a child." His mother dismissed Faith with one curt sentence. "I'm no fool, Stone. If you think you're going to con me into believe—"

"I don't care what you believe." He put a hand on Faith's back, feeling the rigid tension in every muscle. Deliberately he slid his palm under her collar to the smooth, bare flesh at her nape, gently massaging the taut cords, his big hand curving possessively around her slender neck. "Faith and I have known each other since we both were children. I've been waiting for her to grow up and she has. When you made me your offer, I realized there was no reason to wait anymore." He exerted a small amount of pressure with his fingers, tugging Faith backward against him. "Right, darling?"

She turned her head to look up at him and he could see the uncertainty in the depths of her bottomless gray eyes. "Right," she replied, her voice barely audible. Her face was white, probably from shock. He doubted she'd ever had words with *her* mother that were anything like this scene. She couldn't have looked less like a thrilled bride-to-be, so he did the only thing he could think of to make his case more convincing: he kissed her.

As he bent his head and took her lips, he put his arms around her and turned her to him, pulling her unresisting frame close. The moment their lips met, he felt that punch of desire in his diaphragm, a sensation he still hadn't gotten accustomed to. His head began to spin.

Her lips were soft and warm beneath his, and as he molded her mouth, she made a quiet murmur deep in her throat. The small sound set a match to his barely banked desire, and he slid his arms more fully around her, pressing her long, slender curves to him. Faith lifted her arms around his shoulders and as her gentle fingers brushed the back of his neck, he shuddered. The intimate action moved the sweet swell of her breasts across his chest and rational thought fled as he gathered her even closer.

"Good grief," his mother said. "You can stop now. You've convinced me."

It took him a moment to remember that they had an audience, to make sense of the words. Faith's mouth was soft and yielding, still clinging to his when he broke the kiss and dragged in a steadying breath of air. She kept her arms looped around his neck, her face buried in his throat, and as her warm breath feathered across his throat, his hands clenched spasmodically on her back with the effort it took him not to drag her into a private room to finish what they'd started.

Taking a deep breath, he forced his fingers to relax. He raised his head and looked at his mother over Faith's fair hair. "We weren't trying to convince you," he said roughly. And it was true. He might have started the kiss with that intent, but the moment Faith surrendered to the sensual need that enveloped him every time he touched her, he'd forgotten all about convincing anyone of anything.

Then Faith stirred in his arms, pushing against his

chest until he released her. She straightened her dress and smoothed her hair, uttering a small laugh. "I apologize if we made you uncomfortable," she said to his mother. "When Stone kisses me like that, I have a hard time remembering my name, much less my manners or anything else." She turned to Stone and her voice was steady although her eyes were still soft and dazed. "I'm sure your mother would like a drink, darling."

He had to force himself not to let his jaw drop. She was a better actress than he'd expected, and his own tense demeanor eased as he saw the suspicion in his mother's eyes fade. "Will you join us in a glass of champagne, Mother?" he asked her. "And help us celebrate this special time?"

The rest of the evening went smoothly. He kept Faith close to him, holding her hand or with his arm loosely around her waist, most of the time when they weren't at the table, not giving his mother any opportunity to corner her alone and harass her. It was both heaven and hell to feel her warm curves at his side, and he told himself he was only trying to convince his mother that their marriage was a love match. But he couldn't quite ignore the leaping pleasure in every nerve ending. God, what he wouldn't give to have the right to make her his wife in the fullest sense of the word!

She had recovered her innate elegant manners by the time they went in to dinner. And though she was quiet, he imagined it was simply because he and his mother were discussing business matters much of the time.

Touching her, he decided as they settled on the love seat in the drawing room again after the meal, was like a damned drug. Addictive. He had his arm around her and he idly smoothed his thumb over the ball of her shoulder joint as his mother turned to her and said, "Faith, I hope you'll forgive my earlier behavior. Welcome to the family."

Faith smiled. "Thank you."

"Faith's mother will be moving in with us soon." He didn't know why he was telling his mother this, but he plowed on. "She suffers from multiple sclerosis and we're fixing up an apartment for her on the main floor."

Eliza turned to Faith. "I never met your mother. Has she had MS long?"

"Almost all my life," Faith responded, her smile fading. "I was a late baby and she was diagnosed just over a year later. But I think she had symptoms years before that and ignored them."

His mother nodded. "My first secretary, who was absolutely invaluable during the first years when I stepped into my father's shoes, was diagnosed when she was forty-four. It was terribly difficult to watch her slowly lose capabilities. She passed away last year." Her eyes brimmed with tears; he was amazed. He'd never seen his mother cry, had never even imagined that she could. Which, he supposed, was a sad indicator of the degree to which they'd stayed out of each other's lives. Still, she was the one who had initiated the estrangement, if it could even be called that. There was no reason for him to feel guilty about it.

At his side, Faith stirred and he realized she was passing his mother a cocktail napkin so she could wipe her eyes. "It *is* difficult to accept that there's so little we can do to combat it," she said. "After my father died, my mother's condition worsened rapidly.''

After a few more moments of conversation, Eliza set down her drink and rose. "Call me a taxi, please, Stone. It's time for me to be going."

He did so, then helped her on with her coat and they stood in the foyer for a few moments until the car rolled down the street and stopped in front of the house.

As he closed the door behind her, he turned to Faith, still standing at his side in the foyer. "We did it! We convinced her." He took her hands, squeezing lightly. "Thank you."

"You're welcome." She smiled slightly but he noticed her gaze didn't reach any higher than his chin as she eased her hands free of his and turned. "It's been a tiring day. Could you take me home now?"

"Of course." His elation floated away, leaving him feeling flat and depressed. And there was no reason for it, he told himself firmly. He'd accomplished what he'd intended. So what if he had a raging physical attraction to Faith? She wasn't indifferent to him, either. He was certain of it after that smoking kiss before dinner, but she clearly wasn't any more prepared to step over the line than he was.

And he knew he should be glad for that. Because if she encouraged him, he was fairly certain he'd forget he'd ever drawn that line in the first place.

Faith spent the following Monday packing most of her things and answering breathless questions from Gretchen about her upcoming marriage. The morning paper had carried a tantalizing mention of Stone's impending nuptials and Gretchen had been quick to add up the details and come to the right conclusion.

Stone picked her up just after two o'clock and they made the drive into rural Connecticut where her mother lived in a beautifully landscaped condominium. Her apartment was on the ground floor and was handicap-accessible. Faith had helped her find the place during one of her infrequent vacations from school. Only now did it occur to her that Stone had probably helped her mother sell their old house. And rather than using it to finance this purchase, she was willing to bet he'd used it to pay off her father's debts and had spent his own money on her mother since then.

The thought of him assuming the full financial burden of caring for her mother and her still pricked at her pride, but she was grateful, too. She was practical enough to recognize that she never could have provided her mother with a stable, comfortable home. God only knew what would have become of them if Stone hadn't stepped in. What had her father been thinking?

They probably would never know. Her throat tightened as she thought of the laughing man with hair as pale as her own who had tossed her into the air and tucked her into bed every night. Clearly he hadn't been perfect, but she would always think of him with love.

Thank God, she thought again, for Stone. He'd provided desperately needed tranquillity for her mother and also had given Faith the tools to make her own way in the world one day. And she was all the more determined to repay his kindness during the upcoming year. She'd be such an asset to him he would wonder what he'd done before he had a wife! A momentary flash of disquiet accompanied the thought. Already, it was as though she'd been with Stone for months rather than days. What would it be like to lose him after a year?

Clarice, her mother's day help, answered the door when Stone rang the bell. "Hello, honey," the older woman greeted Faith. "She's really looking forward to your visit."

Faith hugged her. Clarice was a godsend. Widowed at sixty, Clarice had little in the way of retirement savings and was forced to continue to work. Faith and her mother had tried three other aides before they found Clarice, and Faith knew a gem when she saw one. Clarice, in addition, appeared to genuinely enjoy Mrs. Harrell and swore the work was well within her capabilities. Fortunately Faith's mother wasn't a large woman, so it wasn't terribly difficult for Clarice to assist her for tasks like getting in and out of the bath.

Still, Faith worried. Her mother was steadily losing mobility and motor control and the day was coming when she would need more than occasional assistance and handicapped facilities in her home. But as she entered the condo with Stone behind her, she felt less burdened, less worried than she had in some time. For the next year, her mother would want for nothing. And as soon as Faith got her degree and a job with decent pay, she planned to find a place she could share with her mother that would meet both their needs.

"Clarice," she said, "this is Stone Lachlan, my fiancé." She was proud that she didn't stumble over the word—she'd practiced it in her head fully half of the trip.

"Hello," said Clarice, "Faith's never brought—" Then the import of Faith's words struck her. "Well, my lands! Come in, come in. Congratulations!" She pumped Stone's hand, then hugged Faith. "Does your mother know?"

Faith shook her head. "Not yet. Is she in the living room?"

The older woman nodded. "By the window. She loves to look out at the birds. I put some feeders up to attract them and we've been seeing all kinds."

Faith felt another rush of gratitude. Clarice was indeed a gem. She wondered if there was any possibility of convincing her to come with her mother to live in New York. Deciding not to get ahead of herself, she let Clarice lead them into the living room.

"Mama." She went to the wheelchair by the window and knelt to embrace her mother, tears stinging her eyes.

"Hello, my little love." Her mother's arms fumbled up to pat at her. Her speech was slow but still reasonably clear, although Faith had noticed some change over the past year. Then her mother said, "Stone!"

"Hello, Mrs. Harrell." He came forward and Faith was surprised when he knelt at her side and gave her mother his hand. "It's nice to see you again."

"You, also." Naomi Harrell clung to his hand. "Did you drive Faith up?"

He nodded. Then he looked at Faith, and she smiled at him, grateful to him for sensing that she wanted to be the one to tell her mother of their marriage.

"Mama, I—we have some news. Stone and I are engaged to be married."

"Engaged?" Naomi slurred the second "g" and her eyes, magnified by the thick glasses she wore, went wide. "You're getting married?"

Stone looked at Faith again, still smiling, and for a moment, she was dizzied by the warm promise in his eyes, until she realized he was putting on a show for her mother's sake. "We are," he said. "This Friday, at eleven o'clock. We'd like you to be there, if you are able."

Naomi Harrell looked from one of them to the other. "I didn't even know you were dating," she said to Faith.

The comment shouldn't have caught her off guard but it did. "We, um, haven't been going out long," she said. Understatement of the year.

Stone slipped one steely arm around her shoulders, pulling her against his side. "I swept her off her feet," he told her mother, then turned again to smile down at her. "I was afraid if I waited until she was finished with school, the competition might edge me out." He paused, looking back at her mother. "I wasn't about to lose her."

Her mother nodded slowly, and Faith wasn't surprised to see tears welling in her eyes. Naomi Harrell had known that kind of love for real. She accepted the idea that her daughter had found the same happiness more easily than Stone's mother had. "I'm glad," Naomi said. "Faith needs somebody."

Faith knew her mother only meant that she didn't want Faith to be alone in the event anything happened to her. It was an upsetting thought. "That's not all, Mama," she said, anxious to get it all said and done. "Stone and I would like you to come and live with us after we're married. Stone has an apartment on the main floor of his home that you could have. There's plenty of room for you and Clarice, too, if she'd consider leaving this area."

But Naomi was shaking her head. "New-ly-weds," she said, enunciating carefully, "should have some time alone."

Stone chuckled. "Mrs. Harrell, my home is big enough for all of us. Your apartment can be completely self-contained. There's even an entrance from the back. You don't even have to see us if you don't want to."

Naomi smiled. "I want to. But I don't want to be in the way."

"Mama, I'd really, really love it if you'd come to live with me." Faith took her mother's hands. "I miss you."

"And besides," Clarice piped up, "this way we'll be right there when the grandbabies start arriving!"

Oh my Lord. If there was any way she could put those words back in Clarice's mouth…she felt herself begin to blush.

At her side, Stone stirred, bringing his other hand up to rest over hers and her mother's. "We aren't ready to think about that yet," he said. "I want Faith all to myself for a while. A long while."

"And besides," she added, "I have to finish school and get established in my career." Well, at least *that* wasn't a lie.

"Yes, I can't seem to talk her out of this obsession with working." Stone's voice was easy and colored

with humor, but she sensed a grain of truth beneath
the light tone. She was sure it wasn't her imagination.
Thinking of the tension between him and his own
mother, she wondered just how deeply he'd been
scarred by his parents' split when he was a child.

She recalled the acid in his voice the night he'd
suggested that his mother knew the way out—it had
been a deliberate attempt to hurt. And judging from
his mother's slight flinch before she controlled her
expression, the shot had hit its mark. She felt badly
for Eliza Smythe even though she didn't agree with
the way she'd apparently put business before her
young son more than two decades ago. Eliza's face
had shown a heartbreaking moment of envy when
Stone had told her about Faith's mother moving in
with them. Again, she suspected he'd done it because
he knew it would hurt. Or maybe he'd *hoped* it
would, she thought with a sudden flash of insight.
Children who had been rejected often continued to
try to win their parent's attention, even in negative
ways.

She sighed. She'd *liked* her new mother-in-law-to-
be. Was it too much to hope that during her year
with Stone she could contribute to mending the obvious rift between them?

Her year with Stone. As they said farewell to her
mother and Clarice, Faith was conscious of the large
warm shape of him at her side, one big hand gently
resting in the middle of her back. He smelled like
the subtle, but expensive, cologne he always wore,
and abruptly she was catapulted back to Saturday
night, when he'd taken her in his arms. That scent
had enveloped her as he'd pulled her to him and
kissed her.

He'd kissed her! She still thought it might have been a dream, except that she could recall his mother's wry, amused expression far too well. No wonder she'd been amused. For Faith, the world had changed forever the moment he'd touched her. And when his firm, warm lips had come down on hers and his arms had brought her against every muscled inch of his hard body, she'd forgotten everything but the wonderfully strange sensations rushing through her. Her body had begun to heat beneath his hands. She'd wanted more, although she didn't quite know what to do next to get it. But when she'd lifted her arms and circled his broad shoulders, the action had brushed her sensitive breasts against him and she'd wanted to *move,* to cuddle her body as close to his as she could get, to press herself against him even more. When he'd lifted his head, she'd simply hung in his arms as he'd spoken to his mother. God, the man was potent! She had been too embarrassed to face Eliza Smythe for a moment, then she'd simply told her the truth. She *did* forget everything when Stone kissed her.

Covertly she studied him from beneath her lashes. Stone's big hands looked comfortable and confident on the wheel of the Lexus and she shivered as she remembered the way they'd slid restlessly over her body as he'd kissed her. Would he do it again?

She wanted him to. Badly. In fact, she wanted far more than his kisses. She was almost twenty-one years old and she'd never even had a serious boy-friend. Soon she would have a husband. She studied his chiseled profile, the jut of his chin, the solid jaw, the way his hair curled just the smallest bit around his ears. She'd been half in love with him practically her whole life and being with him constantly over the past few days had only shown her how much more she could feel.

Quickly she turned her head and looked out the window before he could catch her staring at him like a lovesick fool. He didn't love her, only needed her for the most practical of reasons. But still...her heart was young and optimistic, unbruised and whole. He might not love her, but he certainly seemed to desire her. Wasn't that a start? Maybe, in time, if they got close...physically, he'd begin to need her the way she was realizing she needed him. It was too new to analyze. But she knew, with a not entirely pleasant certainty, that if she couldn't change his mind about making this a longer than one-year marriage, she wouldn't be able to leave him behind easily.

Not easily at all. In fact, she wasn't sure she could ever forget him. What man would ever measure up to Stone in her estimation?

She was afraid she knew the answer to that.

Four

Back in Manhattan, he headed home.

"Where are you going?" Faith asked.

He glanced across at her. She'd been very quiet the whole ride, apparently lost in her own thoughts. "Home."

"My home or your home?"

"Our home." He put a slight emphasis on the pronoun.

"It won't be our home until Friday," she said, using the same emphasis. "And I need to go to my apartment in any case. I still have things to pack."

"I can send someone to finish the job. We have things to do."

"I'd rather you didn't," she said mildly.

"It's no problem. And it will save you—"

"No, thank you." She shook her head, her blond hair flying and her tone was definite enough to warn him that he was traveling a narrow path here. "No. I would like to pack myself. There's not that much."

"Can I at least send someone to pick everything up and move it for you?"

She smiled, and a small dimple appeared in her soft cheek, enchanting him. "That would be nice. They could come Friday afternoon."

"Friday afternoon? Why not tomorrow? Surely you don't have that much stuff to move."

The smile had disappeared. "I'm not planning on moving in until after the ceremony on Friday."

"That's silly," he said sharply, acknowledging more disappointment than he ought to be feeling. There was an unaccustomed tightness in his chest. "I want you there as soon as possible. Why wait until Friday?"

"Because my mother would expect it," she said heatedly.

"Your mother would—oh." Belatedly he realized what she meant. He almost laughed aloud, to think that someone would still be so concerned with observing the proprieties. Then he saw that she was dead serious. He sighed in frustration, bringing one hand up to roughly massage his chest. "All right. But I still think it's silly." *Especially given the fact that nothing will be changing after you do move in.*

"Fortunately," she said in a honeyed tone, "I don't particularly care what you think."

"Yes, you've already made that plain," he said, recalling the way he'd found out she quit school after the fact.

Then she homed in on the rest of his original statement. "What things do we have to do?"

"Wedding dress," he said briefly, glancing at her

again to gauge her reaction. "And wedding plans."
Faith wasn't quite as pliable as her quiet nature suggested, a fact he seemed to be learning the hard way.

Her eyes went wide and then her fair elegant
brows drew together. "Absolutely not. I'm not wearing a real wedding dress. I have an ivory silk suit,
fairly dressy, that ought to do."

"I have a woman meeting us at the house at one
with a large selection." He took a deep breath, fighting the urge to bark out orders. Faith wasn't one of
his employees and if he shouted at her, she was liable
to bolt. "If you don't want a big, fluffy wedding
dress, that's fine. But our mothers—not to mention
the press—are going to expect you to look something
like a bride."

"It's really none of the press's business."

"I know. But when you have as much money as
I do, you wield a certain amount of influence. And
influence leads to attention, even though I don't seek
it out." A quick glance at her expression told him
she hadn't bought it yet. "Like it or not, we're going
to be of interest to the public. Think of yourself
as…sort of a princess of a minor kingdom. Royalty
interests everyone. And since there's no royalty in
America, the wealthy get pestered."

She sighed. "It's that important to you?"

He hesitated. There was an odd note in her voice,
though he couldn't decipher it. "Yes," he said finally. "It's that important to me. This has to look
real. If anyone should suspect it isn't…" He looked
over at her while he waited at a light, but she had
linked her hands in her lap and was studying them.
He was sure she was going to object again, or perhaps even refuse to marry him. He took a deep

breath, deliberately expanding his lungs to full capacity, but still he had that taut, binding sensation gripping him.

Then she said, "All right. I'll come to your home and see these dresses."

His whole body relaxed and the air whooshed from his lungs with an audible sound.

She shot a questioning glance at him. He'd better get a grip. She was going to think this meant more to him than it did. All he wanted, he reminded himself, was to inherit the company that had been his mother's family's. He'd known before he'd ever embarked on this course of action that this was to be a marriage with a finite limit of time. And in any case, he had no business even thinking about Faith in any terms other than those of a…a what? A guardian and his ward was definitely too archaic. A sister? No, there was no way he could ever condition himself to think of her as a sister. A friend? There. They could be friends. That was by far the most suitable description of their relationship, both now and in the future.

Inside him, though, there was a little voice laughing uproariously. *A friend? Does kissing a friend get you so hot and bothered you barely remember your own mother is in the room?*

Shut up, he told the voice. Just—shut—up.

But all he said aloud to Faith was "That's great. Thank you."

Friday morning finally arrived. Standing in the courthouse with his mother, he checked his watch. Almost time. Where the hell was Faith? He knew he should have made her move in before this. Then he could have kept an eye on her, made sure she didn't get cold feet.

It had been a surprisingly long week. He'd caught himself glancing at his watch throughout meetings and conference calls practically every hour since he'd dropped Faith off at her apartment to pack on Monday after her private showing of wedding dresses.

Which she hadn't let him see.

He frowned. Whoever would have suspected the stubborn streak hiding behind that angelic face? It would be bad luck, she'd told him.

Just then, an older woman walked around the corner. Spying him, her face lit up and she hurried forward. "Hello, Mr. Lachlan. We're here."

It was...what was her name? Clarice. Faith's mother's...friend. Caregiver. Whatever.

"Hello, Clarice," he said. "Have you seen Faith?"

"Oh, she's here. We all came together." Clarice extended a hand to his mother. "Hello. I'm Clarice Nealy, Faith's mother's companion."

He felt a dull embarrassment at his lapse of manners. "Oh, sorry. Clarice, this is my mother, Eliza Smythe." The two women shook hands.

His mother only smiled at him. "We forgive you." To Clarice, she said, "He's going to have a stroke if he doesn't get to see his bride soon."

Stone ignored that and consulted his watch. "It's our turn. What is she doing?" Impatiently he strode toward the corner, but Clarice's voice stopped him.

"No, no. You go in. Faith and her mother will be here in a moment."

He frowned, but when his mother took his arm, he sighed and led her into the room.

The justice of the peace stood at the front of the room in front of a wooden rail. To one side of him was a massive raised bench behind which the man presided over his courtroom, with state and national flags displayed behind it. He looked a little startled as Stone and his mother walked forward. "Hello. You are Stone Lachlan and Faith Harrell?"

Eliza Smythe started to chuckle. "No. The bride isn't here yet."

Just then, the door to the small chamber opened and he caught a glimpse of Clarice's beaming face as she held it wide. Faith's mother, seated on a motorized scooter, whirred into the room and stopped just inside the door. Then Faith stepped into the doorway and reached for her mother's hand.

The whole room seemed to freeze for one long moment as he simply stared. His heart leaped, then settled down to a fast thudding in his chest.

She looked stunning. As she walked toward him, pacing herself to the speed of her mother's scooter at her side, he had to remind himself to breathe.

She had chosen a short dress rather than anything long and formal. An underlayer was made of some shiny satiny fabric that fit her like a second skin, showcasing her slender figure. The satin, covered by a thin, lacy overlayer, was strapless and low-cut and against his will his eyes were drawn to the shadowed swell of creamy flesh revealed above its edge. Over the satin, the sheath of fine sheer lace covered her up to the neck, though it clearly wasn't designed to hide anything, but rather to enhance. This layer had long close-fitting sleeves and extended in a lacy scallop just below the hem of the underdress.

He took in the rest of her. Her hair was up in a smooth, gleaming fancy twist of some kind and she wore flowers in it, arranged around a crown of shining gems. As he recalled his reference to royalty, he had to suppress a grin. She'd done that deliberately, the little tease. She carried the small but exquisite trailing bouquet of palest peach roses, Peruvian lilies and white dendrobium orchids with touches of feathery greens that he'd sent to her. The subtle touch of color was the perfect enhancement for the glowing white of the dress.

It didn't escape his notice that she'd chosen pure, virginal white for her wedding day. Probably a good thing, since it served to remind him of the liaison they had—and its limits.

Limits. God, what he wouldn't give to be able to show her the pleasures of lovemaking. For an instant, he allowed himself to imagine that this was real, that the beautiful, desirable woman coming toward him would be his wife in every way. If this was real, it would be just the beginning. He would enjoy the incredible pleasures her soft body promised, and come home to her warm arms every night. In due course they would add children to their family—

Whoa! *Children?* He gave himself a firm mental kick in the butt.

Faith had reached his side by now and he surveyed her face as she turned to kiss her mother and then his. She wore more makeup than usual and the normal beauty of her features now approached a porcelain perfection. Her skin seemed lit by an inner radiance. She'd curled small wisps of her hair and it gently bounced around her face in soft, shining waves that made him want to sink his fingers into it simply to experience the texture. But he couldn't do that. He couldn't touch her in any but the most innocuous of ways.

The justice cleared his throat and Stone realized the ceremony was about to begin. His mother flanked him and Naomi maneuvered her scooter to Faith's far side. Clarice took a seat in the small rows of chairs behind them. He extended his arm to Faith and she took it, smiling up at him tentatively.

He didn't smile back. The reminder that this was a forced union of sorts had ruined the moment for him. This was a ridiculous charade, necessitated by the intransigence of his mother. It was, at best, an inconvenience, an interruption, in his life as well as Faith's. There was nothing to smile about.

The smile faded from her face when he didn't respond and she dropped her gaze. Her face abruptly assumed the serene contours he knew meant she was hiding her thoughts from the world, and she turned toward the official who was beginning the ceremony.

Too late to catch her eye, he regretted his action. Now he felt like a real bastard. She'd clearly wanted a little reassurance. He glanced down at her fine profile as she stood beside him, one small hand resting in the crook of his arm. To his dismay, he realized she was blinking rapidly, her silver eyes misted with a sheen of tears. Damn!

Acting on instinct, he raised his free hand and covered hers on his opposite arm, squeezing gently.

She looked up at him again and offered him a wobbly smile. Remorse shot through him. She was only twenty years old. He doubted this was what she'd envisioned when she'd dreamed of her wedding day, even though she'd insisted on this extreme simplicity when they'd discussed it.

He smiled down at her as he passed an arm behind her back and gave her shoulders a gentle hug. She felt small and soft beneath his hand, and he liked the way her slender curves pressed against his side far too well. Tough. He wasn't going to do anything about *that* but he could make this day less of a chore for each of them.

The ceremony was short and impersonal as the justice of the peace sealed the bonds of matrimony with swift efficiency. Faith spoke her responses in a quiet, steady tone, looking down at their hands as they exchanged rings and in a shockingly brief matter of minutes, they were legally bound.

The justice looked incredibly bored; how many of these things did he perform in a week's time? "You may kiss your bride," the man intoned.

Stone set his hands at Faith's waist and drew her toward him. As his mouth descended, she raised her face to his and his lips slid onto hers. He froze for an instant, nearly seduced by the sweet, soft flesh of her full lips and the memory of the way she'd melted in his arms on Sunday night. But this couldn't be. It *couldn't be,* he told himself fiercely. Faith wasn't experienced enough to know that sex and love were two distinct issues in a man's mind. He would be courting a messy, emotional disaster if he couldn't keep his distance from her. And so, steeling himself to the powerful allure of her person, he kept the kiss brief and impersonal, then drew back.

He felt her go rigid beneath his hands, and he nearly apologized, but as the words formed, he re-

alized how strange *that* would sound to the wit-
nesses, so he swallowed the apology and settled instead for, "Are you ready to go?"

Faith nodded. She wouldn't look at him and he
gritted his teeth against the urge to raise her chin and
cover her lips with his own again.

Oh, hell. No, no, and *no!* He wasn't going to do
anything stupid with Randall Harrell's daughter. His
ward. This marriage was just a business arrangement,
of a sort.

Of course it was.

Faith woke early on her first morning as a married
woman. For a moment, she didn't recognize her surroundings and then it all came flooding back. Yesterday she had married Stone.

Married. She raised her left hand and her new
rings sparkled as the faceted stones caught the light.
If it weren't for these she'd think it had been a
dream. Slowly she got to her feet and headed for the
bathroom. As she showered and dressed, she couldn't
keep herself from reviewing the wedding ceremony,
like a child who couldn't resist picking at a healing
wound.

Stone had looked so handsome in the severe cut
of the morning suit he'd worn. As she'd come into
the courtroom, she'd allowed herself to fantasize, for
one brief instant, that she was a real bride, flushed
and brimming with love for her husband, taking his
name and becoming part of his life forever. But then
she'd looked into Stone's eyes and seen nothing.
Nothing. No feeling, no warmth. No love. He'd
quickly tried to cover it up, but that first impression
was indelibly stamped on her mind.

She felt her bottom lip tremble and she bit down on it fiercely. For the first time, she allowed herself to acknowledge the depths of her disappointment. She hadn't married Stone entirely because of their bargain. She'd married him because somewhere in the past week her silly, girlish crush had gelled into a deeper, more mature emotion.

Oh, it hurt even to think it and she shied away from deeper examination of her feelings.

Instead she replayed the wedding scene in her mind again. And she realized her shattered heart had forgotten something. He did have *some* feelings for her. Recalling the look in his eye the first night he'd kissed her, she knew with a deep inner feeling of feminine certainty that he wanted her, at least in the physical sense. And yesterday, for the briefest instant before his gaze had grown cool and distant, she'd seen the poleaxed look on his face as he absorbed the sight of her in her wedding dress. And she'd been gratified, because she'd chosen the unconventional wedding dress, her makeup and the soft, pretty hairstyle for the express purpose of making him notice her.

Yes, for that one unguarded moment, there had been no doubt that he wanted her. If she was going to remember the cold shoulder, she needed to cling to this memory, too. And though she knew it was foolish to believe she could parlay that basic sexual desire into a more lasting emotion, that was exactly what she hoped.

He wanted her. It was a start. And she…she wanted him as well. Wanted him to be the one to teach her the intimacies of the sexual act, wanted him to make love to her. Maybe she could attract his feelings the same way her body attracted his.

Perhaps they would begin to communicate better when they went on their honeymoon. Though she knew Stone hadn't planned one, he'd told his mother they would be going away a few weeks from now. He'd only said it because Eliza had very pointedly asked where he intended to take Faith, she was certain. And she knew he would follow through if only to assuage any doubt in his mother's mind about the veracity of their marriage.

Buoyed by the thought, she made her bed and headed downstairs. The newspaper was lying on the kitchen counter and there was fresh coffee, signs that Stone must already be up. She hunted through the cupboards until she found cereal and dishes, and ate while she leafed through the paper. But all her nerve endings were quivering, alert, waiting for him to enter the room.

When she heard him coming down the hall, she quickly ducked her head behind the paper again, looking up innocently as he entered. "Good morning."

"Good morning. Did you sleep well?" He barely glanced at her as he headed for the coffeepot and poured himself a cup.

"Quite, thank you. And you?"

"Fine." He sounded grumpy. Maybe he wasn't a morning person, though he certainly looked like he was awake and alert. Lord, it simply wasn't fair for the man to look so absolutely stunning first thing in the morning. He was as handsome to her as always and her heart rate increased as a wave of tenderness swept through her. She was his *wife!* Then she realized he was saying something else.

"Your mother and Clarice will be moving in today. I have a company bringing her household up late this morning. Will you help her arrange everything when it arrives?"

"Of course." It shouldn't bother her that he hadn't asked her opinion. Although she'd have preferred to go down and help Clarice pack, she knew this way would be much faster and more efficient.

Stone seemed unaware of her thoughts. "I know it's Saturday but I have to go in to my office for a few hours, so I'll leave that to you." He opened the door of the refrigerator and she saw a large casserole dish. "That's a chicken and broccoli casserole the housekeeper made and froze. I set it in there to thaw. If you want to invite your mother and Clarice to eat with us tonight, that's fine with me."

She nodded. "Is there anything else you'd like me to do? Until the summer sessions begin, I'm going to have a ton of time on my hands. I have some accounting skills and I know my way around a computer. Maybe I could help in your office—"

But he was chuckling. "I employ people to do all that," he said. "Just consider the next two months a vacation."

Disappointment rushed through her for more than one reason. She hated to be idle. And working for him would give them something in common. "Oh, but I could use the experience—"

"Tell you what," he said, cutting her off again. "I know something you could do that would help immensely."

Thrilled, she sat up straighter. "What?"

"The den," he said.

The den? *What* in the den?

"I've never had it redecorated," he continued. "It's something I've thought about a lot and just never gotten around to doing. But it needs a facelift desperately. The easy chair my father sat in for years is still in there." Now he looked at her hopefully. "Would you consider taking on that project?"

"Of course," she said. "Just tell me what color scheme you like. But also, I—"

"I trust your judgment," he said. "Anything fairly neutral." He headed for the door, coffee cup in hand. "I've got to get going. I have an early meeting this morning. Enjoy your day."

"Oh, yeah, it ought to be a blast," she muttered as she heard the front door close. Redecorate the den. Was he serious? She'd intended to help him at the office. She didn't care if she was a receptionist. It would certainly be better experience than redecorating the stupid den! She should have told him how insulting she'd found that…giving her a little wifely project to do when what she really wanted was to be working for him, in whatever capacity he could use her.

Yikes. Her mind took that last thought and gave it a distinctly sexual twist as the memory of his hard, hot body pressed against her side while they spoke their vows set her heart racing again. She still was trying to get used to the perpetual breathless state that being around Stone left her in since the night he'd kissed her in front of his mother and turned her world upside down.

He'd kissed her when they'd gotten married, too, and though that had been only the merest correct meeting of lips, she was sure it had short-circuited some of her brain cells. It certainly had sealed her fate. And with that thought, she forced herself to face the truth.

She hadn't married Stone Lachlan because he needed her help. And she hadn't married him because it was a way to pay him back for his financial support, or because he'd promised to take care of her mother, or because he had promised to help her finish school. No, she'd married him because she was in love with him.

She took a deep breath. *Okay, you've admitted it.* She'd loved him, she supposed, for years under the guise of having a crush. Only the crush had deepened more and more as she'd come to know him, as she'd seen what a decent, honorable man he was, what a thoughtful, caring person—and how incredibly potent his appeal was.

And that was her misfortune. He'd made it abundantly clear, over and over again, that this was a business arrangement, not one in which emotion was welcome.

Well, tough. He might consider it business, but she was declaring war. She had a year. Three hundred and sixty-five days. Surely within that time she could make herself such an integral part of his life that he'd wake up one day and realize he loved her, too.

Having Faith's mother and Clarice around the house wasn't the burden he'd expected it to be, Stone thought a week later as he sat at the kitchen counter nursing a cup of coffee. In fact, it was a distinct blessing.

He'd encouraged the older women to join them for

dinner each night. And though they'd both protested at first, he'd made it his goal to charm them. And he'd succeeded. He hadn't had to spend more than a few moments alone with Faith all week. Yes, inviting her mother here had been a great idea.

It might be the only thing that kept him from grabbing his young bride and ravishing her for the remaining fifty-one weeks of what was shaping up to be one damned long year.

He heaved a sigh, propping his elbows on the counter and pressing the heels of his palms against his temples. God, but Faith was making it difficult to be noble! He had no intention of seducing her. It would be despicable of him to use her that way for the brief term of their marriage and then discard her when they split up, as they intended to do.

And maybe if he kept telling himself that long enough, he'd believe it. He could hear her first thing in the morning, moving around in her bathroom, humming in the shower, removing hangers from her closet and replacing them. His active imagination supplied visual details in Technicolor. She joined him over breakfast, no matter how early he got up, and her soft farewell was the last thing he heard before he left. In the evening, she always came to greet him at the door with a smile, taking his coat and preparing dinner while he changed into casual clothes. It was a treat not to have to eat alone all the time.

And then there was her relationship with her mother. Faith and Naomi were closer than they had any right to be, considering how little they'd really seen of each other during Faith's adolescent years. They teased and smiled, shared stories about Faith's father, worked crossword puzzles together, and genuinely seemed to treasure each moment spent together. It was such a marked contrast to his relationship with his own mother that he could get jealous if he let himself think about it long enough. Sure, he'd imagined that normal families had relationships like that, but until he'd seen exactly how close and loving Faith and her mother were, it had been an abstract concept. Now, thanks to them, it was a reality.

He could hear them laughing right now as they came in from an early walk—or drive, in Naomi's case—through Central Park, across the street from the town house. In a moment, they were in the kitchen.

"We're back." Faith greeted him with a smile as she helped her mother out of her coat and took it to hang in the closet. "It's a beautiful day. Spring is definitely on the way."

"The prediction is for snow by the first of the week," he warned her.

"But it won't last," she said confidently.

Naomi directed her motorized scooter toward her own apartment down the hall from the kitchen and the two of them were left alone. An awkward moment of silence passed.

Then Faith cleared her throat. "Do you have anything planned for today?"

"Um, nothing special," he said. "Tonight there's a dinner and ball but we have most of the day before we have to start getting ready for that."

"That reminds me," she said, snapping her fingers. "Is there anything in particular you'd like me to wear to the ball? I have those dresses we bought last week, remember?''

He remembered. And his blood heated. Though she hadn't modeled them for him, he'd had several long, detailed daydreams. "How about the blue?" he said.

"All right." She cleared her throat. "Actually, if you have time, I'd like you to look at some fabric swatches and paint colors for the den. I can order things next week."

He didn't really want to spend any more time alone with her than he absolutely had to, but she vanished before he could think of a good reason not to look at the samples. A few moments later she reappeared clutching a large folder and two wallpaper books. He folded up his paper and efficiently, she spread everything out on the counter. Her slim figure, clad in blue jeans and a clinging pale yellow sweater, was so close he could smell the clean scent of her hair, and her shoulder brushed against his side as she moved. "Here you go." She pulled one of the wallpaper books toward them. "The first thing you need to do is decide on the walls. Then we'll go from there."

"You're really happy to have your mother here, aren't you?" Good God. Why had he said that?

Her fingers stilled on the books. "Yes. Thank you again."

"No," he said impatiently. Hell, he'd started this, he might as well find out what he really wanted to know. "I mean, you're enjoying her company, not just putting on a polite act."

Her eyebrows rose. "Why on earth would I do that? Of course I'm enjoying her company. No, I take that back. I'm *loving* it. At school, there were nights when I cried myself to sleep, missing her so much. It wasn't that the school was a terrible place,'' she said hastily as he frowned. "The staff members were actually very caring and mostly I was happy. And I could call Mama every day if I liked. But it still wasn't the same."

"No, I guess it wasn't." He could hear the longing in her voice as she relived those days and he felt a surprising kinship. "But you understood how difficult it would have been for her to try to care for you at home. You knew she would have done it if she could."

She turned and looked at him, her gray eyes far too wise and understanding. "I think your mother cares, too. Maybe it wasn't as easy for her to leave you as you think."

"I don't think about it," he said. He didn't want her pitying him, thinking he'd had a miserable childhood. "My father and I got along fine without her."

She didn't say a word, only studied him.

"She could have pretended she cared," he said, goaded by her silence. "Would it have killed her to let a little kid think he meant something special to her?"

Faith laid her small hand on his arm and he realized how tense he was. "I don't know," she said. "Have you ever asked her?"

He consciously relaxed his muscles, feeling the tension drain out of him. "No." He reached forward and pulled the wallpaper books toward him. This conversation was pointless. "It doesn't matter anymore. Now why don't you show me what you have in mind?"

She continued to gaze at him for a long moment, and he kept his eyes on the books. He didn't want her pity. Sure, he'd been hurt by his mother's indifference when he was small, but he was a grown man now, and her approval had long ceased to matter to him.

"All right," she finally said. She rested one hand on the back of his chair and opened the topmost book with the other. The action placed her breasts just below eye level, inches away, and he couldn't prevent himself from covertly assessing the rounded mounds. "Here you go. The first thing to decide on is—"

"Look." He pushed back his chair and rose before he gave in to the fantasy that had leaped into his head. "I want you to like the den, too," he said. "I don't need to approve it. I'm sure whatever you choose will be fine."

"You're the one who's going to have to live with it after I leave," she pointed out.

After I leave… The words echoed in the air around them and he was shocked by the strong urge to blurt out "Don't leave!"

But he didn't say it. Instead images of his life a year from now, when Faith and her family were gone and he was rattling around this place alone again, bombarded him. He *liked* having Naomi and Clarice around, dammit! And he more than liked having Faith around. For one brief instant he allowed himself to imagine what it would be like to grow old with her, to stay married to her on a permanent basis. The thought was so tantalizingly appealing that he immediately shoved it away.

Abruptly he turned his back and started out of the room. "I don't have time to deal with this now."

Five

That evening, Faith showered and shampooed, then rubbed silky cream into her skin and rolled her hair in large hot rollers that left it frothy and bouncy around her shoulders. It would be a lie, she thought as she applied a heavier-than-normal makeup suitable for evening, if she didn't feel the slightest bit pleased by his reaction to her in the morning. When she'd stood close to Stone at the breakfast bar, he definitely had been uncomfortable. And she was pretty sure it wasn't because he was worried about her decorating skills. She'd noticed him looking at her body out of the corner of his eye. And before that, he'd talked about his mother.

Okay, those few sentences weren't much to go on, but she couldn't expect him to be too voluble at first. That would come later, after they'd gotten closer, she hoped. She slipped into a strapless bra and panties

and donned the pretty Escada with the silver trim that
Stone had asked her to wear. The Prada heels and a
small silver clutch bag completed the ensemble and
as she glanced into the full-length mirror in the bathroom, a small thrill ran through her.

She'd never owned anything so beautiful before.
Thanks to the snug bodice of the strapless dress and
the bra beneath it, she had genuinely respectable
cleavage. The silver and blue layers of the full skirt
swayed as she left her room and walked down the
stairs to meet Stone.

He was standing in the archway to the formal front
room with his back to her as she rounded the turn
on the landing and continued down toward him, one
hand lightly trailing on the banister as a precaution,
since she wasn't used to such high heels. When he
heard her footsteps he turned—

And for one long, strangely intense moment, the
air seemed to shimmer between them. His gaze
started at her toes and swept up her body, leaving
her quivering in reaction and her steps slowed and
stopped as his eyes bored into hers. She simply
stood, halfway down the steps, held immobile by that
gaze and she felt her breath quicken as a heavy, unfamiliar pressure coiled low in her abdomen.

Finally Stone cleared his throat. "I'll be the envy
of every man in the room."

The spell was broken but she was warmed by his
words. "That would be nice," she said, finishing her
descent and stopping in front of him. "I'll try to be
an asset to you."

Stone smiled but it looked a little strained and she
realized the barrier he'd put between them earlier in
the day was still firmly in place. Then he smiled.

Silhouette ROMANCE® 1444
$3.50 U.S.
$3.99 CAN.
MW

DIANA PALMER

MERCENARY'S WOMAN

SOLDIERS OF FORTUNE

We'd like to send you **2 FREE** books and a surprise gift to introduce you to Silhouette Desire®.
Accept our special offer today and
Get Ready for a totally Refreshing Experience!

HOW TO QUALIFY:

1. With a coin, carefully scratch off the silver area on the card at right to see what we have for you—2 FREE BOOKS and a FREE GIFT—ALL YOURS! ALL FREE!

2. Send back the card and you'll receive two brand-new Silhouette Desire® novels. These books have a cover price of $3.99 each in the U.S. and $4.50 each in Canada, but they are yours to keep absolutely free!

3. There's no catch. You're under no obligation to buy anything. We charge nothing—ZERO—for your first shipment and you don't have to make any minimum number of purchases—not even one!

4. The fact is, thousands of readers enjoy receiving books by mail from the Silhouette Reader Service®. They enjoy the convenience of home delivery...they like getting the best new novels at discount prices, BEFORE they're available in stores...and they love their *Heart to Heart* subscriber newsletter featuring author news, horoscopes, recipes, book reviews and much more!

5. We hope that after receiving your free books you'll want to remain a subscriber. But the choice is yours—to continue or cancel, any time at all. So why not take us up on our invitation with no risk of any kind. You'll be glad you did!

SPECIAL FREE GIFT!

We can't tell you what it is...but we're sure you'll like it! A FREE gift just for giving the Silhouette Reader Service® a try!

Visit us at
www.eHarlequin.com

"The first time I ever met you, you had a ponytail so long you could sit on the end of it. It's a little disconcerting to see you looking so grown-up and gorgeous."

"Thank you. I think." She wasn't particularly pleased with the hint that he still thought of her as a child, and she knew he'd done it deliberately. But she didn't comment. "You look very nice, too. I've never seen you in a tux before."

"A necessary evil." He dropped her hand and turned away, picking up a small box from an etagere beneath a large gilt-framed mirror. "I have a wedding gift for you."

She was dismayed. "But...I didn't get anything for you."

"Agreeing to this charade was gift enough." He lifted her limp hand from her side and pressed the velvet case into it. "Open it."

Automatically she lifted the other hand to support the box, which was heavier than she'd expected. "Stone, I—"

"Open it," he said again, impatience ripe in his tone. "Don't forget you're Mrs. Stone Lachlan now. People would talk if I didn't have you dripping with gems."

Slowly she nodded, then bent her head and pried open the hinged box. And gasped.

Nestled on black velvet was a necklace of brilliant blue sapphires and diamonds. The alternating colored stones glinted gaily in the light from the crystal chandelier overhead, smaller stones back near the ornate platinum clasp gently graduating in size to a significant sapphire anchor in the middle. Matching teardrop earrings were fastened to the velvet as well.

She was speechless. Literally. Her mouth was as dry as a bone. There was nothing she could do but stare at the striking jewelry, not even blinking. Never, in her entire life, had she seen stones like these up close and personal. Unless you counted the glass display behind which the Hope Diamond rested at the Smithsonian in Washington.

Stone took the box from her and removed the necklace. "Turn around."

Obediently she turned around, and in a moment she felt the cool weight of the platinum and gems against her skin as Stone's fingers grazed her nape. This felt like a dream. Just weeks ago, she'd been waiting on customers at Saks; today she was married to one of the wealthiest men in the country and he was showering her with clothing and jewels. A few months ago, she'd been a college student with no idea that every penny of her education was being paid for out of the goodness of someone's heart.

Flustered and agitated, she whipped around to face Stone. "I can't do this."

"Do what?" He raised his hands and clasped her upper arms gently, rubbing his thumbs back and forth over the sensitive flesh.

She shivered as goose bumps popped up all over her body and a quick *zing* of mouth-drying, breath-shortening attraction shot through her. She was so close she could see the flecks of amber and gold amid the blue in his irises when she looked up and abruptly she realized her change of position had placed them in a decidedly intimate pose. Her breasts grazed the solid expanse of tuxedo-clad chest and the way in which he held her made her feel strangely small and delicate.

"You know." She stepped back a pace and raised her hands to try to unclasp the necklace. "Pretend to be your wife—"

"There's nothing pretend about it, Faith," he said. "You *are* my wife."

"Not in every way," she said steadily though she knew she was blushing and her whole body felt trembly and weak.

His hands dropped away from her as if her skin burned his flesh. "No," he said. "That was our agreement."

"We could…change the terms, if we wanted to." She didn't know where she'd found the courage to speak to him so frankly, but she was conscious of every hour of her year sliding by.

But he was shaking his head. "No. It's normal for us to be attracted to each other in a situation like this. But acting on it would be a huge mistake." He took the box from her and removed the earrings, then handed them to her as matter-of-factly as if they hadn't just had the most intimate conversation of their acquaintance. "Put these on and then we'll go."

She wanted to say more but she didn't have the courage. He'd turned her down flat, crushing her hopes. Numbly she fastened the earrings through her ears and picked up her small purse again.

"Aren't you even going to look at them?" Stone took her shoulders and angled her to look in the mirror over the table. Reflected back was an elegant, beautiful woman wearing a stunning sapphire-and-diamond collar and matching earrings. Behind her, his hands possessively cupping her shoulders, was a tall, handsome man in a tuxedo, confidence oozing from every pore.

A perfect match. She turned away from the mirror, fighting tears. They looked so right together, confirming her feelings. How could he think making love would be a mistake?

"What is this fund-raiser for?" Faith asked as they stepped into the grand ballroom a little while later.

Stone grinned, feeling a spark of genuine amusement as he anticipated her response. "It's not quite the typical political occasion," he said. "It's for WARR."

"War?" Her eyebrows rose.

"Wild Animal Rescue and Rehabilitation. The organization rescues lions, cheetahs, tigers, elephants, bears...you name it, from bad situations. They restore them to health and place them in zoos, parks and other habitats where they'll be able to live in peace."

She nodded, her eyes lighting up. "That's wonderful. I read an article about Tippi Hedren's efforts with the great cats recently. It's horrifying to hear some of the stories about the way those poor animals are forced to live."

"It's also horrifying that people think they'll make great pets." He took her hand and directed her toward a large display near the entrance, where guests were perusing photos and stories about WARR's work. "A child in Wyoming recently was killed by a tiger that her neighbor owned as a pet—uh-oh." Catching sight of the woman bearing down on them, he squeezed her hand once in warning. "Brace yourself. We're about to face the inquisition."

"Stone Lachlan!" It was a woman's voice, booming and imperious. "Where have you been hiding yourself?"

Stone kissed the rouged cheek of the tiny woman who approached. "Mrs. deLatoure. What a pleasure. I've been working rather than hiding, but I'm glad I took a break tonight. Otherwise, I might have missed seeing you."

The little woman beamed. "Outrageous flattery. Feel free to continue."

Eunicia deLatoure was the widowed matriarch of one of the country's wealthiest, oldest wine-making families. Her sons had taken over the business a few years ago when her husband had passed away but the widow deLatoure was still a force to be reckoned with. Rumor had it that her sons ran every major decision by her before plunging into anything. Having met her quiet, deferential sons before, Stone didn't doubt it.

He slipped an arm around Faith's waist then and drew her forward, enjoying the feel of her slender body in his grasp as he made a perfunctory introduction. This night was going to be both heaven and hell. Especially now that he knew what she was thinking. Did she have any idea what she was asking for? He seriously doubted it. He was pretty sure she was still a virgin. Damn, *that* was the wrong thing to think about!

"Your bride! I just read about your engagement a few days ago." The woman's eyes flew wide and the stentorian tones turned heads throughout a solid quadrant of the ballroom. She leveled a piercing gaze on Faith. "Congratulations, my dear. I assume this is a recent development."

"Very recent. We're still in the honeymoon stage."

Stone answered before Faith could open her mouth. "And we're feeling quite smug to have kept it a secret from the press."

The matriarch chuckled. Then her gaze sharpened as she pinned Faith with that gimlet eye again. "It's delightful to meet you. Is your family in attendance tonight?"

It was a blatant attempt to ferret out Faith's pedigree, he knew. "No." He answered before she could speak. "Just me." He pulled her closer to his side. "It's good to see you, Mrs. D. Say hello to Luc and Henri for me."

As he steered Faith away, she said, "I could have spoken for myself, you know. The woman probably thinks you married a mute."

He registered the slightly testy tone in her voice. "Sorry. I just didn't want her to grill you. She can be merciless." As he continued across the room, he muttered in her ear, "We don't have to worry about spreading the news anymore. I bet every person in this ballroom knows we're married within ten minutes."

"That's what you wanted, isn't it?" Her gaze was steady and there were unspoken issues dancing between them.

"Yeah," he said, ignoring everything but the words. "That's what I wanted." Purposefully he moved through the crowd enjoying drinks and canapés, introducing Faith as they went.

The band switched from background music to dance tunes and the floor filled immediately. When he heard the strains of the first slow dance, he took her glass and his and set them both aside. "Do you like to dance?'' he asked as he escorted her to the floor.

"I don't really know,'' she said. "I've never done much of it.''

"You're kidding. What did they teach you at that school?''

"Latin, physics, biology…little things like that. It was a *real* school.''

"Point taken,'' he said, amused. "All right, I'll teach you to dance. Just step where I step and hold on to me.''

"How about I just stand on your feet like I used to?''

He laughed. "Let's see how you do learning the steps before we resort to that.''

When they reached the dance floor, he pulled her into the rhythm of the steps with ease, guiding her with one big hand on her back. His fingers grazed her skin just above the place where her dress stopped. God, he wanted to touch her in so many other ways. This was torture. But it was necessary. They had to appear to be a happy newly married couple. The first few weeks were bound to be the toughest, until their marriage faded from the radar screens of the gossip-mongers.

"Are you doing all right?'' he asked. She was following his lead easily, as if they had danced together a hundred times before.

She nodded, the action stirring the soft curls against her neck. "Fine.''

"Good.'' He hesitated, then said, "I'm going to hold you closer. The world is watching and I want them to be convinced we're newlyweds.'' *Uh-huh, ri-i-ight,* said his conscience, but he firmly squashed it.

"All right." Her voice was breathy, her color high. Her gaze flashed to his, then away, and the desire she felt was so transparent he felt scorched by the heat that leaped between them.

Dammit, this was impossible. Knowing that she wanted him was the worst kind of aphrodisiac in the world. If she were more experienced, he wouldn't hesitate to take what she offered. But she wasn't. And he had no intention of changing their situation. Someday she would thank him for it. He hoped so, anyhow, because if she didn't appreciate how hard this was for him, he might just strangle her.

How hard...bad choice of words. Very bad choice of words. He drew her in, tucking their clasped hands to his chest and sliding his arm more fully around her, bringing her body closer to his without pressing her torso against his. Thank God she was wearing that puffy-skirted dress that made it hard, er, *difficult* for him to get too close. She'd probably be shocked silly if she realized exactly what she was pressed against, because for all her delicate dancing around a very touchy subject, he knew her experience was extremely limited. The first time he'd kissed her he'd sensed that she hadn't had a lot of practice at it. But she'd learned fast. Thinking about her passionate, searing response to his kiss was a bad idea. A really, really lousy idea, in fact. He tried to concentrate on the music, the couples around them, but all he could seem to absorb was the feel of her in his arms. She startled him then by turning her face into his throat, tilting it slightly upward so that her breath caressed his throat and resting her head against his shoulder and without thinking, he slid his hand up over the bare skin of her back to caress her nape.

She shivered involuntarily, and he smiled against her hair. "Sorry. Did I tickle you?"

"N-no."

"Good. Relax." *Was she kissing his neck?* No, of course she wasn't. It was only his prurient imagination in overdrive. "People are watching us. You do realize we're going to be the hot topic of tomorrow's gossip column, don't you?"

"I hope not." Her breath lightly feathered his skin.

"We are. But as I said, they'll soon be on to some newer gossip. We'll be so boring they won't have anything to write about."

"Good." Her answer was heartfelt.

They danced in silence for a long while as the music flowed from one song into another. He thought he probably could hold her, just like this, all night. Their silence wasn't strained, and though his body was well aware of her nearness, there was a strangely satisfying peaceful sweetness in simply dancing with her in his arms. The thought of doing this week after week for an entire year was powerfully appealing. His blood fizzed and bubbled like fine sparkling wine in his veins and reluctantly, he acknowledged that he was going to have to put some space between them or he was going to do something he would definitely regret.

"Faith?"

"Hmm?"

"When this song ends, we're leaving."

She raised her head from his shoulder and immediately he missed the warmth. "It's barely ten o'clock. Isn't that a bit early?"

"Not for newlyweds. They'll think they know exactly where we're going."

"Oh." Her eyes widened and her gaze clung to his for a long moment. Then she dropped the contact and looked steadily at his right shoulder, which he knew was all she could see from her angle. She'd withdrawn from him, he realized. And a second later, he also realized he didn't like it one damn bit.

"Faith?"

"Yes?" She didn't look at him.

The hell with distance. He had to taste her again or die. "I'm going to kiss you."

"Wha—?" Her eyes flew open and she instinctively tried to pull away from him, but he controlled her with such ease that he doubted anyone even realized she'd just lost a bid for freedom. "Why?" she asked bluntly. "You said I—you said you didn't want me—"

"Appearances." His voice sounded strained to his own ears. "I'm going to kiss you so there's no doubt in anyone's mind why we're leaving." *Liar.*

"Oh." It took the wind out of her sails and he almost could feel her droop against him. She was so vulnerable that one short comment had wounded her. It was a puzzle. How could a woman as lovely as Faith think she wasn't attractive? Then he realized that she'd simply never been exposed to large quantities of men who would undoubtedly drool over her. He sighed, unable to let her continue thinking that she didn't turn him on.

"It's not you," he said gruffly. "You're the most desirable woman I've ever known and if you want the truth, I'm having a hell of a time keeping myself from, uh, doing something rash.''

There was a silence between them.

Finally she said, "Really?" and her tone was distinctly doubtful.

"Really," he responded dryly.

"It, um, wouldn't be rash," she said, looking up at him with such hope in her eyes that he felt ten feet tall.

His body urged him to take her somewhere private and plunge into the maelstrom of passion she offered—but he resisted. He still wasn't going to make any moves they both would regret later. He had to kiss her, but he would keep it short. Just a taste to get him through this ridiculously adolescent longing. "Selfish, then. Your whole life is ahead of you. You need time to experience the world."

She didn't say anything, just lowered her gaze to his shoulder again, giving him a subtle but definite cold shoulder.

Now he knew exactly what his married buddies called "the silent treatment." And he knew why they didn't like it. Well, the hell with that. Letting go of the hand he held in closed dance position, he took her stubborn little chin in his fingers and tipped her face up to his. And then his lips slid onto hers and the world exploded.

He initially had intended to give her a light, gentle kiss that would look romantic to the many eyes covertly directed their way. But the minute he began to kiss her, Faith relaxed against him with a quiet hum of approval, delighting him and pushing his already eager body into a far-too-serious awareness of the girl who was, in the strictest sense of the word, his ward until her twenty-first birthday. God, she was so innocent! He could taste the inexperience in the sweet soft line of her lips as she passively let him mold them, and he moved carefully, determined not to scare her.

But she didn't seem to be in any danger of being frightened. He suppressed a groan as her lips began to move beneath his. Slowly he lifted his mouth a breath away from hers, knowing he couldn't take much more. They were on a dance floor in the middle of a crowded ballroom; even if he intended to deepen the kiss and teach her how to kiss him back the way he longed for her to do, he wasn't going to do it here.

You aren't going to do it ever.

Ever. He looked down at her, taking in the glaze of passion in her eyes and the way she ran her tongue over her lips in reaction as she said, "Stone?" in a bewildered tone.

"That should convince them." He forced out the words, ignoring her unspoken appeal. "Thanks."

Her eyes widened and her body went stiff in his arms. Carefully she pushed herself away from the close contact and let him continue to lead her through the motions of the dance. But she'd lowered her head and withdrawn into herself again. He could feel the distance between them and abruptly, he led her off the dance floor.

No matter how much he wanted to pull her back against him and teach her all the things that were playing in his mind right now, he wasn't going to. They had to live in each other's pockets for twelve months. He was her guardian, he reminded himself rather desperately. He respected her too much to cheapen their relationship with casual sex. He was almost thirty years old and he'd learned by now that sex without commitment wasn't all it was cracked up to be. He didn't love Faith that way and though he wanted her badly, he didn't want to mislead her. She was so innocent she'd probably confuse sex with love. Which wasn't what was between them. Not at all.

Love wasn't an emotion with which he was familiar. In fact, he was pretty sure it didn't exist, except in poets' imaginations. It was just a pretty word to dress up desire. Physical attraction. He'd never seen two people in love yet who weren't physically attracted to each other, proving his point. And when that attraction wore off, there often wasn't enough basic compatibility to keep them together. His parents were a prime example of that.

Things were strained between them during the rest of the evening, though he doubted anyone else would notice. Faith dutifully smiled and made small talk as he took her around the room to introduce her to a few more people who would be offended if he didn't. But she didn't meet his eyes. He kept a hand at the small of her back or lightly around her waist most of the time, just for show.

She was still silent on the drive home.

He said good-night to her at the foot of the stairs, then left her to rustle up the stairs in her pretty gown alone while he moved into his study on the pretext of checking his e-mail. In truth, he didn't really want to be in his room, imagining her disrobing just on the other side of an unlocked door. He trusted his willpower but there was no sense in being stupid.

She was young and beautiful, slim and warm, and his body knew she was available.

Just say no, he reminded himself. He'd seen Nancy Reagan's famous slogan, intended to help kids resist drugs, plastered on billboards. Somehow, it seemed appropriate under the circumstances.

Two weeks passed. Forty-nine more weeks with Stone after this one, she thought to herself one Wednesday morning. Although that time would do her little good, she thought morosely, when the man barely set foot in the same room with her. He left for work at dawn and often worked well past the dinner hour. She'd eaten dinner with her mother and Clarice almost every night and kept a plate warm in the oven for him. Her days were incredibly long and, well, boring.

The one bright spot in the tedium of her current situation was the time she got to spend with her mother. Yesterday, they'd gone across Central Park to the West Side and toured part of the Natural History Museum. Naomi's face had been one big smile the whole time, although Faith worried a little bit that the trip was too tiring for her.

"Tiring?" her mother had said. "How can it be tiring? All I'm doing is driving this scooter."

But privately, Faith could see that her mother had lost a lot of ground in the past year. She was unable to get from bed or chair to her scooter without Faith's or Clarice's assistance. Eating was becoming more difficult due to the tremors that often shook her hands and arms. And on Monday, they'd taken her to the ophthalmologist because Naomi had thought she needed stronger glasses. The ophthalmologist did give her a new prescription, but while she was picking out new frames with Clarice, he'd taken Faith aside and told her that her mother was developing double vision, a common problem with MS. She should see her primary care physician, he'd emphasized, since there were advances in medicine all the time and he didn't know that much about multiple sclerosis.

The worries about her mother's health made every moment they spent together even more special. She thought of Stone, and the way he'd reacted to his mother, and she remembered what he'd said: *Would it have killed her to let a little kid think he meant something special to her?* His resentment was deep-seated and not without cause. But she'd also seen the pain in Eliza's eyes on more than one occasion when Stone had brushed her off. Whatever she'd been or done in the past, she cared about him. And Faith couldn't imagine that a woman who cared about her child would absent herself from his life for extended periods without good reason.

Acting on impulse, she went to the kitchen and found the telephone book, then placed a call. A few moments and two receptionists later, she was speaking with her mother-in-law.

"Faith! What a pleasant surprise!" The CEO of Smythe Corp. sounded delighted to hear from her. "How are you adjusting to marriage?"

"Quite well, thank you." Dangerous subject. She'd better move to the reason for her call. "I was hoping you could join us for lunch one day soon if you're not too busy."

There was a momentary silence on the other end.

"I would love to," Eliza said, and Faith could tell she meant it. "When and what time?"

On Saturday night, Faith and Stone attended the opening of a new Broadway show in the Marriott Marquis. It was a stirring musical based on the life of Abraham Lincoln. It ended with shocking effect with the shot that took Lincoln's life and the audience held their applause for a hushed moment of silence before breaking into wild clapping.

Faith wore another of the dresses Stone had purchased for her and the sapphires again. Might as well let him get his money's worth. She felt constrained in his presence tonight, all too aware of the distance he insisted on imposing. He'd been that way in the weeks since the WARR ball, staying so busy she barely saw him, spending what time he was at home in his office working. Some days she hadn't seen him at all. Others, he'd made charming small talk with her mother and Clarice over dinner, including Faith just enough to make a good showing for the older women. She resented it, but she knew she had no real reason to complain. This was the bargain they'd made. He was living up to his end and expected her to do the same.

"Well," Stone said as they moved toward the room where a private reception to celebrate the opening night was being held, "I predict a long and healthy run." He didn't meet her eyes, though, as he spoke, and she was all too aware this was a public performance.

"I agree." She pointed as they entered the ballroom. "Oh, look at the ice sculpture." There were several stations scattered around the room for hors d'oeuvres and at each one was a towering ice sculpture. The one nearest them was a stunningly faithful representation of Lincoln in profile.

They got plates of pretty sandwiches and other bite-size morsels and Stone brought her a glass of club soda as she'd requested. But he didn't sit down when he returned with her drink. "I see some people I need to speak to," he told her. "I'll be back in a few minutes."

"Oh, I'll go with you." She started to rise, but he put a hand on her shoulder.

"No, it's business. Go ahead and eat. We'll dance when I get back."

She watched him walk away through the crowd. *It's business.* He was determined to keep that part of his life separate from her, it seemed. And to keep himself away as much as possible, too. She ate, and waited. And waited some more. She was getting quite tired of waiting when she saw a small knot of people off to her left. As she scrutinized the group, she realized that they were clustered around a youngish looking dark-haired man. And a moment later, she recognized him as one of the actors from the play.

Well. If Stone wasn't going to entertain her, she'd find someone to talk to on her own. She might never have had the nerve to approach the actor if there hadn't been a ring of fans already around him, but she'd been quite impressed with his performance and wanted to tell him so. Rising, she walked toward the crowd and waited patiently as person after person shook the actor's hand and effused about the show. The man glanced up, and his gaze sharpened as he caught her eye. She smiled and extended her hand.

"I wanted to tell you what a fine performance you gave tonight. I suspect this will keep you employed for quite some time."

The actor laughed, displaying dimples and perfect white teeth. "That would be nice!" He didn't let go of her hand, but turned, tucking it through his arm. "I'm starving. Will you accompany me to the buffet?"

She allowed him to turn her in the right direction.

"What's your name? I'm at a disadvantage—you know mine." His blue eyes twinkled as he looked down at her.

And indeed she did. "I'm Faith," she said. "Faith—Lachlan."

"It's nice to meet you, Faith. Please tell me you aren't here with anyone."

Vaguely alarmed, she released his arm. "Sorry," she said. "My husband is here with me."

"He doesn't seem to be taking very good care of you."

"He is now."

Faith jumped and half turned. Stone had approached behind her. His voice was distinctly chilly. She felt his left hand settle at her waist; the right he extended to the other man. "Stone Lachlan. I take it you've met my wife."

"Sorry," said the actor, backing away, a wry grin on his face. "She was alone. I assumed she was single because no man in his right mind would leave a woman like her alone..." and he turned and headed in the other direction.

Stone's hand slid from her waist and he braceleted her wrist with hard fingers. "Dance with me."

"All right." But he was practically dragging her toward the dance floor.

"Did you tell him," he said through gritted teeth as he swung her into dance position, "that in eleven more months you'll be free to flirt with anyone you want?"

What? She was so shocked by the unexpected attack that she was speechless as he took her in his arms and began to move across the dance floor. "I wasn't—"

"Save it for later, when we don't have an audience," he said curtly.

"I will not!" Finding her voice as outrage rose, she stopped dancing, forcing him to halt as well.

"Faith, you're making a scene." His voice was tight.

"Maybe you should have thought of that before you started slinging around unfair accusations." She tugged at his arm around her waist but it was like pulling on a steel bar. He didn't give an inch. "Let me go," she said. "I want to go home."

"Fine. We'll go home."

"I said I, not we." To her utter mortification, tears rose in her eyes. "I did nothing to deserve to be treated like that. Let me go!"

"Faith—" He hesitated and there was an odd note in his voice. "Don't cry."

"I'm not crying. I'm *furious!*" But that wasn't strictly true. She was devastated that he would accuse her of such a low action. "I wasn't flirting. And if you didn't want me talking to other people, you shouldn't have left me sitting alone for an hour."

She tried to wrench herself away from him but instead of releasing her, Stone merely wrapped his arms around her and lifted her off her feet, moving from the dance floor to a partially private spot beside a large pillar. "Baby," he said roughly, "I'm sorry—"

"Not as sorry as I am," she said. She deliberately made her voice and her face expressionless, retreating in the only way she knew how, forcing herself to ignore his big, hard body so intimately pressed to her own.

"Look," he said desperately, "I was wrong. I was jealous and I didn't handle it very well. Please don't cry." And before she could evade him, he bent his head and covered her lips with his.

She'd longed for his kisses, dreamed of them constantly. As his warm mouth moved persuasively on hers, she tried to hold onto her anger but it was quickly overridden by her body's clamoring response to the man she loved. With a small whimper, she put her arms around his neck and tried to drag him closer, and between that heartbeat and the next, the kiss changed. Stone growled deep in his throat and his arms tightened. He slid one hand down her back to press her up against him and she gasped as his tongue slipped along the line of her lips.

Oh, she wanted him! Her pulse beat wildly at the realization that he wanted her, too. *I was jealous...* The husky words echoed in her head, melting her anger and softening her heart as wonder stole in. He'd been jealous. She could hardly credit that in light of the way he'd been carefully avoiding any contact with her, but...he was *kissing* her now, his mouth moving possessively, his big hands splayed over her body, holding her tightly against him.

But in a moment, he began to lessen his grip and

his kisses became shallower and more conventional. "My wife," he murmured against her lips as he finally set her free. "You're *my* wife."

His wife…was that all she was to him? Her rising hopes crashed into a flaming abyss once again. Had he only kissed her to establish a claim? To show the world that she was his?

She couldn't quite let herself believe that, not after that kiss. She looked up at him, but he already was leading her out of the ballroom, claiming their coats, hailing a taxi and bundling her in. As he tipped the parking attendant who'd gotten the cab and slid in beside her, she cleared her throat. "Stone?"

"Hmm?"

"Where do we go from here?"

He looked at her questioningly. "Home."

"No." She waited until he braked at a red light and she caught his eye again. "I mean, you and I. Our relationship."

"Faith." His gaze slid back to the street and his voice was firm and resolute. "We've had this discussion before."

"Yes, but—"

"The answer is no. It doesn't matter what you want, or what I want. It would be a huge mistake for us to get involved in a physical relationship."

"Are you trying to convince me or yourself?" she challenged, frustrated beyond belief by his hardheaded refusal to see what they could have together.

"Both, probably," he said grimly.

Six

"Hello, Faith. Thank you for inviting me." Eliza Smythe entered the foyer two weeks later and handed Faith her coat and handbag. "I've been hoping we could get to know each other better."

"So have I," Faith responded, leading her mother-in-law into the dining room, where she had set two places at a small round table near the fireplace. "Please, sit down." She waited until the older woman was seated before she took her own place. "I'm so sorry Stone couldn't be here. He had some pressing things to take care of at his office."

"Pressing things?" Eliza laughed cynically. "I bet they became a whole lot more pressing when he found out I was coming for lunch."

Faith felt herself flushing. She was unable to deny it.

Eliza leaned forward, her face growing serious. "I

hope your invitation didn't cause trouble between you and Stone.''

''It didn't.'' That was perfectly truthful. For there to be trouble between them, they first would have to talk. Stone's only reaction, when she'd told him his mother would be coming to lunch was a curt, ''I have meetings all day, so count me out.'' Gee, what a shock.

''Good.'' Faith's mother-in-law smiled warmly at her. ''So tell me how you like married life. Has the press been too intrusive?''

''Not as bad as I feared, actually,'' Faith confessed. ''But Stone has taught me to keep a low profile in public. That's helped.''

''He'll be less interesting now that he's married,'' predicted Eliza. ''Unless,'' she added, smiling wickedly, ''you keep giving them moments like those photos from the Lincoln reception. That was hardly what I'd call low-profile.''

Faith felt the heat rise in her face. The week after the disastrous evening, there had been a series of three photos of them in the Star Tracks section of *People* magazine. In the first frame, Faith was with the actor she'd met, with her arm tucked warmly through his. The man's head was tilted down so that he could hear something she was saying. It was a decidedly intimate-looking pose.

The second photo showed Stone, scowling, pulling her toward the dance floor and the other man could clearly be seen walking away in the background. But the third shot was the one that had made her cringe. It had been taken during their heated kiss behind the pillar. Stone had her locked against him, nearly bent backward beneath the force of his kiss. She clung to him on tiptoe, one hand in his hair. The sly, amusing captions had mentioned his jealous reaction—and she doubted the author would ever know how true it had been. Unfortunately, she thought, Stone hadn't been reacting out of any personal feeling. He just didn't want anyone coming on to his wife. She was pretty sure he viewed her as an extension of property.

She ducked her head. "Stone wasn't very happy with that," she admitted. "We'll have to be more careful in the future." Her mother-in-law was still smiling, though, and she decided that the revealing photos probably had helped Stone's cause in his quest to convince his mother of the authenticity of his marriage.

Faith picked up a spoon then and started on the soup she'd set out for the first course. Her mother-in-law followed suit and they talked of other things during the meal. Eliza asked after Faith's mother, and Faith found herself sharing some of her concerns about the future. To her pleasure, Eliza spoke freely about her business. If only Stone would do the same! She longed to share his life, but it seemed he was never going to give her the chance.

"So," the older woman said as they relaxed with coffee an hour later, "we got sidetracked after I asked you how you liked married life. Has it been a big adjustment?"

"In some ways." Faith hesitated, then decided it wouldn't be inappropriate to share her feelings with her mother-in-law. "The boredom is driving me crazy," she confessed, "if you want the truth. I can only spend so much time with Mama—she needs a lot of rest and quiet."

"I thought you were a student. Don't you have classes?"

"I took this semester off." Faith doubted Eliza even knew about Stone taking on financial responsibility for two additional people. In any case, she couldn't explain the details of her "semester off" without the risk of giving away the true reasons for her marriage. "My classes don't start again until June."

"That's not so far away," Eliza pointed out.

Faith raised her eyebrows. "You wouldn't say that if you were the one sitting here twiddling your thumbs. I've asked Stone if I could help at the office but—" she rolled her eyes and tried to sound mildly aggravated as an indulgent wife might "—he told me to redecorate the den." Her opinion of *that* was evident in her voice.

"Well, it is a project," his mother said, playing devil's advocate.

"One I accomplished in a few days," Faith said. "The painters are here right now. The wallpaper, carpet and new furniture have been ordered."

Eliza chuckled. "And you're twiddling your thumbs again." As Faith nodded, the older woman cleared her throat. "I might have a project for you, if you're interested."

A project? Faith was cautious. "Such as?"

"I have a significant amount of data from one of my plants that recently was restructured. The last man was an incompetent idiot and he left a huge mess with a number of damaged files that need to be recovered. It needs to be straightened out. It would be a short-term job, of course, but it might be perfect for your situation."

Faith's spirits soared immediately. She nearly clapped her hands. Then something occurred to her. "Wait a minute. How do you know I'm capable of doing this job?"

Eliza's slim shoulders rose and fell in a wry gesture. "I confess I did look into your background a little bit. You have quite a gift with computers, it seems."

She didn't know whether to be flattered or annoyed. "I'm beginning to see where Stone gets his autocratic nature."

Her mother-in-law winced. "I'm sorry if I've made you angry."

"It's all right." She wasn't really angry. "The job sounds like a challenge. I like challenges. But I'll need to talk to Stone about it."

"All right." Eliza rose. "Thank you for lunch. Whether or not you take the job, I hope we can continue to get together from time to time."

"That would be nice." And it would be. "Perhaps Stone will be able to join us next time."

Eliza made a distinctly unladylike sound. "Not if he finds out I'm going to be there."

The words were filled with pain, as were her eyes. Faith hesitated. She knew Stone wouldn't thank her for getting in the middle of his relationship with his mother…still, she couldn't simply ignore this. "I'm sorry," she said. "Maybe, in time, he'll soften." But she doubted it.

Eliza sighed. "You don't believe that and neither do I. Stone thinks I abandoned him. And he's right. I did." Her face looked as rigid as marble. The only sign of life was the leaping, snapping flames in her eyes. "When my father died, I was a young wife with a small child. And suddenly, I was the heir to this company—which was struggling to keep its head above water, something my father had never told me. I was determined to keep Smythe for my son. Maybe I should have hired someone else to lead it, but at the time I felt like...oh, I don't know, like it was my destiny or something.'' She tried to smile. ''Or maybe it just makes me feel better to tell myself I had no other choice but to take over and lead the company myself.''

''It must have been a good decision,'' Faith said, realizing what a difficult choice Eliza had been forced to make. ''Look at what you've accomplished.''

The Smythe Corp. CEO shrugged. ''But look at what I sacrificed. My marriage fell apart when my husband realized I had no intention of walking away from Smythe Corp. I should have refused to cooperate when he told me to leave. I should have taken Stone with me. But he was so close to his father...I didn't think it would be fair.'' She shook her head. ''Of course, I never thought my husband would try to keep me from seeing my son, either. And once I'd moved out, the courts *did* view me as a poor parent.'' Her shoulders slumped. ''I guess we all have things we wish we had done differently.''

Faith was stunned. Stone thought his mother hadn't wanted him! All these years he'd thought she didn't care...he couldn't have been more wrong.

''You, ah, wanted to see him more often?''

His mother looked beaten. ''Yes, but when his father got full custody he was able to severely limit the time I spent with Stone. After a while, Stone seemed to view my visits as a chore and it was easier not to go as often." She shook her head regretfully. "I'm very sorry now that I didn't continue to be a presence in Stone's life no matter what."

Then she glanced at her watch, and Faith could see her shaking off the moment of painful truth. "I have enjoyed this tremendously, Faith. Thank you again for inviting me. It's time for me to get back to the office."

"Thank you for joining me." Faith rose and laid her napkin aside, then led the way to the front door.

Eliza put on her coat, then turned once more. "Let me know if you're interested in that job. It wouldn't just be something I've made up to keep you busy. I really do need to get someone on that project soon."

"I'll let you know by the end of the week," Faith promised. "I appreciate the offer more than you know."

She was just coming down the stairs to breakfast two days later when she heard Stone calling her name. His voice sounded alarmed, unusual for him, and immediately she doubled her speed.

He was in the breakfast room. So was her mother. But Naomi was lying on the floor near the table with him crouched at her side.

"Mama!" Faith rushed forward, taking in the scene. Her mother was conscious, though she lay awkwardly on her side. "What happened?"

"She says she was transferring from her scooter to the table. She had a muscle spasm and she slipped," Stone said. As Faith dropped to her knees, Stone rose and left the room, returning a moment later with the telephone as well as a blanket, which he draped over her mother. "It's a good thing it's

Saturday," he said, "or I might not still have been home. She could have lain here for a while except that I was in the kitchen and I heard her."

"Where's Clarice? And why were you trying to do this alone?" Faith knew her voice was too shrill but she was frightened. Naomi shouldn't have been trying to move without supervision.

Clarice had agreeably offered to work six days a week. Sunday was the only day she took off and even then, she often was gone only a few hours. She had no children and, Faith assumed, no other family.

"I sent her to the deli," said Naomi. "They have wonderful fresh bagels. I thought I could...I thought..." Her voice trailed off and she started to cry.

"It's okay, Mama." Faith stroked her hair. "It's okay. How do you feel? Do you think anything is broken?"

"Don't try to move." Stone's voice brooked no opposition. "Let me call an ambulance and we'll go to the hospital so you can be checked."

"No emergency service," Naomi begged.

Stone shook his head as he punched a speed dial button. "I won't call 9-1-1. I'm calling your doctor first."

Clarice returned just as Stone hung up from explaining the situation to Naomi's doctor. The caregiver was as upset as Faith had ever seen her, and it was as much work to calm Clarice as it was to comfort her mother. Things moved rapidly after that. Naomi's doctor sent a private ambulance and she was transported to the hospital where she was met by her doctor. Faith, Stone and Clarice waited impatiently until a nurse appeared to take them to the room in which they'd settled Naomi.

The doctor who oversaw her care met them in the hallway and took all three of them into a small visitors' lounge before they saw Faith's mother.

"Your mother is experiencing an increase in spasticity that worries me. It's important that we begin a physical therapy program in order to keep it from worsening. Passive stretching, maybe some swimming, that kind of thing. Also, she absolutely should not attempt transfers from one place to another without physical assistance. Sometimes the spasms can be severe enough to knock a patient right out of their wheelchair."

"Is she going to have to start using a wheelchair now?" Faith asked apprehensively.

"I'm not ready to take that step yet," the doctor replied. "Let's see if we can't control the spasticity first."

"Exactly what do you want us to do?" Stone's voice was authoritative and Faith was happy to let him direct the conversation.

"I would recommend one of two things: either hire trained therapists who can work with Mrs. Harrell, or consider placing her in a facility where she can be cared for."

"You mean a nursing home," Faith said dully. She'd worried about this edict for years. Now, suddenly, here it was. And she was no closer to accepting it than she had been before.

"She won't need a nursing home." Stone put his arm comfortingly around her shoulder as he addressed the doctor. "But if you could give us the names of some reliable sources of personnel, we'll get more help at home.''

Stunned, Faith stared at him and he glanced down at her and smiled.

A moment later, the doctor left.

Clarice rose. ''I guess you won't need me now,'' she said in a small voice. ''I don't know how to help her exercise.''

''Oh, you're not getting away from us,'' Stone told her in a firm voice, removing his arm from around Faith and standing. He took Clarice's hands in his. ''Unless you want to, that is. Naomi depends on you, and so do Faith and I. If you agree to stay, you'll be in charge of any personnel who come in to help. It'll be your job to make sure they're doing theirs, and that everything is going smoothly.''

Clarice stared at Stone for a long moment. She opened her mouth, but no sound came out. Faith realized the older woman was on the verge of tears. Finally she said, ''Thank you. Thank you so much. I don't have any family and I've gotten really fond of Naomi. I would have hated leaving all of you.''

''And we would hate to lose you,'' Faith said, rising and hugging the older lady. ''We're your family now.''

Clarice went ahead of them to see Naomi as Faith turned to Stone. She swallowed with difficulty and took a deep breath. ''I appreciate your support but I know you hadn't counted on this when we made our agreement. I won't hold you to anything you said to that doctor.''

''I know you won't. But I still intend to hire additional help and keep your mother in our home.''

''You've done enough for us already,'' she told

him unsteadily. "I don't think your father meant for you to support us for the rest of our natural lives." She tried to smile at the weak joke.

Stone put his arms around her and pulled her head to his shoulder, just holding her for a long, sweet moment. "Your mother means a lot to me, too," he told her. "She and Clarice have made the house a warmer, livelier place."

She pulled back and searched his gaze for a long moment. He appeared to be completely serious. "Thank you." She didn't know how she ever would repay him, but she would swallow her pride to make sure her mother was happy and well-cared-for. Putting Naomi in a nursing home would have been devastating for her as well as for Faith.

"Don't thank me," he said, still holding her loosely in his arms. "I mean it. Keeping her at home is really an act of selfishness on my part."

"Right." Although she could have stayed in the comforting embrace forever, she forced herself to move away from him. "You're a good man," she said quietly, touching his cheek with a gentle hand before turning to leave the room.

They visited briefly with her mother. She hadn't been badly hurt, just severely bruised and she'd broken a bone in her wrist. She would be staying overnight at the hospital for some additional tests and would be released tomorrow. Faith was relieved the fall hadn't been worse.

Clarice decided to stay at the hospital for a few hours and told them she would take a cab home later. On the ride home, Stone said, "I haven't told you how good the den looks. I really like my new chair." He flexed his fingers on the wheel. "I believe my mother must have chosen the old furnishings. I don't ever remember it looking any different.''

''Your mother did a lovely job,'' she told him. ''The things she chose lasted a long time.''

''Longer than she did.''

''I'm not sure that was her choice, entirely.'' It was a risk, talking about his mother, but she felt she had to try to share with him his mother's version of the past.

The car was uncomfortably quiet for a moment. Then he said, ''It's old news.'' He shrugged, frowning as he drove. ''Who cares anymore?''

You do. ''She does,'' Faith said. ''She didn't want to leave you behind but your father fought her for custody. And limited her visits. She's always wanted to be a bigger part of your life than she was permitted to be.''

''And I suppose she told you this during your cozy little luncheon.'' His voice was expressionless.

''Yes.'' There was another awkward silence. She waited for him to ask her what she meant, what his mother had said. But he never did.

Instead he finally said, ''We got off the track, I believe. We were talking about the changes in the den.''

''I'm glad you like the new look and the new furniture.'' She was disappointed that he hadn't listened to more of his mother's story, but at least he hadn't bitten her head off. ''I really wasn't sure about it, but since you told me to go ahead...'' Then she followed up on the opening he'd given her. She'd been trying to figure out a way to approach him again for several days. ''Now that the job is finished, I'm finding myself with a lot of free time. You know, I'm not sure you appreciate the extent of my computer skills. Surely there's something at your company that I could—"

"There really isn't," he interrupted her. "But I did want to ask you to do something else." Without giving her a chance to respond, he said, "I've received several wedding gifts at the office and I know we've begun to get quite a few more at the house. Would you please write thank-you notes to everyone? I'll supply you with the addresses you need."

"I've kept a list of everything. The files are on the computer in your home office," she told him, disappointment shading her tone. "I'd thought perhaps it was something we could do together."

But he shook his head. "I really don't have the time. I'm sorry. At the end of the week I'll be leaving for China for a nine-day trip."

"China!" She couldn't believe he hadn't mentioned this before. How long had he intended to wait before telling her?

"Yes. We have an incredible opportunity to get our foot in the door with some steel exports." Unaware of her thoughts, he sounded as excited as she had ever heard him. "And I want to investigate the possibilities of setting up an American division of Lachlan Industries in Beijing."

It had been a strange conversation. He'd taken her to the heights of exasperation but now he was sharing his business plans with her...something she'd wanted for so long. Cautiously, afraid he would clam up again, she said. "Lachlan Industries in Beijing?"

"Uh-huh. The world really has become a global marketplace. If I want Lachlan to be a player on more than a national level, I have to establish a pres-

ence around the world. Our plants in Germany pro-
duce a number of products for the European market.
One in Beijing could serve a sizable portion of the
Far East, including Taiwan and Japan.'' He was
warming to his theme and his tone was enthusiastic.

''Now I understand why people say you have the
Midas touch,'' she said. ''You never stop thinking
of ways to improve.''

''I can't,'' he said simply, ''if I want to stay on
top. I'm always looking for the next opportunity. It's
a full-time effort.''

''When you take over your mother's corporation,
how will you manage both companies?''

Instantly the light in his eyes flattened and cooled.
She saw immediately that she'd said the wrong thing.
He shrugged, elaborately casual. ''I'll probably work
out some kind of merger. Get everything under one
umbrella so I don't have so many balls to juggle.''

His too-casual tone, coupled with an explanation
that sounded wooden and rehearsed, alerted her to
the realization that this wasn't just business for
Stone. Merge the two companies?

Some of the pieces of the puzzle that was her husband clicked into place as she recalled the odd note
of near-desperation in his tone on the night he'd laid
out his proposal. Her heart ached for him as a flash
of insight showed her the truth. He didn't want
Smythe Corp. because it was a good deal, or even
because it was a family tradition. A merger was
something he could control as he hadn't been able to
control the disintegration of his family when he'd
been a child—and in a very tangible if symbolic
sense, he would be putting his family back together
again.

She wondered if he understood that some things could never be fixed. Quietly she said, "You know, merging these companies is nice, but it isn't going to help you resolve your differences with your mother. You really ought to sit down and talk with her."

But she could tell her impassioned words had fallen on deaf ears. His face drained of expression and when he looked at her, his eyes were as cool as the blustery spring weather outside. "Funny, but I don't remember asking you for your opinion on what I ought to do with my mother. All I require of you is that you play a part for ten more months."

She felt as though he'd slapped her. As a reminder of the time limit she had, it was fairly brutal. She didn't speak again, and when they arrived home, she got out of the car before he could open her door and hurried inside, heading for her room. *Fine,* she thought angrily. *Let him go to China. Let him count down the days until he rids himself of me. Let him refuse to give me anything meaningful to do.*

With that thought, she remembered Eliza's offer. And she reached for the phone.

"This place is awesome!" Faith's former roommate Gretchen bounced into the kitchen of the town house as they completed a short tour of the house several days later. She turned to face Faith, her expressive pixie face alight. "I still can't believe you're married to him."

"I can't believe it, either," Faith said wryly. "It's a little overwhelming sometimes."

"He's really been great about your mom living here." Gretchen flung herself onto one of the bar stools. "Tim would wig out if I asked him to let my mother live with us."

"It's a slightly different situation." Faith felt compelled to defend Gretchen's steady beau, one of the nicest guys she'd ever met. "I mean, it's not as though we're tripping over each other like we would in a small place."

"Yeah, I guess the money makes a difference." The redhead made a little moue of frustration. "Money. I wish it didn't exist."

"Amen." Gretchen couldn't know how much Faith meant that. Then her friend's woebegone expression registered, and she focused on Gretchen. "What's wrong?"

Gretchen shrugged. "Nothing, really. Tim asked me to marry him—"

"When? Why didn't you tell me?" Faith leaped from her own seat and embraced her friend. "Congratulations!"

But Gretchen raised a hand and indicated that she should calm down. "Well, frankly, it isn't that big a deal yet. Tim says he wants to marry me, but he wants us to save some money first. He's thinking we should buy a house in New Jersey."

"And you don't want to do that?"

"Are you kidding? I'd love it!" Gretchen waved her hands about. "Big old trees, a little white picket fence and a house with shutters. We could get a dog…we've even talked about children." Her big eyes sparkled with tears. "But he wants to wait until we can make a down payment on a home to get married. I love the stupid man and I want to marry him *now!*"

"Why should you wait?" Faith tried to think

about it from Tim's point of view. And failed. People who loved each other should marry. What did money have to do with love?

"Beats me."

"I don't get it, either." Faith sighed heavily. "I'm sorry. Men are such dolts sometimes."

"You said it, girlfriend." Shedding her sad mood, Gretchen eyed Faith over the rim of her coffee cup. "That sounded like you had one specific man in mind."

Faith smiled slightly. "Without question."

"Problems with the tycoon?"

"A few." If her friend only knew!

"Sex," said Gretchen.

Faith nearly choked on the coffee she'd just swallowed. "What?"

"Men are amazingly easy to manipulate if you start with a little physical T.L.C."

"They are not."

"That's what all the magazines say." And that, as far as Gretchen was concerned, made it fact. "So you just have to dazzle him with incredible, unforgettable sex and then talk about whatever's bothering you. He'll be much more malleable then."

"You are *terrible!*" Faith began to giggle as she saw the glint of humor lurking in her friend's eyes. But her amusement faded away as she thought about her marriage. "Anyway, that's not an option. We don't—" Oh, my God. She stopped, appalled at her runaway tongue.

Gretchen was staring at her as if she'd sprouted a second head. "Tell me you are kidding. You have a platonic relationship with one of the most gorgeous men in North America?"

"Um, yes, that's about right." Faith squirmed beneath the incredulous stare.

"Don't you love him?"

Faith nodded sadly. "I do. I never knew it was possible to care for someone the way I care for him. But that doesn't mean it's mutual."

"Well, if he doesn't love you and you're not having wild, bed-wrecking sex every night, then why the heck did he *marry* you?"

Well, there was no backing out of it now. If there was a more persistent woman than her redheaded friend on the face of the planet, Faith would have to meet her to be convinced. "He married me because he feels responsible for me," she said miserably. To an extent, that was true, and it was the only thing she could say to her friend without breaking Stone's trust. "His father and mine were best friends. When they were killed together, Stone became my guardian."

"Your *guardian?* How Victorian!" Gretchen's eyes were wide. "And because of that he felt compelled to marry you?" Her eyes narrowed and she gave a snort of disbelief. "Uh-uh. I don't buy it."

"It's true," Faith said glumly. "That's why we haven't—we don't—"

"Give me a break." Gretchen hopped off her stool and paced around the kitchen. "Look me in the eye and tell me that if you were as homely as a mud fence he'd have married you." When Faith's brow wrinkled and she hesitated, Gretchen stabbed her index finger at her. "See? I knew it! No man would sacrifice himself like that. He wants you."

"He doesn't." Faith stopped, remembering the

passionate kisses they'd shared, and her expression reflected her lack of conviction.

"Ha! I knew it." Gretchen was grinning at the look on her friend's face. "He *does* want you. He's just trying to be, I don't know, noble or something. I guess he's got some hang-up about that guardian stuff. Still…if he's hot for you, there's hope. You just have to seduce him."

"*Seduce him?* You are insane."

"No, no, I'm serious." And her freckled face did look surprisingly sober. "I might have been kidding before, but I am so totally not joking about this. Faith, you were meant to be with this guy. And he was meant to love you back. He's just too dumb to know it. You're going to have to go after him big time."

"No way." She shook her head, remembering the way he'd rejected her before, and the way he'd reacted two days ago when she'd tried to encourage him to mend his fences with his mother. "He's made it clear what his position is."

"Oh, come on. Aren't you the girl who came to town without a job *or* a place to live, and found both the very first day? If you really want him, he's toast. You just have to go for it."

"This is a ridiculous conversation." Faith rose and began stacking dishes. "Come on, I'll take you in to meet my mother and her companion before you have to get back."

But Gretchen's words lingered in her mind long after her old roommate had left. *If he's hot for you, there's hope.*

Seven

The trip to China lasted three days longer than he'd planned. By the time Stone left LaGuardia behind and slipped his key into the lock of his town house, he was exhausted. The meetings had been long and ultimately fairly successful from a business standpoint. But the strain inherent in communicating his ideas effectively to people of another culture had worn him down. But it wasn't only that. For the first time in his life, he'd been impatient to conclude his business and get home. Not so that he could get back to work, but so he could get *home*.

Impatient. Right. How about so nervous he couldn't even spit? He checked his watch. It was nearly ten in the evening. He'd been away for twelve days and they'd seemed like twelve hundred.

He'd hated traveling. No, he thought, trying to be honest. He'd hated traveling alone. God, he'd never imagined feeling lonely simply because a certain woman wasn't at his side. He'd never expected to be seized with a barely controllable urge to hop a flight and fly home simply because that's where she was. He'd never, *ever* thought about a woman so much that it shattered his concentration and turned his brain to mush in the middle of important meetings.

But thoughts of Faith had done all that to him and more. He'd lain awake aching for her, knowing that even if he were in New York he'd still be aching for her...and wishing he were there, anyway, because then at least he'd be close to her.

He must have been crazy when he'd married her, he decided as he took the stairs two at a time. How could any man be expected to ignore the temptation of her lithe young body day after day after day? It was natural for him to want her, to ache for her. It was just a physical reaction.

He walked through the house, noting the lamp that was always lit now in the hallway that led to the kitchen. Faith had begun leaving it on for Clarice, in case she came to get something from the kitchen at night. He'd gotten used to seeing the small glow.

He walked down the hallway to his bedroom door, noting that Faith's was firmly closed. Would she come to greet him when she heard him moving around? Probably not. He'd have to wait until morning.

Morning. He realized he'd actually missed mornings at home. On the days he hadn't run from the house at dawn, he'd shared breakfast with Faith and sometimes her mother and Clarice. He'd always imagined he'd find having other people around first thing in the morning annoying, but it was surprisingly pleasant.

It might not be so pleasant now, after the way he'd left things with Faith. But even then, knowing that she was likely to be cool and formal with him, something eased in his chest because at long last he was home again, and she was sleeping right in the next room. He hoped he could make things right with her. He missed her smile, and the habit she had of humming beneath her breath as she moved around the house.

She hadn't done much humming the past few days before he'd gone to China. Their parting had been strained, stiff, the way things had been between them since the day of her mother's accident. He should have apologized for the things he'd said to her about her interference with his mother. Faith had a good heart and a wonderful relationship with her own mother; it probably was beyond her capabilities to understand the way he felt.

He stepped into his bedroom and dropped his suitcase inside the door. A startled squeak made him jerk his head around to locate the source—and there she stood.

She must have just finished in the shower because she had a towel wrapped around her torso and her hair was pinned atop her head. He could see droplets of water gleaming on her shoulders.

Immediately he felt a rush of desire begin to radiate through his body, making him take a short, tense breath as every inch of his skin seemed to sizzle with an electric charge. He'd been thinking of her, wanting her for so long that it only took moments to make him worry that she'd notice the burgeoning arousal pushing at the front of his pants.

"Hello," he said, and his voice was husky. "I didn't mean to scare you."

"It's all right." She smiled at him, and the radiance of her expression tightened every muscle in his body. "I'm glad you're home. I missed you."

"I, uh, missed you, too." He couldn't look away from her. She was smiling, her gray eyes shining, so beautiful that he ached with the need to cross to her and crush her to him. She apparently had forgiven him. Or forgotten their argument. Hah. He doubted Faith would forget something like that.

Then she put her hands up to the top of the tucked-in fabric and his whole body tightened. She took a deep breath, uncertainty flashing in her eyes so fast he wasn't sure he'd seen it to begin with. And before he could say a word, she dropped the towel.

As it fell away from her, he made a strangled sound in his throat. She was as beautiful as all his fevered imaginings, long, slim, sleekly muscled. Her breasts were high and round with deep rosy nipples that puckered beneath his gaze. Her bare feet curled into the carpet and he couldn't prevent his gaze from sliding up her long elegant legs, over the splendid curve of her hip. At the junction of her thighs, a thatch of blond curls protected her deepest secrets.

As he devoured her with his gaze, she fought an obvious battle with shyness and modesty. Her hands came halfway up her body in a defensive posture before she deliberately let them relax at her side again. A rosy blush suffused her neck and climbed into her cheeks, but she held out her arms to him, still smiling into his eyes. "Make love to me."

His blood surged heavily, nearly propelling him into her arms. He wanted her, and he hated himself for it. She was too young.

She's not too young. She's legal.

Well, she was too young for him.

Ten years isn't a huge age gap.

"Stone?" She came through the dividing door into his bedroom and began to walk across the room toward him, her eyes flickering with nerves even though her voice was steady and warm. "This is the part where you're supposed to respond."

She obviously hadn't noticed just how *responsive* he was. He felt himself beginning to sweat. "Dammit, Faith, just stay over there." He backed around the other side of the bed, putting some space between them, appalled at the panicked note in his voice. "You don't want this."

"I do." Her voice was as soft as ever but there was a note of determination in it that shook him. "I thought about it the whole time you were gone. I've been thinking about it since the day you asked me to marry you." She took a deep breath and he couldn't prevent his gaze from dropping to her breasts as the firm mounds rose and fell "I want my first…first time to be with someone I trust and care for. I want it to be with *you.*"

"No, you don't." But her words sent unpleasant images bolting into his mind, images of Faith with another man, and he had to bite back the snarl that wanted to escape.

"I do," she said again. She reached up and took the clip from her hair, tossing it onto his dresser as the silky blond tresses fell down her back and framed her body. She came around the end of the bed and walked to him.

He put out a hand like a traffic cop to hold her off but she slipped inside it and pressed herself against him, her hands sliding up to curl around his neck as her lips grazed the sensitive skin where his shirt collar exposed his throat.

He groaned at the feel of her slim young frame pressed against him. She smelled fresh and sweet, and despite his good intentions, his extended hand dropped to her back, sliding slowly up and down her sleek spine, testing the naked, resilient flesh, moving dangerously down to trace the cleft in her buttocks. His hand clenched spasmodically on her soft flesh, pressing her hips hard against his aching arousal. "We won't be able to get an annulment." His voice sounded hoarse and unfamiliar to his ears.

"I don't care." She kissed his throat again. "How can this be so bad when we both want it so much?"

"I haven't changed my mind about this being a mistake." But he had. The words she'd said, that she wanted *him* to be the one, danced through his head. If he refused…he couldn't even complete the thought. Instead he ran his hands over her silky skin everywhere he could reach, savoring the soft, sweet feel of her as common sense warred with pure carnal need. Finally need won. He dropped his head and sought her mouth, wrapping his arms around her. His kisses were hard and wild, his tongue plunging deep. She gasped and he remembered how innocent she was, so he reined himself in with gargantuan effort, gentling his kisses, stroking the inside surfaces of her mouth with his tongue and teasing her until she followed his lead, her tongue hesitantly joining his, exploring his mouth as fully as he explored her. Finally he tore his lips from hers, breathing heavily. He kissed her cheek, slid his mouth along her jaw and down the side of her neck. She smelled of scented bath soap and the unique flavor of her silken skin.

He raised his head, capturing her gaze, and his face was rigid with the control he was exerting to rein in the need he felt. "No," he gritted. "I can't do this anymore. I can't fight myself and you both. I can't pretend I don't want to make love to you when every hour of every day, I'm thinking about doing *this*." He slid one hand boldly around to cup her breast and his thumb found the tip of her nipple, rubbing gently back and forth. Her eyes closed as he watched her face, and her lips parted as her breath rushed in and out. Then he bent his head and replaced his thumb with his mouth, suckling her strongly, and her eyes flew wide. Wildly she arched against him as she cried out.

"And this," he muttered against her breast, sliding the same hand down over her rib cage and the softness of her belly, stroking gently before plunging firmly down between her legs to her most intimate feminine secrets. She was moist and slick, surprisingly ready for him. He cupped her, sliding his fingers between her legs as he used his thumb on the small bud hidden beneath the sweet curls. Her body arched again at the new sensation and she gasped. Then she set her hands against his shoulders, trying to push him away, instinctively wary and nervous of such implacable male determination.

"Ah, no, baby, don't fight me." He lifted his head and took her lips again, understanding her momentary panic. Despite her brave invitations, she was still an innocent. The act of giving herself to a man made a woman intensely vulnerable. And so he simply let his hand lay against her as he resumed kissing her until she felt secure with him, permitting him access to her mouth without restraint as her legs relaxed. Then slowly he resumed the intimate caresses. He slid one finger inside her, groaning at the tight, wet feel of her clinging flesh and his hips surged forward as he tried to ease the harsh need driving him. "That's it," he growled. "I want to make you feel good. We're going to be so good together."

Withdrawing his hand from its nest, he slid both arms beneath her and lifted her into his arms, moving the short distance to his bed. She put her arms around his neck and lifted her face to his and he sat down on the side of the bed, kissing her and stroking her, torn between the need to bury himself deeply within her and find release, and the desire to explore her hidden treasures for hours. But then she shifted against him, her hip pressing hard against his full flesh, and he knew he wasn't going to be able to wait hours.

She lifted her hands and inexpertly began to unbutton his shirt. He rose, laying her on the bed, then quickly shed his shirt and jacket in one movement, removing his shoes and socks, taking off his belt, all without taking his eyes from the bounty of her bared body.

She was watching him, too, and he saw her pupils contract as he tore off his shirt. She lifted one hand from the bed and laid it over the rigid, throbbing flesh that distended his pants and he nearly jumped out of his skin. He tore at the fastenings, pushing his trousers down and off along with his briefs. Her eyes widened again as his need for her came fully free, and her gaze flashed to his. "Can I...touch you?" she whispered.

He gritted his teeth at the unconscious sensuality of her request as her body turned toward him. "Sorry, baby." He caught her wrist and linked his fingers with hers. "That would be a really bad idea right now. This would be over before it ever really got started."

She smiled and her voice was nearly a purr when she said, "Then I'll wait."

He came down on the bed beside her, sighing as his naked flesh met hers for the first time. His erection pressed against her hip and he could feel the moisture he couldn't hold back dampening her flesh. He shuddered, hoping he could wait long enough to make it good for her.

Quickly he smoothed his hand down over her downy belly and feathered his fingers over the sweet folds between her legs again. Her gaze was fastened on his and he caught a hint of apprehension in her beautiful eyes. Leaning forward, he kissed each of her eyelids as they fluttered shut. "Relax," he whispered. "I'll take care of you." He leaned over her and took her breast, suckling firmly until she moaned and tried to arch toward him. His fingers grew bolder, parting her and opening her for him, and he shifted his weight onto her, his arms shaking with the effort it took not to simply shove himself into her and ride her until he exploded. But Faith was a virgin. And she was...special. He wanted it to be as good for her as it was going to be for him. He pulled his hips back and let his shaft rub her, then reached down and opened her further until the slightest surge forward caught the head of his aroused flesh within her.

She gasped.

He groaned.

She raised a hand, and wiped away a drop of sweat that trickled down his temple. "Is this hard for you?" she whispered.

He chuckled deep in his throat. "No, it's hard for *you*." Her eyes widened as he probed her, alert to the barrier that signaled her virginity. Just within her, he met resistance. "I'm going to try not to hurt you," he warned her, "but the first time might not be much fun." She watched him wide-eyed as he moved his hand between them and found again the pouting bud he'd exposed. As he began to lightly press and circle, her eyes closed and her back arched, pushing him a little deeper.

"That's—too much," she panted. "I can't...I can't..."

"You can," he breathed. "Let it build, baby." He kept his tone soft, his voice low, watching the flush that spread over her fair skin as she gave herself to her passion, to him. In a moment, her hips began to respond to his encouraging touch, rising and falling, and he had to steel himself to withstand the seductive lure of her body caressing the tip of him.

"Stone," she cried, "hold me!"

"I've got you, baby," he crooned. "Let go, let go, let go..."

And she did. He saw the shock in her eyes as her body convulsed, shuddering beneath him, and as she arched wildly up to meet him, he plunged forward, burying himself deep within her responsive body.

"Oh!" Her legs came up to wrap around his hips,

possibly the most erotic feeling he'd ever known, and as her sweet channel continued to rhythmically caress him, he began to move, stroking heavily in and out, teeth clenched, body shaking. He was so ready that it took only moments until he erupted, falling over the edge into her soft arms as he emptied himself deep, deep within her. Pleasure shattered his senses as it spread throughout every cell in his body, rendering him momentarily deaf and blind.

As he began to regain his senses, he looked down at her. "Are you all right?"

"I'm fine."

"I didn't hurt you?"

"Only a tiny bit." She smiled at him, her fingers rubbing the back of his neck. "You were wrong. The first time *was* fun."

He chuckled as he slowly lowered his weight onto her, conscious of her slight frame. But she kept her legs and arms around him when he would have shifted himself to one side, holding him close until he let himself go boneless in her embrace. He rested his forehead on the pillow next to her and moaned as her fingers lightly kneaded up and down his back.

"Stone?"

"Hmm?" He was so relaxed it was an effort to move enough to reply.

"How long before we can do it again?"

His eyes flew open. He started to laugh, lifting himself on his elbows to inspect her face, then dropping his head to kiss her. "A little while, at least," he told her. "I'm pretty tired. But on second thought—" he moved his hips experimentally "—I'm feeling much more rested already."

She smiled, her gaze warm and contented and he

kissed her again, lingering for a moment before he levered himself up and began to withdraw—

And froze. He swore vividly, and Faith's eyes widened in shock.

"What?" she demanded.

He pulled himself back to his knees, then stood and cursed again, his hands on his hips, his still-erect flesh cooling unpleasantly. "No protection," he said grimly. "How the hell could I have been that stupid?" he asked the ceiling. But he knew exactly how stupid he'd been. He'd been so focused on completing the act of making her young, virgin body his that protection had been the last thing on his mind.

Faith went very still, probably as horrified as he was. After a moment, she sat up and eased herself to the side of the bed. Her brow wrinkled momentarily and she winced; he realized she was feeling some discomfort. But she stood, and stepped forward to slide her arms around his waist and press herself against him.

"It's all right," she said. She kissed his collarbone and then looked up at him. "I love you. I wouldn't mind if I got pregnant."

His body had reacted automatically to the soft feel of her curves but her words were a shock of ice water on his rising passion. "Faith," he said grimly, taking her by the shoulders and holding her gently but firmly away from him, focusing on the only part of her statement he could allow himself to believe. "*I'd* mind. This marriage is only going to last a year, remember?"

She simply gazed at him. And he was the first to look away.

"I know you think you love me," he said, desperate to convince her. "It's natural when two people make love for feelings to get mixed up with basic human needs. But trust me, you won't love me in a year."

Still, she regarded him silently. Finally she opened her mouth. "You're wrong. I'll still love you in a year. I'll still love you in ten years, and in twenty."

"Look," he said, frantic to erase the echo of those seductive words, "let's not get into a fight about this."

She smiled at that, and he stared at her, mystified. What the hell was so funny? "I wasn't planning to fight with you," she said. "I want to make love again." She stepped forward, pressing herself against him, burying her face in his neck. Her warm breath stirred the curls on his chest and he shuddered, knowing that she surely could feel the arousal he couldn't prevent.

"This isn't lovemaking," he said above her head. "This is sex."

"Okay." She nuzzled his chest and he leaped a foot in the air when her lips grazed his nipple. "You call it what you want and I'll call it what I want."

If he was smart, he'd walk away from this right now, and not compound one error by making another. But his arms came around her without his permission, and his head lowered and sought her lips all on its own. His body knew what it wanted even though his mind knew better. "And we use protection," he decreed, trying to retain some control of the situation. She was a twenty-year-old recently deflowered virgin. How could she be so unshakably certain of herself?

"If that's what you want," she said agreeably. Her

small hand slipped slowly down his body and his stomach muscles contracted sharply. "Is it okay to touch you now?" she asked.

He closed his eyes and exhaled in surrender. "Yeah," he said, giving himself to this night and this moment. He'd worry about tomorrow later. "But only if I get to touch you, too."

She awoke before dawn, aware of her body in a way she'd never been before. She lay on her side, her back cuddled into the living furnace of her husband. Stone's left arm was draped over her hip, the other was beneath the pillow on which both their heads lay.

With dreamy satisfaction, she relived the hours just past. He'd scared her silly when he'd walked into his bedroom without warning. Even though he'd told her his flight would be in that night, she hadn't really expected to see him. He'd warned her that he'd probably get home in the wee hours.

It was probably just as well that he'd surprised her. If she'd been prepared, she'd never, ever have had the nerve to approach and seduce him the way she had! She took a deep breath, remembering the moment of sheer terror she'd felt when she'd decided to drop her towel and take Gretchen's advice. At first, she'd thought he really was going to refuse. But then she'd seen his hands clenched in fists. She'd felt the barely contained desire he kept on a tight leash and she'd pushed a little more until the volcano had erupted and he'd swept over her with the force of a hot lava flow, incinerating her modesty and her virginity with his sheer delight in her body and his blatant encouragement of her sexuality. She might know another lover someday, but she knew without question that she'd never meet another man who pleased her like Stone did, who anticipated her every need before she even realized what she wanted.

She loved him so much. He still couldn't let himself see that they were perfect for each other. He'd led her to believe it was because of their age difference but the truth was, Stone was terrified of intimacy. Not physical intimacy, but emotional closeness. She knew he'd had scores of lovers in the past, but she was certain none of them knew him the way she did, knew his secret need for a stable home, the sorrow and resentment that threatened to permanently damage his relationship with his mother, the unacknowledged wish for a family of his own.

A family. A baby. How amazing that she hadn't even been thinking much about that kind of future until he'd introduced the possibility. She'd always thought of herself as a good girl. Going to her marriage bed a virgin was simply a given. But it shook her a little to realize that it wouldn't have mattered if she'd been married to Stone or not. If he'd ever tried to seduce her, he would have had her anytime he'd wanted. And it scared her more than a little that she hadn't even thought about protection once she was in his arms.

His grim panic from the night before shot into her mind. The very fact that he hadn't even thought of birth control had shocked him beyond belief. She hadn't thought of it, either, but then again, she wasn't worried about a pregnancy. Had she subconsciously expected him to take care of it? Or had she simply not cared because she knew she wanted his child? Regardless of the reasons for her memory's short-circuits, she'd known the moment he'd said it that very little could make her happier than to bear Stone's baby.

She was married to the man she loved and she knew instinctively that a child would change their lives forever. Stone would never let his child grow up in a broken home. If she did become pregnant, they'd stay married.

And then she'd have much more than a year to show him that he loved her, too.

But she had no desire to trap him in any way. She'd never imagined a man could be so scared by a few little words, she thought tenderly. Though she hadn't expected him to respond in kind, it had still hurt a little that he had so easily dismissed her feelings. Obviously he had never considered love to be a part of their relationship. She could only be patient now, and hope that her confession would get him thinking about love, about her, about making their marriage a forever one.

A surge of love so strong it shook her moved through her. Slowly she reached back with her left hand and let it rest on his hip, gently running her thumb back and forth across his warm flesh, simply needing to touch him. After a moment, his even breathing changed. So did something else, she discovered with pleasure, wriggling her bottom back against him a little more.

"Good morning." His voice in her ear was deep and sleep-roughened. The hand at her hip slid up to cup her breast, plucking lightly at her nipple until it contracted into a small, hardened point that sent streamers of arousal down into her abdomen.

"Good morning," she returned. "Welcome home."

"I thought you already did that."

She giggled. Then all coherent thought fled as he leaned over her and caught her mouth in a deep, sweet kiss. When she had to breathe or die, he lay back again behind her. For an instant he rolled away, and she heard the sound of a foil packet tearing, then heard him quickly fitting himself with protection. He'd insisted on using protection the second time last night, too, though she'd told him he didn't have to. He'd gone still for a moment, then simply sighed, shaken his head and kissed her.

In a moment, he was back. His hand slid down over her body to her thighs and he urged her top leg up, draping it over his as he angled himself into the hot, tight crevice he'd made. She felt the column of blunt male flesh prodding at her and he lifted her leg a little higher, until suddenly, he flexed his hips and slid smoothly into her. She moaned, impaled on pleasure, and slipped her hand back to his taut, lean buttocks to pull him even closer, even deeper.

"Are you sore?" He stopped abruptly. "I didn't even think—"

"I'm fine," she said, shifting her hips and stroking the smooth, hot length of him, "now."

Stone nuzzled her hair aside and kissed the joining of her shoulder and her neck. He flattened his hand on her lower stomach, holding her steady as he moved against her. And again, she welcomed him home.

Afterward, he rolled to his back. She pulled the sheet over her, not comfortable enough with nudity yet to ignore her own modesty, watching as he disposed of their protection.

"I meant it, you know," she said quietly as his gaze met hers.

"Which 'it' are you referring to?" he asked cautiously.

"Everything," she said honestly. "I do love you. And if a baby is a result of this—" she indicated them "—I would be thrilled."

"What about school?" His voice was challenging. "Starting your own business? Or is that all just so much talk?"

"Of course not." She refused to let him pick a fight over this, though she suspected he would feel better if he were able to make her angry. "Having a family and a career don't have to be mutually exclusive." The moment the words left her mouth, she realized that to Stone, who had been the victim of a marriage in which that very thing had indeed been an issue, the two goals were in direct conflict with one another.

"Are you kidding?" He sat up abruptly and swung his feet over the side of the bed. "Women can comfort themselves with that 'I can do it all' mantra as much as they want. But the reality is that something suffers when they try to juggle too many balls." He slapped an angry hand down on the bed between them. "I have no intention of bringing children into this world to be tossed to whichever parent isn't as busy at the moment. In fact, I never plan to have children at all!"

Faith stared at him, shocked by the declaration. She understood that he felt he'd been the casualty of his mother's determination to have a career but she'd never imagined he would let it affect him to such an extent. If only she could get him to walk in his mother's shoes long enough to realize it hadn't been the simple, power-hungry decision he assumed it had been. Her heart ached for him as she understood exactly what his parents' differing points of view could cost him.

Could cost them both.

Slowly, seeing that insistence would only make him more intractable, she said, "I apologize for not understanding how you feel. We have plenty of time to think about children—" unless he threw her out when her year was up "—and I certainly would never try to talk you into doing something you don't want."

There was a long, tense silence.

Finally Stone heaved a huge sigh. He turned toward her, not away, and she knew an overwhelming relief as he took her in his arms. "I'm sorry, too," he said. "I shouldn't have gotten angry with you. We never talked about children because I didn't think it would ever be an issue. Hopefully it still won't be." He pressed a gentle kiss to her forehead. "Can we just enjoy this for now?"

"Of course," she murmured. She tilted her face up to his and kissed him sweetly, deeply, without reserve. With any luck at all, each day that passed would bring them a little closer, and he would see what a long life together could be like. And how very special it would be to add a child born of their love to their family.

After a final kiss, he rose from the bed and went into the bathroom. She rolled over to watch him walk away, admiring the way his wide shoulders tapered down to a lean waist, the way the muscles in his buttocks flexed as he walked, the strong, well-shaped columns of his legs. As he disappeared, her gaze fell on the clock beside the bed.

"Oh, no!" She suddenly realized it was Thursday, one of the days she'd set up to work for Smythe Corp. And she was going to be late if she didn't hurry. She bolted from the bed and headed for the door that connected their bedrooms.

Stone came out of the bathroom and followed her, unselfconsciously naked. She wrapped her robe around her then rushed to her dresser for fresh undergarments and panty hose, wishing she could be as blasé about her nudity.

"What's the rush?" He rested a shoulder against the doorway of her closet as she picked out a sedate gray-charcoal suit. "Do you have plans this morning?"

"I, um, yes." She skirted him and started for her bathroom, but he caught her by the waist and dragged her back against him.

"Can they wait?" He dropped his head and trailed a line of kisses down her neck, and she shivered as his hot breath blasted her sensitive nerve endings. "I thought we could take a bath together and then have breakfast."

She swallowed, tempted by his words, and her body heated at the image of the two of them in the big Jacuzzi tub in his bathroom. "I—can I take a rain check?" She cleared her throat. "I really do have some place I need to be. And don't you want to get back to your office?" Instinct warned her that explaining she was working for his mother probably wasn't the wisest course of action she could take.

"I've been in touch by phone, fax and e-mail," he said. "I hadn't planned on going in early today after traveling for all those hours. Where are you going?"

There was no help for it. She took a deep breath. "I have a temporary job."

His brows snapped together. After a moment, he said, "I thought you wanted to be able to spend time with your mother?"

"It's only a part-time thing," she said. "And it hasn't interfered with my time with Mama. She rests a lot."

"Where are you working? I'm surprised you were able to find anything suitable."

He meant that didn't expose her to the public, she knew. She took a deep breath. The thought of lying to him flitted across her mind and was rejected in the same instant. "Your mother offered me a position straightening out some records that were left in a mess by a departing employee."

"My *mother?*" His expression grew even more forbidding.

She swallowed. "The day we had lunch she asked me to consider it…"

"Why the hell didn't you say no?"

She squared her shoulders and lifted her chin. "Because I was bored. I wanted something to do, some kind of work and you wouldn't even consider it."

"You *have* things to do," he roared.

She'd never thought of herself as a temperamental person but the unfairness of his expectations refused to let her quail before his displeasure. "No," she said stonily. "I don't. The den is redecorated, the thank-yous are written and sent. I still have time to take on any other little projects you throw my way, but two days a week, I will be working at Smythe Corp.''

Stone eyed her expression, apparently deciding he was going nowhere fast. "Fine," he said angrily. "Have a great time." He stalked back to his own room, closing the door between them with a definite snap and she winced, holding back tears.

She'd known he was going to be unhappy about her new job but she hadn't really thought he'd react quite so...strongly. Did it bother him because she would be in steady contact with his mother or because he simply didn't like not being able to control her every move?

Eight

He'd been an ass.

A horse's ass. A *big* horse's ass. Stone stared moodily out the window of his office at the gray Manhattan day. It was raining. He'd really been looking forward to some sunshine this morning, but when he'd stepped out the door to start the jogging that he tried to fit in four or five times a week, he'd been soaked to the skin in less than a minute. The only good thing about it was that Central Park had been nearly deserted, except for a few other hardy exercising idiots like himself.

God, what had he been thinking, to lay into Faith like that?

He hadn't been, he supposed. He was still jet-lagged from the unbearably long flights home. And he certainly hadn't gotten what he could call a full night's sleep last night.

He pinched the bridge of his nose between his thumb and forefinger. Last night.

The mere thought of it was enough to make him start to sweat. He'd woken with her in his arms and as his body had reacted to the sweet, soft lure of hers, he'd acknowledged what he'd been avoiding for days: he enjoyed having Faith in his life. He wanted to make this a real marriage, at least for the time they had left. He'd tried to stay away from her, but fate and Faith had tempted him until he couldn't resist anymore.

He couldn't quite remember why he'd thought it was such a bad idea. There was no reason they couldn't have a physical relationship while they were married. Unless, perhaps, he counted the fact that she might never speak to him again after the way he'd stormed off.

One thing that was certain—perhaps the only thing—was that he owed Faith an apology. He might not like her working for his mother, he might even—if he admitted the truth—feel betrayed in a small way, but he didn't own her. They had an agreement to which she was living up and anything she did that didn't jeopardize that was none of his business.

He didn't like the way that thought made him feel. *He wanted it to be his business, dammit!* He wanted her to be his wife in every way there was. He didn't just want her hostess skills or even her wonderfully responsive young body. He wanted her mind, her emotions, her commitment.

He shoved himself from his chair with an explosive curse. Oh, hell. Oh, no. Oh, hell, no. He was not going to fall into her trap.

Faith had made sure he knew how she felt—that

she wanted to make their marriage a reality in every way. And the knowing was powerfully seductive, the future calling to him with almost irresistible force. But long-term commitments were for other people. He wasn't dumb enough to believe he'd feel like this about Faith forever. Sure, he had friends who appeared to have happy marriages. But he also had friends whose marriages had wrecked them emotionally and financially, and even, in the case of one buddy whose wife had shot him for sleeping around on her, physically. His own parents, with all their money and resources, hadn't made it work.

He knew better than to believe in happy endings.

Still, she had said she loved him. And maybe she did. But his cynical side, the side that was doing its level best to preserve him from stupid, ill-conceived ideas born of passion, that side of him said, *Gee, the timing surely is convenient.*

Her mother was getting worse. He'd given Naomi Harrell a home, kept her companion, offered to provide her with more care. Faith cared deeply for her mother and would naturally appreciate his support. But would she tell him she loved him simply because of that?

She might if she were worried about what was going to happen once you cut her loose. She might if she wanted to ensure that you kept the funds flowing.

No way. His mind rejected the ugly notion. Faith had integrity and honor enough for two people. She'd been determined to secure care for her mother through other efforts before they'd married. She wouldn't stoop to the easy solution.

Would she?

Of course not. She was as aware of the terms of their marriage as he was. But damned if he was happy with them. When he tried to imagine what would happen next March, he failed utterly. He couldn't see himself without Faith. He couldn't see his home without her quiet influence or even, ridiculous as it seemed, her relatives. Before Faith had come, his elegant, upscale town house had been little more than an address to identify him. Sure, it had come to him from his father. But frankly, his memories of growing up in this house were less than stellar. It was a mausoleum. Or at least, it had been.

Now it was a home. When he came to breakfast, Clarice had brought the paper in for him already. Faith almost always saw him off, holding his coat and waving him out the door. When he came home in the evening, Faith and Naomi often were in the den, ensconced by the fireplace playing a board game. Sometimes Faith read to her mother, since Naomi's eyesight was deteriorating to the point that she was becoming unable to read. He had a wonderful new chair in the den, too, one that Faith had picked out herself.

And last night, he'd had just about the best night of his life.

So why was he still planning on getting rid of his wife at the end of a year?

He didn't know. And thinking about it was giving him a royal headache. What he really ought to be thinking about was how to get back in Faith's good graces. And if he were smart, he'd be thinking about what he could do to keep her so busy she wouldn't have time to go hunting for work, for his mother or anyone.

And then he had an idea.

* * *

She hadn't had the best day of her life. Though the assignment Eliza had given her was indeed a challenge, Faith's mind had drifted continually, re-hashing the angry exchange with Stone that morning.

It just wasn't fair. Last night, he'd made her hap-pier than she'd ever thought she could be. Then this morning, her happiness was ripped away with the angry words he'd thrown at her.

Faith sighed as she walked briskly from the sub-way station to the town house. Love was supposed to make people happy, not miserable.

When she came through the door, she was struck by the same feeling she always got when she entered her home...it was cozy, despite its size, and welcom-ing, despite her husband's anger. It had truly become home. Leaving it was going to be one of the hardest things she'd—

An odd scrabbling sound behind her startled her as she hung her coat over a hook on the coat rack. She whirled. A small furry creature was barreling toward her, skidding and slipping on the smooth pol-ished hardwood floor.

A puppy!

"It's for you," said a deep male voice, and she looked up to see Stone lounging against the door frame at the end of the hall.

She dropped to her knees and gathered up the puppy, talking nonsense to the wriggly little black-and-tan bundle, giving herself time to collect her thoughts. He didn't sound angry anymore. Cau-tiously she said, "What kind is it?" as she held the puppy up to her cheek. She laughed as the little tongue lapped at her cheek.

"She's a German Shepherd," he said. "Do you like her?"

"She's adorable! She's so tiny."

"She won't be that size for long. I thought she would be a good companion when you're walking around the park alone." He walked forward as she got to her feet with the puppy in her arms and to her shock and pleasure, he drew her close. "I'm sorry about this morning." He dropped his head and sought her mouth before she could speak, masterfully teasing her into a response that flared wildly between them. Then he tore his mouth away from hers. "Will you forgive me? It's none of my business what you do with your time."

She was stunned. What had produced this sea change? "Of course," she said, resting her head against his shoulder. "I'm sorry I didn't tell you before."

"Well," he said in a teasing tone, "I seem to recall that we were somewhat preoccupied...before." Then he set her away from him. "What should we name her?" he asked, nodding at the puppy.

"I don't know! Have Mama and Clarice seen her yet?"

He laughed. "Yes. They were bitten by the love bug at first sight. Or should I say first lick?"

She giggled. Then she snapped her fingers. "That's perfect. How about Lovebug?"

"Lovebug?" He looked dubious. "You'd really make me stand on the streets of New York with a German Shepherd named Lovebug?"

When he put it that way…"Oh, well," she said. "Back to the drawing board."

"It's got a certain cachet, though," he said. "Lovebug." He bent his knees so that he was eye level with the dog in her arms. "Are you a love-bug?"

She smiled at him. "You sound just like a doting daddy."

"That's what I was afraid of."

There was an instant of awkward silence as they both remembered the night before.

"We'd better take her out," he said at the same time that she said, "What will we do with her at night?"

They both laughed, and the moment passed. He put a hand at her back and guided her to the back of the house, where they took Lovebug outside. Then he showed her a crate in the kitchen. "The breeder told me it would be a good idea to get her used to being crated," he said. "For trips to the vet, or if we're away, or if we have parties and we want to protect or confine her. Apparently a lot of dogs like them so much they voluntarily sleep in them if the door is left open." He pointed to the table, where several books and a variety of leashes and toys lay. "I got a few things the breeder recommended."

She shook her head, amused. "You don't do any-thing halfway, do you?"

"Why don't you let me show you?" His voice dropped intimately.

A thrill of arousal shot through her. "What will we do with Lovebug?"

"Try out the crate?" he suggested. So they did, and to her amazement, the puppy sniffed around her new domain, wrestled once or twice with a large stuffed parrot, and then circled three times and fell asleep on the fleecy dog bed Stone had purchased.

"Hot damn!" he said. "Shall we try out the tub?" He took her hand and pulled her up the stairs into his room.

"We haven't even eaten dinner yet," she protested.

"Later." His voice was a rough growl. He tugged her into his arms and wrapped them around her tightly, so that every inch of her was locked against every inch of him. "I want you," he said. "I didn't get a damn thing done today because all I could think about was you."

She was stunned. And so happy she thought she might just burst. He'd brought her a puppy. A puppy that wasn't going to be anywhere near full-grown in less than a year, meaning...? She couldn't even let herself hope.

But now, now he was telling her things that she'd longed to hear, that she'd never imagined she would. He wanted her. He'd thought of her all day. "I thought of you, too," she said. "I—" But she didn't get a chance to tell him she loved him.

His mouth closed over hers as he bent and lifted her into his arms. He carried her up the steps and into the bathroom, where she discovered that he hadn't been kidding about trying out the tub.

Later, they ordered a pizza and ate it in front of the fire. Stone propped his back against the couch afterward and pulled her against his side, stretching his long legs out and sighing. "I'm still acclimating to the time change. I'm beat."

"Was your trip fruitful?" she asked, curling against him and laying her head on his shoulder. She kept her voice light, trying for an easy conversational tone as she stroked the puppy that lay in his lap.

He rolled his head, stretching the taut muscles in his neck. "Yes. We're going to begin the application process to open a plant in Beijing. With a little luck and a lot of greasing of official palms, we might be up and running in twelve more months or so."

He was talking about his work! She hid her elation and said, "Isn't there an awful lot of corruption in China? How are you going to control your costs?"

"I've factored in a certain amount of overhead simply because of that. And I'm using American managers, at least for the setup, until we get a true cost picture. Once things stabilize, we might hire local managers."

"But by then you'll know the costs and if things changed drastically you'd know something funny was going on."

"Exactly." He hesitated. "I'm going to have to go away again next week."

"Oh." She let her disappointment show in her tone. "Where to this time?"

"Dallas."

"I'll miss you."

"And I'll miss you." He turned his head and kissed her temple, and her heart doubled its beat. Stone wasn't just acting like a man who had the hots for a woman. He was acting as if he really cared for her. Then he spoke again. "I thought about asking you to go along, but I'll be so busy you probably would see very little of me. I've managed to schedule five days of work into three, though, so it won't be a long trip."

"Good." She traced a pattern in the thick mat of

hair that covered his chest, exposed by the shirt he'd thrown on and hadn't bothered to button. "I can see I'm going to develop an aversion to your absences."

"Then I'll just have to devote extra time to you while I'm here." He lifted the puppy and surged to his feet, starting for the kitchen. "Let's put her in her crate and go to bed."

"That would be nice," she said demurely.

He looked back as he straightened from the crate, catching the gleam in her eye, and laughed as he started toward her. "It'll be a whole lot more than 'nice,' and you know it."

The following week raced by at the speed of light. He made love to Faith every chance he got, and if she could be more radiant, he couldn't imagine how. She lit up whenever he came into the room, her pleasure in his presence clearly apparent. Stone decided that if all marriages were like his, no one would ever get divorced.

The thought sobered him slightly. When they'd married, he'd planned a quiet annulment at the end of twelve months. Now there was no chance of that. He and Faith would have to divorce. The very word left a bad taste in his mouth.

He was scheduled to leave for Dallas on an afternoon flight. That morning, he went in to the office for a few hours, then came home to pack. Faith sat on the bed and watched as he efficiently gathered his clothing and folded it into the suit bag he was taking.

"You're awfully good at that," she said. "I guess you get a lot of practice."

"Practice makes perfect," he parroted. He looked at her, seated cross-legged on his bed—and suddenly,

he knew he was going to have to have her one more
time before he left. Her lovely face was woebegone
at the prospect of separation; he knew just how she
felt. The thought of sleeping without her was making
him more than a little desperate.

Setting aside the briefs he was stuffing into corners, he stepped toward her, his hands going to his
belt, swiftly opening his pants.

"Stone!" she said. "You've already had your
send-off."

"Ah, but that was goodbye." He put his hands on
her thighs and slid them up beneath the skirt she
wore, dragging down her pantyhose and the thong
he'd watched her shimmy into that morning, throwing them across the room. "This," he said, position-
ing himself and bracing his body over hers as he
slowly pushed into the hot, welcoming depths of her
body, "is my incentive to hurry home."

Her eyes were dazed, her expression so sensually
intent that it set fire to his already raging need for
her. He lifted her thighs and draped them over his
shoulders, beginning a quick, hard rhythm. She bit
down on her lip and moaned, then her eyes flared
wide and she arched up to meet him. It was a fast,
frantic coupling. He was driven by a need he didn't
fully understand, some primitive urge to stamp her
as his, and he hammered himself into her receptive
body until she convulsed in his arms. Immediately
he followed her, feeling himself spilling forcefully
into her until he lay over her, panting.

Faith lifted her arms, which had fallen limp to her
sides, and clasped his head in her palms. She gave
him her mouth in a sweet, deep kiss that he returned

in full measure. When she tore her lips from his, she gasped, "I hate it when you're gone."

"I know, baby." He grinned at the pouty expression on her face, kissing her again. Faith wasn't generally moody; she must really be minding this. "I'm sorry. I'll try to cut down on my traveling from now on."

"I'd like that," she said. "I had visions of spending the next couple of decades watching you pack a couple of times a month."

"Faith—" Her words were entirely too seductive, slipping into his mind and twining around the need for her that he couldn't admit, even to himself. With an effort, he recalled his original proposition. One year. That was all he'd ever promised her.

"I love you," she said. He closed his eyes against the stark emotion pooling in hers, defensive anger rippling through him. Hadn't she understood anything he'd said that first night they'd made love? But she continued. "I know you think you don't want children now, but you might change your mind one of these days, and I'd hate for our child to grow up wondering where Daddy is half the time. As it is, Lovebug is going to be devastated. She worships you. I thought in a couple of years maybe we could get her a companion—"

"Faith!"

She finally stopped, and her shock at his tone was evident.

Fighting himself as well as her, he said, "I told you before that I don't want children. And does the phrase 'temporary marriage' ring any bells with you?" The words were harsh with frustration.

Immediately he regretted the question. She recoiled from the words as if he'd struck her. Slowly, she said, "We've been talking—sharing—everything, which I assumed meant we were growing closer. You got the dog, which I assumed meant we'd be sharing her in our future. You've made love to me every chance we got, which I assumed meant more than simply sex. Did I assume wrong?"

He was sweating. Pure fear took over. What if he let himself believe her? He wasn't sure he'd survive if she left him one day. "You knew from the very beginning that this arrangement had a definite end in sight." Forget the fact that he'd been wondering if there was any need to end it. Ever.

Her whole body stiffened. She immediately pushed at his shoulders, trying to free herself. He held her down with implacable force, their bodies still joined, but she turned her head to the side, shutting him out. Tears trickled from beneath her eyelids and ran across the bridge of her nose to disappear into the hair at her temple. He swore, dragging himself back away from her and shoving his clothing roughly into place.

Faith scrambled backward away from him, off the far side of the bed, where she bent her head and ignored him while she pulled her skirt into place, ignoring the fact that she was wearing nothing beneath it. Finally she took an audible breath and raised her head. Her gaze was so tortured and filled with pain that it struck him like a blow.

"I asked you a question earlier. You haven't answered it." Her voice was steady but her eyes were swimming with tears. "I assumed our lovemaking was more than sex. Was I wrong?"

No! Admitting anything would make him vulnerable. He hesitated.

And in that fatal second, he saw that whatever he said wasn't going to be enough.

"Never mind," she said. She turned toward the door.

"I told you before that it was easy to confuse love and lust," he threw at her back, furious at her for forcing this confrontation. "You're too young to know the difference."

She stopped. Turned. And shot him a look of such fury that he was shocked. Then the fury drained away, right before his eyes, leaving her face a stark study in anguish. "You're wrong," she said, her voice breaking. "But if all this is to you is a case of lust, don't expect sex when you come home again. Because I'll be looking for someone to *love*."

"Wait," he said, but she was already gone, the slam of the door echoing around his bedroom. He sank onto the bed, putting his head in his hands. What in hell had just happened? Guilt tore through him. He'd broken her heart. Deliberately. Using words like weapons to hurt her.

And he was afraid she was never going to forgive him.

Why? *Why* had he done that? He could have made his point in a gentler way. But she'd rattled him so badly that he hadn't been able to think for the panic clouding his brain.

He rose, intending to find her and demand that they talk this out, to apologize and grovel if it would keep her from looking at him as if he were lower than an earthworm. She would forgive him. She'd been the epitome of patience and understanding since they'd married; it was only to be expected that she would get frustrated and lose it occasionally. But she'd forgiven him before, each time he'd hurt her by reminding her that the marriage was temporary, that her feelings were transient. Once she calmed down, she'd forgive him again. *She had to.*

Why? asked the smug little voice in his head. *You didn't want her emotions.*

But he did. He took a breath so deep that his shirt seams strained. Oh, God, he did. He wanted her love, her understanding, her happiness, every emotion she felt.

Then the unmistakable sound of the back door closing caught his attention. He rushed to the window in time to see her slide into the smaller of his two cars and disappear down the street.

He was astounded. His gaze shot to the intimate apparel she'd left discarded on the floor. Unless she had underwear stashed in her purse or something, Faith had just left without even bothering to get fresh underwear.

Knowing her as he did, that realization alarmed him more than anything. Faith was the most ladylike of ladies outside their bedroom door. She would never do something so risqué without extreme provocation.

And that seemingly small action told him far more effectively than any words that *she considered their marriage to be over.*

The panic he'd been trying to subdue punched him full in the chest. Too late, he saw what had been within his reach all this time: a long happy life with the woman he loved at his side. But he'd driven her away with his selfish, self-protective actions...

And now he had nothing.

* * *

He canceled the Dallas trip, clinging to a dwindling hope that she would come home and forgive him.

But Faith never came home that night. He called her former roommates, the only friends he knew she had, but they professed not to have seen her.

He went to work the next day because the alternative was answering unanswerable questions from Clarice and Naomi. He had a lot of time to think while he sat in his office trying unsuccessfully to work. He'd tried to call Faith at home several times, but every time the machine had picked up. He'd known, in his heart, that she wouldn't answer even if she were there, but he'd had to try.

More than once, he picked up the phone to call a private investigator to track her down. But each time, he'd set the phone back in its cradle unused. Lunch was as unappealing as breakfast had been and he barely touched his meal.

That night, he explained to Naomi and Clarice that he and Faith had had a misunderstanding and that she'd gone away for a few days. Her mother was clearly alarmed, saying over and over again that Faith would never just go off without telling her. Stone spent an hour reassuring her, telling her that he was the messenger Faith had chosen, that she would be back.

And he'd see that she did return. Even if it meant him moving out.

Five days passed, with the weekend sandwiched in between. On the morning of the fifth day, Faith finally acknowledged that Stone wasn't coming after her. She knew what kind of determination and drive he had. If he'd wanted to find her, he'd have made it happen within hours of her leaving.

He didn't want her.

She lay in the spare bedroom of the apartment that Eliza Smythe's receptionist had offered to share with her when she'd learned of Faith's dilemma and sobbed silently into her pillow. She should be dealing with this better. Hadn't she already cried enough to fill a bathtub?

It was time to contact him, she decided. To let him know she would return and honor her commitment. The very thought brought fresh tears. But she'd made a promise and she intended to keep it. The only change would be that she planned to move into the set of rooms her mother and Clarice shared. That way, she could avoid Stone altogether, except for times when they had to appear publicly.

She couldn't imagine how she was going to get through the rest of the year.

Still, people didn't die from broken hearts. She'd be starting school in another month, and since she had nothing else to think of, she could double the class load she'd intended to take. That would keep her from simply giving up. She hoped.

She couldn't give up! She had responsibilities that were bigger than her own problems. Once she had her degree and a full-time job she could cover the cost of her mother's care herself. And maybe if she worked hard enough and long enough, she'd be able to forget the man she loved.

The man who didn't love her.

* * *

He headed for his mother's office, praying that Faith still was coming to work there twice a week. The shock on the face of the young receptionist at the front desk would have amused him at any other time. Today, all his concentration was focused on meeting with his mother.

He was directed to Eliza Smythe's office, but as he strode down the hallway on the third floor, his mother came to meet him. "Stone! Welcome to Smythe Corp."

"Thank you." He realized abruptly how small she was. She had looked tiny and defenseless as she came toward him.

"I presume this isn't a social call," Eliza said briskly. "Come into my office and we'll talk."

Defenseless. Hah.

He followed her through a quietly elegant outer office to her own, a feminine mirror-image of his, with all the necessary bells and whistles softened by quiet colors and soft fabrics.

"Have a seat," his mother invited. She seated herself in one of the wing chairs flanking a small glass table rather than behind her desk.

He took the other seat and inhaled deeply. He'd spent his life rejecting his mother. It wasn't easy to ask for her help. "Faith has left me," he said abruptly.

Eliza's expression became guarded. "I'm sorry to hear that. I like your wife."

"So do I. I want her back."

His mother studied him for long enough to make him repress the urge to squirm in his seat like a schoolboy. "We don't always get what we want. Why do you want her back?"

"Because." He floundered, unable to force himself to say the words that would leave him vulnerable. "She's my wife."

"Well, that's sure to sway her," Eliza said. She leaned forward. "Why did she leave?"

"We had a...disagreement," he said. "I came here to find out if she's still working for you. I need your help to get her to talk to me."

"Why should I help you?"

"You're my mother!"

"Interesting that you should remember that now." She was unmerciful. "Look, Stone, I made no secret of the fact that I thought your marriage was just a ruse to get your hands on Smythe Corp. But once I saw you two together...I was pleased. And as I've gotten to know Faith better, I think she's perfect for you."

"She *is* perfect," he said. "I just didn't figure that out until too late."

"You wouldn't just be trying to convince me of this because of our agreement regarding your inheritance?"

"There's nothing I want less at the moment than this company." And he meant it. "If it would bring Faith back, you could give it to the first stranger on the street."

His mother's eyebrows rose. "You're serious," she said, and there was pleased wonder in her tone.

"Very." He sighed. "You weren't wrong. Faith and I had a bargain. I married her to satisfy your conditions. She married me because in return I agreed to take care of her mother."

"Which you were doing, anyway."

He was startled. "Says who?"

"I did a little checking into your life before I made my offer," she said coolly. "Imagine my surprise when I found out you were supporting the Harrell ladies lock, stock and barrel."

"Faith was equally surprised," he confessed. "She just found out a few months ago."

"Ah. She confronted you, did she?"

Was his mother a mind reader? "All that's history now," he said. "I just want her back."

"Maybe she doesn't want to come back. What did you do to make her leave?" Eliza hadn't gotten to be a success by dancing around the issues.

"I, um, let her think I didn't love her," he said. It was hard to admit it, much less say it aloud.

"I see." She steepled her fingers. "And you want me to do what? Convince her that you do? Tell you when she's working?"

"All I want," he said, desperate and not caring anymore if he sounded it, "is a chance to talk to her. Then, if she still wants to leave, she can."

"You would lose Smythe Corp." Eliza reminded him, probing the depth of his sincerity.

"I don't give a damn!" he shouted, finally losing patience with explanations. "Hell, I'd even sell Lachlan if it would bring Faith back."

There was a moment of profound silence in the room. He glared defiantly at his mother. Eliza rose and walked around her desk. His heart sank. She wasn't going to help him. It was poetic justice for all the times when she'd tried to be a part of his life and he'd shut her out.

Well, he'd sit in the street and wait for Faith to come out if that was what it took to track her down.

Eliza hit a button on her speakerphone. "Hallie, would you send Faith in here, please?"

"Yes, ma'am."

A moment later, the door opened and Faith started through. His gaze was riveted to her. In the part of him that wasn't absorbed in steeping himself in his wife's presence, he was astonished. His mother must have sent for her when he'd arrived!

But then Faith saw him. She stopped in her tracks and her face was weary and wan, her eyelids puffy. She looked ill. After one quick glance, she ignored him and spoke to Eliza. "You sent for me?"

"There's a visitor to see you," Eliza said.

"There's no one that I want to see." Her voice shook and she bent her head, studying the carpet. He restrained himself from going to her and forcing her to acknowledge his presence, to grab her and hold her so she could never get away from him again. It was obvious that Faith was going to turn right around and walk out the door if he didn't let his mother handle this. The irony didn't escape him. How could it be that his mother, who had been absent for so many years when he'd have given anything for her attention, was the only person who could make his world right now?

"Faith." The president and CEO of Smythe Corp. waited until Faith looked up again. "My son is a very smart man in many ways. But in others, he's…a little dim." She smiled fondly at him. "And since I contributed to his desire to protect himself and avoid commitment, I feel bound to try to repair the damage. Will you listen to him?"

"That's all I want," Stone said quickly. "Just listen. And then, if you still want to leave, I won't stop you."

She had swung her gaze to him when he began to speak, and he saw doubt, sorrow, hope, and myriad other emotions tumbling in her eyes before she made her face blank again. She shrugged. "All right," she said in a barely audible voice.

Nine

"**W**hy didn't you just hire someone to find me?" she asked. She looked at the floor because she was afraid if she looked at him, the love she couldn't banish would be written all over her face. She didn't have any intention of letting him trample her heart more than he already had.

He shook his head. "It was my mistake. It was mine to fix."

"You could have sent me flowers, or jewels, to ask me to come home."

"Baby, I'll shower you with both if that's what you want," he said huskily. "But those are things. Anyone could send gifts. I didn't think that was the way to your heart."

"I didn't think my heart had anything to do with our marriage." She couldn't hide the note of anguish and her voice wobbled as she fought back tears.

He winced. "I didn't, either, in the beginning," he said quietly. "But I've found that your heart is essential, not just to our marriage but to my survival." He started across the room toward her. "And I've also found that I have to give you mine in return, because it's withering away without you."

She lifted her head and stared at him, rejecting the words. The moment she moved, he stopped immediately, as if he were afraid of startling her into flight. "You don't have to tell me that," she said wearily. "I'd already decided I have to come back and stay for the rest of the year."

"How can I convince you that I love you?" he asked her. "How can I convince you that I need you to love me?"

"You don't have to say that!" she cried. "I just told you I'll keep my end of our bargain."

"There is no bargain," he told her, his gaze steady and warm with an emotion she couldn't let herself believe in. "I told my mother she could give her company to someone else. I don't want it if it means I can't have you."

Her heart skipped a beat, then settled into a mad rhythm that threatened to burst out of her chest. "You can't do that. This company has always been in your family." *And part of your dream is to put your family back together.*

"Watch me." He rose and walked to the door, opening it. "Mother, would you please come in here?"

Eliza appeared in the doorway, her gaze questioning first one of them and then the other. "Yes?"

"What did I tell you before you brought Faith in here?"

His mother looked perplexed. "You mean about loving her or about giving up the company?" She turned to Faith. "Actually I believe his words were, 'I'd even sell Lachlan if it would bring Faith back.'"

Faith's face drained of color. Stone leaped forward, afraid she was going to faint as she groped for a chair. His mother went out again, closing the door behind her but he barely noticed. He gathered his wife into his arms, turning to sit in the wing chair and pulling her into his lap.

She didn't even struggle, just lay passively with her face buried in his shoulder.

She was warm, smelling of the indefinable essence of her, a scent he would recognize anywhere, and he nuzzled his nose into her hair. "God, I've missed you." His voice shook, surprising him as he savored the weight of her body pressed against him. She still didn't move, didn't respond, and he started to worry. "Faith?"

Slowly, she pushed away from him and sat up. "You think I'm too young to know the difference between love and sex."

"No." He shook his head slowly, holding her gaze, trying to communicate the depth of his feeling to her. "The truth is, I was *afraid* you were too young. I felt like I was taking advantage of you— you hadn't known enough men to know whether you loved me or not. And whether or not I wanted to admit it, I was falling for you. I was afraid. Afraid you'd grow up and fall out of love with me, afraid to believe in forever." He ran his palms slowly up and down her arms. "Now," he said, "now I don't give one flying damn if you're too young or not, because *I* know the difference." He swallowed, his throat closing up. "And what we have is love."

He saw her face change, just a slight relaxation of the tense muscles. She believed him! "I love you," he said again. "Forever."

"Forever." Her voice wobbled. "I love you, too."

He sought her mouth, relief almost a painful sensation as she kissed him back. God, he'd been afraid he'd never know her kiss again. He lifted his head a fraction. "As long as we live."

She gazed earnestly into his eyes. "It's all right if you don't want children. We'll have each other."

He considered her offer. "Thank you, but I've changed my mind about so many things I think I'll change it about that, too." He took her face in his hands. "I want to give you babies. I want to be there when they're born, and every day of our lives after that. I want to see your mother's face the first time we put her grandchild in her arms."

"And your mother's." Tears glimmered in her eyes but she was smiling.

"And my mother's," he repeated. He glanced around the room. "I guess she's going to be smug about this for the rest of my life." But his tone was fond. Somewhere inside him, he'd discovered that he could accept his past. He knew he and his mother would have to talk, because she felt obliged to explain. But he also knew it wasn't going to matter. She would be a part of his future.

Faith laughed. "How did she know to call for me?"

"If I had to guess, I'd say that little receptionist out front probably gave her the headsup. She looked like she'd seen a ghost when I walked in."

"'That little receptionist' happens to have become a friend of mine," Faith told him. "I've been staying with her."

Another mystery solved. "I guess I have to thank her, then, for taking care of you."

"We might have to buy her new pillows," she said. "I've sobbed into all of hers so much they're permanently soaked."

He stroked her cheek, sobered by her words. "No more sobbing. Promise?"

She smiled tenderly, her hand coming up to stroke the back of his neck. "Promise."

He kissed her again, pulling her close and the caress quickly turned to a searing passion as he stroked her body, unable to get enough of her after the days of worry. "I want you," he said in a low voice. "I want to get started on making a baby right away."

"Not here!" She straightened immediately, looking shocked.

"It is going to be my office some day," he reminded her, loving the prim and proper streak that was as much a part of her as her love for him.

"Well, it isn't yet!"

He laughed, intoxicated by the feel of her in his arms again. "Then let's go home, wife, so I can show you how much I love you and need you."

* * * * *

*Look for Anne Marie Winston's
next Silhouette Desire,
BILLIONAIRE BACHELORS: GARRETT,
in May 2002.*

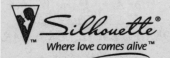

This Mother's Day
Give Your Mom
 # A Royal Treat

Win a fabulous one-week vacation in
Puerto Rico for you and your mother at
the luxurious Inter-Continental San Juan
Resort & Casino. The prize includes round
trip airfare for two, breakfast daily and a
mother and daughter day of beauty
at the beachfront hotel's spa.

INTER·CONTINENTAL
San Juan
RESORT & CASINO

Here's all you have to do:

Tell us in 100 words or less how your
mother helped with the romance in your
life. It may be a story about your engagement,
wedding or those boyfriends when you were
a teenager or any other romantic advice
from your mother. The entry will be judged
based on its originality, emotionally
compelling nature and sincerity.
See official rules on following page.

Send your entry to:
Mother's Day Contest

In Canada
P.O. Box 637
Fort Erie, Ontario
L2A 5X3

In U.S.A.
P.O. Box 9076
3010 Walden Ave.
Buffalo, NY
14269-9076

Or enter online at www.eHarlequin.com

PRROY

HARLEQUIN MOTHER'S DAY CONTEST 2216
OFFICIAL RULES
NO PURCHASE NECESSARY TO ENTER

Two ways to enter:

• **Via The Internet:** Log on to the Harlequin romance website (www.eHarlequin.com) anytime beginning 12:01 a.m. E.S.T., January 1, 2002 through 11:59 p.m. E.S.T., April 1, 2002 and follow the directions displayed on-line to enter your name, address (including zip code), e-mail address and in 100 words or fewer, describe how your mother helped with the romance in your life.

• **Via Mail:** Handprint (or type) on an 8 1/2" x 11" plain piece of paper, your name, address (including zip code) and e-mail address (if you have one), and in 100 words or fewer, describe how your mother helped with the romance in your life. Mail your entry via first-class mail to: Harlequin Mother's Day Contest 2216, (in the U.S.) P.O. Box 9076, Buffalo, NY 14269-9076; (in Canada) P.O. Box 637, Fort Erie, Ontario, Canada L2A 5X3.

For eligibility, entries must be submitted either through a completed Internet transmission or postmarked no later than 11:59 p.m. E.S.T., April 1, 2002 (mail-in entries must be received by April 9, 2002). Limit one entry per person, household address and e-mail address. On-line and/or mailed entries received from persons residing in geographic areas in which entry is not permissible will be disqualified.

Entries will be judged by a panel of judges, consisting of members of the Harlequin editorial, marketing and public relations staff using the following criteria:
- Originality - 50%
- Emotional Appeal - 25%
- Sincerity - 25%

In the event of a tie, duplicate prizes will be awarded. Decisions of the judges are final.

Prize: A 6-night/7-day stay for two at the Inter-Continental San Juan Resort & Casino, including round-trip coach air transportation from gateway airport nearest winner's home (approximate retail value: $4,000). Prize includes breakfast daily and a mother and daughter day of beauty at the beachfront hotel's spa. Prize consists of only those items listed as part of the prize. Prize is valued in U.S. currency.

All entries become the property of Torstar Corp. and will not be returned. No responsibility is assumed for lost, late, illegible, incomplete, inaccurate, non-delivered or misdirected mail or misdirected e-mail, for technical, hardware or software failures of any kind, lost or unavailable network connections, or failed, incomplete, garbled or delayed computer transmission or any human error which may occur in the receipt or processing of the entries in this Contest.

Contest open only to residents of the U.S. (except Colorado) and Canada, who are 18 years of age or older and is void wherever prohibited by law; all applicable laws and regulations apply. Any litigation within the Province of Quebec respecting the conduct or organization of a publicity contest may be submitted to the Régie des alcools, des courses et des jeux for a ruling. Any litigation respecting the awarding of a prize may be submitted to the Régie des alcools, des courses et des jeux only for the purpose of helping the parties reach a settlement. Employees and immediate family members of Torstar Corp. and D.L. Blair, Inc., their affiliates, subsidiaries and all other agencies, entities and persons connected with the use, marketing or conduct of this Contest are not eligible to enter. Taxes on prize are the sole responsibility of winner. Acceptance of any prize offered constitutes permission to use winner's name, photograph or other likeness for the purposes of advertising, trade and promotion on behalf of Torstar Corp., its affiliates and subsidiaries without further compensation to the winner, unless prohibited by law.

Winner will be determined no later than April 15, 2002 and be notified by mail. Winner will be required to sign and return an Affidavit of Eligibility form within 15 days after winner notification. Non-compliance within that time period may result in disqualification and an alternate winner may be selected. Winner of trip must execute a Release of Liability prior to ticketing and must possess required travel documents (e.g. Passport, photo ID) where applicable. Travel must be completed within 12 months of selection and is subject to traveling companion completing and returning a Release of Liability prior to travel; and hotel and flight accommodations availability. Certain restrictions and blackout dates may apply. No substitution of prize permitted by winner. Torstar Corp. and D.L. Blair, Inc., their parents, affiliates, and subsidiaries are not responsible for errors in printing or electronic presentation of Contest, or entries. In the event of printing or other errors which may result in unintended prize values or duplication of prizes, all affected entries shall be null and void. If for any reason the Internet portion of the Contest is not capable of running as planned, including infection by computer virus, bugs, tampering, unauthorized intervention, fraud, technical failures, or any other causes beyond the control of Torstar Corp. which corrupt or affect the administration, secrecy, fairness, integrity or proper conduct of the Contest, Torstar Corp. reserves the right, at its sole discretion, to disqualify any individual who tampers with the entry process and to cancel, terminate, modify or suspend the Contest or the Internet portion thereof. In the event the Internet portion must be terminated a notice will be posted on the website and all entries received prior to termination will be judged in accordance with these rules. In the event of a dispute regarding an on-line entry, the entry will be deemed submitted by the authorized holder of the e-mail account submitted at the time of entry. Authorized account holder is defined as the natural person who is assigned to an e-mail address by an Internet access provider, on-line service provider or other organization that is responsible for arranging e-mail address for the domain associated with the submitted e-mail address. Torstar Corp. and/or D.L. Blair Inc. assumes no responsibility for any computer injury or damage related to or resulting from accessing and/or downloading any sweepstakes material. Rules are subject to any requirements/limitations imposed by the FCC. **Purchase or acceptance of a product offer does not improve your chances of winning.**

For winner's name (available after May 1, 2002), send a self-addressed, stamped envelope to: Harlequin Mother's Day Contest Winners 2216, P.O. Box 4200 Blair, NE 68009-4200 or you may access the www.eHarlequin.com Web site through June 3, 2002.

Contest sponsored by Torstar Corp., P.O. Box 9042, Buffalo, NY 14269-9042.

presents

A brand-new miniseries about the Connellys of Chicago,
a wealthy, powerful American family tied by blood to the
royal family of the island kingdom of Altaria.
They're wealthy, powerful and rocked by
scandal, betrayal...and passion!

Look for a whole year of glamorous and
utterly romantic tales in 2002:

Where love comes alive™

Into Thin Air

CINDY MILES

A SIGNET ECLIPSE BOOK

SIGNET ECLIPSE
Published by New American Library, a division of
Penguin Group (USA) Inc., 375 Hudson Street,
New York, New York 10014, USA
Penguin Group (Canada), 90 Eglinton Avenue East, Suite 700, Toronto,
Ontario M4P 2Y3, Canada (a division of Pearson Penguin Canada Inc.)
Penguin Books Ltd., 80 Strand, London WC2R 0RL, England
Penguin Ireland, 25 St. Stephen's Green, Dublin 2,
Ireland (a division of Penguin Books Ltd.)
Penguin Group (Australia), 250 Camberwell Road, Camberwell, Victoria 3124,
Australia (a division of Pearson Australia Group Pty. Ltd.)
Penguin Books India Pvt. Ltd., 11 Community Centre, Panchsheel Park,
New Delhi - 110 017, India
Penguin Group (NZ), 67 Apollo Drive, Rosedale, North Shore 0632,
New Zealand (a division of Pearson New Zealand Ltd.)
Penguin Books (South Africa) (Pty.) Ltd., 24 Sturdee Avenue,
Rosebank, Johannesburg 2196, South Africa

Penguin Books Ltd., Registered Offices:
80 Strand, London WC2R 0RL, England

First published by Signet Eclipse, an imprint of New American Library,
a division of Penguin Group (USA) Inc.

First Printing, November 2007
10 9 8 7 6 5 4 3 2 1

SIGNET ECLIPSE and logo are trademarks of Penguin Group (USA) Inc.

Printed in the United States of America

PUBLISHER'S NOTE
This is a work of fiction. Names, characters, places, and incidents either are
the product of the author's imagination or are used fictitiously, and any resem-
blance to actual persons, living or dead, business establishments, events, or
locales is entirely coincidental.

The publisher does not have any control over and does not assume any
responsibility for author or third-party Web sites or their content.

For all the wonderful, wacky women in my life whom I adore: moms, grandmas, daughters, sisters, aunties, cousins, in-laws, and sister-friends. Thanks for the *bleeping* chaos. Without it, life wouldn't be nearly quite as much fun.

And for the most wonderful, wackiest woman of all—my mom, Dale, who happily exclaims her pride and joy for my accomplishments to anyone with a good working pair of ears (and sometimes to those without). Thanks, Mom. I love you.

ACKNOWLEDGMENTS

For the following, I'd like to express my sincere gratitude for their part in this incredible journey.

Jenny Bent, my superduper agent, who guides me and encourages me along the way.

Laura Cifelli, my fabuloso editor, whose fantastic suggestions make my stories so much better.

Sheri Dotson, Tracy Pierce, and Nikki Nixon, my silly, fun, and fantabulous sisters, who support me in everything.

Tyler and Kyle, my wonderful kids, who listen to my ideas and keep me "hip."

Kim Lenox, my best pal and sister-writer, whose constant encouragement, zany sense of humor, and phenomenal brainstorming are the best (said like the boy in *The Sandlot*).

The Denmark Sisterhood, and especially the matriarch, Dona Denmark, for their support, love, crazy-fun spirit, and wonderful afternoon tea parties.

Betsy Kane, Molly Hammond, Eveline Chapman, and Valerie Morton, my demented, rather sick-minded sister-pals, whose nutty humor gives me plenty of fodder for crazy character ideas.

Cynthia Reese, Nelsa Roberto, and Stephanie Bose, all fantastic writers whose friendship and support I cherish.

And for the wacky guys in my life (that'd be all of them), who are probably pouting because I dedicated this book to all the wacky girls in my life.

To all my new reader-fans, including the dedicated ladies at the beauty shop, whose encouraging words of praise for my work continue to truly inspire me.

And to everyone who has given me unflagging support.

Thank you.

Prologue

Northeastern England
A Midwinter's Night
Somewhere in time, high in a blanket of darkness,
three stars furiously blinked . . .

"I'm not at all in favor of this decision, Fergus. I daresay it's rather selfish. Why have They assigned him another charge now? After all, the boy has proven his worth far more than once."

"Pah!" Fergus' starlight sputtered. "You whine overmuch for a Moorish warrior. Dunna be such a ninny, Aizeene. 'Twill give the lad character!"

"Not tae mention secure our promotion," said Elgan.

"But the boy's worked hard these past centuries to shed his wings. There's nothing more he desires and deserves than mortality." Aizeene fretted. "His retirement is less than a pair of fortnights away!"

"Blast you, Aizeene, this is unavoidable! We've no choice in the matter."

"What mean you?" asked Aizeene.

Elgan sighed. "I'm afraid there's a small problem." He coughed. "His charge? 'Tis a girl. She's the *One*."

Aizeene gasped. "Nay. Mean you, the *very* One?"

Fergus snorted. "Aye! She's the boy's soul mate! His bloody Intended! Nigh onto dead, the lass is, and because of her, he may lose that blasted mortality he so heartily desires." He harrumphed. "Lasses. A fickle-minded lot of trouble, if ye ask me."

"The lad has a will stronger than any I've ever known," Elgan interrupted. "He's managed for nearly a thousand bloody years, don't forget, and not once has he lost a charge. Besides, I grow weary of twinkling up here with you witless fools. We need that bloody promotion!"

Aizeene puffed out a blast of star shine. "What of Nicklesby? He used to be one of us. Can he not give any aid at all?"

Elgan blew out a gust, a spray of starlight scattering about. "Nay, other than offer what knowledge he has on the matter on the girl's condition. Besides, he has no inkling of this new development. 'Tis forbidden to inform him likewise and you know it. Now. Like it or no', Gawan of Conwyk is indeed faced with this new challenge, and if he succeeds, 'twill guarantee his mortality as well as our positions. *All* of our positions."

Aizeene relented. "What of the boy's heart, though? What of *hers*? By the saints, there's much at risk." He sighed. "What if he doesn't succeed?"

Elgan drifted closer. "Well then, my old Moorish friend, it appears his fate lies in the hands of an addle-brained modern lass."

Ferguson cleared his throat. "Isn't there anything we can do?"

"You know there isn't, old crow. Fate has a much stronger will than any of us, and 'tis against all rules to interfere," Elgan said. "All we can do is hope. Pray. And watch. Now begone, the both of you, and help me maintain sentry over these two. But brace yourselves, lads, for what you're about to witness is not for the faint of heart. . . ."

Northeastern England
A Midwinter's Night
Present Day

Frigid water lapped at her cheeks, sloshed over her insulated jacket and jeans, seeped into her skin. A howling wind whipped overhead, sucking the air from her lungs. She couldn't move, couldn't open her eyes, and the ache in her head was like being bludgeoned with a sledgehammer. Where the heck was she? It felt like she'd been run over by a team of horses. Before that, though, she'd been floating, gasping for breath, and tasting a lot of salt. Scared. Had she fallen? Finally, rocky sand had been under her feet, and she'd dragged herself out of the water. The next thing she knew, she'd been sailing through the air. God, she'd been *hit*. Car, truck— she didn't know which.

A gruff voice grumbled above her, slurred, disjointed. "Oy, girl, why'd ye have to . . . ? Ye appeared out o' bloody nowhere. . . . No bloody moon out tonight. . . . Aww, Jaysus, I can't let 'em find ye. . . ."

Ye? Who says *ye* anymore? She tried to open her mouth, tried to scream, but no words came out, though she still made an attempt. Who was this guy? *Hey, pal, can you give me a hand? I'm freezing my butt off here. . . .*

In the next second his rough hands tried to lift her from the icy water, but dropped her with a splat. *Oww! Can you go a little easy, guy? Something might be broken.* She tried to move, but her body was dead weight. *Why the heck am I lying in freezing water?*

More disjointed words faded in and out. ". . . too bloody heavy . . . shouldna be here . . . gotta hide ye . . . oy, girl, Christ Almighty, yer already dead. . . ."

Dead?

Those same rough hands shook her so hard her teeth rattled. "Not dead yet, anyway . . ." He grabbed her by the wrists and dragged her over rock and sand.

Oh, God, she was being abducted, probably even murdered. They'd find her dead, frozen body floating in the icy water, all cross-eyed and fish nibbled. *"Ow!"*

Her teeth clacked together as her head grazed a rock, and a dizzy queasiness stole over her. The frosty air touched her soaked body, and she floated, the muffled voice seeming more distanced, yet . . . not. Pain seized her, making pricks of light flash behind her eyelids. She grew colder. And, ugh, that nauseating smell of rotten sea life. What was happening to her?

She felt herself being picked up and settled none too gently on a hard surface. Then an arctic blackness engulfed her. The roar of an engine and the gruff muffled voice faded farther and farther away. . . .

One

Northeastern England
A Midwinter's Night
Present Day

Gawan peered into the drizzly night at the headlights bobbing toward him, and from the looks of it, whoever it was didn't plan on stopping. Probably a lost tourist, he'd wager. Lost, and on a one-track lane, no less.

His one-track lane.

The lights bobbed at an alarming pace, erratic and faster as they grew closer. With a grumble and a curse, and nowhere to go except backward, Gawan slowed, stopped, and put the Rover in reverse. Half turning in his seat, he steered toward the small byway he'd passed, backed in, and waited for the vehicle to go by.

Seconds later, a beat-up farm truck blew by. Not a tourist, he suspected. "Witless fool," Gawan grumbled. The truck didn't belong to anyone he knew—not that he knew many—but he'd be sure to keep an eye out for it. Bent side-view mirror and a missing headlight, both on the same side. He'd bank that to memory. The reckless idiot could kill someone.

Throwing the Rover in drive, Gawan pulled back onto the lane and continued up the track. The rain picked up, and he flicked the wipers on high. Probably not the best of nights to crave a fried Milky Way, but Nicklesby hadn't learned to make the bloody things yet, and Mrs. Cornwell had indeed called him to come round and collect a fresh batch. By the saints, he'd nearly burned the larder down when he last tried to make them himself. "Bleeding priests!"

Gawan slammed his foot to the brake and skidded to a stop. Throwing open the door, he jumped out into the now-pouring rain.

A woman, soaked to the bone, stumbled over the guardrail and landed flat on her bottom. Wet hair plastered her head and hung forward in thick strands to cover her face. She didn't move.

Reaching her, Gawan went down on one knee and placed a steadying hand to her elbow. *"Ti'n iawn?"* he asked. *Not in Welsh, fool.* "Are you all right?" Mayhap she was drunk? He bent close and took a whiff. She didn't smell of alcohol. He looked around. No car, not even a bicycle. He peered over the guardrail. Nothing below. She was drenched, alone, and in the dead of a cold North England's December eve.

This, he suddenly decided, did not bode well.

"Girl, are you ill?" Gawan hooked a finger through her wet tresses and slid them to the side. He bent his head to get a better look. "Are you hurt?"

The girl lifted her face, her eyes rounded and glazed. Rain dripped off the end of her nose, and her lips quivered. But she said nothing. After a quick scan of her person, he noted no blood. Passing odd, indeed.

Standing, Gawan yanked off his weatherproof and draped it over her narrow shoulders. He pushed his own wet hair from his eyes. "You're bound to freeze to death, if not drown in this downpour. Come. I'll take you—"

She shook her head, opened her mouth to speak, and when nothing came out, she cleared her throat a time or two. "No. Um, I mean," she stammered, the words raspy, and in an intriguing American accent, "I'm fine.

Really." She wiped the rain from her eyes and looked around, then shook her head again. "I'm really okay." On shaky legs she stood, patted her thighs, her belly, then down both arms, mumbled something Gawan could not comprehend, then walked with timid steps to the guardrail and peered over the edge. "I, uh . . . is that the ocean down there?"

"Aye."

She looked around, shook her head, and cleared her throat a score of times more before mumbling a bit. She seemed completely lost and bewildered.

"Girl, come with me out of the rain. There's nowhere to go for miles around. I live"—he nodded his head toward the lights at the top of the cliff—"just there. Please." He took a step toward her. "Nicklesby can see you settled into a room for the night."

She stared at him, and crazy as it was, standing on the one-track lane on a frozen Midwinter's night in the icy rain, he noticed with intensity how beautiful she looked.

"Who's Nicklesby?" she asked, the wariness in her eyes evident in the Rover's head beams.

"He's my man," Gawan said.

One of her eyebrows lifted. "Your man?"

Gawan nodded. "Harmless, I assure you. Besides, you can't just wander about in the cold rain. You'll catch your death. Come." He inclined his head to the Rover.

With a final glance around, she pulled the edges of Gawan's weatherproof closer and walked to the *driver's* side and got in.

Gawan tapped on the window. "I vow 'twould be best if I drove, miss."

The door opened and she stepped out. "Sorry," she mumbled, then walked around and slid into the passenger's seat.

"Quite all right," he said, trying to put her at ease. When they were both inside, he shifted the Rover into drive and started back up the lane. "Do you have a name, girl?" he asked. "Or mayhap someone you'd like us to ring?" Out of the corner of his eye, he saw her looking at him. "What's happened to you?"

Then, fidgeting, she placed her hand on the door handle. "Maybe you could just drive me into town." *Because no matter how cute you are, if you think I'm going home with you, you're freaking crazy.*

Gawan's head snapped up. "Beg pardon?"

"I said, maybe you could just drive me into town."

Gawan shook his head. He must have misheard her.

In truth, he knew she was scared and didn't want to give her name, and he wished like hell he could put her at ease. And by the devil's pointed tail, he couldn't leave her. "Nay, miss. I fear everything's closed for the night." He turned his head to look straight at her. "You'll be safe within Grimm's walls. I give you my word."

She frowned, as if pondering, then nodded without saying anything at all and stared out the window into the ink-black darkness. Her hand, though, remained clenched around the door handle. She was ready to bolt, her chin trembling from the cold. At least, he thought it was from the cold.

" 'Twill be fine, girl," he said, and turned up the heater.

Minutes later, the Rover climbed the winding, rocky path to Grimm's barbican gates. The big iron beasts opened as he approached, and Gawan steered through, under the portcullis, and around the drive, stopping at the front entrance. He parked and turned off the engine.

"You *live* here?"

"Aye." Gawan peered through the darkness at imposing Castle Grimm—home for nigh on nine hundred years.

"Who are you?"

"Forgive me, girl. Gawan of, er, Conwyk. Gawan Conwyk." He gave a short nod. "Let's quit this drafty Rover, aye? No doubt Nicklesby has a fine fire roaring in the hall." He jumped out, grabbed his bag of soggy fried

Milky Ways from the dash, slammed the door, and ran around to help her out.

She sat, hesitating. Not that he blamed her.

Finally, she accepted his outstretched hand and stepped out of the vehicle. At that same time, the tall oak double doors of Castle Grimm swung open.

"Young Conwyk, what are you doing in the rain? Do you require aid?" his wiry steward called.

"Nay, Nicklesby," Gawan answered. He tugged on the girl's elbow. "Come."

For a moment, Gawan thought she'd run. Her wide eyes darted from Nicklesby to the barbican gates and back to Gawan.

Should I? Shouldn't I? Should I? Shouldn't I?

Gawan stared at her and cocked his head. Nay, 'twas impossible. How could he hear her thoughts? 'Twas one of the only skills he'd maintained, from before, when he could hear the thoughts of his charges.

"Thanks," she finally said, and started to move.

As they climbed the steps, Nicklesby clucked his tongue. "Oh, dear. Soaked to the bone." He lifted his gaze to Gawan. "I thought you went out for those fried concoctions you fancy."

Gawan stepped into the great hall, and all but pushed his confused visitor inside ahead of him. "I did"—he held up his rather pitiful-looking sack of treats—"and I stumbled across this waif alone in the lane."

Nicklesby eyed Gawan for a moment, no doubt curious. Then he examined the girl. "Her room shall be ready, posthaste." Without another word, he hurried up the stairs.

Gawan bet Nicklesby was all but bursting at the seams with curiosity. Nosy devil, that one.

Gawan ushered the girl to the hearth, where indeed, Nicklesby had an enormous fire roaring.

She took a step closer to the flames, stared into the fire, and rubbed her arms.

"Have you a name?" he asked. "You never did say."

She hesitated. "Where am I?" She turned to face him. And waited. Expectantly.

Gawan scratched his chin. Did she really have no clue? "As I said before, Castle Grimm."

She squinted, staring hard. *Not the brightest bulb in the box, huh, fella?* "No. *Where* am I? What country?"

Gawan blinked. He poked his forefinger into his ear and gave it a good squeaking. He had to be hearing things, for no way was he hearing her aright. Must be one of the others, goading him. Bleeding priests, she didn't even know what country she was in? " 'Tis the North of England. Now, your name?"

She scratched her brow. "England? You're kidding me?" She looked at him. "You spoke to me earlier, out there"—she inclined her head to the double doors—"in another language."

Gawan gave a short nod and ran his fingers through his wet hair. " 'Twas Welsh."

She paced, looking at her feet, and began to mumble to herself. "In the North of England. How'd I get here? In a castle, with a Welshman. Cute, too. Everyone talks funny, saying *nay*, *ye*, *mayhap*, and *aye*. *'Twas*." She shook her head. "Didn't think they still said that stuff. I just don't get it."

"Mayhap I should ring the infirmary? I could send for a helicopter—"

"No! I'm"—she stopped and once more patted her head, then her stomach—"fine, really. I just . . . this is all just so weird."

Taking off his jacket, Gawan tossed it over the back of his favorite chair and placed a hand on the girl's shoulder. She looked up.

And his bloody knees nearly buckled.

Though drenched like a stable rat, Grimm's latest guest had brownish-red hair that hung far below her shoulders in thick, wet hanks to frame a creamy, oval face. Tiny freckles crossed her nose and cheeks. Like-colored brows arched over green—no, blue-green—eyes that stared at him, wide and uncertain.

And scared witless.

God, you're gorgeous, but could you please stop staring at me like that? You're freaking me out.

Nay! Why was he able to hear her thoughts? Damnation, this could not be so! Not *now*.

Gorgeous?

He cleared his throat. "Do you know who you are?" he asked, as gently as he could.

Still wearing Gawan's weatherproof, she pulled the edges together and frowned. "Don't be silly. Of course I know who I am. I . . . I'm"—she glanced around the great hall; then her eyes widened—"Eleanor. That's right. My name is Eleanor."

Gawan cocked his head. "Just Eleanor?"

Again, she moved her gaze around the room, then back to him. "Aquitaine. Eleanor Aquitaine." *It'll do for now, anyway, because I have no freaking clue who I am!*

Oy, by the bleeding priests, this cannot be happening. Gawan forced out a smile that felt rather pasty. "Very well, Miss Aquitaine."

"Call me Ellie."

"The chamber is ready, young Conwyk," Nicklesby called from the top of the stairs. "Come, miss. You must get out of those soaked garments. I have a robe at the ready."

Following *Ellie* up the stairs, he and Nicklesby escorted her to the prepared room. At the door, she turned.

"Thanks for letting me stay here. I don't know how to repay you." *Please, just don't be a pair of freaky murderers who prey on hapless travelers.*

Gawan shook his head and reached into his pocket and withdrew his mobile. "No need." He felt Nicklesby's pointy elbow sink into his ribs, and he smothered a grunt. "Make use of anything you find in the chamber and garderobe. And here," he said, placing his small silver mobile in her hand. "Keep this with you. Local numbers are listed, including the constable." He smiled. "Just to make you feel safe."

Her gaze shifted from his to Nicklesby and back. *What would make me feel safe would not to be in this stupid mess!* "Thank you." She pushed a bit of her hair from her eyes. "For everything."

Gawan gave a short nod. "The pleasure is quite mine."

Nicklesby cleared his throat. "I'll prepare an evening snack. Something other than those horrid fried bars young Conwyk brought home. No doubt you're hungry?"

Ellie stepped into the room. "Starved."

"Splendid. I'll see to it."

With that, Ellie closed the door.

Gawan looked at Nicklesby and lowered his voice to a whisper. "Eleanor Aquitaine."

Nicklesby lifted one silvery-gray eyebrow. "Come again?"

Jerking his head toward Ellie's door, he leaned closer to his steward. "She told me *her* name was Eleanor Aquitaine."

Both silvery-gray eyebrows shot up. "Do say? What a coincidence."

" 'Tis not a bloody coincidence, man. She saw the tapestry hanging in the great hall. She's no more named Eleanor Aquitaine than I. And," he said, "I can hear her bloody thoughts!"

With a nod, Nicklesby agreed. "So right." He quirked a brow. "Then who is she— *What*?"

Gawan grabbed his man's elbow and led him farther down the corridor. "I can hear her bloody thoughts! Not all of them, I assure you. And I vow I don't know who she is. At first, I thought she'd been struck by this witless fool in a farm truck who nearly ran me off the track. Out of nowhere, she all but stumbled over the guardrail and into the lane ahead of the Rover. No car, no one else around. Just her. Didn't even know she was in England."

"Passing odd, indeed," Nicklesby said, nodding. "Apparently, there's something amiss. We both know there is only one reason why you would be able to perceive her thoughts."

"Aye." Gawan looked over his shoulder at the still-closed door of Ellie's chamber. "There must be a mix-up, Nicklesby. This isn't supposed to happen—not now. Mayhap after she eats, she'll remember—"

A small crash sounded from behind them. Gawan looked at Nicklesby, then both hurried up the passageway to Ellie's room.

All was quiet within.

Gawan rapped on the solid oak. "Ellie?" He and his man shared a glance; then Gawan knocked again. "Miss Aquitaine?"

Complete silence.

"Try the door," Nicklesby urged.

"What if she's undressed?" Gawan thought a moment. "Mayhap you're right."

"Oh, for God's sake, move over," a grumbly voice said. The shimmering image of Sir Godfrey of Battersby appeared between Gawan and Nicklesby. Without effort, he poked his ghostly head through the six-inch solid-oak door.

He pulled his head out. "She's gone."

"Impossible," Nicklesby said.

Gawan tried the door, found it unlocked, and pushed it open.

He, Nicklesby, and Sir Godfrey all entered the chamber.

It was, as Sir Godfrey claimed, empty.

As Gawan thought, *not* boding well.

In the middle of the floor lay Gawan's mobile. Beside it, his weatherproof. He bent to retrieve both. "By the bloody priests . . ."

Nicklesby, who'd quickly run his lanky self about the

room, checking every nook and cranny, sighed. "Indeed, she's nowhere, sir."

Crossing the chamber, Gawan threw back the drapes and shoved open the window. Through the darkness, the North Sea crashed against Grimm's rocky base. Thankfully, the spot of ground below the window remained vacant.

Eleanor Aquitaine had disappeared, indeed.

He turned and faced his companions, still trying to talk himself out of knowing what was, in truth, happening. "She couldn't have left the room. We blocked the passageway. And by the saints, she didn't jump."

"Tsk, tsk, tsk," clucked Sir Godfrey. "After all these centuries, you're still learning the ways of the unliving, eh, Gawan?" He shook his head. "Shame, really. A most comely wench, in my own opinion."

Gawan frowned and took a step closer to Sir Godfrey, till they were nearly nose to nose, and asked the question he bloody well knew the answer to. "What mean you?"

Sir Godfrey, previously of Battersby, lately—as in the last five hundred fifty years—of Grimm, folded his arms over his foppy silk and ruffled tunic. "Why, she's dead, of course."

Gawan closed his eyes and swore.

TWO

"Godfrey, you old poop—of course she's not dead," Nicklesby said. "Young Gawan here touched her, and more than once. She had his weatherproof draped about her shoulders, for heaven's sake. Had she been a spirit, 'twould have slipped right through her."

Gawan pinched his brow with thumb and forefinger. A headache surely would plague him soon. Saints, he hated being right.

"Aye, she is dead. Well," Sir Godfrey argued, "she's *mostly* dead, anyhow."

With another frown, Gawan stared at the old knight. Indeed, this was a new one, even for him. "Mostly? What do you mean, mostly?"

"What he means is that she's fluttering about between the living and the unliving," another voice answered. "We like to refer to it as *In Betwinxt*. Rarely happens, of course, and only in the utmost extraordinary circumstances."

All three turned as Lady Follywolle emerged from thin air. Dressed in her usual gown of lace and green pinstripes, her powdered hair coifed into some sort of odd bird that Gawan found highly amusing, she bustled into the room, as she'd done for the last three centuries.

He turned and quit the chamber, Nicklesby, Sir Godfrey and Lady Follywolle close on his heels.

"My good sir, it seems you've a new case on your hands," the lady said, her voice quavering with excitement. "Terrible time for a case such as this, being so close to your retirement. 'Tis understandable, though, that you did not recognize her unusual aura. You'll find it most useful, though, to be able to touch her person, should you need to." Lady Follywolle swooped ahead of him as he ambled down the passageway. " 'Twill boggle the mind, if you let it. But you've not handled a mostly dead lost soul yet." She leaned in close, her ghostly lashes batting furiously. "Have you?"

Gawan jogged down the stairs and crossed the great hall, his mood growing darker by the second. "Nay, I have not."

"My good lady," Nicklesby said from behind, "that's quite enough. I'll explain what I know to the boy."

"Oy, Millicent," Sir Godfrey said. He always called Lady Follywolle by her Christian name. "Let us quit this drafty hall whilst Nicklesby instructs young Conwyk here of his new duties." Godfrey laughed, a loud, boisterous cannon of a sound. "I vow we'll hear the full tale later. Come. Meanwhile, we can inform the others."

Millicent accepted Sir Godfrey's proffered arm and gave Gawan a short nod. "Until later, good sir," she said, smiling.

"By the by," Godfrey said, "the wench's name is of a certainty *not* Eleanor Aquitaine."

Millicent giggled as Godfrey led her through the hearth and they disappeared.

Gawan, still wet from his previous ordeal in the rain, turned to Nicklesby. "They still enjoy tormenting me."

Nicklesby nodded. "I fear they do, sir. But you're passing easy sport, if I do say so myself. 'Tis all harmless, though, I suspect."

"Hmm. No doubt." Gawan shivered from his damp clothes. "I'm going to run through the shower, change, then come down for a bite. *Then*," he said, holding up his hand as Nicklesby opened his mouth to argue, "I'll listen to what you have to say, although I'm fair positive I don't want to."

With a short nod, Nicklesby answered, "Very well, young Conwyk."

Moments later, hot water pelted Gawan's neck and back as he stood in the shower. Damn fine invention, that. It still puzzled him at times, the concept of heated water running through pipes about the castle. Bloody amazing.

Tilting his head back, he rinsed the suds from his hair and let the steaming water run over his face. Quite different from the twelfth century, truth be told. Not all bad. Just different.

Turning off the water, he cracked the door of the stall and grabbed a towel off the electric rack. Heated drying cloths. Who would have ever thought it?

Taking the cloth, he dried first his body, then scrubbed his hair. Wrapping the towel about his waist, he stepped onto the mat and leaned against the sink with a groan. Damn, after nearly a thousand years, his poor body still ached from warring. One would have thought acquiring Angel status would have surely eliminated bodily pains.

Mostly dead. Ellie Aquitaine was mostly dead. A true shame. How? he wondered. What had happened to her? Mayhap she was on borrowed time?

Much like himself.

Only his borrowed time, if things went accordingly, was finally almost up. He'd shed his Earthbound-Angel status and finally gain mortality.

Running water and heated towels he could grasp. The Range Rover, he could grasp. Jets and rockets and men on the moon—all fascinating, but tangible. Hell, he owned a bloody helicopter, for priest's sake. He, a once-twelfth-century-warrior-turned-Angel. But *mostly* dead? One was either dead or one wasn't. Aye?

Nay. He himself was neither dead nor alive. Then again, he was something altogether different. Although he lived as a mortal, in truth, he could not be killed. He had a few paltry Angel powers, such as reading thoughts and coercion of one's mind. He'd lost his higher-up powers when he'd gained Earthbound status. And *that* particular status ran out in less than a pair of fortnights. Now he had Ellie's problem to decipher. *So little time . . .*

Saint's blood, there was something about her that wouldn't leave him.

"My name's not Eleanor Aquitaine."

Gawan jumped at the sound of her voice, knocked his razor from the sink, then grabbed the edges of the towel that had started to slip down his hips.

"Christ's priests, girl!" he said, breathing hard. "You nearly—" He blinked. "How did you get in here?"

"I don't know! God, I don't know anything!"

He turned her around before she started that infernal pacing again. Then he gently shoved her out of the garderobe and into his bedchamber. He followed, clutching his towel, and pushed her down onto the bed.

When she looked up, her eyes widened, then dipped from his face, clear down to his bare toes, then back to linger on his chest. While her voice remained silent, her lips mouthed the shameless word *Wow*.

Gawan crossed his arms, determined to delve into her thoughts only when absolutely necessary. "Where'd you go?"

Her gaze drifted across his upper body, affixed to the scores of symbols tattooed there.

He supposed now was necessary.

Sexy. Wacky, but definitely sex-y. Finally, she shook her head and looked at him. "I told you. I. Don't. Know." She stood and pushed past him. "One minute, I was standing in the middle of the room, wondering what the heck was happening and how the heck I even got here." She crossed the chamber, pulled back the mantle, and peered through the glass. "And why I couldn't remember my own name." Turning, she leaned her backside against the window frame and blew out a hefty breath. "I stole the name Eleanor Aquitaine from that big tapestry downstairs."

Gawan smothered a smile. "Aye. I figured as much."

Grasping the corner of his towel, he gave a short nod. "But until we get things sorted, Ellie will do, aye?"

She nodded.

"Good. Then we have an accord. Can you recall anything of import?"

She thought a moment. "I remember floating in the water. Freezing-cold water. I don't know how long I was there, but I managed to get out, crawl up onto the beach, and then I was hit, I think."

"Someone hit you?" he asked.

The space between her brows crinkled as she frowned. "With a vehicle, maybe. I can't be sure. I remember flying through the air, and it *hurt*. I think someone must have tried to drag me to safety, and then I just passed out." She met his gaze. "Then you were there."

They stood in silence for a moment; then Gawan nodded. "Right. Allow me to change and we'll sup. Nicklesby has food preparing as we speak. Then we'll talk. Mayhap you'll recall a bit more." Throwing her a grin he hoped would put her at ease, he ducked back into the garderobe. With haste, he used another fascinating invention—deodorant. Lo, how that ingenious stick of wax would have made the battlefield a much more enjoyable place to be. He pulled on the jeans and long-sleeved tunic he'd chosen, ran his fingers through his wet hair, and hung his towel over the shower stall. With a flick, he clicked off the light.

Barefoot, he stepped into his bedchamber. "Just let me pull on my boots, then."

He glanced around the large, open, *empty* room. "Ellie?"

Oy. *Gone again.* Poor girl. From what he could tell, she hadn't even a hint that she was, as Lady Follywolle had put it, *betwinxt the living and the unliving.* Damn, he could barely believe it himself, and by the saints, he'd seen quite a lot of strange things. He *was* one of those strange things. But for a tangible body to appear and disappear? How could that be possible?

Pulling on his socks and boots, Gawan thought of what Ellie must be like—taken out of the odd circumstance, of course. He'd seen a vibrant flash in her eyes, and she most certainly was quite bold of tongue. A quick thinker, too, by the way she'd scoured his great hall, found the tapestry of Eleanor of Aquitaine, then filched the name to use as her own.

He grinned. Quirky, clever girl. Somehow, the two brave and tenacious women seemed strangely alike.

Tying back his hair, Gawan hastened to the kitchens to satisfy his empty belly, and to hopefully hear a full explanation from Nicklesby as to why and how the comely Ellie could appear in the flesh, then vanish into thin air. Nicklesby himself was an Angel, once upon a time. He'd certainly have guidance to offer.

As in what, by the devil's hoof, was Gawan to do about Ellie in such a short amount of time?

As he entered the kitchen, Nicklesby met him at the arch, a blue-checked oven mitt on each hand. Nicklesby lifted one mitted hand and rubbed his chin. "Did you by chance mention to the girl anything about your present occupation, or how the outcome of her situation will determine your fate?"

Gawan frowned. "Of a certainty, Nicklesby. Right after I informed her of how I acquired all the markings on my skin nigh onto a thousand years before. And then I stripped me tunic off, called forth me wings, and flapped them a time or two."

Nicklesby grunted. "Passing grumpy today, aye?"

Walking to the open kitchen hearth, Gawan stared into the flames. "Nay, not grumpy. Just frustrated." He glanced at Nicklesby over his shoulder. "Twenty-four days, man. I had twenty-four more days before retirement, and then *her*." He shook his head and returned his gaze to the flames. "Trust me. Over nine hundred years of Guardianship, one starts fancying the idea of living out the rest of a mortal life once and for all *not* as a *gwarcheidiol*."

"No doubt," Nicklesby said. "Sit, sir, and eat your supper. Things will be clearer come the morn."

Never had a night been so black. Of course, it could simply be because there wasn't even a sliver of moon out. Cold, too. Cold and black. Or was it really night? Could be a dark room, right? Things could be worse, though. Much worse.

Couldn't they?

Ellie lifted her hand in front of her face and squinted hard, then blinked several times, trying to make out her appendage. Hmm. Not even a shadowy outline showed. The electricity must be out—

Ellie jumped, trying to get her bearings, yet unsure that her hand waved before her face, unsure that her foot felt for the floor. It was just so dark. And empty.

She smelled . . . hay? No, not hay. Something more earthy. Warmth replaced the cold.

My name's not Ellie. . . .

She thought she closed her eyes as her mind spun, gathering scattered memories. What *was* her name? The man who helped her—what was his name? Talk about intense. Cute, but intense. His looks betrayed an inner strength—the quiet type, she thought. Tall, broad, with shoulder-length dark brown hair that hung in disarrayed curls. Not tight curls, but loose, carefree ones. And eyes so brown, they seemed to have no pupils.

Gawan, he'd said his name was.

She couldn't be sure, but something had seemed odd about him. Maybe not odd, but out of place? His mannerisms, maybe, or was it his speech? Definitely an unusual accent. Cute, too.

Welsh, he'd said.

Sighing, she tried once more to rise, to call out, but the darkness grew heavier, an oppressing force daring her to challenge it. She seriously wanted to, but something held her back.

Then before her mind could recall another thing, the

heaviness began to lift and fade, and a tiny spot of light appeared far in the distance. Headlights? No, she didn't think she was outside. Ellie willed herself toward it, hoping it would at least be someone who could tell her what the heck was going on. . . .

"So what you're saying"—Gawan scratched his brow—"is that Ellie, or whoever, has had something near-fatal happen to her. And she is somehow trapped between life and death?"

"More like suspended," Nicklesby answered. "Her life force teeters precariously, if what I know of the affliction proves aright."

"Oy." Gawan rose from the dining room table and began to pace. "She obviously doesn't realize it."

"Aye, and 'twill be your duty to tell her the tale, being you were the one who rescued her. 'Tis why she can appear in the flesh as she does. Even though your Earthbound powers are limited, they're just powerful enough to gain a few senses of import with a soul who is In Betwinxt." The man clucked. "Just in time, she is. I daresay you've not much to work with."

"What mean you?"

Nicklesby blew out a gusty breath. "Her body has obviously taken a mighty blow, if indeed she was struck by a vehicle. She appears and disappears because she is fighting."

Gawan rubbed his eyes. "To stay alive?"

"Aye. A strong will, that one has." Nicklesby shook his head. "Poor dear. I've no doubt the news will not sit properly with her. 'Tis why you must do the deed with upmost delicacy."

Gawan cringed and followed his man into the kitchen. "I fear I'm not very good at being delicate."

"Poppycock! I daresay you've been most delicate at times, in contrast to your, err, well . . ." Nicklesby coughed. "I have all faith in your abilities, young Gawan."

Leaning a shoulder against the kitchen fireplace mantel, Gawan cocked a brow. "In contrast to my what?"

Nicklesby worried his clean-shaven, pointy chin with a long, bony finger. Then he sighed. " 'Tis no secret of your past, master. One only has to be in close quarters with the markings on your person to know you led a questionable existence, once upon a time. You're a legend, and well you know it." He waved a hand. "No matter. Those days have passed, and you, sir, have fostered your occupation rather well."

"Oh, aye, indeed," a new voice agreed.

Gawan turned to find Lady Bella Beauchamp walking through the larder wall, leaving a ghostly trail of seawater as she made her way toward him. Because she had drowned in the North Sea in August 1802, Bella's lavender-and-lace gown always appeared drenched—as did the massive amount of graying red curls piled high atop her head.

"I've heard tremendous tales of your fierceness, lad, and then of your strength and loyalty whilst serving as Guardian Angel of the Knights all those years past." She shook her soppy head. "The souls you've saved as a mere Earthbound Angel are experiences whispered far and wide about the spirit world and will no doubt be talked about until the end of time." A faraway look hazed her eyes. "To have been your charge would have been glorious. And to think, you're so close to retiring." She clapped her hands and gave him a wide grin. "You more than deserve a mortal life, love, but it appears the deed placed before you is quite an imposing one, to be sure." She glanced at Nicklesby. "Now. Tell me of this newest case. I'm dying to hear all about it. 'Tis far different from your other charges, indeed, as the others have always been quite alive. Now this one is a lovely girl, from what's been rumored, although a bit touched, mayhap?"

Gawan and Nicklesby exchanged glances before Gawan addressed her. "Lady Beauchamp, I do appreciate your kindness. Truly. But I fear there isn't much to tell . . . yet. I've only just learned of the girl's predicament moments ago. Other than that her mortal life is in deep peril, I cannot offer anything else, save I'm the one responsible for rescuing her."

Lady Bella's eyes lit up and she clasped her hands together. "Well, I daresay you should hasten your studies on the subject, Lord Grimm. You most assuredly have your work cut out for you." She smiled and vanished, her ghostly image blurring as she faded. "I'll think on the matter and get back to you, posthaste. Oh, and do promise to show me your wings before you shed them. I've been dying to see them." With a wink and a giggle, she was gone.

Gawan heaved a gusty sigh. "Why *mostly* dead? Why not *all* the way? 'Twould have been much easier to stomach." He rubbed his eyes. 'Twas a lie and he knew it. The thought of Ellie completely dead didn't sit well with him at all. "Where does she go?"

"Lady Bella?" Nicklesby asked.

"Nay. Ellie."

Nicklesby wiped the kitchen counter with a red cloth. " 'Tis a place only she can tell of, I'm afraid. And even she may not know. It depends on the condition her mortal self is in." He stopped and gave Gawan a grave look. "You were chosen for this line of duty, Gawan of Conwyk, because you've proven to have impeccable ways with the living as well as the unliving. Whilst you were alive, you proved to be a most fierce warrior, and since that time passed, you've done a fine job as Guardian." He patted Gawan's shoulder and cleared his throat. " 'Tis why you've been bestowed such a challenge. I've no doubt you'll manage Ellie's affairs with genteel propriety, as well."

Gawan gave a curt nod. "I thank you for such a loyal endorsement, my friend. But those charges in the past whom I could not save were completely dead, not just *somewhat* dead, floating about from one existence to the other. *Not remembering.*" He frowned. "Nor can I recall any of them being quite so fetching."

Nicklesby chuckled. "So you'll have to, say, modify, your design. Aye?"

"Indeed." Gawan turned and started for the kitchen door. "I suppose being an ex-Guardian Knight yourself has lent you the power to interact with Ellie, as well. Aye?"

Nicklesby cocked an eyebrow. "For a certainty, master. But most who've touched the spirit world can interact with an In-Betwinxt soul."

"Then I shall need your aid on the matter. I've but twenty-four days until my retirement. I don't plan on having anything go amiss. Now, I'm off. No doubt this *modified design* will plague my bloody dreams until morn."

"I truly hope so," Nicklesby said with a grin.

At the door, Gawan turned and nodded once more. "*Nos da,* my friend."

Nicklesby gave a low bow. "And good night to you, young Gawan."

As he crossed the great hall and jogged up the steps, Gawan recalled his medieval days as Guardian Knight. Scores of fierce knights in just as many battles unknowingly had Gawan watching their backs, making sure they didn't leave their mortal world until 'twas truly their time to go.

Had he himself but chosen a different path . . .

He pushed open the heavy door to his chamber and stepped inside. Aye, he'd been given a rare opportunity. A gift, really, that few other Guardians received, or even dreamed of receiving: the post of Earthbound Angel. And he was bloody grateful for it. Hopefully, he'd be worthy of accomplishing such a task as Ellie's.

He closed the door, brushed his teeth with that finetasting cleaning paste Nicklesby always purchased, pulled off his clothes, and crawled into bed. On the morrow, he'd have a clear head. Ellie needed his help and he had wings to shed. Mayhap he'd start by returning to the spot where he'd found her.

After a few moments, the low whistle of the night's bluster seeping into the old castle walls lulled him to drowsiness.

Thoughts turned to the past once more, and Gawan recalled Castle Grimm right after construction. 'Twas a sturdy keep, and he'd enjoyed his days here then, as well. Never had the thought crossed his mind he'd be living in the same castle more than nine hundred years in the future.

His eyelids drooped a time or two, and he was nigh onto giving in to much-deserved rest, until a shiver caused him to open his eyes.

He'd forgotten to stoke the fire. He'd freeze to death by morn if he let it burn out. Even with the prestigious title of Guardian, he still faced the same comfort measures as a mortal. All except death, anyway.

With a grunt and several fine Welsh curses, Gawan threw the covers back, raised his naked self from the bed, and crossed the cold floor to the hearth. Grabbing the iron poker, he stabbed and shifted the embers, then set a new log on the grate. As he kneeled before the hearth, he stared into the building flames. 'Twas a generous-enough fire.

Just as he rose, a small intake of breath from somewhere close behind ceased his movement.

Ellie.

Oooh, I shouldn't look but eeek! I can't help it!

Gawan looked for something to shield himself, saw only the damn poker, then changed his mind. He heaved a sigh. "I apologize for my state of undress," he said, peering over his shoulder, "but from the look on your face, 'tisn't overly offensive." He grinned. "Say something, girl, before you make me blush."

Ellie's cheeks glowed. "Good Lord," she whispered, then blinked and looked him square in the eye. "Who—no, *what*, are you?"

Three

Amused. Cocky. No, not cocky. Confident. Definitely that.

Ellie's mouth went dry. Putting aside the fact that Gawan stood before her in all his muscled nakedness, she was fascinated by the tattooed markings, much like the ones across his chest, that decorated his back, from shoulder to shoulder, then down his spine. She couldn't make herself stop looking. Buck naked and not seeming to care, Gawan grinned as he looked over his shoulder. Thank God he had the decency *not* to turn around.

She did, though, just in case his decency slipped. "Sorry," she muttered.

He laughed, mumbled something in what she could only assume was Welsh, then made a rustling noise she sincerely hoped was him pulling his clothes on. Not that he wasn't something *veeery* spectacular to appreciate. Statue material, really, except with a much bigger—

" 'Tis safe enough now, girl."

Ellie turned around. "I really don't mean to keep dropping in on you like this," she said, barely noticing Gawan wore nothing more than a pair of jeans, and his tousled dark curls rested boyishly on his shoulders. He looked like a wild warrior from some medieval movie. "I can't seem to help it. I mean," she said, "I *would* help it, if I could, but I can't." She shook her head. "I don't know what's going on. But for some reason, I feel you do."

Even though he gave her an easy smile, she could tell that something bothered him.

He shrugged into a baggy shirt he'd grabbed off the back of a chair and inclined his head to the door. "Come. There will be plenty of time for speech on the morrow, after you've rested. The chamber Nicklesby readied for you earlier is just next door." He crossed the floor and pulled the door open. "I give you my word, you'll be safe."

"I know that," she said. Somehow, she did. "But no way can I go to sleep without a few answers." She took a step closer. "Please?"

Gawan studied her, scrubbed a hand over his chin, then gave her a nod. "Aye. If it will ease your mind a bit, I'll tell you what I can, which I fear isn't overmuch at present." He closed the door. "Mayhap you should sit."

Sit? Nothing good ever happened after the suggestion to sit before the Telling of Whatever. But since she'd asked for it, and she really didn't have a clue what was happening, or how she kept appearing in this man's bedroom, Ellie found a comfy window seat and sat.

And waited.

Meanwhile, this guy she didn't even know—Gawan Conwyk—paced with his hands clasped behind his back and his dark brows drawn close, as though he were in deep, deep thought.

Somehow, she felt as though she were in deep, deep doo-doo.

Gawan grabbed a straight-backed chair, pulled it up, and sat across from her. He leaned forward. "Can you recall anything else other than what you told me earlier?"

Ellie thought about it. And thought some more. Had it been tonight? It seemed a lot longer than that. "I remember being wet and sitting on the road." She focused. "Wet and cold. Lights, I think. Really bright ones, and then . . ." She looked at Gawan. "You. I only remember you." She took in a hearty breath and studied the room. "I remember getting into your truck, then coming here." She snapped her fingers. "I remember Nicklesby."

A smile lifted the corner of Gawan's mouth. *Cute smile,* she thought. *Cute and comforting. Nice lips. Really nice lips.*

"Nicklesby leaves a grand impression on everyone, I'll warrant." He scrubbed his brow. "Do you know how you came to be in the lane?"

The lane. How *did* she end up on the lane? For that matter, how had she ended up in the north of England? "I just can't remember."

"'Tis fine, girl."

The way he said *girl* came out *gel. Very charming,* she thought.

He brushed a hand over his mouth and tried to hide a smile. She noticed he did that often. Then he cleared his throat and studied her again, hard, those brown eyes boring into her as if he could will the information from her brain. She wished he could.

"Can you recall your family? Do you have siblings? Your mother and sire, mayhap?"

Ellie thought hard. Certainly a normal person would remember their own family? She closed her eyes, thinking for some stupid reason it would help her concentrate. Maybe help her focus better. *Sire? Who said sire anymore?*

Then it came. First pitch-blackness, then a flash of light. Yellowed light, foggy and dim. It illuminated a scene, almost as though she were watching an old movie. It faded just as fast as it had appeared.

"What is it?"

Ellie opened her eyes and stared at Gawan. "Not much. A young girl, maybe eight or nine years old, sitting on a wooden dock with an old man."

Gawan cocked his head. "A wooden dock?"

Ellie nodded. "Yeah. A dock floating over the water. Maybe a river?" She recalled the scene again. "I think it was me. Maybe with my grandpa? But how do I know it's my grandpa?"

"Nothing more?" he asked, his voice calm, soothing.

She nodded. "When I left here, before, I remember being somewhere black, cold at first, then warm. And it smelled very earthy. I couldn't see anything, though. But it felt weird."

Gawan frowned, scratched his jaw, then sighed. "I've something to tell you that may frighten you, but there's no sense in putting the matter off." He reached out a hand, large, with thick veins, callused, and squeezed her own hand. She liked how it felt against her skin. "I beg you, don't be afraid," he said.

The pit of Ellie's stomach lurched. "What is it?"

He cracked his knuckles. "I suppose I should have told you from the first, but you kept disappearing." He sighed. "I have a rather, well, unconventional occupation."

She stared. What did his occupation have anything to do with her situation? Certainly, he had a good reason. "*Sooo*. What is it?"

Those soulful brown eyes rimmed by dark lashes blinked; then Gawan leaned closer. His soapy scent wafted toward her nose. "I sort of . . . see the unliving."

Silence.

"Help them, actually," he said. "Guide them. Along with others in need. Of help, that is."

More silence.

Without moving her head, Ellie glanced around. She scanned each corner of the expansive room, looking for a hidden camera, a hidden camera *crew,* or who knew what lurking in the corner, ready to jump out. Then she locked eyes with Gawan when nothing did.

"You what?" she asked. She scooted closer to the edge of her seat.

He shoved a hand through his hair. "I know it sounds ridiculous, unfathomable, mayhap, but 'tis the truth. I vow it." He cleared his throat. "I'm a . . . Guardian, of sorts. A *gwarcheidiol*, to be exact." He coughed. "Sort of."

Ellie peeked over the very broad shoulder of Gawan Conwyk and eyed the door. The one she'd be going out of at any second. Good Lord, how could someone *that* cute be *that* delusional? Oh, his poor mother.

"Ellie?"

Her eyes darted back to Gawan, who had the look of a wounded puppy. Too bad. Didn't matter how cute and sexy he was—he had *issues*. Major ones. Ones she felt sure she couldn't help him with. And here she sat in his bedroom.

He thought he saw *ghosts*. And he claimed to be a *gwarcheidiol*? What the *bleep* was *that*?

With her fingers digging into the side of the armrests, Ellie slowly stood, and her muscles bunched as she got ready to make a break for the door.

"She's going to bolt!" a gravelly voice barked from behind the large oak door. "Grab her!"

"Hush, Sir Godfrey! You'll frighten the poor lamb."

"Move over, woman! I cannot see a bloody thing!"

Ellie froze as two—images?—sifted, no, fell through the *closed* door. She blinked, rubbed her eyes with her knuckles, and stared.

A strange word grumbled from Gawan's throat. Ellie suspected it wasn't nice.

The images appeared to be a man and a woman, slightly transparent and wispy and looking as though they'd stepped out of another century. They slowly erected themselves. The woman covered her red lips with two fingers and gasped. The man coughed.

The woman had a big bird on her head.

"Now, Ellie," Gawan said. His voice, while deep and a bit raspy, resonated in a low, soothing tone. Sexy, she'd think, if the situation weren't so bizarre. "Mayhap you should sit? Come"—he touched her elbow—"settle back down. I'll explain."

Ellie looked at the man and woman, who simply stood stiff and stared back at her. Blinking.

They'd just stumbled through a closed solid-oak door.

That just wasn't possible.

She slid a glance at Gawan, whose eyes pleaded with her to do something. Sit? No, she wouldn't sit. *Definitely* not sit. Run, maybe. How she loathed being a coward, though. What else was she to do? Gawan claimed to see ghosts, for God's sake, to be a *gwarche* . . . er . . . *gwarcheid,* or whatever that was, and to help them, even, and then . . .

She chanced another peek at the two by the door. The woman with the big bird on her head gave a sheepish grin and a hesitant wave. The man just frowned.

She could nearly see through both of them.

She could see them?

Ellie closed her eyes and squeezed her temples. "Not real. Not real. Not real . . ."

"What in Heavens!" Nicklesby, who reminded Ellie of a slightly older version of Ichabod Crane but dressed in a long, striped sleeping gown and hat, flung open the door and walked right through the bird lady and the man.

"Beg pardon," Nicklesby said over his shoulder. Then he scowled at Gawan and made a beeline for Ellie.

"My dear," he cooed, grasping her hand and giving it a gentle pat, " 'tis all right." He tugged her gently. "Come away from this chamber of madness and let me settle you into another, more *sane* one." He scowled at everyone in the room. "One where you may gain a spot of peace."

Ellie's mind whirled, but she focused and studied Nicklesby. He felt safe. Maybe a blend of Ichabod Crane and a young Ebenezer Scrooge. Yeah, especially in his old-fashioned nightclothes and his gangly arms and legs. And that silly long hat. But if he thought she was about to bunk *here* for the night, he was crazy, too.

Gawan gave a hearty sigh and shoved a hand through

his hair. "Nicklesby, let me. I'll settle her just as comfortably as yourself—I vow it."

The two by the door stared on, watching the exchange, but remained silent. Maybe they couldn't speak? No, they'd certainly spoken earlier, and Ellie had heard them clear as a bell. Or was that her imagination?

In a way, it all struck her as pretty hilarious. She couldn't recall her own name, or where she was even from, but she felt pretty darn sure she'd never had two guys—even if one did look like Ichabod Scrooge—fight over who would do the honors of *settling* her into bed.

In a swirl of mist, her mind drifted away from the room with its entire strange lot of people. Nicklesby's hand remained on her elbow, so she knew she hadn't left. Very, very bizarre.

Who *was* she? And how in the heck had she ended up in Northern England? God, her brain hurt from all the deep, heavy thinking she'd been doing. And none of it had helped.

And *this* guy, Gawan. The self-proclaimed *Guardian*. She was drawn to him, almost like she was *meant* to be drawn to him. Quiet yet strong, emanating a sense of security and power unlike anything she'd ever experienced. His voice, while a bit raspy, was deep but not too deep, definitely not too high, but in fact, just right. Calming. And that strange Welsh accent made it all the more intriguing.

Wait—how did she know she'd never experienced anything like that? She couldn't even remember her own name, or where she'd bought the clothes she had on, or jeez, she didn't even remember getting on a 747 and flying to England.

Gawan claimed to see spirits. Claimed to be a *gwarcheidiol*. (*Note to self: always carry a pocket dictionary, preferably an English-to-Welsh one.*)

Bad thing was, she could see spirits, too.

The headache started to return.

As did the voices . . .

"Honestly, Godfrey, you are bloody irritating, man. Wait, she's coming back round." Gawan leaned close to her. "Ellie? Are you well?"

Ellie blinked and focused on the knee-buckling, handsome face of Gawan Conwyk. His soft, fathomless—ancient?—eyes studied her. "Are you?" he said. "Okay?"

Godfrey? Who was Godfrey?

Again, Ellie glanced around the room. The man and woman had moved closer, now they were only a few feet away and curiously studying her. Nicklesby had stepped back, and Gawan had taken his place at her elbow. Everyone seemed genuinely concerned over her well-being. So why did it all seem so surreal?

"Do not worry overmuch, Ellie," Gawan said, his voice low, his words seemingly meant just for her. " 'Twill be easier deciphered come the morn."

It was at that exact moment—the one where she'd *almost* felt a tiny bit calm, when a small figure burst through the thick stone wall. A young boy, maybe nine or ten years old, dressed in dark knickers and stockings, scruffy ankle-high boots, and a long-sleeved white shirt with dark suspenders, came hurdling toward her. He pulled up short just a few inches away, out of breath. He, too, was nearly transparent.

Not only that, but the outfit he wore made him look like a paperboy announcing the sinking of the *Titanic*.

He stared. Then his nose screwed up and he cocked his head. "Blimey, she don't look much like she's dead," he said in a thick, nearly inaudible British accent. He leaned close. "Sir Godfrey, I thought you said she was dead."

The transparent man, Godfrey, coughed.

"Oy, young Davy," Nicklesby said. "Be you silent!"

Ellie blinked. Too much weird stuff was happening, and cowardly or not, she figured the best thing to do would be to Run Like Hey-el.

Dead?

"I told ye, she's going to bolt!" Godfrey cried again. Just as she bolted.

"Show her your bloody wings, boy!" Godfrey shouted. *Wings?*

Jerking out of Gawan's grasp, Ellie ran, straight through young Davy, slammed into the very narrow and bony shoulder of poor Nicklesby, then right through the flimsy forms of Godfrey and the bird lady, and then straight out the door.

Down the passageway she flew, the hiss of gaslights throwing a pale yellow streak over the stone, reminding her of an old Frankenstein movie. She'd watched that before, right? Good Lord, at least she remembered something.

Down the winding steps, then across the oversized great room, Ellie dashed for the double front doors, voices arguing seemingly right on her heels. Her heart thumped in her chest and her lungs burned, but by God, she was leaving this mad house, sexy guy or not.

Then her body grew light and wispy, and an eerie feeling of her feet not actually touching the ground stole over her. Her vision became very, very blurry.

Gawan called to her, above the ruckus of the others as they quibbled and argued over something, but his voice began to fade, as well.

All just before her body sifted through those thick, ancient double doors . . .

. . . and vanished.

Four

"**W**ell, is she dead or isn't she?" Young Davy Crispin said in one inquisitive breath.

Gawan, winded from his workout, lowered his blade, leaned on the hilt, and waved off his opponent. " 'Tis enough for now, Chris. Until tomorrow morn."

Christian de Gaultiers, recently of Arrick-by-the-Sea, a handful of years older than Gawan and who didn't seem at all winded, smiled and gave Gawan a low bow. He raised a brow, smirk still firmly affixed to his face. "A most worthy opponent you are, Conwyk. With a bit more practice, you could even best my sister, I'd warrant. Mayhap even my grandmother."

Gawan laughed. "Aye, you might be aright on that accord."

"I know I am." Christian grinned widely before he disappeared.

"Well is she?" Davy asked again. "Dead?"

Lowering to one knee, Gawan eyed the squirming lad. "She's In Betwinxt, so I'm told. Caught between the mortal world and yours. Something's happened to her, and I've got to figure out just what."

"Blimey." Davy scratched a place under his cap. "Where'd she go, then?"

"I wish I knew, boy." Davy's curiosity didn't exactly surprise Gawan. Whenever a new subject wandered onto Grimm's lands, the lad clung to Gawan's side, determined to help decipher how the soul had become lost in the first place. No doubt the boy would accompany him on his missions, had he the ability to leave Grimm's lands.

'Twas sad, really. Davy himself hadn't a clue as to the cause of his own untimely demise. Gawan hadn't yet given up on solving that particular case, although the boy rather liked his home at Castle Grimm and didn't seem inclined to move on. Aye, a Guardian Gawan truly was, but he served only those charges assigned. And Davy hadn't been one of them.

"Well, what's gonna happen to her, then?" Davy asked.

Rising from his kneeling position, and not overlooking the popping of his poor knees, Gawan sheathed his blade. " 'Tis difficult to say," he said, meeting the boy's ghostly gaze, "but I vow to do everything in my power to give her aid."

Davy kicked a rock with the toe of his ankle-high boot. "I rather like her. She's quite nice to look at."

Gawan laughed. "Aye, that she is."

Squinting as if in deep thought, Davy looked up. "Why didn't you show her your wings like Sir Godfrey said to? Surely she would have believed you then?

Gawan shrugged. "Mayhap. Mayhap not. 'Twasn't the right time, methinks."

Davy nodded, then peered back up at him. "Nicklesby shouted at me for asking if she was dead in front of her. She doesn't know she's In Betwinxt?"

"Nay," Gawan said. "And I fear she won't take that reckoning very well. Mayhap then I shall show her the wings."

"Davy!" Godfrey's booming voice echoed over the bailey. "Come here, boy! I've a mind to best you at a game of knucklebones!"

Davy grinned. "Gotta go. Sir Godfrey is passing creaky at me for beating him three times past and vows to whip me good." He turned to leave and stopped. "You'll go into the village soon, won't you? To ask questions? I know ye searched about Grimm and yonder yestereve, but the lady's been gone for nearly two nights now."

It more than worried Gawan, as well. But these were precarious matters he dealt with, and he had to utilize his skills with utmost—how did Nicklesby put it? Delicacy?

"Aye, boy, that is my plan, indeed. And I shall report to you straightaway upon my return."

Davy gave a gap-toothed smile and gave a nod. "Right. Now we have an accord." Then he turned and disappeared through the wall of the bailey.

With a heavy heart, Gawan stared over the crags of Castle Grimm and out to the North Sea beyond. A fine morn, actually, all things considered. 'Twas brisk enough for sure, with the chilled sea wind grazing his sweaty skin, but the rain had passed and the sun had just begun to give the clouds a yellowish glow.

As he walked closer to the edge of the bailey, where a sheer drop-off fell straight into the ocean, his thoughts yielded to those of the mysterious Ellie.

He had, in fact, visited the very place Ellie had first appeared—at the guardrail in the lane. That she'd been vastly interested in the sea below caused him to climb down the slope, just to see if anything could be found. There'd been nothing, of course, save the pebbled beach, and without her, he had nothing more to go on. 'Twas a rainy day, though, and he could have overlooked something. He'd stop by once more on his way to the village and go over the area while the fine weather lasted.

It more than unnerved him that Ellie hadn't appeared in two days. Bleeding priests, he hoped she faired well. The odd way she popped in and out meant her physical body was struggling to stay alive. More than once, the unsettling thought crossed his mind that she had indeed passed on.

"Indeed, she has not."

Gawan jumped at the voice, and then drew a deep breath as he recognized it. "Aizeene, I thought I'd finally seen the last of you."

"Not quite, my warrior friend. You've still nearly a fortnight left before your retirement. And so you know why I am here, no doubt."

Gawan studied the white-robed Saracen-turned-Angel. "I've a fair guess."

Aizeene moved to stand next to him, and was silent, staring out over the sea for several moments. "This will be a rather difficult assignment, lad. The girl is In Betwinxt, a most challenging charge, to be sure. You've not dealt with the like in all your years of Guardianship."

"A fine Guardian I've proven to be. I don't know what to bloody do with her."

Aizeene looked at him and chuckled. "You'll save her—that's what you'll do with her. Find her mortal body, before it's too late. 'Tisn't her time yet, lad."

Gawan looked at the Saracen long and hard. "There's something else."

Aizeene moved his gaze back to the sea. "As you know, I cannot advise you further. Other than, of course, to remind you that you'll not remember one another. After."

Gawan blew out a hearty breath. Somehow, the thought of not remembering Ellie bothered him. Vastly. "So you came merely to goad me?"

Another chuckle. "Never. Just to make sure you know the girl is indeed your charge, and that your mission is to save her life. No matter what else occurs, and no matter the cost."

Gawan met Aizeene's gaze, then nodded. "In truth, I knew it from the moment I found out she was *mostly* dead."

Aizeene gave a short nod. "Then I shall be off." He lifted one dark brow. "Do not underestimate your Earthbound powers, Gawan of Conwyk, as they are fine ones, indeed. You have been a most worthy Guardian over the centuries. I have complete confidence that you will conquer this last task." He glanced at the sword at Gawan's hip. "I see you still train. A most satisfying sport, aye?"

Gawan grinned. "For a certainty."

With a slight wave, Aizeene disappeared.

Gawan inhaled a lungful of sea air, then exhaled. A vision of Ellie came to mind.

Ellie Aquitaine. His final charge.

Young Davy had it aright. Ellie was indeed fine to look at. Comely, even soaked and drenched, she was. Vastly different from the women of his time.

Vastly, indeed.

Mayhap 'twas those fetching hose she wore? Damnation, he could see every curve of her legs. Not that he looked overmuch.

An American, she was, with the most intriguing manner of speech he'd ever heard. Aye, he'd heard it aplenty on the telly—another fine invention—but hers was indeed a stranger accent. He rather liked it.

She thought him gorgeous.

Seabirds squawked and dove into the North Sea, and a stiff breeze caught Gawan square in the face. Drawing in the icy air, he wondered briefly if Ellie had a family. A husband? Children? If so, where were they? Had she been in England alone?

A spear of guilt nagged him. Here he was, ogling the poor girl, and she may very well have a man whom she loved dearly, mayhap babes, even.

That didn't sit as well with him as it should.

The hairs on the back of his neck lifted, just before he heard her voice.

"It's quite breathtaking."

He turned, and the object of his thoughts stood no more than two paces away. 'Twould be a bold lie not to admit that a feeling of relief shook him, but he'd keep those womanly thoughts to himself.

"Aye, 'tis a fine enough view." He looked her over. Same faded blue hose—jeans, they were called—same oversized brownish tunic, and a pair of worn leather boots. Fine boots, he'd wager. At least now she appeared dry.

Gawan lifted his gaze to meet hers and his knees nearly gave way. Her eyes were the most fetching shade of blue-green.

"Why do you have a sword strapped to your back?" she asked, slipping her hands into her pockets and inclining her head toward his weapon.

"Just a bit of training," he answered, giving her a smile he hoped would keep her beside him. "How do you fare this morn?"

Ellie moved around him, slowly, as if taking in every inch of his person; then she stepped up beside him and turned her gaze toward the sea. "Am I dead?"

How to answer such? He kept his head out of her thoughts and studied her profile as she stared out across the water. Strong jaw and chin, a nose just the right size for her face, adorned with a splatter of tiny freckles. Very long eyelashes and high-arched brows the color of her hair—reddish brown and in varying lengths, it dropped to the middle of her back.

Aye. Fetching, indeed.

"Am I?" she asked.

Gawan cleared his throat. "Nay, not exactly."

Several seconds passed. "If you see ghosts, then that's what I must be. A dead, lifeless, floating spirit."

Gawan stifled a chuckle. "I see the living, as well. And don't forget Nicklesby. He sees you and he is very much alive." The fact that Nicklesby, as well as himself, had been born centuries before and had served the Higher-Ups certainly didn't need to be brought up just now. He'd reserve that information for later.

She turned and faced him full-on. "Then what's wrong with me? Why can't I remember anything? Where do I go when I go? I mean, you'd think I'd recall boarding a plane and flying to England, but I can't. And trust me, I've tried."

Bleeding saints. Did her voice just quaver? Comforting the dead, or guarding the life of a charge proved to be a much easier task than comforting a weeping In-Betwinxt woman.

Any woman, for that matter.

"Those people in the castle—that man dressed in old clothes and the woman with a bird on her head. Oh, and that kid—I ran right through him." She wrapped her fingers around his forearm. "Ghosts?"

"Aye. Ghosts."

"And yet I can touch you, and you can touch me." Ellie's hand dropped and she returned her stare to the sea. "Good Lord."

Gawan moved to touch her again—just on the elbow—but he retracted his hand. An overwhelming urge to wrap her completely within his arms came over him, but he pushed it aside. "I fear you're In Betwinxt the living and the unliving, Ellie. I cannot explain it fully, but you seem to be teetering."

"On death?" she asked without looking at him.

"Or life." The fact that he was more than just a spirit-seer was something he didn't think she could handle just yet, so he left that bit out, as well.

She chuckled and rubbed her arms. "Well, it sounds crazy. But I guess I really have no choice but to believe you." After a moment, she turned to him. "Can the others—the ghosts—can they hurt me?"

"Nay, nor would they even if it were possible. They're a rather likable lot."

Ellie nodded and turned to the castle, giving it a long, hard stare. She toed the ground with her boot, much as young Davy did. "What is a *gwarcheidiol*?" she asked.

Saint's priests.

Gawan drew in a breath. " 'Tis like a Guardian, of

sorts. Like I said before." He swiftly averted the subject and gave her a nod. "I will do my best to help you, girl."

"Promise?"

Crossing himself, he grinned. "Upon pain of death, I vow it."

Thankfully, that seemed to satisfy her questions. Without another word, they both started for the keep. Across the bailey and through the courtyard, they approached the great doors in silence.

Just as they mounted the stairs, Ellie hesitated. "Why did the man Godfrey tell you to show me your wings?"

Gawan cleared his throat. "Er, you must have misunderstood. You know, his speech is rather ancient. Well over six hundred years or more."

She nodded and inclined her head toward the keep. "Maybe you're right. So, what about the others? What will they think of me?"

"Not to worry. I'll wager they're clambering at the windows at this very moment for first position to greet you properly."

Ellie smiled, studying him as she walked. "You've got a funny way of saying things. Funnier than just Welsh." She continued her bold stare. "I can't put my finger on it, but I like it. Are you sure *you're* not almost six hundred years old?"

Gawan couldn't help but smile. Not only were twenty-first-century women most comely, but they were, of a certainty, bolder of tongue. Gawan rather fancied it.

"I can assure you, girl, I am for a certainty not six hundred years old."

"Hmm."

More closely to a thousand, but who's counting? he mused.

Inside the great hall, Nicklesby greeted them.

"How do you fair, young Ellie?" he asked, hovering about her like a peahen. "It distressed me so, your last leaving. Worried me something awful, I'd say."

She smiled, and Gawan thought it to be rather beautiful, although he glimpsed it just from the side. "I promise from here on out to not freak out too much, Nicklesby. Okay?"

Nicklesby inclined his head. "No freaking out, indeed. And I shall endeavor to aid you in that lofty goal, young lady."

Gawan rolled his eyes at Nicklesby's theatrics, then placed his hand on Ellie's lower back. "Come, then. We'll see if you can last long enough to break your fast."

"I'll see her to the larder, master," Nicklesby said with a frown. "You, sir, need to bathe."

Gawan resisted the urge to sniff himself. "I'll bathe once we've had speech. There's no telling when Ellie may disappear again." He glanced at her and gave her an apologetic nod. "No offense, of course."

"None taken."

He smiled. "Besides, I'd not make you face the Grimm ghosts alone."

"Thanks."

The look of relief on her face was proof he'd made the right decision. "Come, then, before Nicklesby fair drags you to the larder."

As they crossed the hall to the kitchens, Gawan couldn't help but take a peek into Ellie's thoughts. 'Twas one of his most useful abilities, and she just might *think* something she otherwise wouldn't say. Something that could lead to her true identity. Having no idea when the girl was going to next disappear, the notion to peek immediately appealed to him. So, he peeked.

Larder? Break my fast? Where the heck am I? On the set of a King Arthur movie? Sweet mother, if anyone could play a decent Arthur, it would definitely be this guy. He even has a sword.

Gawan fought a grin. Not a bad start.

Okay, think, girl, think. Gawan's going to ask more questions, and it'd be nice if you had something to say other than "Derr, I don't know." Did I mention you're in a castle filled with ghosts? Did I mention you are almost one yourself?

This time, Gawan didn't fight it. He grinned. Damn him, he couldn't help it. Ellie was beyond charming. She had wit. Scores of it.

He couldn't keep his eyes off her.

"Why are you smiling?" Ellie asked.

Gawan cleared his throat, glanced down at her and shrugged. "I thought I had to sneeze."

She studied him for a second or two, as if deciding whether to believe him. She gave a nod as they entered the kitchens. "Okay. I think I'm ready."

Ellie sat down at the table, folded her hands in her lap, and waited. Gawan unsheathed his sword, propped it against one of the chairs, and sat across from Ellie.

"Have you remembered anything else?" he asked.

That spot between her brows knitted together, and then her eyes widened. "Actually, yes. I do remember being dragged against the pebbles and sand. I think my head knocked against a rock." She lifted a hand to a spot on the back of her head and rubbed. "I can't really feel anything, though." She shrugged. "I could have dreamed it."

Gawan rubbed his chin. "I doubt it. You seem to recall bits and pieces of things directly before you were hit." He studied her. "Nothing clear as to what happened *before* you were in the water the first time?"

With both hands, Ellie pushed against her temples. "No." She glanced at him. "Nothing."

"May we come in now, Sir Gawan?"

Young Davy and Lady Bella stood just inside the doorway. Davy's eyes were wide, staring at Ellie. Lady Bella waved.

With an approving nod, Gawan allowed it, and the pair hesitantly came toward the table.

"Ellie, this young pup is Davy Crispin, and this lovely woman beside him is Lady Bella Beauchamp."

Ellie gave a wan smile. "Hi."

Nicklesby hurried about the kitchen, preparing porridge and tea and toast. He stopped and glared at Gawan. "Sir, I beg you. Go bathe before my porridge curdles."

After glaring at Nicklesby, Gawan met Ellie's stare. "Do you mind overmuch if I leave you for just a moment?"

She shook her head. "I'll be fine with Davy and Lady Bella. And Nicklesby."

Gawan gave a short nod. "I shall be gone but for a moment."

Again, she smiled, although hesitantly, and not yet a full-blown smile. "Okay."

Gawan hurried upstairs. Just as he reached his chamber, an amused grumble sounded from a shadowy alcove behind him. As he looked, a fiery ember burned at the end of a cigar as the inhaler pulled a smoke. At least, that was what the illusion was.

Gawan scrubbed the back of his neck. "Aye, Sir Godfrey, what do you want?"

With much bluster, Sir Godfrey illuminated only his ghostly shadowy features. "You fancy the wench, aye?" He chuckled. "Ye might be able to fool some, boy, but not me."

"No doubt," Gawan said. "I'm here to help her. Make retirement. Gain my mortality. Nothing more."

"Even if said wench was beyond pleasing to the eye?" Godfrey added.

With a nod, Gawan smiled. "Aye, even there's that. And I don't need your meddlesome old self giving aide. Now, she awaits, and with Nicklesby, Davy, and Lady Bella, no less." He gave Godfrey a pointed look. "You and the others be gentle with her. She's a modern maid and is having a difficult time coming to terms with things." He waved a hand. "Don't all of you cluster about her so. And do not mention my wings again. If I can accomplish the task without her seeing them, 'twill be better."

A wide, wicked smile stretched across Godfrey's weathered face. "Oh, aye. The poor maid hasn't a clue what a *gwarcheidiol* is, does she?"

Gawan blew out a breath and shoved a hand through his hair. "I told her it was a Guardian of sorts. And that is how it will remain, Godfrey."

The old ghost chuckled. "As you say, boy. But methinks you'll need every trick you can muster, including those fetching wings of yours. And don't fret. We most assuredly will not cluster." Godfrey disappeared with another deep-throated chuckle.

Gawan narrowed his eyes at the empty shadowed space in the wall and turned to his chamber door. No telling what that old busybody knight was up to. But truly, Gawan could do nothing more than pray Ellie was strong enough to withstand it. The ladies, he knew, would be kind, even if a bit overwhelming. But Godfrey? The saints only knew.

In truth, 'twas best that Ellie knew as little as possible about who he was, or his origins. 'Twas bad enough, he thought, that should he save her life, which he fully intended to do, she'd always have a nagging memory of her time spent at Grimm. Not quite a realistic or corporeal memory, of course, but enough of a nuisance to make her occasionally pause and scratch her head.

Thankfully, once he gained his retirement, he'd have no memory of her whatsoever. Which, he thought, didn't sit very well with him, as he already found himself rather enamored with her. But 'twas the unavoidable way of it. 'Twas the requirement of being a *gwarcheidiol*. An Earthbound Guardian.

Rather, an *Angel*.

With that somewhat gloomy thought in mind, he hurried through his washing, anxious to get down to the kitchens before Ellie was overcome by Grimm's resident ghouls. Or disappeared again.

After a thorough brushing of teeth, Gawan pulled on jeans, a warm tunic, socks, and boots. He hastened downstairs to the kitchens, and just as he stepped through the wide arch, he stopped and blinked.

He shouldn't have been oversurprised.

There, at the long table, sat Ellie. And around her, beside her, and atop every flat surface in the larder perched more spirits than even he'd seen over the past fortnight.

So much for not clustering.

As he watched, he had no choice but to admire the manner in which Ellie handled herself. While her face looked more than a bit pasty, she sat with her hands folded, making somewhat of an attempt to answer the deluge of questions being thrown her way.

"What's it truly like, young lady, to be In Betwinxt?" asked Lady Follywolle, the beak of her coiffed swan nearly impaling Ellie's eye.

He couldn't help himself. He *listened.* Again.

What's it feel like? Are you insane? It feels like crap! she said in her thoughts, a thin smile stretching over her very lovely white teeth.

"Does it hurt overmuch?" asked Davy.

Hurt? Nooo, of course not. I feel just fine, sport! The smile widened.

Gawan nearly had to leave the room, he was so overcome with mirth.

The questions kept flying forth, and Gawan scanned the occupants of the room. Christian of Arrick-by-the-Sea leaned against the wall near the pantry, arms crossed over his chest, a bemused look upon his face, thankfully keeping his mouth firmly shut. He glanced at Gawan and grinned.

Gawan shrugged, then cleared his throat. Loudly. " 'Twill be enough, everyone." He frowned at Sir Godfrey, who at least had the decency to pretend to flick a bit of something from his surcoat. "Get you gone from this larder and allow Ellie some peace." He met her grateful gaze. "She's had a taxing day."

"Pah! This maid has more nerve than most of the lads in my garrison," said Godfrey. "Besides, her tales of the modern world are far more interesting than yours, Gawan." Godfrey winked at Gawan.

"Can we see you at supper, lady?" Davy asked. "I've loads more to ask you."

"Oh, yes! I insist you take your repast whilst seated between myself and Lady Bella!" Lady Follywolle exclaimed so fiercely, the swan on her head all but flapped its wings.

Ellie gave a sheepish grin. "Um, sure. I'll be there."

Lady Follywolle clapped her hands. "Splendid! Come, Davy, and lend me your arm whilst we leave the maid Ellie to her doings."

Davy's face screwed up. "All right," he said with a groan and, like a good lad, held out his arm.

Sir Godfrey boomed out a laugh.

One by one, the spirits disappeared. All but Christian, that is.

Ellie's gaze met Gawan's. "Wow."

He laughed. "Aye, wow, indeed." He gestured toward his friend. "This little lad is Christian of Arrick-by-the-Sea. Rather old, but he can still swing a fairly lethal blade."

Christian pushed from the wall to stand before Ellie. He gave a low bow. "Only lethal to those who prompt me, I assure you, and not nearly as lethal as your host." He inclined his head to Gawan. "He tells me you were found in the lane down the way."

"I daresay she doesn't recall much," Nicklesby answered, moving about the kitchen gathering teacups. "Much as we'd like her to."

Ellie propped her chin on her fist. "He's right. I don't remember much of anything before Gawan found me."

Christian looked at Gawan. "Have you searched the beach further?"

Gawan heaved a sigh. "Aye, but I found nothing of

import. I planned to have another look on my way into the village this afternoon. Ellie thinks she may have knocked her head against a rock."

Christian nodded. "I have a mind to look myself, as well. I'll let you know later if I find aught amiss, Grimm." He gave Ellie a smile. "Lady, should you need reprieve from this bothersome wretch, you've only to call." With a slight nod, he disappeared through the wall.

Gawan stifled a snort. Bothersome wretch, indeed.

Nicklesby placed a steaming cup of tea before Ellie, then excused himself. She picked up the spoon and stirred in a bit of honey, but did not sip. She met Gawan's eyes with a look of despair. "This is all so weird. I'm having trouble digesting it all. I feel like I'm watching a movie or something."

Gawan nodded. "In truth, I would as well, were I you." He regarded her closely. "I'll do my best, though, to find the truth, Ellie. I vow it."

For a moment, nothing else existed. She stared at him and the sheer look of uncertainty all but tied knots in Gawan's belly. The way her eyes searched his shook him to the bone. He wanted to touch her, but he wouldn't. That was not what she needed now. She needed to trust him. And the very last thing he needed was to become attached to an In-Betwinxt soul he'd never see again once her life was saved. He even wrestled with the urge to sneak a listen of her thoughts.

Ellie drew a deep breath, and her next words fell out on a sigh. "I believe you."

Those three words struck something deep within Gawan, something that made him know, without a doubt, and no matter the outcome, that he and Ellie were about to delve into an irreversible predicament. One he wasn't convinced would leave either unscathed. It more than unsettled him.

It scared the bloody hell out of him.

Five

The more Ellie tried to wrap her brain around the situation, the more her head hurt. She just couldn't comprehend what was happening. According to Gawan, she existed *In Betwinxt. Mostly dead.* Here one minute, gone the next.

How the *bleep* could someone be mostly dead?

In and out of a deep, deep coma, he'd claimed. When she was lost to unconsciousness, she for some reason appeared at Castle Grimm, particularly in the company of Gawan. When she came to, she disappeared and went somewhere else. Funny. Instead of waking and knowing exactly where she was, or that she was alive, Ellie remembered nothing but pitch-blackness, and the earthy scent that clung to her nostrils.

She groaned and clapped a hand over her eyes. "This is insane."

"Could be far worse," Gawan said.

Ellie peeked through her fingers. "Worse? How could it be worse than memoryless and mostly dead?"

"Well," he said, rising from the table, "you could be completely dead."

"Ugh," she groaned. "Don't remind me." She rose and crossed the floor to the sink, where she poured the contents of her teacup down the drain. Had she even swallowed any? "So I can just fade in and out without a warning?"

"Aye, I fear so."

Rinsing her cup and saucer, she set them in the dish drainer. "And I'm drinking tea, but not *really* drinking tea? Is that it?" She flipped the faucet on and off. "And I'm turning the water on and off, but not *really*?" She rubbed her temples. "And you can witness this because you're a Guardian of sorts? You interact with ghosts and almost-ghosts?"

Gawan followed her to the sink. "I don't claim to understand the whole of it, Ellie, but aye. All what you say is apparently so."

Turning, she grabbed Gawan's arm. "Is this not real, either? My skin touching yours?" She squeezed his biceps, which, she thought after a few more discreet squeezes, was rock-solid, and gave him a bold stare. "Feels pretty darn real to me." She swallowed as Gawan wrapped his long fingers around her wrist.

"Aye, 'tis real enough, Ellie." His eyes smoldered as they stared into hers. "I can feel the heat in your touch"—he gently dragged his knuckles against the top of her hand—"and the pulse of your blood running through your veins, here," he said, pressing a fingertip at her inner wrist. "I wish I could explain it, but I cannot. Yet the more time that passes, the more odd things will become."

"Odder than this?" she asked.

He gave a slight smile.

Strength and confidence radiated from him in waves, like heat rippling off tarmac in the dead of summer. Ellie had the feeling that Gawan could command an entire army with one simple, quiet word. Or a single scowl.

Even right now, the way he stared at her with those dark brown eyes, she felt touched—no, *caressed*—and all without him having moved a single inch. Not only that, but his eyes seemed ancient, all-knowing. As though he'd seen a *lot*.

His head dipped closer, eyes fixed on hers, and Ellie's heart slammed in her chest.

"If ye plan on making it up the way to the village, then ye'd best get going straightaway. There's another storm blowing this way, methinks," Sir Godfrey said out of nowhere, with quite a lot of enthusiasm.

Ellie blinked, and the spell was broken. Gawan's brows tugged into a frown; then he lowered his hand from Ellie's arm and turned toward the old knight now occupying the kitchen entrance.

"Quite the sport you are of late, Godfrey, keeping track of the weather and such," Gawan said, muttering. "A bloody weatherman. We were just leaving, by the by."

"Aye, well, good thing," Godfrey answered.

Ellie, still trying to catch her breath from the almost *something,* inhaled and smiled. "Thanks, Sir Godfrey."

The room took a sudden dip, the air grew light and wispy, and then everything turned dark. Gawan repeated her name over and over, but his voice seemed far off, muffled, as though he were in another part of the castle. Then she couldn't hear him at all.

Another vision, this one of a young girl, thirteen or fourteen, standing at the foot of a hospital bed. In the bed lay the old man, now with a shock of white hair, his face weary. Placing a large, veined hand atop her head, he comforted her with a few pats. She looked into his eyes. They were clear and blue-green, just like her own. His lips moved, speaking to Ellie, but no sound came forth. For some reason, her heart ached.

"Ellie?" Gawan's voice broke through the haze, far away at first but growing closer. "Ellie, look at me."

Ellie blinked and the vision disappeared completely. Once more, she stood before Gawan. His brow was furrowed, his eyes intense. His handsome face was very close to hers.

"Are you well?" he asked. "Another vision?"

Nodding, Ellie rubbed her forehead. "It was me, with the same old grandpa man, this time he was in a hospital bed. He was trying to tell me something, but I couldn't hear what he was saying. His lips were moving but no sound came out. And I felt very sad."

Gawan steadied her with both hands on her shoulders, and her skin grew warm beneath his touch. "We'll figure out this riddle, Ellie. It will all come together. I vow it." He turned her toward the door. "Let's start with a visit to the beach, then a few questions at the village."

Driving down the lane, Gawan watched Ellie from the corner of his eye. Just as before, she sat rigid, hand clutching the door handle as though ready to open it and fling herself out.

The need to tell Ellie about who he really was nearly choked him. Never before had he wanted to tell another—especially a modern mortal—of his past and oddly bizarre present. He did, though, with Ellie. A strong desire to purge every last sordid detail, good and bad. The bad, he feared, outweighed the good by far. And what bothered him so much was, *why her*? Why did he feel the need to tell this bewildered, quirky American who was almost a ghost?

A slight movement from Ellie drew Gawan from his thoughts. A swipe of the back of her knuckles across her eyes. Christ, she was weeping. But before he could say a word, she spoke.

"It's close to Christmas, isn't it?" she said, sniffing.

Gawan needed not to ponder that, as his retirement officially ended at midnight on Christmas Eve. "Aye, *Y Nadolig,* so it is. 'Tis less than a pair of fortnights away."

A heavy sigh escaped her lips. "*Y Nadolig.* That sounds nice. I love Christmas. I think." Then she continued to stare out the window. "Less than a pair of fortnights?"

Gawan smiled. "Less than a month."

"Oh."

Christmas. Or the Yuletide, as he'd once called it.

Strange to think of it now. Joy. Merriment. Mulled wine. The season of giving, of love. Family.

His thoughts traveled back to a less merry time, when he'd been battle-weary and bleeding, the dead of winter surrounding him as he stitched his own wounds in the bowels of a freezing cave on the Yuletide eve. No wonder his bloody bones creaked so. How vastly different things were now.

The guardrail loomed ahead, and Gawan pulled the Rover off to the side of the lane. He turned off the ignition and faced Ellie.

"This is where I found you. Are you sure you're up to exploring?" he asked.

She nodded. "Absolutely. Let's go."

Together they got out, squatted near the guardrail, and inspected the ground beside it. The rain had already flattened the area where Ellie had been sitting.

She ran her fingers over the brown grass, picked up a small stone, studied it, then tossed it back down. Standing, she peered over the rail. "Let's try down there."

Before Gawan could give her a steadying hand, Ellie straddled the rail and was on the other side. He followed her down the slight slope of dead winter grass, stopping here and there to study a bit of something along the way.

'Twas impossible, of course, not to stare at the girl. He simply couldn't help himself. She fascinated him. Not just her beauty, which he thought was passing fair; 'twas her confidence, her sure-footedness as she climbed down the slope, the gentle sweep of her hand over the grasses as she searched for some sort of recognition. The way her brows pulled tight as she immersed herself in heavy contemplation. And by the saints, the quirky thoughts she had of his comeliness all but made him chuckle out loud. Indeed, she was truly something.

A brisk wind caught her hair and tossed it across her face, a thick strand catching on her lip. She ignored it, of course, so caught up she was in her task.

Then she stood, facing the sea, her nose red from the cold. Her hair blew in disarray about her face, her lips trembled, and puffs of white frosty air blew out before her with each warm breath. She shivered and crossed her arms over her chest.

Do I have a husband? Kids? her thoughts screamed.

The air in Gawan's lungs lodged at the sight of her. Beautiful, aye, and she could very well belong to another. With a frown, he shoved his hands deep into his pockets and began to study the rocky sand. Not that he needed to concern himself over that matter. He need only make sure she *lived*.

With an internal shake to rid his pitiful self of distracting thoughts, he studied the ground. Because of the torrential rain, any prints that would have been made were long swept away now. Nothing but bits of broken shell, pebbles, and rocks. Still, Gawan looked hard at the path straight down from the guardrail. He couldn't be certain why. Mayhap because she'd tumbled over that railing?

Ellie joined him, but continued to gaze seaward, and voiced her previous thoughts. "I'd know if I had a husband or children, wouldn't I?" She turned fully, to face him. "I'd *feel* it, right? I mean, how could a mother forget something like that?" Her hand strayed to her very flat stomach.

Gawan knew, then, that no matter how fiercely attracted he was to this wayward almost-ghost, he'd have to steady his course and not become attached. 'Twasn't fair to Ellie, by no measure, and he didn't want to add to her confused state, such as it was.

He cleared his throat. "One never knows, I imagine. With a brutal blow to the head, aye, you could have lost a strong memory, such as bearing a babe." He clenched his hands inside his pockets to keep them secure as a powerful desire to touch her came over him, despite his own chastising. "Mayhap not lost forever, though." He inclined his head toward the path. "Come. Let's be off to the village before this storm blows in full force."

As they made their way back up the rocky path, thick gray clouds swirled overhead, and a light rain began to mist.

A large rock, just off the path, caught his attention. He grasped Ellie's arm.

Ellie stopped. She stared for a moment, then walked toward the rock. Gawan followed. Once there, Ellie knelt and ran her hand over the surface.

Then she brushed her fingers around the base of the rock. Her eyes widened, and then she lifted a small object from beneath.

Gawan bent over and peered into her flattened palm. 'Twas an ear bauble. He fingered the silver stem and light green stone. "Is it yours?"

Her hand flew to her earlobes, and though the holes were present, both were vacant of jewels of any sort. "I don't know." She looked at him. "But something made me search under that rock." She glanced at the bauble. Pushing her hand deep into her jeans pocket, she retrieved something. She gasped as she opened her palm. 'Twas the matching bauble.

Gawan nodded. "So 'tis yours, for a certainty." The rain started heavier now, with big, fat drops splattering the guardrail, making a tinny *clink* with each fall. "Mayhap your memory will slowly recall. Come, then."

By the time they'd reached the village, the raindrops had turned into a heavy mist. The threat of a storm still lingered, though, as if at any moment, the gray clouds could open up.

It was in the first village shop they stopped in that Gawan not only realized exactly what he was dealing with in an In-Betwinxt Ellie, but in the meddlesome lot of annoyances that resided in his keep.

Gawan gave a push to the bookstore door, which boasted a big, piney Christmas wreath lavished with pinecones, nuts, and ribbons, and a bell announced their arrival.

Mrs. MacGillery, the bookstore owner, sat behind a large, polished mahogany podium, which served as her cashier's counter. She glanced up, glasses askew, and she blushed an alarming shade of red. Then she patted the sides of her hair—also askew—into place, looked directly at Gawan, and batted her eyelashes.

"*Bore da*, Mrs. MacGillery," Gawan said with a nod.

Mrs. MacGillery giggled. "Oh! *Bore da* to you, too! I do love to hear you speak the old Welsh. Good to see you this fine misty morn, Lord Grimm! How is that wicked rogue Nicklesby? Do tell him to come by for a visit. Quite the witty one, he is, and keeps me in stitches. Oh! I've something for you." She slipped down from her matching high-perched mahogany stool and came toward him. A wee thing, compact in stature, with brown hair shot with gray and coiffed rather high. "It only just came in yesterday. Now where did I put it?"

Mrs. MacGillery walked straight through Ellie, who stood to Gawan's left.

Ellie sucked in a breath, made a sort of choking noise that Gawan didn't fancy at all, and stared, wide-eyed, at Mrs. MacGillery.

"Wow. She can't see me," Ellie said, mostly to herself. She held her own arms out and studied them, as if trying to see if *she* could see them. Gawan smothered a smile with his hand.

"Aha!" Mrs. MacGillery said, and he and Ellie both jumped. Mrs. MacGillery pulled a heavy leather-bound volume off the shelf from one of the expansive bookcases lining the old shop. "Here it is, right under me nose! All the way from Snowdonia!" She turned, crossed the wood-planked floor, her heels clacking with each step and her long plaid swishing side to side. Again, she made to pass right through Ellie, who artfully dodged the woman this time.

A snort and a laugh erupted from the back of the store.

"Methinks she's besotted, I do," Sir Godfrey said as he materialized, perched on the step of the bookcase ladder. He waved a hand, foppish ruffles fluttering. "The way she flitters about, cheeks turning a blistering blaze and such."

"Aye," agreed Christian of Arrick-by-the-Sea, who now leaned against a large stone hearth with a roaring fire. "She's definitely taken wi' you, Conwyk." He pointed. "Look you there how her eyes beat."

"Lord Grimm?" Mrs. MacGillery asked.

Gawan glanced at her, and indeed she batted her lashes furiously.

Ellie snorted.

"Er, aye," Gawan said. He accepted the book he'd ordered a few weeks before: *Early Welsh History.* "Obliged." He pulled out his wallet and paid for the tome.

Mrs. MacGillery smiled and patted her hair once more. "My pleasure as always, Lord Grimm."

More snickers from his ghostly mates erupted, and Gawan forced a smile. Christ, how he hated to be referred to as lord. He'd begged her before not to do such, but she insisted. "Right. Uh, Mrs. MacGillery, have you by chance happened upon a young woman recently, say, in the past fortnight or so? An American, mayhap?"

Her brows furrowed as she thought. "The past fortnight, you say? Hmmm," she said, tapping her chin. "Odd time of year for tourists, for a certainty. Although," she said, still pondering, "let me see. . . ."

Mrs. MacGillery snapped her fingers. "I've got it! A young American girl did stop in. She wasn't here for very long, though. Lovely girl, with striking blue-green eyes—"

"What did she want?" Gawan asked.

"Ask if she gave her name," Ellie said.

"Or where her bloody lodgings were," Sir Godfrey added.

Godfrey, Christian, and Ellie all drew closer to the bookstore owner.

"Well, a book, of course." She strode across the floor, back to the podium, where she reached down, then lifted a rather old-looking volume. "This one."

Six

Ellie peered around Gawan and stared at the large leather-bound book: *Titled Nobles of Northumberland, Past and Present.*

Why would she want to read that? Bor-ing!

Gawan gave Ellie a quick glance, then turned to Mrs. MacGillery. "Did she by chance leave a name? Or where she was lodging?"

Mrs. MacGillery waved a hand. "No, no, I never take names, love. If the books aren't picked up, I simply slip them onto my own shelves and sell them to another. Of course, I allow plenty o' time for the book to be retrieved first."

"Ask about her bloody appearance! And how bloody long she planned to stay! Come on, boy!" Godfrey said.

Gawan shot him a frown. "Be quiet!"

"Pardon?" Mrs. MacGillery said, one eyebrow raised as she glanced in the direction of Godfrey.

Christian of Arrick-by-the-Sea simply chuckled.

Gawan cleared his throat. "*Mae'n flin 'da fi,* lady. I'm sorry. I've a, er"—he coughed—"frog in my throat."

Ellie giggled. It was like watching the Three Stooges. *Hey! At least I remember Curly, Larry, and Moe!*

"So it seems. Now, let me see," Mrs. MacGillery said. "She did mention that she was here on a research mission of sorts. Genealogy, I think." She winked at Gawan. "You know how those Americans love burrowing into their medieval roots. I believe she claimed to be staying in the area for at least a month, which is why she ordered the book." She shook her head, clacked across the floor, and resumed her perch at the podium. "And as I said, she had striking eyes, and a lovely shade of auburn hair." She giggled. "Although she wore a baggy jumper and denims, she couldn't quite hide that darling figure."

Ellie looked at Gawan and wiggled her brows. "*Definitely* me."

A twinkle lit Gawan's eye, but he didn't say a word.

Mrs. MacGillery patted her hair. "Reminds me of a younger me, actually." She winked at Gawan. "Quite the dish, I was. *Scrumptious*, even."

Godfrey snorted and said something under his breath that was very medieval and probably extremely naughty, because Christian laughed. Loudly.

Gawan coughed again, but Ellie could see he was trying his best not to laugh, too. "I've no doubt there, Mrs. MacGillery. Is there anything else you can recall?"

"Ask her for any minute details—anything I may have said to give away where I was staying," Ellie said.

"Er, anything in regards to her lodgings? A general area, mayhap? Or a name? Possibly a B and B?"

Mrs. MacGillery tilted her head down and peered at Gawan over the rim of her glasses. She grinned, a lazy, all-knowing kind of womanly smile. "She did mention something about freezing her butt off in the drafty old cottage she'd let. Claimed the brisk sea wind all but took off a layer of skin." She laughed and shook her head. "Quite witty, that one. She didn't say where such a blustery cottage was, I'm afraid. But if I recall anything else, I'll be sure to ring you." Her smile widened. "If I didn't know any better, I'd think you were smitten."

Godfrey and Christian snickered.

Gawan strode to the podium, lifted Mrs. MacGillery's hand, and brushed a kiss across her knuckles. "Thank you, my good lady, for the information and pleasantries. I am more than obliged."

"Blimey! Would ye take a look at her face! 'Tis the reddest I've seen it yet!" Godfrey said.

"You make my own heart flutter, Grimm," said Christian.

Ellie rolled her eyes. "I think I'm going to hurl."

The guys laughed.

"Quite all right, young sir." Mrs. MacGillery fanned herself. "No charge for the volume, as long as you send Nicklesby round with it on return." She batted her eyes.

Gawan gave a nod. "I'll see that he does."

With that, they all piled out of the bookstore.

Once outside, Ellie gave Gawan a grin. "I think she has the hots for you *and* Nicklesby."

Gawan blew out a breath. "I daresay you're right. Quite tenacious, that one."

"More than you can handle, I'll warrant," Christian said.

Gawan grinned. "No doubt."

"We're off to Grimm, then," said Godfrey. "All this detective work has me tuckered."

Gawan frowned. "You've done little more than heckle me, you old fool. How can you be tuckered?"

Sir Godfrey ignored the comment. "I've a mind to sit down to a game of chess with a worthy opponent, quite right. Come, Arrick-by-the-Sea! I'll even give you splendid odds."

Christian shrugged and disappeared with Godfrey.

Just then, the spitting rain grew heavy. Gawan pulled the books close to his chest to keep them dry and inclined his head. "Let's put these in the Rover, then visit the other establishments. If Mrs. MacGillery had words with you, mayhap others will have, as well."

Ellie and he went in and out of at least four other stores, yet no one could give any more information than what Mrs. MacGillery had given. Soaked, Ellie and Gawan hurried to the Rover.

"It looks like we're finished here, for now, anyway." Thunder cracked overhead. "We can get back to Grimm, dry off, then go through the book to see if anything jars your memory."

Ellie nodded and ducked her head as the rain picked up. "Sounds good to me."

Minutes later they were headed back up the rocky path leading to Castle Grimm. Ellie stared out the window at the blustery wintry scene. The crags and cliffs of Northern England were stunning, the North Sea a turbulent churning of gray frothy power as it bashed the cliffside. Even through the closed glass, the briny scent of the sea permeated the Rover and her senses. It smelled familiar, somehow. Brave seagulls swept over the water and then disappeared beneath the rocky overhangs. The grass along the cliffs had yellowed and swayed with each gust of icy wind. An old stone wall crept across the meadow, then suddenly vanished. Ellie guessed the original builders of Castle Grimm had carefully laid each stone, hundreds of years before. Once she was home, she'd have to research the area.

Research? *Home?* Good Lord, would things ever be normal again?

"Is there aught amiss?" Gawan said.

Ellie shrugged. "Other than being mostly dead? Nah. Everything's fabuloso." She cocked her head. "I don't get you, Gawan Conwyk. You talk like you're from another century, yet you're as real as Mrs. MacGillery. Certainly, if you were anything *weird,* she'd know it. Right? I mean, she doesn't know you're a *gwarche,* er, a Guardian, or whatever you are, does she?" She shook her head. "You take all this crazy stuff in like it's second nature to you. Aren't you the least bit freaked out by any of it? By me?"

The corner of his very sexy mouth tipped upward into a boyish grin. "Aye, well, your state of affairs is passing odd, girl. Of that, there's no doubt." He shrugged and turned off the lane and through the double gates of Castle Grimm. "But I've been doing what I do for far too long to be *freaked out,* as you say." He glanced at her.

" 'Tis a certainty, though, that you are by far the most fascinating charge I've ever had. And no, Mrs. MacGillery hasn't a clue what I do for a living."

In that slight glance, the chocolaty smoothness of his eyes gave off a glint. Of *what,* exactly, Ellie didn't know.

It gave her a shiver clear to the tips of her toes.

With a rather sly, inconspicuous look, Ellie studied the strong hands gripping the steering wheel of the Rover. Thick, long fingers, blunt nails, big knuckles. Beneath the cuff of his sweater, at his wrist, was yet another tattooed marking. Good Lord, he was riddled with them. Very sexy, she thought, and the markings looked nothing like any tattoos she'd ever seen. The markings were pitch-black, not faded like some ink. And the designs themselves were strange, almost like ancient symbols.

She knew that beneath his wool sweater, those tattoos tracked across his chiseled chest, broad shoulders, and even broader back. Sheesh! She'd seen him in the buff, nude, nekkid as a jaybird, all-out *commando*, for God's sake, and what a blessed sight to behold. And oh, baby, had she gawked. Just like that time in the museum—how old had she been, twelve?—when she'd gotten caught gaping in adolescent awe at the David statue. She'd even copped a feel of the solid marble *appendage* that had captivated her and her friends. Good Lord! Her father would've croaked if he'd ever found out.

She gasped. "Oh! I remembered something!"

Gawan, who had a ridiculous grin on his face for some strange reason, pulled up at the castle entrance, stopped, and threw the Rover into park. He cleared his throat. "Er, what?"

Ellie turned in her seat to face him full-on. "My father! I was sitting here, wondering about all those tattoos you have. Then I thought about how I'd seen you naked that one night and how sexy I thought those tattoos were, and *that* led to a memory of me at a museum feeling up a statue of David, and *then* I thought about how my father would croak if he ever found out." She laughed. "I've got a father! I'm remembering!"

Gawan just stared at her, that funny, almost smothered grin changing, as a slow, easy smile lifted the corners of his mouth.

"What?" Ellie said, and gave him a punch in the arm. "Isn't that great?"

One dark eyebrow rose above one sinfully dark chocolate eye. "You were thinking of me naked?"

Ellie blinked. "Well, yeah."

The grin widened. "And you find me markings sexy?"

Ellie feigned an exaggerated yawn. "Sort of."

Gawan's eyes held hers for a moment, and that darn glint of his was back. The muscles in his jaws flexed, making his features intense, and Ellie's mouth went dry as a bone. That couldn't possibly be a good thing.

With a deep breath, she laughed it off. "Sooo, how 'bout those books, huh?" She gave him another playful punch in the biceps—which, she noticed not for the first time, was quite the rock. "Chop chop! The sooner I'm no longer mostly dead, the better, right?"

Just that fast, Gawan's expression changed. Gone was the playful, flirty look; now a solemn, remorseful one took its place.

Thinking it best to tackle one bizarre thing at a time, the first, of course, being her inconceivable *state of affairs,* as Gawan had called her almost-deadness. She pasted a pleasant smile to her face and jumped out of the Rover. "Come on, Grimm. Get the lead out of your pants. Let's get down to the business of saving *me,* okay?"

She didn't wait for him as she bounded up the half dozen steps and through the castle's wide double oak doors.

Literally *through* the double oak doors.

Gawan blinked. Damnation, Ellie had vanished again. Here one second, gone the next. Bloody frustrating, that was what it was.

He sat in the car and stared at the space she'd just occupied. A feeling of emptiness washed over him, and he wondered why, in all his centuries of being a Guardian, he had not *felt* the same toward any of his other charges. Aye, he'd felt compassion, and he'd done his job well. He'd never lost a soul, not once. He'd never become overattached to any of them, though.

He felt rather attached to Ellie of Aquitaine.

It pained him to think of not remembering his time with her.

Grabbing the two leather tomes he'd acquired at Mrs. MacGillery's, he shut the door to the Rover and stopped as Ellie's words came back to him.

. . . that *led to a memory of me at a museum feeling up a statue of David* . . .

Gawan laughed out loud as he climbed the steps and opened the doors. "The girl's surely mad."

"Sir Gawan! I seen her, but then she disappeared through the bloomin' door!" Davy said, breathless, just inside the hall. "Came straight through the wood, she did, smiled at me so big I seen all her teeth. Then off she went!"

Gawan closed the doors behind him and grinned. "You sift through doors and walls regularly, boy. And I don't think you saw *all* of her teeth."

Davy ran alongside Gawan. "Aye, I did see them all—back ones, too. Could see them in the dark, I s'pose, they're so bloomin' white." He skipped ahead and turned to walk backward, facing Gawan. "Whitest teeth I ever did see, methinks—next to yours." He grinned. "And I slip through doors and such, aye, but I'm a spirit in truth. Lady Ellie's In Betwinxt. That's different!"

Gawan laughed. "Aye, so it is." Striding over to the hearth, he laid the two volumes atop a short, wide mahogany table perched before a leather settee and matching chair. Both the settee and the chair had plenty of stuffing, with the hide softer than any saddle he'd ever straddled, and both were passing comfortable. He'd thumb through the book Ellie had ordered after he looked up all the cottages for let in the area. Hopefully, he'd find the one Ellie had procured.

"Did you find out anything, then, Sir Gawan?" Davy perched cross-legged atop the table, next to the books. "Her name, mayhap? Although I quite fancy the name Ellie."

Crossing his arms over his chest, Gawan studied the young spirit. Although not his charge, Gawan had indeed tried but never solved the mystery of Davy's death. The boy, of course, had no memory of it, and there'd been no clues leading to the boy's family, home, or the events which had caused his unfortunate end. All Gawan, or anyone else, knew of the incident was that young Davy Crispin's nine-year-old body had washed up lifeless at the rocky base of Castle Grimm. His little spirit had never left.

"Sir Gawan!" Davy said, with the force of a nine-year-old's impatience.

"Nay, boy, I did not find out her true name. You may continue to call her Ellie, then."

Davy's face screwed up. "Blimey. We've just got to find out more." He glanced at the volumes on the table. "What are those?"

Before Gawan could answer, Nicklesby pushed through the larder door and hurried across the great hall to stand before him.

"Well, sir," Nicklesby said, "anything at all?" He glanced around. "Where's the young lady?"

"She sifted through the bloomin' door, Nicklesby! I seen her!" Davy shuddered. "Grinnin' one second, she was. Then wide-eyed and scary the next, just as she vanished." He scratched his brow. "Didn't fancy that a bit, I s'pose."

"I'm sure you didn't, lad," Nicklesby said.

Gawan ran his fingers through his still-damp hair. "Aye, and I can assure you that Ellie didn't fancy it, as well." He clapped a hand on Nicklesby's bony shoulder.

"Mrs. MacGillery had dealings with her, though. Ellie stopped in and ordered a book and told Mrs. MacGillery she was lodging in the area—letting a cottage with a fierce sea wind."

Nicklesby nodded. "Passing interesting. Did it spark the lady's memory at all?"

Gawan recalled Ellie's museum memory and struggled to keep a grin off his face. "Nay, nothing useful. Although she did find an ear bauble on the beach, beneath a rock she recalls her head hitting. She had a match to the bauble in her trousers."

"Her memory is sure to come back, then!" Davy cried. "I'm off to tell the others!"

With that, he jumped up from the table and disappeared through the wall.

Gawan rubbed his eyes and his chin, which he found beard-stubbled. Then he shoved his hands into his pockets and faced his gangly steward. "You were once a Guardian, Nicklesby. I vow, I've tried not to grow close to her." He sighed. "I cannot help myself. I can't keep my bloody mind off her." He looked at Nicklesby. "Do you understand? I hate knowing she'll forget me, and I'll forget her."

With hands clasped behind his back, Nicklesby nodded. "Aye, lad. I do. Far better than you know, although I can honestly say I never had the unique experience of having an In Betwinxt as a charge." He grinned. "Nor one quite as fetching." He patted Gawan on the shoulder. "Yet you know as well as I the fickleness of the Higher-Ups. For a certainty, though, They do have a purpose for all They do." He gave Gawan a smile. "Have you ever fancied that thought, my boy?" He grasped Gawan's elbow and steered him toward the library. "Take me, for instance. I'd have never given a second thought to being pulled from my Guardianship to serve in a higher court. But 'tis what happened, and yet, now I'm here." He cocked his head. " 'Tis a glorious gift indeed, to be bestowed a pair of wings such as yours.

You've done great things with those feathered appendages, Sir Gawan, even if you do keep them hidden. Do
not ever forget that."

Gawan grunted. "Wings are highly overrated,
methinks—*hrumph!*"

Ellie, arms and legs flailing, seemingly dropped out of
nowhere and slammed into Gawan. Nicklesby stumbled
out of the way, just in the nick of time.

Gawan, though, took the hit full force and tumbled to
the floor with Ellie atop him. They both landed with a
grunt, nose-to-nose. Their mouths, Gawan noticed as he
stared at Ellie's tempting one, were a mere whisper
apart.

"Oops," Ellie said, a sheepish smile on her face.
"Sorry."

And for the first time since being picked up from the
lane that wintry night, Ellie smiled a full-blown smile.

Gawan blinked. The weight of her body pressed
against him, and the warmth of her breath fanned his
neck. Damn, but he could feel her heart beat against his
chest. So *real*.

How the bloody hell can she be *mostly* dead?

The tightening of his groin at the intimate contact assured him that while Ellie of Wherever was mostly dead,
there was, indeed, a certain part of her that most definitely remained very much *alive*.

Get up, Conwyk, you letch . . .

"Dear girl, take my hand," Nicklesby said, poking out
his bony hand.

Ellie kept her eyes trained on Gawan's and, if possible, gave an even wider smile, annoyingly endearing, and
it was then he thought he saw something. Cocking his
head to the side, he stared, then blinked. 'Twas the most
minute of details, and one he'd obviously missed before:
an unmistakable, barely there imprint at one corner of
her mouth.

He nearly choked. By the devil's pointed hooves, this
was *not* happening. He had to be wrong.

He peered even closer. Nay, he was *right*.

Lo, how he loathed being so right.

'Twas a soul mate's unstolen kiss . . .

Gawan jumped up, at the same time dragging Ellie up and then shoving her into Nicklesby's arms. Both stumbled, then looked at him as though he'd lost his bloody mind.

And in fact, in truth, he thought he just truly had.

Bleeding priest's and saint's curled toes combined. Ellie, the almost-ghost whose only memory was of herself shamelessly groping the male pride of a naked David statue, was his blasted soul mate.

His *Intended*.

Seven

Ellie stood there, Nicklesby's skinny arms steadying her, while Gawan's face turned pale. He shoved a hand through his hair, scrubbed his five-o'clock-shadowed chin, rubbed his eye sockets with the pads of his fingers, and then muttered something under his breath.

Gawan inclined his head. "Mind her, Nicklesby."

Then he pushed his hands into his pockets and stalked off. Mumbling. In Welsh.

Nicklesby took a step toward Gawan. "But, sir?" After a moment, he shook his head.

"What's wrong with him?" Ellie asked. "He looked like he was going to throw up or something." Which was sad, because she could have sworn they'd shared an intimate moment on the floor. Not that she'd meant for it to happen, of course. She couldn't help where she'd fallen. But fallen on him she had. Then that funny look had taken over his sexy features, and the intimacy was gone.

"Hmm," Nicklesby said. "I've not a clue." He grasped her elbow. "I daresay 'tisn't a bothersome stomach, though." He clucked his tongue. "No need to fret, young lady. 'Twill all be well. Most likely a matter of forgotten business came over him. Come." He gave her elbow a tug. "Would you care to see the castle? Mayhap you were here on a tour of sorts before you were interrupted with your work? You Americans love to tour old castles."

"I'll take 'er, Nicklesby!"

Young Davy emerged through the wall at a full run and skidded to a halt before Ellie. "Do you wanna come wi' me, then? You'll fancy the views!"

Wow. Would she ever get used to all this ghosty stuff? It was one thing to sit on the Haunted Mansion ride at Disney World and see the cute little Victorian spirits sitting in the car with you as you passed the mirror. Quite another thing altogether for it to really *happen*.

It made her head swim. But at least she remembered Disney World.

Davy seemed harmless enough, though. Cute kid, actually. He looked like a typical scruffy little Victorian London paperboy.

"Well? Ya wanna come?" Davy asked again, his skinny little knickered legs hopping around with excitement.

What she really wanted to do was sit down and pore over that book they'd borrowed from Mrs. MacGillery. She hoped something in it would spark another memory. A *useful* memory. But a short walk around such an amazing castle surely couldn't hurt. Besides, her head ached from constantly worrying about what was happening to her. A little sightseeing might do her some good. Give her a tiny bit of normalcy, maybe. And somewhere, in the back of her mind, she had the feeling she'd always *wanted* to visit a medieval castle.

The interest in the castle spirits, not to mention the handsome lord of the keep, was a totally new development.

Ellie glanced at Nicklesby, who gave her a warm smile. "Go ahead, young lady. I vow Davy Crispin here does indeed have access to the best views from the keep." He gave Davy a stern look. "Mind the west tower, lad. 'Tis a treacherously brisk wind coming off the sea. While it can't blow you away, it is surely something to be considered for Ellie."

"Aye, Nicklesby!" Davy said, hopping up and down. "Come on, then!"

Ellie grinned at Nicklesby and started after Davy. "Be back in a little while."

As she and Davy wandered off, Nicklesby shouted from behind, "Be mindful of the artillery chamber, lad!"

"Aye!" Davy called back. Then to Ellie: "Hurry! We'll explore the artillery first!"

For the first time since arriving at Castle Grimm, Ellie took a close look. She'd been so consumed by her bizarre predicament, she'd ignored the rugged beauty of the medieval keep. Black timbered beams stretched from one corner of the great hall's high ceiling to the other, the walls covered with tapestries—including the one of the great Eleanor of Aquitaine, from whom she'd swiped her temporary name. The monstrous hearth took up the length of one whole wall, big enough for a few men Gawan's size to stand in it, and before it sat the most comfy-looking leather sofa and overstuffed chair she'd ever seen. Maybe she'd drag the book from Mrs. MacGillery's onto her lap and perch in front of the fire once she finished with Davy's tour. Perhaps she'd even con Nicklesby into making her a cup of tea.

At the mammoth staircase, Davy bounded up each step with the enthusiasm of a puppy. Well, more like he *floated*. She followed close behind, not missing one detail of the castle's interior.

"Come on!" he said. "Hurry!"

More tapestries clung to the walls up the staircase, along with wall sconces—electrical replicas—and once they'd gone up one level, they turned down a long passageway that led to a set of tall double doors. Davy slipped straight through the wood, poked his head back out, and grinned.

"Come on! It's not locked!" he said, then disappeared back through the oak.

Ellie pulled the old handle and pushed open the doors. The room was pitch-black.

"Turn on the light!" Davy cried. "It's just there, right beside you!"

With a tentative hand, in case there may be a spider or something crawling along, Ellie felt for the switch, found it, and clicked it on. Soft light filled the stone-walled chamber, a yellowish radiance that made everything seem ancient.

Ellie's breath caught in her throat as she drank in a sight she was pretty sure not many had been privy to. She wasn't quite sure why it fascinated her so much, since she couldn't remember ever being enamored by medieval weapons before. But this? It was beyond amazing. As with every other room she'd been in within the walls of Castle Grimm, an enormous fireplace dominated the chamber. But along two walls were majestic suits of armor, complete with helmets, swords, and shields, all appearing to be in different styles, or from different time periods, from a very primitive one that was behind glass, to the most modern. Every medieval weapon she'd ever heard of was perched on walls, in the hands of the silent knights, and in every corner.

"Methinks ye fancy this chamber, lady, because your mouth is gaping," Davy said. "Look at this one here first. 'Tis me favorite!"

Ellie pushed the door closed behind her and entered the chilly chamber. She crossed the wood-plank floor to the suit of armor Davy danced around. It was tall with a broad breast plate and a full face shield on the helmet. She could easily conjure up the knight who must have worn it.

Powerful.

Davy feigned swordplay, poking and swiping at an invisible opponent as he pretended to be the armored warrior. "Take that, ye bloody rotten swine!" he said, his little arms flailing as he hefted and swung his invisible weapon.

Ellie studied the other suits, but the one in the far corner, behind glass, caught her eye. Leaving the marauding Davy behind, she crossed the length of the chamber for a closer look.

Peering into a double-paned leaded-glass wardrobe, Ellie felt the air leave her lungs as she stared at the contents. A long shirt of chain mail, hood and coif included, along with a pair of chain mail hose, hung within. A pair of well-worn leather boots sat on a high wooden box, the creases from the wearer's foot bending over and over plainly visible. A lethal pair of spurs sat strapped to each bootheel. Propped against the box, which looked painstakingly carved from what appeared to be a thick chunk of oak, rested a large wood-and-iron shield and a rugged-looking sword. Hanging beside the mail was a long black, sleeveless shirt made of thick cloth, apparently worn over the mail. Both the tunic and the shield carried the same design: black, with a large silver cross over the front.

" 'Tis the garb of a Crusader."

Ellie jumped at the warm, buttery-raspy voice. Turning, she stared up and into Gawan's eyes. *Gulp.*

"You're not going to run away again, are you?" she asked. She gave him a quirky smile. "People might start to talk, you know." She jerked a thumb at the chain mail. "Guys like *this* wouldn't leave a girl standing in the arms of a wiry butler. I can promise you that."

A grin crossed Gawan's face, and Ellie noticed he had the cutest dents in his cheeks when he smiled. Nice teeth, too. *Reeeally* nice lips.

Gawan gave her a slight nod. "My apologies, lady. Something, er, pressing caught me most unawares, and I had to leave at once."

Ellie lifted one of her eyebrows. "How convenient. Don't let it happen again. It's bad enough being half dead. I don't remember much, but one thing I'm sure I know is I don't like being ditched." She poked his chest. "Got it?"

His eyes grew dark as he stared into hers. "Aye. Most assuredly so."

Ellie had quite a good bit of trouble breathing at that point, what with Gawan no more than a foot away, those hypnotic, deep brown eyes staring at her, the muscle ticking in his jaw, and good Lord, he smelled good. He'd let his hair loose, those carefree, boyish curls hanging to just below his shoulders. . . .

"Are you ready to search through your book?" he asked.

The moment, once again, was gone. Definitely gone. Gawan now sounded all business.

"Where did Davy go?" Ellie asked. She glanced around the chamber. "He was just here."

"Aye, well, Sir Godfrey was looking for the lad, so I sent him on his way." Gawan turned to walk off. "The book, then?"

"Um, yeah, but just a minute." Ellie took another look at the chain mail. "You said this was from the Crusades?"

Gawan stopped and looked over his shoulder. "Aye, 'tis so."

"Wow. That would make it—what? Thirteenth century?"

"Twelfth." Gawan inclined his head to the door. "Shall we?"

Ellie ignored him and moved to the next display of armor. "This is some collection, Conwyk. Have you ever thought of getting an alarm system installed? This stuff must be worth a fortune. I know a guy . . . who . . . could . . ."

Gawan stopped, turned, and cocked his head. "Go on."

Frowning, Ellie thought. *Hard.* She rubbed her temples and paced. "I know a guy, and I think he installs security systems. Very thorough and up-to-date, latest technology."

Keeping in step, Gawan paced with her. "His name, Ellie? Do you recall it?"

The amount of thought Ellie poured into her brain actually made it start to throb. "I know him pretty good. I've used him on several jobs, I think. Not legally, of course, but—"

"You've used him on several jobs *illegally*?" Gawan rubbed his chin. "What mean you?"

Ellie stopped and looked at him. "I don't know. Gosh, maybe I'm a professional thief or something?" She closed her eyes.

"What are you doing?"

"I'm envisioning myself dressed in head-to-toe black spandex, easing over alarm beams and slipping around corners on tiptoe." She opened her eyes, only to find Gawan smiling. "I look pretty good doing it, but nope. It just doesn't feel right." Then an image came to her. "Wait. I can sort of see a face, blond hair, a goatee, sort of cute, but no name." She blew out a gusty sigh. "Sorry."

He took her by the arm and tugged. "Come, whilst your memory is intact. Mayhap the book will stir things up a bit more, aye? You can venture up here later and gander all you want at my, er, the armor."

The heat his hand caused on her skin nearly made her jump. Tension rippled from her arm to her belly, and she fought to control the urge just to fall against him, back of hand to forehead, and plead in the most Southern drawl, *Take me, sir. I'm yours!* She glanced up at him. His face was now stern, purposeful, the playfulness of earlier gone without a trace.

Apparently, she was the only one having *those* kinds of feelings. It was obvious she'd been reading those heated looks all wrong. Besides, what did it matter? She was half dead. Almost a ghost.

An idea that, like it or not, she was getting more and more used to with every second that passed by.

Ellie gave a short nod. "Aye," she mimicked, and fell into step with Gawan as they left the artillery behind.

One and a half hours later, Gawan excused himself from their cozy little makeshift office before the great hall hearth and left Ellie, along with her newly acquired entourage to their doings. They'd managed to scour through several pages before that blasted Godfrey and the ladies, along with young Davy, joined in. After that, Gawan had barely had room to pinch off a corner of the table to view the book. Besides, how could he bloody well concentrate *knowing* what Ellie truly was?

He damn well couldn't.

All he found himself doing was staring at that cursed little mark at the corner of her mouth. The mark that, only beknownst to him, branded Ellie as *his*.

Bleeding priests, he was an idiot.

Bloomin' daft, he was, to gaze upon someone knowing she was his truly Intended. Not betrothed, as in the old day, by one's sire, but *Intended*. A mate of souls. 'Twas difficult to grasp, because he'd only known her but for a few sparse days. He actually knew passing little about her, save her quirky yet charming disposition, her incredible wit, and her ease with the spirits. On top of that, she was curvy and fetching enough to make a dead man drool. Quite courageous, as well. And all the while he knew that no matter what sort of mark she bore, they could never be, and all because she was his charge. They'd forget each other even existed once Ellie's life was spared.

'Twould do no good to ponder the matter. No bloody good at all. He'd do his best to save her life. That was the only thing that mattered. He wouldn't even consider the consequences if he failed.

Christ, why did she have to be his Intended? Just knowing it made his heart ache. Mayhap he wouldn't have tried as hard to save her, had he not known. He considered that. Nay, he would have and would still do everything in his power to find her live self, and save her.

Even though it meant living without her.

Recalling centuries of memories, Gawan brought to mind his parents. They'd loved each other fiercely. He'd dreamed of having the same. The only thing that settled his mind was knowing that, even though he'd not have his Intended to love, she'd be safe.

Only if he found her. So he thought his time might be better spent inspecting the cottage rentals in the area online. He'd gather the addresses, then contact each owner and give a description of Ellie. Mayhap, luck would be with them and a clue would emerge.

Gawan climbed the stairs to the second level, strode down the passageway, then ducked into the library and closed the door behind him. Easing over to his desk, he felt for the lamp, clicked it on, then powered up the PC.

It didn't take long to find every cottage rental listing in the area. After jotting down contact numbers and addresses for each one, he set down the pen, leaned back, and rubbed his eyes with the heels of his hands.

" 'Tis quite a list of lodgings there, man."

Gawan didn't bother to look up. He knew his mate's voice well. "Aye."

"I heard you fell and tumbled all over the lass earlier, then fled like a whipped hound."

Gawan logged off and powered down the PC. "So?"

Christian of Arrick-by-the-Sea chuckled. "Do not get me wrong, my friend. I'd have thoroughly enjoyed the tumble." He propped a mailed hip against the desk. "But why did you flee?"

"I did not flee."

Christian leaned forward. "Aye. You did. Everyone saw. Godfrey said your face turned a rather frightening shade of unbaked dough."

Gawan rose from his chair and paced to the hearth.

"I'm being spied upon now—is that it? Mayhap my stomach ached?"

"What made you flee?"

Gawan blew out a hearty sigh. If he could trust anyone, 'twould be this man—or ghost, rather. "I discovered something rather unsettling about the girl, and it vexed me all of a sudden. Caught me off guard, is all."

Christian followed him to the hearth and leaned a forearm on the wide stone mantel. "So what is it? Good God, man, you're killing me."

With a quick glance at his friend, Gawan turned his stare back to the flames. "You sound more like Lady Follywolle every day. Passing nosy."

Christian scowled. "I'm a spirit, Conwyk. I've nothing better to do than hear of your pathetic tales of woe. So hence forth with the woe-ing, man, before I lose my patience."

Shoving his fingers through his hair, Gawan peered at his mate, rubbed his chin, then sighed. "Ellie's not just some wayward lass In Betwinxt. She's different. She is, er, meant to be mine."

A slow smile spread across the knight's face. "Is that so?"

"She's my bloody soul mate, Chris. My Intended. I'm a nearly retired Angel—twenty-two days away, mind you, or should I refresh your pitiful memory as to what that exactly *means*?"

The grin on Christian's face stayed firmly affixed, his memory apparently still pitiful. "She has that little curvy thing at the corner of her mouth, then, aye?" He tapped his own mouth's corner and shook his head. "And only you can see it? Aye, I recall such a conversation in the barn once, when we were squires. Remember? No more than twelve summers, we were." He gave a soft laugh. "I believe you tried to convince me I was seeing that same mouth marking on the luscious lips of Genevieve. My bloody *horse*." He raised one eyebrow. "Although she was a fine bit of horseflesh, in truth." He chuckled. "I vow, you Welsh are vastly amusing. Superstitious beyond conception, but amusing."

The memory nearly made Gawan smile. " 'Tis no amusement this time, my friend, and it's not superstition. I saw it, plain as the nose on my face. 'Tis there."

Turning, Christian rested his gloved hand on the hilt of his sword. "So why the long face? 'Tis something to be joyful about, aye? Now all you have to do is learn to love her."

Gawan moved across the room, crossed his arms over his chest and sat on the edge of his desk. "In a normal situation, aye. 'Twould make a soul nigh onto elation, the finding of that mark." He scratched the side of his head. "This is anything but a normal situation. The lass is mostly dead, and I'm a thousand-year-old Angel, twenty-two days from retirement."

Christian shrugged. "So? You save her life, retire, and live happily thereafter."

Gawan frowned. "Nay. Unfortunately, not." He drew in a deep breath when Christian gave him a lost look. "If I'm able to find her body and save her life, Ellie will only have a vague nagging in her memory of something she can't quite place a finger to. That nagging will be *us.* She won't remember anything concrete, Chris. Nothing." He rubbed his eyes. "Not you, not Nicklesby, nor Davy or the others. *Especially* not me. Being the Guardian who saved her, I'd be the first one stricken from her memory." He rubbed a hand over his eyes and sighed. "Nor will I have even a vague memory of her. 'Tis the way of the Order."

Christian let out a low whistle. "By the saints."

"Aye. So you see why I must keep her at arm's length. 'Tis bad enough, me knowing the truth of the matter. I'm by no means in love with her—by the saints' toes, I've only just met her. But knowing what *could* be is fair temptation enough, I assure you. There's no sense in causing the girl grief by telling her about it, as well."

The ghostly knight grinned. "You're mighty confident in your abilities to woo her successfully, my fierce warrior friend, all on the oath of a mere marking of the lip. How know you that she'd gain any feelings but scorn and distaste for your pathetic self, anyway?"

Gawan met his friend's stare with a scowl. "There won't be any wooing, so therefore it doesn't matter. Ellie's not to know of it, Chris. Not a single bloody word."

"Not a single bloody word of *what*?"

Both Christian and Gawan glanced up at the same time. There in the doorway stood Ellie, and behind her, every annoying castle spirit residing at Grimm. Accompanied by Nicklesby, of course.

Gawan cursed under his breath. *Bleeding priests.*

Eight

Gawan fought the urge to run a finger round the collar of his wool tunic. Damnation, he felt choked. Why was it so blasted hot in the library, all of a sudden? He glanced at Ellie. "Er, what I mean to say is—"

Ellie's face grew pinched and her eyes pierced him straight through. "No, no. That's all right, Conwyk. Gosh, stop all that stammering. You look like you're choking on a chicken bone or something." She moved closer and peered at the list lying on the desk of cottage rentals in the area. "I, uh, do appreciate all your help." She slid a hip against the desk corner. "But I'm not quite sure *why* you're helping me." She rubbed her chin, much, he guessed, in the same fashion he himself frequently did when perplexed. "But that'd be rude of me to ask, wouldn't it?" She tapped him on the nose. "Of course it would. I'm just a goofy, mostly dead girl with no memory of who she is, just lollygagging around the castle for no real purpose, other than waiting on my fate. So, since I really have no other choice but to hang out here and wait on that fate, I think I'll just take Nicklesby up on that guest room he offered."

Gawan sighed. "Ellie."

She stood and cocked her head, studying far closer than he liked. "You know, there's something about you, Gawan Conwyk. Something *so* not normal. Other than the fact that you not only see ghosts, but live with them." Her eyes squinted as she stared at him. "No, it's something waaay different than that, even." She turned, gave Christian a stern look, then advanced to the door, where the silent cadre of Grimm spirits awaited her. "I'm watching you, Conwyk." She made a V with her forefinger and middle finger, pointing first at her eyes, then at Gawan's. "Closely." After a few hard seconds of the thorniest stare-down he'd ever had, Ellie Aquitaine turned, marched through the doorway, passed the lingering ghosts, and shouted over her shoulder, "Sir Godfrey! I've a mind to best ye in a game of knucklebones! I've no idea how to play the bloody game, but I've a mind to best ye, all the same!" She snorted. "Hey! I'm a bloody poet, and I didn't even bloody know it!" Her thick, fake accent grew thicker. "I rather like saying bloody, Godfrey! 'Tis rather amusing!"

Godfrey, the old poop, gave Gawan a dodgy smirk, then clambered after Ellie. "Aye! Ye'd best have a wee pull on the whiskey bottle first, girl! I'm by far the best knuckleboner in all of England!"

Godfrey's booming laugh echoed down the passageway.

Davy, who'd been standing in the doorway, unusually quiet, dashed after Godfrey. Lady Beauchamp and Lady Follywolle stood. Staring. *Soundlessly.*

"Did he just say *knuckleboner*?" Christian said, clapping Gawan on the shoulder. "Well, my unpopular friend, at least you weren't forced to break the Code and lie to the wench." He glanced in the direction Ellie went. "Quite ferocious, that one." He grinned. "I like that in a maid, methinks. If you've no mind to woo her, mayhap I will."

"Oh, *sir*," Lady Follywolle said with distaste, "don't be so vile. The poor lamb is simply confused—"

"And it appears, my good Grimm, that you're keeping something from her apurpose," Lady Beauchamp interrupted. "Tripping over your tongue and such." She *tsk-*

*tsk*ed. " 'Tisn't very becoming of a young man in your position. I do suggest if you're going to keep secrets, discuss the keeping of the secrets in secret!" She turned to Lady Follywolle. "Come, Millicent, let's leave the boys here with those thoughts to ponder."

With that, the two lady spirits looped arms and sauntered out of the library and through the wall.

"Does her bird coif seem more crooked to you this eve?" Christian asked, cocking his head. "I vow, it looks ready to fly."

"The least of my worries, Chris, is the position of Lady Follywolle's bloody coif." Gawan mumbled a curse and strode to the door. "Come first light, we're off to visit the cottage owners. Mayhap something will jog Ellie's memory? The sooner the better." He stepped out into the passageway, and Christian followed. Gawan pulled the doors closed. "A gut instinct tells me I've not much time left to solve this mystery."

Ellie sat curled up in the comfy corner of the leather sofa, and closed the large volume perched on her lap. She'd gone through pages and pages, with nothing at all jostling her memory. Interesting stuff, but nothing familiar. Just a lot of history about the nobles of Northumbria. With a grunt, she slid the heavy text off her lap, leaned her head back, and stared at the flames as they licked the logs. A snore made her lift her gaze, and she smiled as she watched Sir Godfrey's chest rise and fall with each deep breath, his head bent forward, and a long plume from his hat catching each gust and quivering to tickle his nose. He slapped at it a time or two, yawned, smacked his lips, then drifted back off.

He indeed was a champion knuckleboner.

If only she could go to sleep. No, if only she could *wake up*. Wake up from whatever kind of coma she was in so she could recover and live out the rest of her life. With *live* people. Although, she had to admit, Sir Godfrey, young Davy, Christian, and the ladies were all pretty fascinating. Skip the fact that they were spirits from various centuries. That in itself was beyond imaginable. They were all individually interesting people, and they'd immediately taken her under their ghostly wings. They seemed genuinely concerned for her well-being, and for that, she'd be eternally grateful.

No matter the outcome.

Her stare returned to the fire. Gawan, on the other hand, was another story. What was it about him that intrigued her? Okay. He was more than good-looking. That was a given. The guy reeked of pent-up power and male sexuality. Beneath that wool and denim lay a hard, muscular frame that seemed built by sheer physical strength and hard work.

What sort of hard work, she had no clue, other than that he had the ability to help ghosts when called upon. And he did work out with swords. That much she knew.

So who *was* Gawan Conwyk?

She glanced around the great hall. How on Earth did he afford Castle Grimm? It was massive, very medieval, yet cozy at the same time. Safe, maybe? Covered in tapestries and centuries-old relics, it boasted the ambience of times gone by, and she could easily imagine ladies in long, flowing gowns slipping down passageways for trysts in shadowy alcoves, and men in tights and tunics, swords strapped to their sides, striding across the great hall floor carrying roasted leg quarters and shouting *Aye!* at the tops of their lungs.

Ellie suddenly noticed something.

There were no pictures. No photos of parents, of grandparents. No brothers or sisters, nieces or nephews. Didn't he have a family? Anybody? Or was it simply Gawan and the ghosts? And Nicklesby.

Weird.

Uncurling her legs, Ellie rose and crossed the hall to stand before the large tapestry of Eleanor of Aquitaine. The scene depicted a battle, with a regal Eleanor dressed as a warrior and straddling a magnificent rearing steed.

Behind her, an army of others, some on horseback, some on foot. The fine stitching showed the most minute detail, including the adoring looks on the soldiers' faces as they stared upon her.

As Ellie gazed over the tapestry, which looked to be centuries old, one of the soldiers in particular caught her eye. She hadn't noticed the detail before now, but then she hadn't taken the time to study it. A mounted warrior, long, wild brown hair hung in disarray down his back, wearing what appeared to be a heavy, steel-studded leather vest, gripped with powerful, hose-clad thighs and tall boots, the sides of a magnificent black horse. With a sword that looked as big as Ellie poised high above his head, that guy meant *business*. His face was streaked with an indigo blue war paint, so his facial features weren't too clear. But something else was.

Down the length of the bare, muscular arm wielding the sword were markings stitched so tight and fine into the tapestry that Ellie had no trouble at all recognizing them. Tattoos. Ancient markings.

The same ones that Gawan had.

Ellie's memory ebbed and flowed, until something washed up. Eleanor of Aquitaine had been a great queen of both England and France. She was fierce and brave and, according to legend, had led an army into battle during the Crusades. Of course, she'd finally been sent back home, being a woman and the queen. Probably didn't go without a fight, though.

A memory sliced through her . . . voices. . . .

You were named after your great-great-grandmother, Eleanor. Who was named after her great-great-grandmother. All the way back to the greatest of Eleanors.

Oh, Dad, everybody claims to be related to someone famous in history. There're at least ten kids in my grade that say they're related to George Washington. There's no way I'm related to Eleanor of Aquitaine.

Ellie's vision blurred, clouds swirling before her as

though she were lost in a thick, soupy fog. Through it pierced a small shaft of light that grew wider and wider, until a scene appeared before her.

Another great hall. No, just a living room, cozy, much smaller, with a fireplace. A sofa, with a tall, nice-looking man sitting beside a young girl. Fifteen, maybe? Father and daughter. A photo album stretched across both of their laps, their heads bent as they flipped through the pages, pointing and laughing.

The girl suddenly glanced up and looked straight at Ellie.

"Ellie?"

The vision vanished and Ellie jumped at the raspy, lilting voice of Gawan, who was standing right behind her. She knocked her head against the tapestry. "Ow!" she said, rubbing her forehead. Just the sound of the buttery-smooth accent, and in such close proximity to her ear, made her stomach fill with butterflies and, God help her, made her knees go weak.

Dang it.

She really was in no mood, or capacity, to have the hots for some rich, gorgeous, sword-swinging Welshman.

"Sorry," Gawan said. "Is there aught amiss? Are you ill?"

Ellie wondered why he kept staring at the corner of her mouth. Inconspicuously, she slipped a hand to that corner to wipe away any remnants of drool that may be lingering. "Other than the half-dead thing, no, everything's peachy."

He grinned.

Her knees wavered.

"Um, yeah, I was just looking at this tapestry," Ellie said. She pointed to the warrior with no armor. "That guy there? He has the same tattoos you do. Well," she said, sliding him a glance, "you have more, I think." She met his gaze full-on. "Is that where you got the idea for yours? From this tapestry?" She looked again at the stitchings. "He must have been pretty crazy."

Gawan moved closer and stared at the warrior. "Why do you say that?"

Why did she have the urge to lean into him? Touch him in some way? She took a breath and ignored the mushy thoughts. "Well, look at all the other guys," she said, pointing to several other soldiers. "They all have on chain mail and such. This guy doesn't even have head gear on."

"Mayhap, 'tis that this warrior was fierce enough not to need it overmuch."

"Fierce doesn't protect you from the business end of a sword," she said. "I'm sticking to the crazy idea, myself."

Gawan chuckled. "So be it, then. He was indeed daft, for sure."

With a hearty sigh, Ellie shoved her hands into her pockets. "I can't sleep. I feel sort of tired, but I just seem to stare off. Sleep won't happen."

Another loud snore erupted from the corner of the great hall, and both turned to stare at Sir Godfrey.

"It seems to come rather easily for him," she said. "Why is that?"

Gawan looked down and stared into her eyes. "He's completely dead, girl. You are not."

Again, the way he said girl, which sounded like *gill*, or *gel*, was charming. Cute, even. She liked to hear it. "Oh, I see."

"If you're not fearful of the cold, we, er, could make for the wall walk, I suppose."

He was staring at her mouth again.

And before she could stop herself, that same mouth opened and said, "Sure. Thanks."

After retrieving two thick, wool cloaks—literally *cloaks,* complete with cowls and big metal brooches of sorts—Gawan helped her into one, adjusting it over her shoulders and wrapping it just so, before clasping it snuggly. He threw the other one over himself, as though he'd been doing it forever, and inclined his head. "Come."

Gawan led her to a single door tucked around the corner of the hall entrance. He flicked a light switch on the wall and opened the door. Through the soft, hazy lamp light lay a set of narrow winding steps leading upward. A thick rope stretched from top to bottom, secured tightly. She *hoped,* anyway.

"Grasp the rope, Ellie, and mind your step," he said, right behind her.

"You don't have to ask me twice."

His chuckle seemed right against her neck, and it made her shiver.

As he urged her with his hand to the small of her back, which made her shiver even more, she began the climb upward. Ellie felt the heat from his skin sear through the wool. Good thing, too, because it was so cold in the stairwell, she could see her breath. "How far up do we go?" she asked, walking on the balls of her feet as they climbed higher. "I'm not positive, but I think I have a thing about spiders and webs," she said, looking around. "I think you need to tell Nicklesby to come up here with the shop vac."

Another laugh, warm, deep, and very male, came through her hair and brushed her neck. "I vow you've a wit about you, Ellie Aquitaine. Through that door, just there," he said.

A few more steps and a landing appeared, and Ellie opened the door. Gawan's hand no longer easily rested against the small of her back, but rather gripped her hip instead.

She liked it.

"Easy, girl. Stop and put your back against the wall here," he said.

She did, and he proceeded to squeeze by, their bodies no more than an inch apart. He stepped out into the cold December night, his breath frosting before him in white puffs, and turned. "Give me your hand."

Just for a split second, she stared at him. The moonlight shined behind him, throwing almost a halo of light around his head. The icy air whipped at his hair, which hung loose to his very broad shoulders, and it brushed across his jaw. The way he looked in that long, dark cloak, with that untamed hair, made Ellie think of the warrior on the tapestry. Fierce, powerful, feral, without the first bit of fear . . .

She gave Gawan her hand, the roughness of his palm scratchy but quite nice. It engulfed hers, protectively, and she ducked through the doorway and stepped out onto the wall walk.

The frigid blast hit her square in the face, and she sucked in a breath. But the sheer beauty of the moonlit North Sea from the outside of the castle made her hold it for just a second longer.

" 'Twill be less windy on the western side," Gawan said. "Here, take a firm grip on my arm, and hold fast."

She did, and his muscle bunched beneath her touch. She found that she liked the feeling. A lot.

The wall itself, which encircled the castle on two different levels—the one they were on, and the extreme top—came to just above her waist. "Somehow, I feel heights aren't exactly an issue for me," she said. "This is fantastic."

"Aye, well, many a man has fallen to his death by cocksure footing. Mind your step and hold on just the same."

She smiled and sneaked a peek at Gawan's face. Cast in silver by the wedge of moon hanging in the sky, he was absolutely the most breathtaking man she'd ever laid eyes on. Chiseled features, strong jaw, lips that promised a slice of heaven. At least, she thought so.

Again, she wondered about him. "So are you going to tell me anything about yourself?"

"Like?"

"Well, what do you do? As in a job? No way can you

maintain this castle by helping out a few ghosts. The taxes alone must kill you."

He laughed. "Aye, not quite like in the old day, I can promise you." He cleared his throat and glanced down at her. "I work for an elite security service. I guard certain clients. Very wealthy clients. They pay rather well."

Ellie blinked. "You're a bodyguard?" She whistled. "You must be good at what you do."

"Vastly."

Ellie gulped. "Well, I should feel extra-safe in your hands."

"Blimey, Cotswald! Come back 'ere!"

Out of nowhere, a large—no *huge*—dog appeared and bounded straight for them, Davy close on his heels, shouting and waving his arms. Ellie's heart jumped and she dropped her hand and darted to the right before she could think, knocking into the waist-high wall.

A squeal, accompanied by a very unladylike word fell from her mouth as Davy and the dog scrambled right through her and Gawan, disappearing down the wall walk.

"Sor-ry!" Davy shouted from nowhere.

Gawan muttered a harsh Welsh curse—she recognized it from before—and grabbed the scruff of her cloak, just as she tumbled over and stared at the business end of Grimm's rocky base over the edge of the wall. In one solid yank, he pulled her around and against him. Her face squashed against his chest, the wool of his cloak warm and smelling like firewood and soap. She stayed there for a few seconds, content, before she noticed a rapid thumping near her ear. It was his heart. Hers suddenly matched it.

When she moved her head from the comfy spot against his thumping chest, she lost her breath along with all coherent thoughts. Snowflakes drifted down from the black sky, landing on her cheeks and on Gawan's. Their gazes fastened on each other's, his jaw tensed, he slid a quick glance to the corner of her mouth, and then muttered another curse. A new one.

She gulped.

Just before he lowered his head.

She gulped again.

And then Gawan Conwyk kissed her.

Nine

Warm lips settled over hers, full, startling, strong. *Delicious.*

Gawan's mouth moved over hers, and at the same time, both of his hands threaded through Ellie's hair and held her head steady, tilting it with just the right amount of pressure until their lips fit more closely. Snowflakes continued to fall against their cheeks, their eyelashes, and the icy North Sea air whipped around them. Neither cared. Only the moment mattered.

A rush of pleasure soared through her as Gawan deepened the kiss, drawing in first her top lip, then her bottom, before sweeping his tongue, warm, confident, against hers. He dragged rough knuckles over her jaw, then angled her chin to better gain access.

And better access he did gain. Lusciously so. She wanted to just melt right into him, but he held her steady.

Potent. The man was raw potent male bound by a loose thread of proper gentleman. *Very* loose.

The slide of his lips over hers—until he kissed, then suckled, then lingered at the corner of her mouth, that same corner he'd stared at more than once—drew every ounce of air from her lungs. It was *exquisite.* And dear God, she didn't want it to end.

She cracked open an eye, only to find their warm, mingled breath caused a puff of frost against the night air between them, and Ellie, surprised but definitely not disappointed, closed her eyes and kissed Gawan right back with all the gusto a girl in her precarious In-Betwinxt quandary could muster.

Until, that is, she felt herself grow flimsy-light, as though she floated just above the ground. She peeked again, and Gawan's mouth stilled against hers. His eyes opened, looking crossed because of their extreme close-ness, and then he pulled back and frowned. A hearty sigh escaped the full lips that had just been kissing the boots off her.

Ellie glanced at her arm, wrapped around Gawan's neck, and gasped. Nearly transparent and fading by the second, she lifted her gaze and met his.

Then they both swore, he in Welsh, she in good old-fashioned American-style English.

Just as she vanished into thin air.

Gawan stared at the space Ellie had just occupied, at the cloak she'd been wearing lying in a heap at his feet. He drew a deep breath, rubbed his jaw, then gripped the wall and breathed in the North Sea air. What in hell had he done? Bloody daft idiot, he was.

"I vow you have the foulest of tongues for an Angel."

Gawan grunted. "Warrior. Remember?" Gawan cocked his head and narrowed his gaze at Nicklesby. "What were you doing? Eavesdropping?" He reached down and picked up Ellie's cloak.

Nicklesby, dressed in a thick black wool overcoat, a bright striped scarf, and a black wool cap pulled low and snug, tapped a rather big bulge on the side of his head that was one of his two very large ears. "Spectacular hearing, I'd say."

Gawan snorted. "Nosy, I'd say." He glanced at him. "You heard, then?"

Nicklesby stared out over the sea. "Aye. Saw as well, I'm afraid. You know, sir, you really should be more careful."

"I *know* that," Gawan said. "Damn me, Nicklesby,

but I couldn't help myself. I vowed not to touch her, but, damn, the girl is different."

With a nod, Nicklesby agreed. "Aye, 'twould seem as much, seeing that she's nigh onto becoming a spirit."

"That's *not* what I meant." Gawan turned and started back up the wall walk, Nicklesby hurrying behind him. "She's marked."

"Marked? Marked for what?" Nicklesby said.

Reaching the door leading to the stairwell, Gawan grasped the handle, pulled, then ducked inside. "For *me.*"

Nicklesby gasped behind him, then pulled the door closed. "Your Intended?"

Gawan grunted.

"By the saints."

Gawan grunted again.

They reached the bottom of the stairs and went through the door. The great hall sat empty, save the roaring fire in the hearth.

Gawan strode to the sofa and flopped down on it. "Nigh onto a thousand years, Nicklesby. A *thousand.* Not once have I ever encountered the mark on any woman. And now"—he pressed the pads of his fingers to his closed eyes—"now I find her, the bloody *one.* A *mostly dead one,* but the one just the same." He laughed and met his old friend's questioning gaze. "Twenty-two days away from retirement, Nicklesby—"

The tall mahogany grandfather clock against the west wall chimed out, twelve deep-pitched chords as the hours counted. At the stroke of twelve, Gawan sighed. "Twenty-one days, rather. I have to save her life in twenty-one bloody days."

"She still has no inkling of what you are, exactly?" Nicklesby asked, taking a poker and stoking the fire.

"Nay."

"Not even"—Nicklesby set the poker down and flapped his skinny arms—"your you-know-whats?"

"Damn, man, stop beating your arms about. Of course

she doesn't know about *those*." He narrowed his eyes. "And she bloody well *won't* know about them. 'Twill do naught but complicate things. Over much so. 'Tis too much for her to take in." Gawan pushed his hands through his hair and rose. "I'm going to bed."

"Off to the cottages tomorrow, then?" Nicklesby asked.

Gawan waved as he crossed the hall and mounted the steps. "Aye. We'll see what that proves. *Nos da,* old friend."

"And to you, sir," Nicklesby called from below. "I'll have your morning fast at the ready."

Moments later, Gawan stormed through his chamber door and kicked it shut behind him. "Bloody stupid fool," he muttered to himself. With haste, he brushed his teeth, stoked the fire, and flung off his clothes. Beneath the coverlet, he cursed himself again, turned over a time or two, punched the pillow, and then flopped over onto his back.

Could he have not left the girl alone? Why had he been so compelled to taste those alluring lips? 'Twasn't as though he'd never tasted others before. Aye, Ellie indeed bore a comely face and a most luscious form, to be sure. Glorious locks, to tell the truth of it, long and thick draped about her shoulders. Oy, just the thought of her softness pressed against him, even through the heavy cloaks, made him ache.

He considered it a minute. Nay, 'twasn't it. 'Twasn't the bloody reason he dragged her against him and kissed her. Well, not the whole of it, anyway. He'd stolen that mark at the corner of her mouth. And had done it *apurpose.*

Had he not known she was his Intended, would he still have had the same reaction to her? She indeed possessed a vast amount of clumsy charm, which he'd found endearing from the moment she'd climbed into the wrong side of the Rover that first night. Aye, he rather fancied that. The way she'd knocked her forehead against the tapestry, and how she squealed, then cursed when Davy and Cotswald had rushed by—

"By the saint's curled toes, man, you are besotted." Christian shook his head and propped a mailed hip against the bedpost. "Pitifully so."

"Damn you, Arrick," Gawan said, sitting up. "Go haunt another chamber. I need not your evaluation."

"Ha-ha, little lad, I fear you do." Christian moved to the hearth. With the flickering firelight behind him, Gawan could see clear through him. "What are you going to do, Conwyk? Now that you've sampled her and can't get enough?"

Gawan draped his arms over his knees. "Sampled? She's not a trencher of stew, fool." He frowned. "Who else saw?"

Christian squatted by the flames, as if he could gain heat from the fire, and rubbed his hands. He threw a grin over his shoulder. "Everyone."

Gawan slapped his forehead and fell back. "Bleeding priests, I reside with a lot of old, meddlesome peahens."

With a smirk, Christian rose. "Be grateful I convinced Millicent not to address you this eve. She and that sopping wet crony of hers were nigh onto making their way to your bedside, just to give you what's what." He crossed his arms over his chest. "I warned them that you slept without nary a stitch on." He chuckled. "They scampered away like jackrabbits. I saved your pitiful arse, Conwyk, for I can promise you, they were not in a charitable mood. Not after seeing you paw and slobber—"

"Get out, Chris."

Christian bowed. "You're in a rotten mood, man, and I think a bit of time with the blades will sweeten your humor. On the morrow, then? Before daybreak?"

He didn't wait for Gawan's response. Christian disappeared. *Chuckling.*

Gawan turned over, still frowning. "I do not paw and slobber."

Christian's laugh reverberated through the stone wall.

*   *   *

Funny. Coming around from the dark place felt similar to the sensation of a foot slowly waking up after being propped under one's backside for too long. Tingly. A bit of pain, but more like smack-your-funny-bone-on-a-corner pain.

Funny.

With her eyes slowly focusing, Ellie peered through the darkened haze of Gawan's bedroom. Although not quite yet daybreak, his bed sat empty. His covers were all bunched up in a big wad as though he'd gone a few rounds in the ring. And *lost.*

Thoughts of his firm, full lips wrapped around hers sent a blush to the roots of her hair and a shudder that reached clear to her toes. The man could *kiss.*

A shiver made her teeth chatter, and she wrapped her arms around herself. Through the open window, the clank of metal against metal rose on the air and drifted in, accompanied by several harsh words, and then a deep, deep laugh.

Followed by a cacophony of feminine giggles.

Easing over to the window—who would keep it open in the middle of December?—Ellie peered out and searched for the makers of the giggles, laughs, and curses. There was nothing but the North Sea, and the snow-dotted rock cliff on which Castle Grimm perched on.

Hurrying out of Gawan's room, Ellie slipped into the passageway, then pulled up short when she came face-to-face with one of the lady spirits.

The one with a big white bird on her head.

Lady Follywolle—Ellie could now see it was her hair shaped into a swan—gave a warm, friendly smile, the corners of her ghostly eyes crinkling with mirth. And *devilment.*

Ellie liked her.

"I know of a wondrous spot from which to observe the match, dear." She gave Ellie a slight nod, the swan on her head taking a tiny dip south and to the left. "I find myself in it often. Come. You'll certainly fancy the watching of this."

In the passageway, Lady Follywolle turned and made her way through the dark. Ellie noticed she was nearly transparent, but not all the way. The woman had no doubt once been quite elegant, because even as a spirit, she moved with grace and poise.

Or, Ellie thought, the ghostly floating gave her that effect.

Together they wound their way to the other side of the castle, until finally, they stopped at a massive twin oak doorway.

Lady Follywolle inclined her head, the beak of her coiffed swan dipping so precariously close to Ellie's nose she had to back up to avoid being pecked. "This chamber has the best views of the battlements. 'Tis where Sir Gawan and Sir Christian take up their blades nearly every morn." She grinned. "A fine treat to behold, indeed, and neither is even remotely aware of it. And we shan't tell them." With ease, the spirit sifted through the door. From the other side, she whispered, "Hurry."

Hurry she did, as Ellie pulled on the heavy latch and slipped inside the monstrous room. A comfy-looking sage chenille sofa covered with several large throw pillows perched before yet another immense fireplace, and Lady Follywolle stood at one of the four tall double-hung windows. She waved a gloved hand for Ellie to join her.

Once at the window, Ellie edged in beside Lady Follywolle and glanced down one level and then to the right. She stared, let loose a gusty sigh or two, and then felt her mouth slide open in pure appreciation. An itch, a prickle—no, a *shuddering thrill*—shot through her as she watched the man who had given her the most startling kiss she *thought* she'd ever had. A guilty pleasure of voyeurism swept over her as she, *ahem,* took private inventory of the Best Kiss Giver Ever.

Bare to the waist, save the leather straps crisscrossing his back and chest. Dark hair wild and loose atop very broad shoulders, the long bangs pulled back and secured. Ancient-looking tattoos visible, moving with each flex of his muscle as he parried and thrust. Some sort of form-fitting, dark brown pants tucked into a pair of midshin, well-worn boots. A short knife sheathed into one of the straps. As frosty air met his warm breath, a puff of iciness came with each exerted grunt.

Good *Lord.* The man was *beautiful.*

Ellie studied the knighted spirit dodging each thrust of Gawan's sword—Christian of Arrick-by-the-Sea— who gave it back to Gawan full force.

Not too shabby, either, for a dead guy, but definitely not Gawan.

"If Christian is a ghost, then how is it Gawan's sword can strike his?"

Lady Follywolle simply smiled. "Sir Gawan has many talents, love. You'll have to ask him the particulars, I'm afraid, although I do believe Sir Christian somehow conjures the illusion and sound of his own steel."

"Hmm."

"Quite the spectacle, wouldn't you say?" Lady Follywolle said, her voice all dreamy and soft. She sighed and propped her shoulder against the window frame. "Fine specimens, indeed." She pointed a long, elegantly gloved finger. "See you there, next to young Davy, Lady Bella and her cousin, Lucinda? You've not met her yet. Dear, dear, they are a naughty pair. They were in life, as well. Lady Lucy made an appearance at Castle Grimm just this morn, you see, after being on a century-long haunt with a traveling opera troupe. Lovely lot, I'm told." She sighed. *"Sooo,"* she cooed and turned to Ellie, "do tell me one thing, love, because I cannot take the not knowing of it a single moment longer. How on *Earth* does it feel to be kissed by an *Angel*—"

"Here now, dear Ellie! Do come away from that gaping window before you topple through it!"

Ellie jumped at the interruption and turned to find Nicklesby, all skinny arms and legs and knobby knees and floppy ears askew, hurrying to her side. Ellie didn't miss the stern look he shot Lady Follywolle before grasping her elbow and giving it a tug. "Come, now, young Ellie. I've bubbling porridge on the stovetop at the ready. You musn't frequent the elements thus. You'll catch your death."

Ellie gave him a dopey grin—as if she hadn't already almost caught *that*—then glanced out the window again. Gawan and Christian had stopped their duel, or whatever it was called, and were both looking up in her direction. Even though they were probably more than a hundred yards or more apart, her nerve endings snapped and sizzled just *knowing* Gawan stared at her. If a mere kiss made her insides turn all gooey, she could only imagine what would happen if, well, more happened.

Though to be fair, it was hardly a *mere* kiss.

All at the same time, her head snapped up as a thought hit, Nicklesby pulled on her arm with a bit more strength than she thought his skinny self capable of, and her gaze caught Lady Follywolle's, whose one white brow lifted high into the tail feathers of the swan's backside.

"What did you call him?" Ellie asked her.

Nicklesby all but jumped up and down, reminding Ellie of the Scarecrow from *The Wizard of Oz*. "Why, she didn't call him a thing! Silly girl! Now, come along, sweetling, before my porridge bubbles over! 'Twould be disastrous!"

Ellie narrowed her eyes at Lady Follywolle.

The lady ghost's matching white brow rose to join the other one, and her red lips mouthed the word Ellie had *thought* she'd said, just before Nicklesby succeeded in pulling her away.

Angel.

Ten

"Nicklesby, slow down!" Ellie said, scurrying along to keep up with Grimm's steward. His lanky frame, clothed in a Victorian-era brown wool proper gentleman's suit, minus the top hat, shuffled even faster down the passageway. Rounding the last bend, they hurried down the steps and skidded into the great hall.

Ellie put on the brakes and nearly yanked poor Nicklesby's arm out of its socket. "Nicklesby! What is going on?"

The hurried panic on Nicklesby's face from before faded, replaced by a sheepish look of pure, out-and-out *guilt.* "Er, why, nothing, my dear girl. 'Tis just that I have your morning repast prepared, and—"

"Ooh, Nicklesby, you big fibber! You didn't even know I'd returned!" She stepped up to him and frowned. "Why did you just drag me out of that chamber, and *what* did Lady Follywolle mean when she asked how it felt to be *kissed* by an *Angel*?" With a forefinger, she poked him, and felt the bones in his chest through the wool of his topcoat. "Angel? What the heck that mean?"

"Why, er," Nicklesby stammered, his face growing paler. "It, er, well—"

"First off," she interrupted, "the only way you'd know about that kiss was if Gawan told you, or you'd watched— Oh, Nicklesby! You didn't!"

"Well, I, er—"

Ellie gasped. "Watched, and *tattled*." She wagged a finger. "Shame, shame on you, Nicklesby!"

"What's going on?"

At the sound of Gawan's voice, she turned. Really, she felt only slightly embarrassed. It was a kiss, for crying out loud, not lewd sex in a back alley somewhere.

Young Davy skidded through the wall and stopped beside Gawan. "I could hear Nicklesby stammerin' clean through the walls!" he said. "What's the matter, lady?"

Great. Now she felt like an idiot. To carry on would just make a bigger deal out of it than was necessary. "Oh, nothing," she said with a wave and a smile. She gave Nicklesby a firm clap to the shoulder. *Extra*-firm. "We were just going to the kitchen for some bubbling porridge. Weren't we, Nicklesby?"

"Right, we were, indeed," he said.

Gawan narrowed his eyes at first Nicklesby, then at Ellie. He studied them both for what seemed like minutes, nearly long enough to make her squirm. Finally, he spoke. "I'll be down shortly."

With that, he turned and jogged up the steps.

Ellie watched, partly out of curiosity, mainly just to gawk. He looked as if he'd just stepped out of medieval times. *Scrumptious*. "Why on Earth is he wearing that?" she whispered to no one.

A scuffling sound made her turn, and when she did, Nicklesby had made it to the kitchen archway without a backward glance.

"Chicken!" she called out. "I'm not finished with you."

"Finished wi' what?" Davy asked. He wiped his nose with his sleeve and cocked his head. "Wanna play me in chess later?"

Ellie pushed murderous thoughts of Nicklesby and lusty ones of Gawan aside and looked at Davy. The old soft hat he wore sat cocked, as usual, to one side.

"Or we could play wi' Cotswald. Only we have to go outside. Nicklesby don't allow no dogs in the hall—even ghost ones." He kicked at an imaginary something with the tip of his beat-up boot. "I'm sorry I nearly made ye take a tumble last night." He lifted his gaze. "I was busy after Cotswald and didn't think ye'd jump aside, seein' how we'd just slip on through ye. But Nicklesby says yer still gettin' used to bein' mostly dead. Aye?"

Wow. Talk about a serious *reality check.* She wasn't anywhere close to getting used to the idea of mostly dead. To dwell on it made her panic, made her remember she couldn't *remember,* and that she had no choice but to lean on Gawan for help.

The smile Ellie pasted on her face felt stiff. The kid was cute as could be, and seemed genuinely concerned about her welfare—alive or mostly dead. "It's all right, Davy. Really." She lifted her hand to ruffle his hair, but clenched it into a fist and put it behind her back instead. "Tell ya what. After I get back from checking out the cottages, we'll play with Cotswald first. Then I'll take you on with the chessboard." She gave him a mock glare. "Me. You. Here." She drew close, nearly nose-to-nose. "Later."

Davy's ghostly features lit up, and he cracked a gap-toothed smile. "I'll be 'ere!"

With that, he turned and sifted through the wall, calling *Cotswald!* as he disappeared.

On her heel, Ellie turned to the kitchen, where she could finish drilling Nicklesby about the whole Angel comment, which made no sense whatsoever. Still, curiosity gnawed at her gut, something she couldn't put her finger on. Or was it that knowing look that had been plastered to Lady Follywolle's face? Instead, though, an idea struck, and she paused.

Mostly dead or not, she wanted a shower and a change of clothes.

Badly.

Certainly, she could wear one of Gawan's sweaters. It'd be nice and baggy and comfy. No way would his pants fit, though. Nicklesby's, on the other hand . . .

With the idea of a nice, steamy shower and a change of clothes in mind, Ellie bounded up the steps and made for Gawan's chamber, mentally comparing Nicklesby's measurements to her own. The picture that fell to mind nearly made her laugh out loud. Nicklesby's pants would probably be too tight. At least no one would *see* her.

Not outside of Castle Grimm, anyway.

Gawan shifted his backside in the seat for what seemed the hundredth uncomfortable time, gripped the steering wheel, and then eased another swift, inconspicuous glance to his left at the quirky woman beside him.

Ellie. Mostly dead. Can vanish into thin air without warning and reappear just as hastily, with as much tangibility as himself. And he could barely keep his pitiful eyes off her.

All while she wore her hair bound in a horse's tail, one of his tunics that drooped so much, she had to roll the cuffs up several times, and a pair of Nicklesby's wool gardening trousers that hung several ridiculous inches too long at the ankle, yet cinched vastly snug across the rear.

Adorably so.

It amazed him, in truth, that even in her state of being, he could smell her fresh-scrubbed skin, and remember just how that skin tasted.

Saint's robes, he was an idiot. That kiss would stay emblazoned in his mind, at the ready to torment. At least, that is, until midnight on the Yuletide's Eve. Then, the memory of those soft, supple lips entwined with his own would disappear forever. Until then, though, he'd treasure it.

He quickly averted his gaze forward, so as not to get caught.

Ellie had been uncharacteristically quiet since they'd left Grimm, and Gawan could only assume she felt uncomfortable about the kiss they'd shared. Saints, he'd thought of nothing else, except how he would get her out of the bloody mess she was in. He felt like a bumbling idiot, and hardly knew what to say to her. Mayhap: *"Er, sorry, gel, for stealing your Intended's kiss without your permission the other night, even though you know not that I am indeed your Intended, nor that you even possess such a luscious mark as the one at the curve of your mouth. I vow, 'twas an overwhelming sense of pure lunacy that claimed me, all of a sudden-like. And whilst I'm spurting forth my scruples, I've a pair of bloody wings strapped to me back. . . .*

"Is there something wrong with you?"

Gawan jumped from his thoughts so hard, his backside nearly left the seat cushion. *See, Conwyk? Bumbling idiot.* He covered the ridiculous motion up with another shift and a cough. "Er, nay. Why do you ask?"

Ellie half turned in her seat and stared a hole through the side of his head before she spoke. "Look. You don't have to act all stiff and weird around me now. Forget the stupid kiss. It was nothing more than atmosphere. Getting lost in the moment. You know, mist, snow, nightfall, moonlight, a ghost kid and his ghost dog nearly knocking me off the side of a castle." She waved her hand in dismissal and turned to stare out the window. "It was nothing, so forget about it and lighten up, okay?" She snorted, then muttered under her breath, "You're not the first guy I've ever kissed, you know. Sheesh."

Gawan let out a hearty sigh. "Ellie—"

"Hey, look!" she said, pointing, and thus dismissing Gawan once more. "Standing stones! I've read about them, maybe? I've seen those in a travel magazine, maybe. I've always wanted to see standing stones. I think." She glanced at him, finished with their kiss discussion. "How old are those, do you suppose? A thousand years old, maybe?"

Gawan thought the best thing to do was to drop the subject. For now, anyway. He followed her finger across a craggy hill covered in yellow-brown winter grass, chipped rock, and a few scattered grazing sheep, to the three tall blue-gray Pictish stones standing sentry amidst the snowy edge of the cliff top. 'Twas a breathtaking sight, to be sure, and behind them, just down the way, stood the ruins of a kirk. "Aye, at least a thousand."

"Wow," she said. "That's amazing. Let's stop there on our way back, okay? I've got to see them up close."

Gawan wondered if it would amaze her as much to know that he'd known the dozen or so men who'd erected them.

Minutes later, they followed a winding, narrow, two-lane track into an even smaller village than Grimm's called Newbry. Gawan remembered when it was nothing more than a craggy meadow. After a quick stop at the petrol station to fill up the Rover, they continued on, past a corner Safeway, a chippy, a pub cleverly called the Rusty Dagger, and a B and B with the faded sign reading Maggie's B&B swinging from a red wooden post by the front stoop.

"Is the cottage far?" Ellie said, staring out the window.

"Nay. Just a couple of kilometers past the village." He glanced at her. "I don't have much hope of finding anything at this particular holiday cottage. The owner claims the lass who let it did so nearly a month ago, and I have a suspicion you've not been here that long."

"You never know, though," she said. *Gosh, he thinks he knows everything!*

Gawan fought a smile. In truth, he needed to reserve the spying of Ellie's thoughts for more necessary times. "Aye, one never does." Gawan knew she held dearly to any form of hope, and for that, he couldn't blame her. He'd hoped for answers, too, when the owner claimed an American woman indeed had rented the seaside cottage from him. The owner had not been overgenerous with information, since he was in the process of selling the cottage to another landowner. But he did divulge that the transaction had taken place completely over the

Internet, and while he did indeed have a name and other pertinent information, which he withheld due to confidentiality, he'd had no visual description and Gawan's gut told him the woman and Ellie were not the same.

He prayed his gut was wrong.

It, of course, was most assuredly right.

At the end of a long, single-lane track banked on either side by long grass and sod lay the small stone crofter's cottage on the cliff's edge. It overlooked the North Sea, and indeed, a rather brisk icy wind came off the water.

Ellie, wrapped in the same thick cloak from the night they'd kissed, turned into the bluster. The cowl flew back from her head and hanks of that reddish-brown hair whipped about her, slapped at her creamy skin, and caught on lips he remembered opening for him all too well.

He blinked. Ellie looked as though she could have been standing on the sea cliff a thousand years before. . . .

"Let's go in?" she asked, her blue-green eyes wide.

"Of course," he answered, and they made their way to the front stoop. There, Gawan reached above the door and grasped the key, just where the owner had said it would be. Quickly, he unlocked the cottage door and pushed it open.

Ellie bustled inside, rubbing her arms and clacking her teeth together. "Brrr."

He followed her inside and closed the door.

"What's that smell?" she asked, sniffing.

"Peat," Gawan said. He pointed to the small hearth. "See you the remnants in the fireplace? 'Tis peat. Makes for quite a nice fire."

She sniffed again. "Smells good, too." After a quick glance at him, she slowly walked the circumference of the small, two-room cottage.

Inside, a hearth, of course, accompanied by a plaid sofa, a wooden-backed chair and footstool, a table and lamp. Facing the sea, a small kitchen with white-painted cabinets. Two rooms, on either side of the cottage, one with a single bed, the other with a bed for two. A solitary guarderobe made up the interior of the only local seaside cottage having been rented to an American girl in the last several months.

Ellie quietly walked around, her fingers drifting over a piece of furniture, the mantel, the back of a kitchen chair. Gawan kept quiet, allowing her to make her own decision. Finally, she did.

"This isn't it." She blew out a gusty sigh. "I think I'd feel something if I'd been here before, right?" She glanced around, then drew her gaze to his. "Everything's cleaned out. I'd have left *something* behind, wouldn't you think?"

Gawan balled his fists and shoved them into his pockets to keep from touching her. "We'll venture into the village on the way home. 'Tis finer weather today, and mayhap one of the vendors has remembered something." He ducked his head to catch her lowered gaze. "I like you better when you're barmy, girl, shouting over your shoulder at Godfrey, king of knuckleboners."

That, at least, won him a smile. Christ knew he might not win anything else.

"Come," he said, and dared to remove one of his tightly clenched fists from deep within his trouser pockets to wrap his fingers around Ellie's shoulder. Certainly, he could control himself. He gave a tug. "Let's get to the village before the chippy closes."

Just then, the purr of an engine, right outside the cottage, revved, then stopped. A car door slammed.

Before Gawan could make a move, Ellie placed a single finger over those luscious lips, hissed a *shh,* then grabbed him by the elbow and pulled him to hide just behind the door.

What, by the saints, was she *doing*?

"Ellie," he said.

"Shh!" she said.

Worse yet, why was he going along with her?

A stomping of feet, just on the other side of the door-way sounded. Big feet. Heavy, booted feet. A pause. *Silence.*

Then the door swung open, right into Gawan's nose.

Eleven

"By the saints!" a deep voice boomed from the other side of the doorway.

"Good Lord!" Ellie shrieked, trapped behind that same door.

Gawan, who'd already become acquainted with the door, held his nose with one hand, and the back of that very door with the other, to keep it from hitting Ellie.

"Stay," he said to her in a low growl.

Somehow, Ellie couldn't stop herself. She ducked under his arm, just as whoever it was on the other side of the door stepped in.

Gawan muttered something naughty in Welsh.

Ellie could see nothing but a *wall*—a huge, massive muscled wall of brown leather, ivory sweater, black hair, and faded denim. Somewhere, embedded deep inside her, an instinct kicked in. One she wasn't, of course, aware of.

It emerged, that unknown instinct, all of a sudden, without warning, full force.

And it happened in less than five seconds.

Somehow, during those five seconds, and without putting much thought to what she was doing, Ellie had solidly kneed in the you-know-whats and had—quite efficiently if she said so herself—forced a very *large* man to the ground, where he lay gasping for air and . . . cursing?

At least, Ellie *thought* it was cursing. It sounded quite French. Sort of.

It took less than a second for realization to smack her right between the eyes.

How had she been able to knee the guy?

Beside her, Gawan stood, holding his accosted nose. First he stared at the man, whose head was still down while he was apparently trying to catch his breath. Then Gawan lifted his eyes, met Ellie's, and quirked a brow. Ellie could tell he thought the same thing she had. Then he voiced it.

"How the bloody hell . . . ?" He let the words drift off in what Ellie thought was utter amazement. He looked at the man she'd just taken down. "You may have just winded the owner of the cottage."

The big man on the floor wheezed.

Ellie's eyes darted to where he knelt, groping his way-laid *groiny parts.* "Oops." She took a hesitant step closer to the man, struggling to rise on one knee. Leaning way around, she gave a laugh that came out gurgly and choked. "Um, excuse me?" She tapped his massive shoulder with her index finger. "Geez, you know? I'm really . . . sorry. . . ."

The man lifted his head and peered through a curtain of shoulder-length wavy midnight hair with the most amazing pair of sapphire blue eyes she'd ever seen.

Wow.

With a loud clearing of his throat, Gawan set Ellie gently aside and grasped the man's elbow. "Sorry, mate. We weren't expecting anyone."

"Give me a bloody moment," the man said in a strained voice Ellie was sure to be a few notes higher than usual.

After a few seconds, the man nodded and Gawan helped him rise.

And then both Gawan and the gorgeous stranger stood and faced each other, and right away, Ellie watched with fascination while the demeanor in both men changed.

While he was at least three inches taller than Gawan, the stranger's back stiffened, his dark brows pulled into a frown, and his eyes narrowed.

Gawan did the same.

Both men inspected the other from top hair to boot toe.

Both men, at the same time and in the same breath, muttered what Ellie guessed to be something *very* naughty, each in a different language.

They *knew* each other?

A twitching pulled at her lips, and Ellie recognized it as the overwhelming urge to open her mouth and say something. For once, though, she decided to be quiet and listen.

"Grimm," the man spoke, his frown still affixed.

"Dreadmoor," Gawan said, his stoic features unreadable.

Dreadmoor?

Ellie couldn't be positive, but she was pretty darn close to believing she'd *never* seen anything quite like either of the frowning men before in her life. Really. How many stunning, jaw-dropping, drool-inducing guys did a girl encounter personally in her entire life? Not that many.

Yeah, snort, snort, *and I've got firsthand experience of how the cuter one kisses. . . .*

Both guys broke their studious concentration of the other's person to turn and stare at her.

It was then, she realized with only a small amount of mortification that she'd just snorted out loud.

As if she could help it. These guys were *wow*. Add Christian of Arrick-by-the-Sea into the mix, and she figured she'd just about encountered the most gorgeous men *ever*. Funny thing was, while Christian was, in fact, a medieval warrior, Gawan and this Dreadmoor guy didn't seem all that far off.

Dreadmoor glanced at her with those sapphire eyes. "If this spirited wench here is in search of employment, I've room for another guardsman." The corner of his mouth quirked. "I vow, 'twould be a much-added improvement to that lazy lot standing sentry over my wife and keep."

Ellie stared, blinked, and then chanced a peek at Gawan.

The corner of his mouth quirked, too.

This time, she didn't ignore her twitching lips. "What's going on?" She glanced from Gawan to Dreadmoor. It was bad enough she had no idea who she herself was. She didn't need another chunk of confusion to add to her already confused state.

The gorgeous Dreadmoor guy barked out a laugh and grabbed Gawan in a tight embrace. Gawan laughed, wheezed as more air than he'd probably have liked left his lungs, and returned the hug with just as much enthusiasm.

Ellie could do nothing but stare. Silently.

Gawan clapped Dreadmoor on the shoulder. "Damn me, man, but I didn't believe the tales were true. Given the source, I hesitated to believe such drivel."

Dreadmoor, or whatever his real name was, clapped Gawan on the back. "Aye, no doubt 'twas that Lady Follywolle and her sopping-wet friend. I've noticed them up at the keep of late, gawking at the men whilst they train. My lady wife has befriended the ghostly pair, of course, and by the saints, they stay until dark nigh onto every eve."

Ellie gaped. He knew of Lady Follywolle?

Then Dreadmoor turned and met her gaze, which she suspected looked pretty stupid at this point. He smiled, his eyes remaining on hers. Had she been a weaker woman, she'd have fainted dead away, just from the sheer sexiness of his gaze.

"Grimm, introduce us, man, for I've neither the patience nor the stomach to wait another bloody second to meet this lovely woman of yours.''

Gawan cleared his throat. "Forgive my rudeness. Ellie, er, Aquitaine, the big thug you injured actually lives just down the way from Grimm, some several kilometers to the south.'' He inclined his head. "Tristan de Barre of Dreadmoor.''

"Aquitaine, aye? That explains your fierceness. You'd no doubt make a fine addition to my garrison, then.'' Tristan grasped her hand, lowered his dark head, and brushed a warm kiss across her knuckles.

Wow.

Then he smiled, gave her a low bow, and patted her hand.

Double wow.

Ellie noticed, rather suddenly, a hint of a scowl on Gawan's face, which vanished so quickly, she wasn't sure it had even existed.

With a grin, Ellie shoved her hands as deep into Nicklesby's snug-fitting wool gardening trousers as she could. "I'm really sorry about, you know"—her eyes darted to his groin and back before she could stop them—"before. At the door. I mean, back there. I don't know what came over me.'' She winced. "Are you okay?''

Tristan smiled, dimples pitting his cheeks. "Aye, well, I shall know if I cannot sire babes, won't I? Thank the saints, though, that I'm a competent sort from hearty stock and have already bequeathed to my lady wife, who carries my babe in her belly this very minute.''

Ellie blinked. *What the heck did he just say?*

Gawan chuckled. "What he means, girl, is that despite your attack, he'll be fine, and he and his wife are already with child.'' He clapped Tristan on the back. "Well done, man! 'Tis rather difficult to imagine you a *sire*.''

"Aye, in truth.'' Tristan strode to the kitchen window, pulled back the white lace curtain, and glanced outside. "It grows darker, and I vow 'tis icy in this croft.'' He turned to meet first Ellie's gaze, then Gawan's. "We've much to discuss, Conwyk. What say you two sup with us this eve? I know Andrea would love a bit of female companionship." He winked at Gawan. "*Live* female companionship, at that."

In Gawan's defense, he sort of cringed at Tristan's words. All it did, though, was reconfirm to Ellie that there was a lot more to Tristan de Barre than bulky muscle, gorgeous hair, honey-thick charm, and snappy blue eyes.

A *lot* more.

He saw *ghosts*, yet, apparently, couldn't detect that she was nearly one herself. Speaking of which, how did he not only see her, but *touch* her? Heck, he probably even toted a sword around, like Gawan. She wondered briefly if Tristan was a . . . What had Gawan called it? A *gwarcheidiol*? Some sort of Guardian, he'd said.

Nah. No way would she encounter two of those things in one lifetime. Or almost un-lifetime. Whatever existence she floated around in.

Should've paid a little more attention in church, smarty-pants. You'd think getting thumped in the back of the head once for goofing off while the sermon was being preached would have been enough. If only Kyle had sat somewhere else. Rotten brother . . .

"Oh!" she said, and grabbed Gawan's arm. "I've got a brother! I just remembered something else! You see, I used to be really naughty in church services—especially when my brother, Kyle, would sit next to me. My grandpa used to thump the back of our heads for playing around during the sermon! Hurt, too."

Tristan joined them from the kitchen window. He flashed Ellie a smile, and then leaned his head to Gawan's ear. As if a deep, booming voice like Tristan's could whisper.

"Saints, man, I vow I didn't realize the lass was addled," Tristan said in his not so whispery whisper. He tapped his temple with a forefinger.

Gawan cringed again.

Ellie chuckled. Sort of. "I'm not addled, really. I'm In Betwinxt." She crossed her arms over her chest. "Which is why I'm so curious to know how it is that you can see me?"

With a quick glance at Ellie, Gawan looked at Tristan, whose expression revealed much confusion. He shrugged. " 'Tis true."

Tristan rubbed his chin. "Damn me. I don't think I've ever crossed paths with such before. 'Tis almost unheard-of."

Gawan's gaze returned to Ellie's and remained there. "Aye. Which is why we're here." He inspected the contents of the small croft they stood in. "Something occurred, and I've not a clue what, which took Ellie's memory, and nearly her life. She's getting bits back here and yon, but nothing solid as to why she's here, or who she truly is." He shoved his hands into his pockets. "We'd found evidence that she'd stayed in the area, but from the looks of things, 'twasn't here."

"That's because I employed a cleaning service to give the place a good scrubbing." Tristan shrugged. "I just purchased it, actually, and came here today to inspect the services rendered."

Ellie wrapped her arms about herself and looked up at Tristan. "Then you didn't see the woman who rented this cottage?"

"Aye, and 'twas a shuddering experience, to say the truth of it. Massive, not pudgy, by any means, but nigh onto looking me squarely, eye to eye." Raising his hand, he held it level to his own head. "Came to here, every inch." He gave a lopsided grin. "Almost offered her employment, as well. Strapping lass, that one."

Gawan chuckled. What a change his old friend had made. In his youth, he'd been boisterous yet carefree, a complete jester. Then, *after,* well, he remained boisterous, aye. But solemn. Cranky. Passing grumpy, Gawan would even say.

With all good sense and sane reason, of course.

Being a cursed spirit for more than seven hundred years tended to make a body *grumpy*.

Aye, they had much to talk about, indeed. He sorely wished he'd been present for the ordeal. According to Lady Follywolle, it had, indeed, been an outstanding occurrence.

A clicking sound drew Gawan's attention, and he quite suddenly realized, 'twas Ellie chattering. "Let's quit this drafty cottage, before the girl here cracks all her fine teeth and her lips turn bluer than they are already."

"Grand idea, Conwyk. I say put your woman in yon iron carriage and turn the fire up, full blast. I'll have a moment with you whilst she roasts."

Gawan heartily wished Dreadmoor would cease referring to Ellie as *his woman*. It made him do nothing but think of how her lips felt beneath his.

As Ellie made for the door, shivering, she passed Gawan and whispered, "Please. Hurry and put me in *yon iron carriage,* will ya? And don't forget to blast me with fire. I'm freezing my bloody arse off." With that, she opened the door and walked out.

" 'Twould be only fair of me to warn you, mate. Those modern American lasses are decidedly stubborn. And that's just the beginning of it."

Staring out the open cottage door, Gawan watched Ellie make straight for the driver's side of the Rover, open the door, stand there for naught but a moment before slamming that same door, muttering something he could only guess was foul, then tromp to the other side and climb in. *Clumsily charming,* he thought.

"And that's a most besotted look stretched upon your pitiful face, Conwyk." Tristan shook his head and slapped Gawan on the back. "Lo, how I know the sentiment well."

Gawan pinched the bridge of his nose. "She's my Intended."

Tristan paused. "But she's *In Betwinxt.*"

"I know that."

"By the saints."

Gawan met his friend's dubious stare. "Aye, and their curled toes, as well."

Tristan scrubbed his jaw. "Well, that certainly does muck things up a bit." He lowered his voice. "I didn't want to say aught in front of the girl, but we've more than just old times to catch up on, you and I."

Gawan cocked his head. "What do you mean?"

Tristan's eyes drifted to the Rover, to Ellie, then back. "One of my properties, just up Northumberland way, has been leased for the past month. To an American lass." He zipped up his jacket and shoved his hands into the pockets. "Normally, I'd not have need of any knowledge of who leases or buys my properties. My solicitor handles the matters and does so with a swift hand and a keen eye. But this, I unavoidably recall."

The Rover's horn blasted. Gawan glanced over, and Ellie shrugged her shoulders, held up her wrist and tapped it with a finger—a silent scolding that she wanted to leave, he knew. He waved to her and turned back to Tristan. "Aye? What is it, man?"

"My solicitor suggested that, since I'd just had the cottage refurbished, to send a photographer round to take pictures to post for advertisement. So I did, and once the job was finished, he placed them in the post and sent them to my solicitor. Once he inspected them, he couldn't help but notice the flame-haired beauty who'd been caught unawares in the photo. 'Twas the same maid who'd just picked up the keys and directions from his office. He was quite taken with her, methinks, and made it a point to flag her photo with a note when he dropped the mailer into the post for me to inspect." Tristan glanced toward the Rover and inclined his head. " 'Twas your girl there, Conwyk. . . ."

At the same time, Gawan followed Tristan's inclining head. He then noticed what had stopped his friend's words in midsentence.

Ellie of Aquitaine had indeed disappeared once again.

Twelve

Being that daylight waned at such an early hour during the winter months in the north of England, Tristan had convinced Gawan with very little effort to follow him directly to Dreadmoor after leaving the rental cottage. Since he had no clue when Ellie might reappear, he'd accepted. After all, Tristan claimed to have a photo of the girl—their only solid lead so far. And Gawan was most anxious to get his hands on it.

After ringing Nicklesby on the mobile to say he'd not sup at Grimm that eve, he followed the fading tail lamps of Tristan's newest toy—a sleek black Jag—down the North Sea's winding coastline, to the imposing keep perched high above the sea atop an ancient shelf of earth and rock. Much like Grimm, in many ways, although Grimm was nearly a century older, Dreadmoor certainly possessed its own distinct character.

Up until quite recently, 'twas filled with naught save one crusty old mortal steward and a seven-hundred-year-old garrison of medieval ghosts.

Tristan himself included.

Yet somehow, the doomed knights had managed to overcome the most incredible odds Gawan had ever heard of, including Sir Tristan finding himself a lady wife in the process.

One who, according to the gossipy female spirits of Castle Grimm, had not only fallen in love with Tristan, known far and wide as the Dragonhawk, the dreaded scourge of England, but had done so whilst he was still a cursed spirit. She had even wanted to wed him in that unsavory state of nonsubstance, Gawan had heard.

He couldn't fathom the vast amount of love the woman must possess for de Barre.

Lucky whoreson.

Gawan thought about the past year and how little time he'd spent at Grimm. 'Twas whilst he'd been away on an assignment, when Tristan and the lads, along with Tristan's wife, had broken the ancient curse. And all due to a storm blowing over that bloody oak in the bailey. He'd come home to Lady Follywolle and Lady Beauchamp, all giggly and gossipy about the events that had occurred. He'd barely believed the tale.

Until now.

The thought of big, boisterous Dragonhawk being brought to his poor knees by the devious moves of Ellie of Aquitaine made Gawan want to laugh out loud. The girl had moved like lightning, hitting just the right place in order to bring down a man who outstood her by a foot and a half, and outweighed her by more than ten stone, easily.

Who, by the devil's cloven hooves, had taught her such a move? And damnation, why hadn't she been able to use that skill on whoever had nearly taken her life? Unless 'twas of naught but sheer accident that had placed Ellie in such a state.

Had the events not occurred, though, he and Ellie would have never met. A rather selfish reflection on his part, not that their meeting had accomplished much, save make him crave something he could not have. Rather, *someone.*

Ellie.

How his head ached.

It was nearly an hour later when the daunting walls of Dreadmoor came into view. Through twilight and mist the dark keep and surrounding buildings rose, sinister and impenetratable. 'Twas a fine fortress, to his notion. Tristan, indeed, had done a superior job with the design.

As he followed Tristan through the gatehouse, Gawan gave the guard, Will, a nod, and the lad, ever so stern, waved him through without so much as a smile or welcome. Gawan motored up the path and across the drawbridge, then parked the Rover beside Tristan's car and started up the massive steps to the double front doors.

Before he and Tristan reached the top step, the doors swung open, and a petite young woman with darkish hair, much like Ellie's, except shorter, stepped out. Wrapped in a wool plaid, she gathered the material about her and waited as Tristan closed the space between them and then pulled her into his arms.

The top of her head reached no farther than his chest.

Much, he couldn't help but think, as Ellie's did his. Only Ellie stood a shade taller than the lady Dragonhawk, as her head nearly reached Gawan's shoulder.

Priest's robes, why would that womanly thought come to mind?

Witless. 'Twas no other way to describe his stupid self.

"Conwyk! Remove that scowl from your visage thusly and greet my wife. 'Tis bloody freezing out here."

Gawan cleared his throat, decided to set all thoughts of Ellie aside for the moment, and gave Tristan's wife a low bow. " 'Tis an honor, Lady Dread—"

"Andi," she interrupted, and then grasped his hands with her small cold ones. "Welcome to the House of Testosterone." She cocked her head and inspected him toe to eyebrow. "From the looks of it, you'll fit right in."

Tristan's laugh boomed over the bailey. "Come." He inclined his head to the door. "The lads will be more than pleased to see you've finally decided to call upon us."

Andi smiled and slipped her arm through Gawan's. "Come on in. We'll go plop down by the fire and talk while we wait for dinner." She pulled him through the door. "Jameson has something cooking that smells like heaven."

"Don't get too cozy with my wife wrapped about you, Conwyk. I've a mind to peel her away from you at any minute as it's been nigh onto a full day since I've last clapped eyes on her."

He glanced at Tristan, whose eyes were indeed now clapped onto his lady, and Gawan noticed immediately that the once-fierce warrior bore the most ridiculously besotted expression he'd truly ever seen.

He found himself to be vastly jealous.

Andi leaned toward Gawan. "Don't mind him. Ever since that curse was broken, he's been impossible to live with."

Tristan in fact did peel his wife from Gawan at that point, which won him a playful squeal. "You mean impossible to live *without,* aye?" Tristan winked at Gawan over Andi's head. "She fancies me saying *aye,* as well as being called *wench.* An American thing, methinks, and I do both as oft as I dare."

"Sir Gawan! I've been wondering when you'd come round! 'Tis wondrous, about Sir Tristan and the rest of us, aye?"

Gawan turned and watched the tall, lanky form of Tristan's youngest knight hurry across the great hall. Clad in modern garb in the form of a wool tunic, denims, and boots, Jason of Corwick-by-the-Sea hastily scampered across the hall's oak plank flooring, with his sword slapping heartily against his thigh. When the lad stopped, he grasped Gawan's hand in a firm shake, a wide grin splitting his face in twain.

"Wondrous it is, lad." Gawan studied him. "Methinks you've grown a bit, boy. Being a mortal seems to suit you rather well."

Jason glanced down at himself, then lifted a gaze full of mischief. "Aye, in more ways than one, sir. How long are you here for?"

Tristan clapped Jason on the shoulder. "At least long enough to have a go at the blades, lad. I daresay Conwyk needs a good flesh-and-blood bit of swordplay, aye?"

The grin on Jason's face grew wider. "Most assuredly, aye."

Andi groaned. "Like I said, House of Testosterone. Jameson!" She turned and walked off. "I'm starving over here!"

All three men watched the lady Dragonhawk saunter across the hall and disappear into the larder.

Gawan grinned. "House of Testosterone it may well be, but I daresay yon maid there has the running of this hall firmly in her wee grasp."

"If you only knew the half of it," Tristan muttered. But, Gawan noticed, he muttered with the utmost respect and love.

Just then a thunderous stomping of booted feet sounded at the stairs, and four big knights, all garbed in modern clothes like Jason, yet none without their blades, hurried down and across the great hall. With much jostling, backslapping, and handshaking, greetings were passed all around.

Aye, 'twas more than wondrous, as Jason had said. 'Twas a bloody miracle, these lives restored with Dragonhawk and his once-doomed knights.

Gawan thought it couldn't have happened to a more deserving lot of lads.

"Oy, Conwyk," said Tristan's captain, Kail, a bloody giant to Gawan's notion. He stroked his chin. " 'Twas just the other day, as a matter of fact, that the lads and I were pondering when you'd come calling for a bit of *live* sport."

Sir Richard elbowed Sir Christopher and winked. "Was wondering, even, if ye was a bit, oh, I dunno, *scared*?"

"Not that your mate Arrick-by-the-Sea isn't a damn fine bit of spirited sport," Sir Christopher said. "A mighty warrior, indeed, whilst still a ghost. Although 'tis a bit more, er, challenging, when fighting one of the flesh."

Gareth, a rather large lad from the Highlands, leaned toward Gawan. "We've just installed new floodlights in the lists, Conwyk." A broad smile split his face as he palmed the hilt of his sword. One dark eyebrow lifted. "What say you?"

Gawan couldn't help the surge of excitement that rushed through him. "Aye, little lad, and 'twill be your blade I'll send sailing through the air first—*umph!*"

"Damnation!" All of Dreadmoor's knights cried out scores of various curses at once.

As they scattered.

Just as Ellie, once again, literally dropped out of nowhere to land unceremoniously atop Gawan's unsuspecting self. Although his body jerked in an attempt to brace himself against her weight, it failed to keep either of them upright. Instead, Gawan found himself with an armload of soft, flailing woman as both he and Ellie tumbled to the floor.

When Ellie opened her eyes, she met the intense and surprised stare of Gawan. Nose-to-nose and clearly sprawled all over him, she passed a quick thank-you to the Lord for her having chosen Nicklesby's trousers and Gawan's sweater to wear instead of a skirt. God knew what a sight that would have made.

Heat seared her lower back, where Gawan's large hands had a firm grip. They were pressed breasts to chest, which was quite an interesting position.

They were on the floor, her atop him. *Again.*

A slow frown pulled at the corner of Gawan's mouth.

And then, quite suddenly, Ellie had a *feeling* creep across her. Forget the fact that she was lying on top of the most absolutely drop-dead-gorgeous guy she'd ever seen. Forget that the same guy had a chivalrous, charming characteristic about him that she was beginning to seriously adore. No, no, that was something altogether separate. Ooh, and there was that annoying half-dead, amnesia thing that was becoming all too normal lately. This was something *else*. Slowly, without moving her head, she slid her gaze first to the left, then to the right.

Gawan and she were surrounded by several pairs of big, worn, leather boots.

Someone above them chuckled.

Although he was still frowning and Ellie couldn't figure out why, Gawan's gaze dropped from her eyes to her lips, which made her stomach do a flip. Then his eyes moved back up. His jaw tensed. "Could one of you lads give us a hand?"

"By the saints, girl, forgive me," she heard Tristan say, just before his strong hands grasped her around the waist and hefted her none too gently off Gawan.

"There now," Tristan said, giving her a firm, awkward pat on the shoulder. He inclined his head. "Er, lads, this is Ellie Aquitaine, Gawan's lady, although I daresay neither will admit the like." He grinned. "Lady, the knights of Dreadmoor. Well, some of them, for the most part."

Gawan knelt and then rose to stand beside her, just as she turned her head in a half-circle to meet the gaze of the four big boot wearers. They all had hair to their shoulders, or at least it would have been, if they'd worn it loose, and while they were dressed in normal clothes, they each had a *sword* strapped to their hips? As she studied each one, they either gave a short nod, smiled, or lifted an amused eyebrow. One, who looked the youngest, winked. Tristan simply stood, legs braced wide apart, arms crossed over his chest. *Smirking.*

"Um, hi, guys," she said. Leaning closer to Gawan, she tugged on his arm, and when he lowered his head, she rose on tiptoes to whisper in his ear, "Where the heck are we?" She knew they weren't at Castle Grimm, and she'd have definitely remembered meeting all these guys. It was one thing to encounter Gawan, for God's sake. But now there were four more? She briefly wondered why they didn't seem too fazed by the fact that she'd just dropped out of thin air.

Gawan's eyes met hers. "We're at Dreadmoor, lady. Tristan's hall." He gave a nod in the direction of the other guys. "And these lads are some of his men."

Before Ellie could address *that*, the sound of scurrying drew her attention across the room, and when she looked, she found an older man dressed in a proper black suit, with perfectly combed gray hair and a slight scowl on his face, hurrying toward them. Beside him was a pretty young woman.

They almost seemed to be *racing* toward her.

"What in Heavens is all the fuss about?" the older man said. "My dear girl, are you quite all right? You lads, there, give her a bit of room."

Ellie smiled, although she didn't think she'd ever be quite all right for the rest of her life. "I'm fine, really."

"Hi, I'm Andi, Tristan's wife, and this is Jameson," the young woman said, smiling and grasping Ellie's hand in hers. "Would you like me to rescue you from these overgrown brutes?"

Before Ellie could happily accept, the front door slammed open, sending in a blast of frosty air. She blinked. Several more overgrown brutes filed in. All with long hair, some tied back, some worn wild around the shoulders. All wearing *chain mail*? And all carrying swords. And they all stared at *her*.

Good *Lord*.

Ellie glanced at Andi. "Do you have your own football team?"

Andi laughed, as did several of the others. "You'd think so, wouldn't you? You should see the grocery bill around here." She tugged on Ellie's arm, which had somehow become firmly attached to Gawan's. "Come on. We could use some help in the kitchen." Andi glanced at the older man. "*Right,* Jameson?"

Jameson, who had a bored look upon his weathered features, heaved a small sigh. "If you insist, my lady. Let's hurry, then, before the stew becomes lumpy."

As Ellie started to follow Andi, Gawan tugged her to a halt. He leaned forward and brought his lips to her ear. " 'Twill be fine, girl. Go with the lady. I'll be along, posthaste, after I've had speech with Tristan."

They stared for a moment, before she allowed Tristan's wife, who seemed to think the whole situation all too typical, to pull her away. Certainly, Andi didn't realize she was In Betwinxt?

And it was only then that Ellie realized that yet another mortal—when had she started thinking of people as mortal or immortal?—was able to touch her.

Hurrying across Tristan's great hall, being pulled by Tristan's wife, and surrounded by a bunch of guys who carried swords, Ellie decided right then and there that even if she couldn't remember anything, she could still sense that these people knew something she didn't.

And she wasn't going to leave Dreadmoor Castle until she found out just what that something was.   .

Thirteen

"So the lass recalls naught?"

Gawan rubbed his chin. "Not her namesake, her sire, nor her family—just a few random memories." Including one memory involving the improper fondling of a certain naked statue. "I've checked with each infirmary between Northumberland and London. They all said their nay."

"Did you use your"—Tristan tapped a forefinger to his temple—"Angel mind-control thing that you do—"

"Whisst," Gawan hissed. "Keep your voice down. She knows naught of my skills. But aye, of course, I used it. They wouldn't gain me information otherwise."

"Surely you jest," Sir Robyn, a tall, sandy-haired knight said. "You've not told her?"

"Damn, Conwyk," Sir Richard said, scratching his head. "Methinks 'tis a powerful important detail to leave out of one's artillery of need-to-know things."

Several ayes and grumbles rounded the circle of knights gathered before the great hall hearth.

"Now, lads," Tristan said, "there's more to this sordid tale, to be sure." He pinched the bridge of his nose. "She's Conwyk's bloody Intended."

Several manly gasps filled the air at once.

"Mean you," Kail said, dabbing his large, clumsy fingertip to the corner of his mouth, "she has that wee mark, just here?"

"But your retirement grows ever so near, sir," Jason

said. "I thought 'twas the absolute rule that all memory of those charges you've given aid to be stricken from you?"

Gawan's skull throbbed. Nay, it slammed against whatever useless bit of matter that lay within. "Aye. 'Tis so."

More gasps, even more manly than before.

Sir Stephen paced before the hearth, hand on sword hilt. "We could make sure the two of you are reunited, aye?" He rubbed his chin as he pondered. "If she's your Intended, then no matter that you can't recall these past events. She's still yours. You'd grow again to love her."

When, by the saints, had these thickheaded fools decided that he already loved Ellie?

Not that it mattered if he did.

Gawan stood and shoved his hands into his pockets. "I thank ye for your efforts, Stephen, but nay, 'twould not work. Because the girl nearly died, and is In Betwinxt, and *I* found her. She became my charge, in truth, right then. That changes everything."

"Methinks that bloody law of yours is passing overrated," Stephen said. "By the by, there's one thing even *They*"—with an index finger, he pointed upward, whilst whispering the word *They*—"cannot control, and that's a fierce desire between a warrior and his maid. 'Twould be naught but a simple thing, to reintroduce the two of you."

Jason scratched an ear. "Aye, that certainly is a wondrous plan, sir. 'Tis more than obvious that you two are most mad about each other."

A low rumble of grunts of agreement sounded.

"Lads, you sound like a gaggle of peahens. There's much more to this than desire. Her bloody life is at stake here, and so far I've been fair useless as a Guardian. She crossed many miles to come here, and I cannot even find out *why,* no matter how many thoughts I read, nor how many minds I coerce. Useless powers, they are, unless I find the right person. Or persons."

How, he wondered, could something such as his desire for Ellie be so bloody obvious to a garrison of medieval knights? They knew of swords and bloodshed and battle and fisticuffs, not of matters of the heart. He shoved a hand through his hair and sighed. "Christ, 'tis maddening."

"Does she know?" Sir Christopher asked, jabbing a poker into the blazing hearth. "That she's your Intended?"

Gawan pushed out a gusty sigh, then swore in Welsh. "Nay. She does not."

Tristan, who'd risen and come to stand beside Gawan, placed a hand on his shoulder. "All this secrecy may be for naught, my friend."

Gawan met Tristan's gaze. "What mean you?"

"Have you ever thought to allow the girl to make up her own mind regarding your position as a nearly retired Angel Guardian *and* her Intended?"

Gawan gave a short, incredulous laugh. "You jest, aye? The girl is addled. She barely comprehends her own state of being, not to mention the fact that my hall is filled with a pushy lot of meddlesome specters." He met Tristan eye to eye. "Are you suggesting I burden her with all of this, as well?"

Tristan's smile was annoyingly cocksure. "Aye, man. 'Tis exactly what I'm suggesting."

"Aye, Conwyk," said Kail. "You're no' God Himself, for Christ's sake. You're merely one of His Guardians, and not for too much longer at that. 'Tis not your decision, the keeping of such matters of import to yourself. The lass has a bloody right to know."

"Or did you forget the Code you swore by?" said Robyn. He waved a hand in the air, big, cocky oaf that he was. "I recall one verse in particular—er, what is it, lads? Help me out."

"Never lie" was grumbled in unison by all knights.

Gawan rubbed his eye sockets with a thumb and forefinger, then stared into the fire. Damnation, what a predicament. The lads were right, of course. Annoyingly so. But by the saints, he had a bad feeling about it all.

He rubbed a hand over his jaw and met Tristan's gaze. "We've yet to visit the cottage Ellie let from your solicitor. I daresay we should have done so before coming here."

Just then, the front hall door slammed open against the wall. Snow blew in, as did the last three Dragonhawk knights. One of them pushed the door closed, and they stood there, just inside the hall, swords clenched in fists, their chain mail covered in frost.

Sir Jon, a fierce warrior from the Black Isle, pointed his blade at Gawan and smiled a most unappealing smile. "You're snowed in, little lad, and the drawbridge has been raised." His grin grew even more wicked. "Methinks you're in sore need of a *decent* bit of training, Grimm. Or have you forgotten how you acquired those ancient markings on your flesh?"

The other two stood there, staring. Grinning. And waiting.

Mayhap, 'twas *exactly* what he needed, Gawan thought.

As if Tristan would have given him a choice.

With a hearty slap to the back, which nearly sent Gawan hurling into the flames, Tristan said, "Do not worry, friend. Hopefully, the storm will have ceased by the morn, when we can dig ourselves out of the snow and travel to the cottage. I've already spoken to my solicitor, who is faxing over the documents he has on Ellie's rental agreement this very eve. Besides, 'twould do none of us a bit of good to try it now, unless you want to sprout those feathered appendages of yours? Although I daresay 'twould be best to investigate in the full daylight."

"Unfortunately, I gave up the use of those appendages when I accepted this almost-mortal job." True, he could still call those feathered reminders forth, stretch them out a bit, only to have to tuck them back into place. 'Twas just as well, he thought. "We'll wait 'til the morn."

"Well done, Conwyk," Tristan said. Then he turned to his men. "Gear up, lads! Whilst the maids tend the larder, we shall put aside all these womanly discussions and behave like bloody warriors!"

The hall echoed with a raucous lot of medieval war cries as those knights not geared for the elements scrambled to their chambers to change.

Tristan grinned at Gawan. "Come with me, the fiercely known Gawan of Conwyk. Looks like we're having a sleepover." His gaze moved over Gawan. "And by the devil's cloven hoof, you can't train in that sorry garb. Do you have in your car boot your blade? Your mail? Never mind. I've got plenty to spare." He faced him, full on. "We'll take a look at that photograph tonight, and go over the faxes, once you've informed your lady of the *situation*."

Situation, indeed. With a quick glance over his shoulder at the larder, where Ellie assisted Tristan's wife and steward with the lumpy stew, Gawan took the stairs two at a time behind Tristan. Mayhap after a brisk skirmish with the life-and-blood knights of Dreadmoor in the icy snow, he'd gain the courage to face something far more terrifying than that murderous lot of bloodthirsty lads.

Ellie of Aquitaine.

"*Oooh,* Jameson, love. You certainly do know how to conjure up a most delightful stew, indeed."

Ellie's gaze darted to Jameson, to get his response to Lady Follywolle's glowing review of his stew making.

Jameson rolled his eyes so far back, they all but disappeared.

Andi gently kicked Ellie beneath the table, and when she looked, Tristan's wife's face was pinched with laughter.

"My, my, Millicent, I do believe you're right. Look you at how he grips the *shaft* of that stirring spoon, just so," Lady Beauchamp said, floating closer to Jameson. "My dear cousin Lucy will be sorely disappointed that she decided to stay about Grimm to keep Nicklesby company. 'Tis far more interesting here."

Jameson's face turned an alarming shade of red.

Millicent, rather Lady Follywolle, bent her head to inspect Jameson's gripping of the spoon shaft, and the beak of her coiffed swan all but dipped into the stew.

Jameson jumped, and Andi barely stifled a giggle.

Jameson, on the other hand, had obviously had enough. He placed the tool in question on a spoon rest and wiped his hands on a dish towel. "My good ladies, while your compliments are most appreciated, as always, I must ask you to adjourn to the table there with the other females and have . . . I don't know . . . female speech of some sort. You're most distracting, indeed."

The two spirits from Grimm giggled, and then eased their way to the table, where they made a big production of sitting down properly.

Andi glanced at Ellie and grinned.

"So how are things over at Castle Grimm?" Andi asked. "How's Nicklesby?"

Lady Follywolle patted her swan. "I daresay he's rather pouty this eve, being left behind with no one about save young Davy Crispin and the lady Lucy to keep him company."

"Although," Lady Beauchamp said, "the little lad is quite good at knucklebones. I'm sure they'll all three pass the time fair." She grinned first at Ellie, then at Andi. "But 'tis far more exhilarating over here at Dreadmoor—isn't that right, Millicent?"

Lady Follywolle bobbed her head. "With a certainty, 'tis so. How, by the saints, Lady Dreadmoor, can you stand being in constant company with so many *fine* specimens milling about?"

Andi feigned a yawn, which made Ellie grin. "Oh, someone has to do it, I suppose."

Jameson cleared his throat.

"Well," Lady Follywolle said. " 'Tis quite exciting at Castle Grimm these days, what with the young mistress Ellie here showing up."

"Causing quite a stir with Himself, too," Lady Beau-

champ added. "I've never seen Sir Gawan so stodgy."
She slid a knowing gaze at Ellie. "In a pinch, most of
the time. You must really ruffle that boys feathers, my
dear."

Ellie listened to the chatter of the two lady ghosts, but
couldn't quite get a handle on what they were saying.
Definitely, she knew there was an attraction between
Gawan and her. That'd been proven with the kiss she so
eloquently claimed she'd forgotten ever even happened.

As if.

Ellie cocked her head. "I make him *stodgy*?" What
the heck did *stodgy* mean, anyway?

"Haven't you noticed? He's always in such a bluster
when you're about." Lady Follywolle said, head tilted to
the side. "Why, my dear girl, hasn't he told you—"

"Y-you how terribly bad he wants to help you, and
that not finding adequate clues is making him stodgy,"
Lady Beauchamp finished.

Ellie glanced from lady ghost to lady ghost, then to
Andi, who shrugged; and then she narrowed her gaze at
Lady Follywolle.

She may not know who she is, but one thing Ellie *felt*:
her mother didn't raise a fool.

"What hasn't Gawan told me, Lady Follywolle?" Ellie
asked. She sighed. "Please, tell me. It's bad enough, not
remembering. But to keep things secret from me?
Why?"

Andi reached across the table and grasped Ellie's
hand. "Maybe we should just wait and talk to Gawan
and Tristan?"

A squeak erupted from Lady Follywolle, and then another. Then a hiccup. Out of a pocket from her gown,
she withdrew a white lace hankie, pressed it to her
mouth, then started to sniffle.

"Oh, dear," warned Lady Beauchamp.

"I . . . I . . . oh, my dear girl, I can't stand it a minute
longer!" cried Lady Follywolle, ghostly tears streaming
down her cheeks.

"Hush, Millicent! Do not—"

"It breaks my heart, poor little lamb," Lady Fol-lywolle continued, with another hiccup. " 'Tisn't fair, I say. Not fair at all."

"Oh, dear, indeed," Jameson said quietly.

Ellie glanced at Andi, who now stood, pulling on El-lie's arm. "Let's go find the guys and get this all straight-ened out, okay? Lady Follywolle, *really,* it'll be okay. You don't have to cry—Jameson, *help* me!"

Lady Follywolle kept on. "B-but, he's an *Annn-gel,* for Heaven's sake! Why can he not change the course of events?"

Ellie blinked. This was the second time Lady Fol-lywolle had referred to Gawan as an Angel. "I'm sorry. What did you say?"

While Lady Beauchamp fretted and wrung her hands, Lady Follywolle wailed even louder. " 'Tis so unfair! The boy's waited for nearly a thousand years." She bur-ied her face into her hankie, and then muttered some-thing Ellie couldn't understand.

"Lady Follywolle, what is it?" Ellie asked, not com-pletely sure she wanted to hear the answer. She moved closer.

The ghostly lady looked up and blew her nose. "He's an Angel, love. Your Guardian angel. And your beloved *Intended—*"

"Come, my good ladies, and I'll escort you to the west solar," Christian of Arrick-by-the-Sea said, just as he walked through the kitchen wall. He grasped Lady Fol-lywolle by the elbow. "There you'll find a fine view of the lads at their swordplay. Come now, you're making a mess of that lovely face of yours. And look." He pointed at Lady Follywolle's head. "Your nicely coiffed bird is all askew."

He glanced at Ellie, then at Andi, gave a tight smile, and managed to coax both distressed spirits from the kitchen.

Before they disappeared through the wall, Lady Follywolle glanced over her shoulder at Ellie. "I'm ever so sorry, my dear girl. Truly, ever so sorry, indeed."

And with that, they vanished.

It felt as though someone had knocked her over the head with a brick. Dazed, yet *ouch*!

Turning, Ellie glanced at Jameson, who cleared his throat and flicked a bit of something from his coat sleeve.

When she looked at Andi, the lady of Dreadmoor simply smiled and shrugged. "Weird, huh? A year ago, and no one would have ever made me believe ghosts even existed."

"I really appreciate everything. I do," Ellie said, pasting a smile to a face that didn't feel much like smiling. "And I by no means want to sound ungrateful. But what in the *heck* is she talking about?"

Andi chewed on her bottom lip as she pondered.

Ellie fought not to chew her own lip *off*. Angel? Beloved Intended? God, was it possible to become even more confused? Apparently so. "Okay. When Lady Follywolle says *Angel*, does she mean *haaa-lle-lujah*! type Angel, or, just that he's a swell kind of guy? And Intended? Intended for *what*? What does Intended mean?" With both hands, she massaged her temples. "Oy," she mimicked Gawan, "my head hurts."

Suddenly, Ellie felt Andi's hands on her shoulders as the other woman guided her back down to the chair. When she opened her eyes, Andi had crouched beside her, hand on knee.

"Ellie, I'm afraid most of what I know came to me just hours ago over the cell phone with Tristan. He sort of gave me a heads-up, so to speak. You know, of everything that's going on with you."

Ellie nodded. "Go on."

With a hefty sigh, Andi continued. "Well, part of what I know, I've known since meeting Tristan and the guys. The other part, I just found out a while ago." She drew in a deep breath and patted Ellie's hand. "Gawan's not a serial killer, or anything like that. Honest. He's a really nice guy." She ducked her head and gave Ellie a smile. "The guys are on the lists training. Trust me, that's not something you want to miss. So let's go watch them for a bit, and then I can tell you a little more of what's happened here recently that may help you deal with your situation a little better. Okay?"

It'd have to be one whopper of a story to top hers.

Ellie was sure it wasn't going to be *totally* okay, but she'd have to trust the people who'd taken her under their wings and did their best to see her through whatever it was she needed seeing through.

After Jameson gathered a pair of thick wool coats and gave them each a plaid wool wrap, Ellie and Andi bundled up and started across the hall to the west tower chamber, a place Andi claimed to have the very best balcony view of the lists. Whatever lists were.

Just as they reached the wide winding staircase, Ellie placed a hand on Andi's elbow and pulled her to a stop.

"Just tell me one thing, because it's eating a hole straight through my head. Gawan, is he really an Angel?"

Andi's expression softened, and she smiled. "Yeah, he really is."

Ellie tried to wrap her brain around it but found it even more difficult than accepting the fact that she'd been having conversations with centuries-old ghosts. "What about my being his Intended? What does that mean?"

Andi smiled. "That you'll have to squeeze out of Gawan."

Fourteen

Once Andi and Ellie reached the west tower, which happened to be an enormous and comfortable turreted bedroom, they stepped through a set of heavy double-hung doors that led to a balcony. A blast of icy wind and snow hit them both, but once the doors were closed behind them, the wind wasn't completely intolerable. Snow fell in a constant sheet, though, and after watching Andi drape the plaid wool blanket around her head, leaving just her eyes showing, Ellie did the same. She glanced down.

Good *Lord,* they were high up.

Then the shouts reached her ears.

"Lop off his head!" That, Ellie noticed, was Sir Godfrey.

"Damn me, but you fight like a drunken wench!"

Andi huddled close to Ellie, then poked a finger through the crack in her blanket and pointed down and to the left a fraction, to a scene Ellie hoped would never, for the rest of her days whether as a living mortal or a wispy ghost, leave her memory. Her breath left her in a puff of white mist, and she wasn't quite convinced it was due to the icy wind.

The guys she'd encountered in Tristan's hall—wow, she counted a few more now—stood in a half-moon around two others, dressed in chain mail and circling each other with sure-footed steps. Gawan and Tristan.

And they were hacking at each other with very big swords.

"Come on, Dreadmoor! Can't ye get any closer to the bumblin' oaf?"

" 'Tis like watching me grandmum, I'd warrant!"

All the men burst into laughter.

"Wow," Ellie said.

Andi sighed. "Uh-huh."

With utter amazement, respect, and—oh, yeah—lip-smacking lust, Ellie allowed her gaze to follow Gawan. Determined and confident, he moved with the grace of a man half his size, as though he'd been fighting with blades all his life. With sword held poised in the air, broad shoulders taut, his gaze never faltering from his opponent, he moved on muscular thighs in a slow dance around Tristan. The only evidence that either man was winded showed as each warm breath escaped their nostrils and mouths, creating a wisp of frosty whiteness before them. Tristan matched Gawan step for step. Both were predatory, beautiful. Warriors.

Gawan all but knocked the wind from Ellie's lungs.

"Magnificent, huh?" Andi said in a half whisper.

Ellie pulled her blanket tighter. "Definitely."

It was then that one of the knights hollered to Gawan, "Are you not feeling a bit confined in all that steel, Conwyk?"

"Aye, methinks he's gone soft, indeed," said Kail, who elbowed the guy beside him.

At that moment, Gawan held up his hand, and Tristan stopped. Jason ran up to stand beside Gawan. Tristan took his sword, then Jason helped Gawan pull off the big chain mail shirt he wore, followed by some thick sort of jacket below it. Leaving him bare chested.

Ellie's mouth went dry, and a small gasp escaped Andi.

The men all whooped and shouted, and Gawan and Tristan continued their predatory dance.

"Won't he freeze to death?" Ellie said out loud.

"I doubt it, but he must be insane," Andi said.

Ellie glanced at the others, some circling the two opponents, some leaning on the hilts of their swords, all in medieval chain mail. Clapping, swearing, laughing, and egging the two fighters on.

Ellie's head snapped up and she settled her gaze on Gawan. His hair wild and loose around his shoulders, and while she was too far away to make out the markings across his back and chest in perfect detail, she could see them from where she stood. She recognized him, just like that, but she watched him a minute more, unable to tear her eyes away.

With each heft and swing of that mighty sword, his biceps and the muscles across his back and chest moved, and the power he emanated from where he stood nearly knocked Ellie from the balcony. He was no mere man. Not even a mere Angel.

He was that wild, ferocious, tattooed warrior from Gawan's own great hall tapestry, the one who'd fought beside Queen Eleanor of Aquitaine.

From the twelfth century.

"Close your mouth, Ellie, before your tonsils freeze off," Andi said, her voice muffled by the blanket wrapped over the bottom half of her face. Then she laughed. "Don't worry. It just takes a little getting used to."

Ellie blinked and glanced at all the men. While she was having a little trouble remembering things, she knew there weren't many men like *those men* left. Not in the twenty-first century. No way. Twenty-first-century men were businessmen, suit wearers, clean-nails-and-smooth-palms sort of guys. Yeah, there were the labor workers, who were a bit rougher than the business guys, but . . .

A gasp of realization slipped out of Ellie's mouth. "No way," she said, mostly to herself.

It was then that Gawan must have caught sight of Ellie, and for just a moment, his gaze met hers, and he let the distraction pull him out of his swordplay. That was all Tristan apparently needed. Gawan's blade went flying over his head, wrenched away by Tristan's deft and very tricky move.

The men burst into rowdy laughter.

Which, of course, only made Gawan lean over, grab up his sword, and move toward Tristan as if he really *did* plan on lopping off his head. The two picked up where they'd left off before Gawan had noticed Andi and her watching.

With a heavy sigh that sent icy air pluming out before her, Ellie turned to Andi. "So you know I'm In Betwinxt?"

Andi nodded. "I have to admit, I didn't think anything else could make me pause and consider." She met Ellie's gaze. "Not after everything that's gone on around here. But, wow. Yeah. *Mostly* dead is a pretty bizarre condition." She glanced back to where her husband hacked at Gawan. "Trust me. If anyone can help you, it's Gawan."

"How is it that you and everyone else here can see me, yet other mortals can't?"

Andi shrugged. "I can only guess it's because of my experiences here. Same with Jameson."

"So what happened here? Exactly?"

Andi didn't answer right away. Her eyes were fixed on the group below. Ellie watched, too, and had to admit that when she called to mind the vision of an Angel, that vision certainly didn't come in the form of a bare-chested, fighting-in-the-freezing-snow, sword-hacking warrior like Gawan Conwyk.

Suddenly, something Lady Follywolle had said earlier interrupted Ellie's thoughts. *Why, he's waited for nearly a thousand years. . . .*

"Tristan and his men," Andi began, still watching the scene below, "are thirteenth-century knights."

Ellie glanced at Andi, then down at the guys, then back at Andi. "Okay." It wasn't okay, but what else was she supposed to say?

Andi turned to face Ellie straight-on. "They were all murdered, here at Dreadmoor, in the year 1292. When

I came here to excavate a medieval hoard and a body of bones that had been buried beneath the roots of a seven-hundred-year-old tree, I met Tristan."

Ellie nodded. And waited.

A twinkle lit Andi's hazel eyes. "And I found out really fast he and his knights were all cursed ghosts." She shook her head. "I didn't want to believe it, at first. I'm a scientist, for God's sake. Firmly rooted in reality." She snorted. "Well, that's all changed now."

Ellie studied the guys below the balcony. Snow clung to most of them, and she especially regarded Tristan de Barre as he tried to fight off the ferocious thrusts of Gawan's sword. Gawan, the Angel, and Tristan and his men, the once-cursed ghostly knights turned mortals.

And she, Ellie of Wherever and Whoever, was almost a ghost herself.

How could all of this be *real*?

"It's kind of like trying to swallow a whole piece of chewed-up bread." Andi grinned. "Not very easy."

Ellie had to agree on that as she imagined a big ball of dough in her mouth. "Disgusting simile, but I get it."

Andi laughed. "We'll have to tell you the whole story over dinner. Tristan and the guys love to tell about their adventure."

Finally, to much groaning, swearing, and poking of fun from the men below, Tristan and Gawan called a truce. Both were breathing hard, white clouds of frost puffing from their mouths and nostrils as they leaned on their swords.

Ellie stared at Gawan, and as though he could *feel* it, he turned and stared back.

The sight of him made her mouth go dry.

He looked *nothing* at all like an Angel.

Tall, broad, muscular, ferocious. Wild hair frosted with snow, and those wicked tattoos streaking his skin. A ripped abdomen moving with each labored breath.

Not a winged, pudgy, cherubic Angel by any means.

More like a feral medieval warrior.

"My dear ladies, whatever are you still doing out there in the snow? It's been nearly an hour."

Both she and Andi turned to the closed double doors behind them at the sound of the muffled words. Jameson stood, ramrod straight, arms to his side, his crisp black suit pressed to perfection. One eyebrow disappeared into his thick, perfectly groomed white hair as he stared through the glass.

He opened the doors, clucked, then inclined his head. "You girls come in here this instant, before you catch your deaths"—he gave Ellie a blank glance—"or in your case, before you catch your complete death." He clucked again. "Come, now. 'Tis passing frigid out here, you know, and you did say you'd only be out there a short spell."

Andi looked at Ellie, shrugged, then allowed Jameson to tug her through the doorway. Once they were inside, he closed both doors and flipped the lock.

"Geez, Jameson, you don't have to be such a worry-wart," Andi said, grinning.

Jameson stiffened. "I most certainly do, young lady, as long as you're carrying my godchild in your belly. Now, the stew is ready and the hall is prepared for the evening meal." He waved a hand. "Shed those damp-ened snowy garments and come along." With an arm held out, he waited.

Andi smiled, unwrapped herself from the plaid wool blanket and jacket, then draped them over his awaiting arm. "Bossy pants."

Jameson ignored Andi's comment, nodded his ap-proval, then awaited Ellie.

She did the same, then followed Dreadmoor's satisfied steward through the castle and back to the great hall.

And just as she and Andi were coming down the stairs, Gawan and Tristan, followed by Sir Godfrey, Sir Christian, and all of Dreadmoor's knights, came bustling through the main doors, stomping boots, shaking off snow, laughing, and sheathing swords. All, that is, except Gawan, whose eyes were now glued to *her*.

Still, Ellie couldn't wrap her brain around it all. None of it. Including her own ridiculous situation.

So tell me, my dear. How does it feel to have been kissed by an Angel?

Ellie stifled a gasp at the memory of Lady Follywolle's words. She *had* been kissed by an Angel.

Why had he done it?

While Gawan stood, *staring,* Tristan pushed past him and made his way directly to his wife. He gathered her up, chain mail creaking, and planted a big smacking kiss right on her mouth. The knights all whooped and whistled.

Andi gave Tristan a halfhearted push away. "Ugh, Dreadmoor, you're all sweaty and your mail is freezing. Go take a shower. Then you can kiss me some more."

With a gloved hand, he lifted Andi's chin and lowered his head. "I will hold you to that, wife." And with that, he turned and bounded up the stairs.

Andi, on the other hand, looked as though she might fall over in a faint. She smiled. "Cute, huh?"

Ellie nodded. Yeah, Tristan was certainly cute. But even cuter was their uncanny relationship. The depth of the love he had for Andi, and she for him, all but lit up the great hall.

She wondered briefly how it would feel, being loved that much. Much like the ghostly situation at Dreadmoor and Grimm, she could barely grasp it.

"We need to have speech," Gawan said, suddenly standing right in front of her. "Soon. This eve."

Ellie looked at him. He was wrapped now in a thick blanket, his mail throw over one arm while his sword hung from a leather covering at his thigh. She noticed just how intense his eyes were; they were fastened to hers as though looking straight through to her insides. She barely managed a nod. "Okay."

With a knuckle, he grazed her jaw. "We've much to discuss, Ellie of Aquitaine."

Breathing, Ellie thought, *used to come fairly natural.* And she hardly ever thought about doing it. It just *happened.* Now, standing in front of this warrior Angel, she found that breathing was just about the most difficult thing she'd ever done. Other than meeting the powerful stare of his dark brown eyes and not tipping over, of course.

Sheesh. She wondered how her real, completely *alive* self would feel about all this mushy stuff. She wondered even more if she'd ever find out.

It seemed then that Gawan's body took up all the space around her, crowding in on her, and she could do nothing but watch, really, and stare back at him. She knew what it felt like to be wrapped in those strong arms, yet somehow, even though she'd sworn to forget it ever happened, she found herself yearning to experience it all over again.

Yearning? Good *Lord.* Somehow, she felt her real, completely alive self would have popped herself in the head for thinking such.

But, God, she couldn't help it. She felt an attraction to Gawan Conwyk that she couldn't explain, probably wouldn't *want* to explain, either.

He moved closer.

"*Phew!* Jameson! Did you stoke the fire? It is blazing hot in here!" Andi said, grinning. She took Ellie by the elbow and tugged. "Come on, before you two set my castle on fire." She smiled at Ellie. "You can borrow some of my clothes, if you want, although the jeans might be a little high waterish on you. Probably a better fit, though, than"—she glanced at her pants—"are those Nicklesby's?" Andi giggled, then gave a frowning Gawan a glance as she pulled Ellie back up the stairs. "Don't worry, Conwyk. I'll bring her back in one piece. We'll meet you guys at supper, okay?"

Gawan didn't answer. He just kept right on staring.

"Grimm, I vow you'll tip the lass over if you dunna quicken yourself up to the showers," Gareth said, walking by and waving a gloved hand in front of his nose.

Richard clapped Gawan on the shoulder. " 'Tis a good bit of advice there, man. I'd do it, were I you."

A slight smile broke the corner of Gawan's mouth at the knight's joking. "Aye. Mayhap you're right."

As Andi pulled her up the steps, Ellie glanced around. Gawan stood at the bottom, watching them climb. He met her gaze briefly, gave her a short nod, then fell into step with the other knights and joined in as they made fun of how much the other one smelled.

Truly, truly amazing, Ellie thought. She turned and hurried up the steps with Andi.

The thought of having an intense private discussion with Gawan made her stomach turn to knots. If the things Andi had told her stunned and amazed her, she could only imagine what she'd do with the information Gawan had to offer her.

Quickly, her mind flashed to the many times she'd simply disappeared into thin air, and for the first time since finding herself in Gawan's company, she prayed heartily she wouldn't just up and do something silly. Like *vanish.*

"Come, ladies," Jason said, appearing at their side. "Let me accompany you ahead of these brutes, safely to your chambers. I'll walk behind you in case their stench topples you over."

Despite the weirdness of the entire situation, Ellie grinned at the young knight. The knight who had once been murdered, cursed, and then ghostly for nearly seven hundred years, all before becoming mortal once again.

Ellie could barely wait for supper.

Fifteen

Funny, Ellie thought, how she couldn't remember her true self, or her own family, but she remembered other things.

Like how the giant, long oak table in the great hall lined with big, ancient, loudmouthed warriors strangely reminded her of *The Waltons*.

Except for the ladies Follywolle and Beauchamp, who sat to her right, the men—ghostly and unghostly—took up the seats of both sides of the long table, talking, laughing, making bawdy jokes. One seat remained empty to her left, as did the seat at the head of the table.

Which meant Gawan and Tristan were still upstairs.

The great hall, Ellie thought, was pretty impressive. Much like the great hall in Castle Grimm, its interior walls were covered in tapestries depicting knights at battle. Sconces set into the stone walls cast a faint glow of light, while dark timbers crossed the expanse of ceiling.

Straight across from Ellie sat Andi, who gave her a grin. "Don't worry. They'll be down in a—" She glanced at the steps. "Oh, here they come now."

Ellie turned, and for the hundredth time that day, her breath caught. Both men crossed the hall, side by side, and although the lord of Dreadmoor was quite a handsome guy, her gaze passed right over him and landed on the powerful man who walked beside him.

A small gasp escaped Lady Follywolle, or maybe it

had come from Lady Beauchamp. Ellie couldn't tell which one. Nor could she blame either.

Gawan was, hands down, the most beautiful man she'd ever seen.

Freshly bathed, he had his damp hair pulled back in a ponytail—or queue, as Andi had corrected her. His skin stood in contrast to the long-sleeved ivory shirt he wore, tucked in to a comfy-looking pair of worn jeans. The most bizarre mix of twelfth century and twenty-first century she could ever imagine. Dark brown boots moved that tall, powerful frame across the great hall floor to the long table.

And straight toward her.

Rather, the empty seat beside her.

As Gawan sat down, a waft of soapy skin drifted past her, and she inconspicuously drew in a big whiff. Nothing, she thought, smelled better than a freshly showered man.

Other than the two giant pots of stew that Jameson had brought to the table, along with three plates of buttery rolls. Ellie's mouth all but watered at the prospect.

Too bad, she thought, that her tummy simply refused it.

Gawan regarded her. "You look most comely in the lady Dragonhawk's garb, although I rather fancied Nicklesby's gardening trousers." He grinned. "A far better look than on Nicklesby, I assure you."

"Gee, thanks," Ellie said, but she still felt her neck and cheeks grow warm. Good Lord, was she blushing? How embarrassing.

"Lady Ellie, aren't you going to eat?" Jason asked. " 'Tis the best stew in all of England."

Ellie glanced down at her bowl. Her stomach growled just at the sight of the steaming brown gravy and chunks of beef, carrots, and potatoes. Yet the thought of actually putting any of it in her mouth—no way. "It looks great," she told Jason. "You seem to be putting quite a dent in that pot yourself."

Jason gave a crooked grin, then looked at the pot, probably checking it for a real dent. She kept forgetting these guys took most everything she said literally.

"Is there aught amiss?" Gawan said in her ear. "Young Jason's right. You've not touched your meal. Did you eat earlier?"

Ellie shook her head. "No. I don't know. It smells wonderful, but I just can't eat." She turned and gave him a smile. "I'll be fine. Besides," she said, inclining her head to his second bowl, "you're eating plenty for the both of us."

"Conwyk, she's got that aright. What's wrong? That lanky twit Nicklesby not feedin' you enough over there at Grimm?" said Kail.

The knights all laughed.

Gawan, on the other hand, didn't look amused at all. His dark brows furrowed, he studied Ellie more closely for what seemed several minutes, and then he turned to Tristan. "The sooner we get this matter settled, the better."

It was then, in the next second, that an ever-so-familiar feeling began to creep over her. Lowering her hands, she gripped the sides of her chair, hoping that would keep her from falling over and causing a scene. Heck, maybe no one would even notice.

"Damn me, but the maid's face looks rather pasty, Grimm," someone said. "Grab her, man."

"I know that," Gawan said, very close to her. "Ellie? Another vision?"

Ellie glanced around, first at Gawan's taut features, then at the knights who'd stopped eating to watch. She saw one of them cross himself.

"I'm right here," Gawan assured her, closer this time, yet his voice faded, just as the surprised *Ochs!*, *Oys!* and *Damnations!* of the knights muttering around the long table did.

Tristan's deep-voiced *By the bloody saints* was the last thing Ellie heard.

*   *   *

"Shall we douse her with water, sir?" Jason asked as he knelt at Ellie's chair. "I've seen it work before. She does look passing ill."

"Mayhap a pat or two to the maid's cheek will help," Stephen said, flexing his fingers as if to do the patting. " 'Twould rouse her from that blasted frightening open-eyed sleep she's in."

"I daresay she'd be better off on the couch, there in front of the hearth," Jameson said, "instead of sitting upright where she is."

"Aye," Tristan agreed. " 'Twould do her little good to fall face-first into Jameson's stew."

"I'm sure Gawan knows what to do for her," Andi said.

Gawan, appreciative of the lady Dragonhawk's support, gave a nod. "Nay, lady, she's not done this before. But Jameson's right. I'll move her to the couch."

Gawan had to admit that Ellie did indeed look fairly frightening, what with her eyes open and glazed over at the same time. He wondered what she was seeing behind that glaze, but he knew she'd tell the tale once she awoke.

After much scooting of chairs and plates and cookery clanging together, Gawan swept Ellie up into his arms, carried her to the couch, and settled her comfortably.

"What do we do now, sir?" Jason asked, ever so attentive.

"We wait," Gawan answered.

Jason nodded, and the others all found some object or another to lean on. And waited.

It didn't take long for Ellie to come round.

At first, she only blinked, as though trying to focus on her surroundings. Then her body tensed, and her hand immediately sought his.

Gawan thought he'd give ponder to what *that* could mean, exactly, later on.

Ellie's fingers squeezed Gawan's hand, and she drew

in a deep breath. Her gaze right away hunted his. He briefly wondered if she knew she did it.

"What did you see, lady?" Jason asked.

Ellie shook her head, as though trying to clear the fog. "A book or log. A ledger, maybe. That's it. A leather-bound ledger." She thought a moment. "It was *me,* kneeling in front of an old bureau, and I have this ledger open on my lap."

"Is there aught in the ledger, then?" Tristan asked.

Her gaze moved from Tristan's back to Gawan's. "Yes. Pages upon pages of writing." Her eyes narrowed as she pondered. "I must have only read a small portion of it in my vision. It says *Northumberland, England, by the seaside. Lad murdered, body not found. Another lad, disappeared, assumed dead. Titled. Gone.*" Her eyes widened. "And a signature. Phineas."

"Does the name mean anything to you, girl?" Gawan said. "Or the ledger?"

"Aye, or does it shake loose a memory?" asked Sir Godfrey, who'd moved closer to Ellie.

Ellie glanced around, and then shrugged. "The vision *feels* familiar, yet I don't remember *doing* any of it."

"So you think that's what brought you here?" Andi asked.

Ellie nodded. "Possibly." She closed her eyes. "Maybe if I concentrated a little harder."

Gawan's heart twinged a bit at the look on Ellie's face, so desperate was she to find answers. Not a single emotion could she hide. Not even when she'd announced, with great fluster, that the kiss they'd shared had meant nothing.

It had meant far more than she could possibly imagine. Christ, he'd stolen her Intended's kiss.

He'd do the same again.

Closing his fingers around hers, which had surprisingly remained with a firm grip, he tugged her up. "Come, Ellie of Aquitaine."

Her eyes flew open and met his.

"There are a few things we must discuss." He glanced around at the Dreadmoor knights, who all had leaned just a bit more forward. "Alone."

Several disappointed grumbles sounded through the men.

Tristan waved a hand in the air. "You men, cease that wailing, and hasten to the sports solar. There's an American football game on satellite we don't want to miss."

The grumbles quickly changed into shouts of excitement. All except the lady Dreadmoor, who simply rolled her eyes.

"Gawan, Ellie, if you need me, I'll either be in the library, or facedown in a carton of Ben and Jerry's in the kitchen with Jameson," Andi said, then smiled. "Seriously. Just holler if you need me."

"We shall indeed holler, should we need you," Gawan said. Then he gave her a nod and guided Ellie to the staircase.

"Where are we going?" she asked.

"Somewhere quiet, and I vow it won't be anywhere close to the sports solar."

Just as they reached the stairs, Tristan pulled Gawan aside. "Be strong, lad. I've heard great tales of your fierceness on the battlefield—you've even the markings to prove it." An annoying smile cracked the Dragonhawk's face in twain. "But as I stand here, you look as though you're quite close to losing your supper stew."

Gawan wouldn't admit that was *exactly* how he felt. "Many thanks, my friend. I shall endeavor to keep said stew in my belly at all costs."

He and Ellie continued up the stairs, and Tristan's irritating laughter echoed behind them through the great hall.

Ellie remained quiet as Gawan led her through the corridors and passageways, to a chamber he felt positive he'd gain a bit of peace.

The north tower.

Tristan had mentioned he'd done a bit of renovating after the curse had been broken, and that this chamber in particular was his Brooding Chamber. Gawan remembered it as being a turreted room at the top of Dreadmoor, indeed, but enclosed, all except the arrow slits and a rather small window opening. A room, in Gawan's mind, that was more suited for solitary confinement.

"Good Lord," Ellie said as they began the climb to the tower, "where the *bleep* are you taking me? To the roof?"

Gawan chuckled, glad for the break in silence. It settled his pitiful nerves, somewhat. "Aye, 'tis in fact the roof. Rather, the tower." He glanced down at her. "Why do you oft say *bleep* in place of a curse?" He thought it vastly charming.

As she climbed the stairs, her breathing became a bit more arduous. "I'll . . . tell you . . . once . . . I . . . remember."

They made it to the top, and Gawan reached in front of Ellie, opened the massive oak door, and gave it a push. Ellie walked in first.

"Oh, wow," she said, her voice breathy, and not completely because of their grueling climb. "This is great."

Gawan stepped in, and, indeed, his reaction was the same. "Wow is right."

Tristan had, in truth, created a most becoming Brooding Chamber. Gone were the arrow slits. Gone was the small window. 'Twas like a garden room, only at the top of the bloody castle. The hearth had remained against the left wall, but the turreted walls, which faced the sea, had been knocked out and replaced by no less than seven-foot windows. Six in all, they gave the Brooder an uninterrupted view of the tumultuous North Sea from all angles. Gawan knew the scene during the fullness of daylight would be fair breathtaking.

Gawan closed the door, then guided Ellie to the one piece of furniture in the chamber: a large overstuffed leather sofa, which, of course, faced the tall windows.

"Here," he said, moving in front of the sofa, "sit down."

Ellie gave him a skeptical look and raised one eyebrow.

He drew in a breath and smiled. "Please."

She did indeed sit, and not for the first time, Gawan noticed that the lady Dreadmoor's clothing did rather flatter Ellie's lovely curves. She wore a softish-looking brown wool tunic, a pair of jeans, and a rather comfortable-looking pair of leather boots. All of that glorious hair was left hanging freely down her back, and Gawan knew then he'd never seen a more beautiful sight. He wanted mightily to thread his hands into that hair.

"Um, hello?" Ellie snapped her fingers in the air. "Earth to Conwyk."

Gawan blinked, then gave a nod. "Right. I brought you here to discuss matters, not gawk at your beauty. Forgive me."

Now Ellie blinked, and then her cheeks turned a rather charming shade of pink. "Oh." She squirmed, then shifted on the sofa and tucked one leg under her bottom. "Please tell me you're going to sit down to talk. You're making me nervous, standing over me like that."

With a gusty sigh, Gawan sat down on the opposite end of the sofa, in the corner, and sprawled his legs out in the most comfortable of positions he could think of.

"I already know you're an Angel, if that's what you're so worried about."

Gawan regarded her. "Lady Follywolle?"

Ellie nodded. "She sort of spilled the beans in the kitchen. No, actually before that," she said, tucking a long strand of hair behind her ear. "Back at Castle Grimm—only I didn't put two and two together at the time."

Rubbing his chin with a knuckle, he grinned. "What made you put it together this time?"

"Well"—she glanced at him—"Lady Follywolle

started wailing and crying, and Lady Beauchamp tried to get her not to say it." She shrugged. "But I pried it out of her anyway." Now Ellie regarded him, a slow perusal before staring hard into his eyes.

He all but squirmed in his seat.

"How did it happen?"

This, Gawan thought, he could handle with a bit of tact. 'Twas the *other* thing—that Ellie was his *Intended*—he was rather nervous about.

He hoped his stew did in fact find a comfortable place in his belly soon.

After a glance at Ellie, who hung on his every word, he wasn't so sure anymore.

Bleedin' priests, he could fair believe himself not only to be an Angel, but an ex-warlord. With a deep calming breath, he began what he hoped to be a decent version of his own odd predicament.

Saints be with him.

Sixteen

"I was born in the year of our Lord 1115 in the north of Wales. It's passing odd to think of those times now, yet they seem as close as yesterday." Gawan shook his head. "My sire was a fierce warlord, and I followed directly into his footsteps, as was expected. By the time I'd reached nine winters, I'd already killed—I can't recall how many men. Hardly a month passed that we weren't at odds with the English, or the Norse, or an angry neighboring clan." He shrugged. "Fighting was all I knew, and I became rather good at it. Especially with the blade."

"That's pretty obvious," Ellie said. "You're amazing to watch." Her face softened, maybe even saddened a bit. "I can't imagine you as a little nine-year-old boy killing someone."

He gave her a slight nod, although her lack of mortification at his young character gave him more courage than he cared to admit. "Aye, 'tis a skill I was rather determined not to lose—with my sword, that is—despite the blood that had been shed because of it in my early years. And aye, nine was rather young, but 'twas how things were managed in my day. 'Twas a brutal time."

"I see that." Ellie shifted again, to more fully face Gawan. "But before today, nobody could have possibly convinced me that you'd shed any blood." She shook her head. "You're levelheaded." She smiled. "Sweet, even. But after the sword hacking I saw you do with

Tristan earlier? Yeah, I can believe it now. Definitely amazing."

With a laugh, Gawan, too, turned to more fully face her. "I daresay I was anything but sweet. I was a disgusting, dirty, bloodthirsty heathen in those days, lady. 'Tis no secret that whilst I did what I had to do to survive, I also took pride in the number of enemies I'd slain."

"Show 'er your markings boy, an' get on wi' it!"

Ellie jumped, and Gawan shook his head and glanced at the door. "Sir Godfrey, could you please escort your nosy self—along with the Grimm ladies, who no doubt have their ears pressed to the door—*away*? This is a private discussion."

"We want to hear all about it, young Conwyk," Lady Follywolle said, her voice somewhat muffled. "Do promise you'll give us full details later?"

"Godfrey, now," Gawan said.

All three sighs, overdramatized, to Gawan's notion, could be heard on the other side of the door. "Very well," Godfrey said. "Come on, ladies." Then a mumbled curse, followed by "Blasted party pooper."

Gawan glanced at Ellie, who had her fingers pressed to her lips, smothering a grin. Or, rather, keeping a laugh from falling out.

"Meddlesome peahens," Gawan muttered. But a smile pulled at his mouth.

"So that's what those tattoos are across your chest and back?" Ellie said, and moved her stare across him. "And your arms? Marks of how many men you've killed?"

Gawan glanced down at one of the black symbols, barely showing beneath the cuff of his tunic. It was the very last one he'd burned into his flesh as a mortal. He ran a thumb over it. "Aye. They're ancient Pict symbols."

"Don't forget to tell her what they mean, Conwyk!"

Gawan rubbed a hand over his brow. "Godfrey, by the saint's robes, begone!"

"Fine, then. Just makin' sure you don't scare the girl off."

Gawan rose and headed to the door. "I'm not going to scare the girl off, Godfrey." God, he prayed he didn't, anyway. Mayhap she thought him a barbarian, no matter that he'd done his bloodshedding centuries before. 'Twas a gory existence he'd once led.

He yanked open the door and poked his head out. The corridor was indeed now empty. "Stay gone. And I mean it."

Ellie's giggle sounded behind him, which made him feel that mayhap she didn't think him an animal. When he shut the door and turned around, Ellie, too, had risen from her spot on the sofa and now stood, staring out of one of the massive windows.

He moved to do the same, yet kept a safe distance between them. He didn't want to make her feel hemmed in.

Although, he admitted to himself, he wanted nothing more than to hem her in. Pull her soft body against his, slide his fingers through that fine mass of hair. *Saints.*

"Okay, so you were a stinky bloodthirsty, warlord." She turned, smiled, and regarded him. "What do the markings mean?"

Dolt. Can you keep your lecherous mind to task for a single second? "In truth, they're sort of a number system. Each symbol stands for a certain number, a specific battle. A cluster of enemies, if you will."

Without warning, Ellie stepped toward him and reached for his hand. She lifted it, and he allowed it, and then she pushed his cuff up and brought it closer to her eyes. She studied it for several seconds, and then, damnation, she traced it with the very soft pad of her index finger. His entire bloody arm tingled.

"So this symbol here," she said, still tracing the mark. "How many does it represent?"

Without hesitation, Gawan said, "Twenty-five." And well he should easily remember. The last had been naught but an innocent boy.

Ellie lowered his hand, but she did not let go of it. "Let me get this straight." She looked at him. "Each symbol represents a specific battle and a cluster of men you've killed."

"Aye."

"All in battle?"

Gawan nodded, his eyes unable to look directly at hers, so he stared out the window instead.

She stepped closer, and blast her, she threaded her slim fingers through his own. "So tell me, Mr. Stinky Warlord. If you were so horrible, as I can tell you seem to think you were"—she moved in front of him, her back to the glass window, forcing him to look at her—"then how did you become an Angel?" The smile she offered was soft and, dared he hope, understanding. "They don't let just any old smelly, bloodthirsty swordswinger become an Angel, last I heard."

She smiled. By the saints, she understood.

His heart melted.

At that moment, she gently dropped her hand from his and moved away, just a bit, and continued staring toward the sea. 'Twas a good thing, to his mind, because a minute more and he would have had her pressed against that blasted window, his lips moving over hers, *tasting*. . . .

"Ooo-kay. So. How *exactly* did you become an Angel?"

Shoving his hands into his pockets to keep from touching her, he continued. " 'Twas in a battle. I found an injured boy. A warrior, in truth—he certainly had a lethal blade in his hand—but a boy, just the same. No more than twelve, I suspect, and he had a nasty slash"—he pointed to the left side of his chest—"just here. As I dragged him to safety, another warrior attacked."

She turned from the window to face him, her face tense. "That's when you were killed?"

"Aye. 'Twas the lad's father, no less, thinking I'd killed his boy." He shrugged. "I'd have done the same."

"But the boy, even though he was young, was still on the opposing team, or the guys you were fighting. Right?"

" 'Twas a Moor, indeed. During the Crusades. Still"—he shook his head—"if only I knew then what I know now."

Silence stretched for what seemed like minutes. Far too long for Gawan's liking. Then Ellie spoke softly.

"It's you in that tapestry in your great hall, isn't it?" Her eyes searched his. "The only warrior without battle gear on, riding beside Queen Eleanor."

So many centuries ago, yet it seemed like yesterday, Eleanor of Aquitaine herself delivered the stitching. "Aye, 'tis me." He shrugged. "Rather, a depiction of me. The medievals—we were a dramatic lot, you know."

"Right. I knew it the first time I saw it, up close. Well," she said, turning and pressing her nose against the window, "I had a feeling that warrior looked familiar. Same tattoos, same hair. I knew it was you." She sighed. "Look, you can see the snow falling through the moonlight, and the waves in the ocean. It's so beautiful out there"—she tapped the glass with her fingernail, making a *click-click* sound—"it almost hurts to look at it."

Christ, how he knew the feeling. He studied every inch of her, from the way her little nose pushed upward from the pressure against the glass, to her long lashes that brushed her cheeks when she blinked, to every small movement her lips made when she spoke.

Besotted, Tristan had called him. Aye, he truly was that.

He cleared his throat and spoke, before he did something ridiculous, like act on that besottedness and kiss her again.

"Aye, 'tis a magnificent view, indeed."

"So you were awarded Angelhood, or whatever it's called, by saving the life of your enemy when you really didn't have to. Right?"

"Right."

She began to pace, pondering out loud in that charming way she had. "That was what year, exactly?"

"1145."

She whistled, long and low. "God, you're old."

Gawan chuckled. "Aye, so I am."

At the hearth, she turned, a grin on her face. "You know what I mean. So you were, what? Thirty, when you died?"

"Closer to thirty-one, but aye," he said, following her to the hearth. He'd thank Jameson later for building such a fine fire. The room was justly warm, not too much so.

Stretching her hands toward the flames, she rubbed her palms together. "Okay, bear with me as I try to piece all this together. You've been an Angel for nearly a thousand years, because of the selfless act of trying to save the life of your enemy in battle. Right?"

"Aye."

"So why didn't you want to tell me any of this before?"

Now the Brooding Chamber was beginning to feel like a bloody furnace.

"I am"—he now had to count, having lost track of the days—"nineteen days from retirement, Ell. You're my assigned charge, and I have to see your situation settled properly before the Yuletide's eve, at midnight."

She moved closer, blast her. "Or?"

He sighed and swiped a hand over his jaw. "Or I lose my retirement."

"Which means?"

Damn, he sounded like an idiot. "Which means—"

"He'll lose the only chance he's got at livin' out his mortal life!"

Gawan closed his eyes, muttered a fine Welsh curse or two, then opened his eyes again. "Godfrey, by Christ—"

"Fine! I'm leaving. Just don't forget to tell the girl everything, lad. Everything!"

Ellie's face had gone decidedly pasty. "There's *more*?" She clapped a hand over her forehead. "Oh, gosh, I can't believe I've possibly altered a retiring Angel's pending mortalism."

Damnation, how he didn't want to tell her another bloody thing. He knew, though, with little thanks to Godfrey, that lace-wearing peahen, that she'd pester him until he *did* tell. " 'Tisn't your fault, Ell, and I vow to set things aright before long. We've nearly three weeks."

She slid her hand over her eyes, then peeped through a crack made between two fingers. "Stop skirting, Conwyk. Tell me *everything*." She dropped her hand and narrowed her eyes. "And I mean it."

He cleared his throat. Best to get this over with now. "You're my—er, let me start over. We, um, you see, damn." A hank of hair fell from his queue and into his eyes, and he let the bloody thing stay there. "You're my Intended, Ellie of Aquitaine. We"—he waved a hand between the two of them—"are each other's Intended."

There. He'd said it. He'd told the bloody telling of it.

And he waited for her response.

That stew from earlier suddenly did not want to stay put. . . .

Ellie couldn't help it. A bubble of something—not gas, thank God, but something—welled up inside her. She tried oh so mightily to stop it from finding an exit. But it found one anyway.

She snorted.

Quickly, she covered her mouth with her hand, just in case another one slipped out.

Gawan just looked at her. Blank face—no, take that back. He looked ready to *hurl*.

She stepped backward, just in case.

With her thumb and forefinger, she grabbed her lips

and pinched them together for, oh, as long as she could stand it without hollering. It was a method she'd perfected as a kid, when her brother was whispering something wicked in her ear, trying to make her laugh at the most inappropriate times.

Gawan quirked a brow and cocked his head. "Is there aught amiss with you?"

Finally, she got a grip. "Sorry. But for some reason, it just struck me funny." She met his stare. "What, exactly, does that mean? *Intended*?"

His eyes darted to the corner of her mouth. "Forever mates of the soul, Ell."

Whump. Talk about heart falling to bottom of stomach.

Although, she quickly reflected, it was pretty darn cute, the way he kept referring to her as *Ell* . . .

"Do you understand, girl?" he asked.

"Well, sort of," she said. A flutter of excitement she couldn't explain grew within her. "Tell me more." She took another step toward him. "Lots more."

Gawan's face visibly blanched. "Er, aye, well"—he scratched his ear—"we're destined, sort of, by Fate to belong to, mayhap, each other." He coughed. "Forever."

Where her boldness came from, she hadn't a clue. She *knew* there was more than simple attraction between them. Knew it. Nah, she didn't *really* know it. Secretly wished for it, though.

She stood before the fire, maybe a foot away from Gawan. She looked up, into his eyes. "How did you know? That I was your Intended, I mean."

For a long moment, Gawan didn't say anything. He looked down at his shoes, flicked a piece of something off his jeans, rubbed his brow. Then, as if a button had been pushed, he looked up.

And Ellie all but had to back up to the wall to stay upright.

Dark brown eyes had turned smoldering, and a muscle flexed in his jaw. His brows pulled not into a frown, but into *determination*. "The Welsh believe in many things, girl. Some may call it lore, but we believe in it, wholly and in truth. 'Tis said that a man can recognize his one and true Intended by a wee mark in the corner of her mouth." His eyes grew even darker. " 'Tis unmistakable, that mark. And you have it."

Ellie gulped. "You mean"—she lifted her finger and touched the side of her mouth—"here?"

Gawan closed the small distance between them, and moved her hand away. "Nay," he said, his voice quieter, and lifted his finger to graze the other side of her mouth. "Here."

Ellie's heart slammed against her ribs so hard, she thought the bones would break. The fact that Gawan kept his finger to the corner of her mouth made her breath catch in her throat.

"Is that why I feel this ridiculous attraction to you?" she asked. "Because there's a mark on my mouth?"

"Mayhap," he answered, barely, his eyes now liquid chocolate. "Damnation, Ell . . ."

Lifting her hand, she placed it on Gawan's wrist, and his muscles tensed at her touch. "The night you kissed me, I remember you especially took your time on that particular corner." God, she felt drunk, even as she moved her hand to cover his, the one still touching that crazy mark she didn't even know she had. "Why?"

Gawan didn't even have to touch her for Ellie to feel the barely restrained control he had building inside that powerful frame. He all but hummed with it, and it wrapped around her like a hot, heavy blanket, and she *liked* it.

His head lowered, slowly, but his eyes remained fixed on hers. "Because, girl"—his breathing had grown raspy, even more so as his finger traced the tiny scar beneath her bottom lip—"that night, I—"

His words were lost as Ellie rose and kissed him.

Seventeen

Somehow, even in the heat of the most passionate kiss she'd ever experienced, Ellie knew it was a kiss to defy all kisses in the history of Best Kisses Ever. Better than Burt and Deborah's roll-in-the-surf kiss in *From Here to Eternity*. Better, even, than the sexy yet desperate kiss between George Bailey and Mary Hatch while that jerk Sam Wainwright blabbed on the phone in *It's a Wonderful Life*. Better than the first Ross and Rachel kiss, for crying out loud. Better than Mulder and Scully's first kiss on *The X-Files*. She'd waited *forever* for that one.

Even better—dared she think it—than the famous upside-down *Spider-Man* kiss.

As Ellie pressed her mouth against Gawan's, she felt the world tilt as he took complete control. That pent-up energy she'd felt emanating from him before broke loose, and her skin all but burst into flames everywhere he touched her. And golly, did he ever touch her.

As one hand slid beneath her hair to cup the back of her neck, the other skimmed her jaw, held it in place, tilted it just so, while his mouth devoured hers. There was no hesitancy this time, no tender tasting of that funny mark on the side of her mouth. It was an all-out, you're-*mine* kind of kiss, a sort of *branding,* she thought, and Gawan left not one millimeter untouched.

Thank *God*.

Her own hands first held on to his arms for dear life,

but then Ellie found, with fascination, they'd crept up to Gawan's face, where she felt the rough texture of his stubbled jaw, then closer to his mouth, *their* mouths, as their passionate kiss spiraled. Finally, she fastened her hands around his neck, fingered the knot holding his queue, and then loosened his wild boyish curls.

Gawan made a deep noise in his throat or his chest—she couldn't determine which. It sounded hungry. Untamed. Feral.

Determined.

His mouth moved over hers in a way that nearly made Ellie cry out, not in pain, but in fear of him *stopping*. He was everywhere, and in one place, all at once, tasting her lips, grazing her tongue with his, as if he were an animal, and she his very last meal. Only *sexier*.

Somehow, they'd moved, and Ellie found her back pressed against the rough stone of the Brooding Chamber's wall. Gawan's one hand remained close to her mouth, holding her jaw or, more likely, guarding that crazy corner of her mouth. His other hand moved possessively down her side, over her hip, and—golly, Moses!—beneath her sweater to graze her ribs.

Breathing suddenly became difficult as his callused palms skimmed the skin of her stomach, inched higher, hesitated, then came back across her side. She was pressed hard against him now, and her one hand tangled in his long hair, the other—how on earth had she found her way into his buttoned-up, tucked-in shirt?—caressing the hard muscles of his abdomen. She *felt* just how *Intended* she was for Gawan of Conwyk.

"Christ Almighty, girl," he muttered, his mouth leaving hers, only to find a new place to taste her neck.

And God, his accent, which was completely sexy, was decidedly much thicker than usual, almost to the point where she had a hard time understanding what he'd said at all. The way *girl* came out *gel* . . .

And then she felt it. Knew what it was as though an aura before a seizure. Quickly, she tugged his mouth back to hers and kissed him deep, took control, made him simmer down.

She opened her eyes to find his staring back, passion-filled and beautiful. Their lips still pressed together, Ellie smiled against his mouth and moved to whisper in his ear, just as his touch became less solid, and she started to feel light. She heard him swear, ever so softly, in medieval Welsh.

She kissed his earlobe. "I'll be right back."

Then she vanished into thin air.

Gawan closed his eyes, leaned against the wall, and tried to get his bloody breathing under control. Sweet Christ, had she not vanished, he would have taken her on Tristan's Brooding Sofa. He hadn't been able to control himself, and by the bloody saints, she'd been no help, slipping her deft little hands inside his tunic. She might as well have drawn and quartered him, rather than skim his stomach with her soft fingertips. Oy, how it left him in pain.

"By the"—he pushed forcefully off the wall—"bloody . . . damnation!" he shouted, then followed those useless words with a litany if Welsh curses.

Then he stopped. Froze, truth be told. A noise, a whisper, mayhap? He couldn't be sure. He strained his ears.

And then, by Christ's robes, he *frowned*.

With as much stealth as he could muster, Gawan eased over to the door, flexed his fingers a time or two, and then in one fluid motion flung opened the massive oak door.

Several Dragonhawk knights tumbled through the doorway. There were more, all of them, in fact, including the Dragonhawk himself, crammed into the passageway. Along with, Gawan noted, Godfrey, Christian, and the Grimm ladies.

The only two occupants of Dreadmoor Castle missing were the lady Dragonhawk and Jameson.

Gawan stood, arms crossed, *glaring* at the witless fools trying to stand upright after falling over one another.

"Damnation, Grimm," Sir Stephen said, "ye took a fair amount of time, aye?"

"And ye still didn't tell the lass all there is to know," Sir Robert said, elbowing another out of his way. "By St. Michael's boots, you should have told her."

"Damnation, I had no chance," Gawan said, even knowing he probably did. "I tried to."

Jason, younger and usually quite a bit more light-hearted than the others, gave Gawan a stern look of disproval. "Shame on you, sir, an Angel such as yourself, taking privileges with the lady. And her *In Betwinxt*." The lad shook his head, then turned around and walked off.

"I couldn't bloody well help it!" Gawan said, somehow feeling put to place by a lad not yet twenty. "Fine lot you all are, listening in at the doorway." He glared at Godfrey. "I told you to stay away."

Sir Godfrey offered a slight nod, the oversized plume in his hat bouncing forward. "Aye, ye did, in truth, but I've never been one to listen very well, I'm afraid."

"We only wanted to make sure the girl was told everything," Lady Follywolle said. " 'Tis a delicate matter at hand, you know."

"I do bloody well know," Gawan said under his breath. "Far more than you can possibly imagine." That he said in Welsh.

Lady Follywolle gasped.

"Listen, my friend," Tristan said, placing a hand on Gawan's shoulder and leading him away from the door. "We didn't hear everything, in truth, really—just a lot of harsh breathing."

"Don't forget the *Christ Almighty* that a certain *some-one* growled out," one brave knight said.

All the knights roared with laughter.

"You men, cease your mockery this instant, and allow me to have a spot of decent, *private* speech with Con-wyk here."

Tristan and Gawan walked to the massive windows.

"I speak for all of us when I say we have only your—and the lady Ellie's—best interests at heart." He shrugged. "And a bit of curiosity, as well, I suppose. 'Tisn't every day that a thousand-year-old Angel finds his Intended."

Gawan considered that. "Aye, Tristan, 'twould be quite fascinating if my Intended wasn't firstly, *In Betwinxt* and, secondly, my *charge.*" He rubbed his eyes, where a pounding headache had slowly started developing. " 'Tis hopeless, but by Christ, I can't live without her."

The Brooding Chamber, Gawan noticed, had become decidedly quiet. When he turned, several of the knights had a most ridiculous expression stuck to their faces, which they covered up rather fast by grumbling, swearing, and pushing one another out of the room quite fast. One of them belched, they all laughed, and it was then determined that the best place to hasten to would be the larder, to seek out a bit of Ben and Jerry's before the lady Dragonhawk ate it all.

Sir Godfrey gave a low bow, his plume waving. "I shall escort these fine ladies back to Grimm, young Conwyk, as I see you've things under control here." He turned to Tristan. "Dreadmoor. Pleasure, as always."

Tristan gave a nod. "You Grimm folk are welcome here, as always."

Lady Follywolle sighed, and Lady Beauchamp giggled.

"We shall see you thusly then, Lord Dreadmoor," she said with a curtsy. "Come, Godfrey, whilst the night is still young."

Godfrey took each Grimm lady by the elbow, threw a grin over his lace-and-velvet shoulder, and the three disappeared through the wall.

Christian of Arrick-by-the-Sea remained quiet, taking everything in, standing near the hearth.

Gawan tossed him a glance. "And what say you, Chris? You're usually so bloody bold of tongue."

Christian joined Gawan and Tristan by the window.

With a slight grin, he stared out into the darkness. "You won't like what I have to say, Conwyk."

Gawan chose to ignore that and instead replied, "Had I known but a bit of mushy speech would have kept the lads away, I would have said it to begin with." Gawan stared out into the darkness, the moon slicing into pitch like a farmer's sickle.

He couldn't stand it another second. Turning, he faced his ghostly friend. "What? You might as well say it, Arrick, for I know you well enough that it won't stay bottled up inside you for long."

Tristan chuckled.

"Very well, then," Christian said, a somber grin fixed to his face. "What I think, Gawan of Conwyk, is that you should do well and true to make the very best of your situation with your Intended, such as it is. At least you'll have your mortal life to live out, even if it's not with her." He inclined his head. "And Dreadmoor here, well, he surpassed his odds, true enough. But look you what he's found after all. Over seven hundred years of roaming, and he now lives and breathes the breath of the living. He has a lovely wife, who carries his babe." He glanced back out into the darkness. "His men, as well, broke free from their curse." He shook his head and gave Gawan a nod. "Methinks you'd do best by accepting what you are given, whether that be little or bountiful. Either way," he said, fading away, " 'tis far more than a ghost shall ever endeavor to have." He placed a hand on the hilt of his sword. "I'm off, mates. I've a queer feeling about my own homestead of late, of which I feel the need to investigate straightaway."

"How fairs the old caretaker?" Tristan asked. "Getting on in years, I imagine."

Christian nodded. "Aye, but full of spice, that old girl." He scratched his jaw. "But I've noticed her of late meeting with a few of her cronies up the way at her cottage, and then 'tis been nearly a sen'night now, I've not seen her at all." He shook his head. "I just feel the need to check on her." He gave another nod. "Until."

With that, he disappeared.

Gawan sighed. Put in his place once again. He did have a mortal life to look forward to—something Christian de Gaultiers of Arrick-by-the-Sea desired every waking moment of his ghostly existence, but would never have. He raked a hand through his hair and sighed again. "Mayhap he's right."

Tristan clapped him on his back. "Aye, in truth, he may very well be." He turned and started for the door. "But we've a photo to look over, and faxes to read. The storm hindered my solicitor from sending them earlier, but mayhap they've come through." He stood at the doorway. "Come, Conwyk, and we'll make an attempt to pry that iced concoction from my wife's sticky hands, gobble up what's left, and then try to figure out just what we can do to make sure you get to keep your Intended." He smiled. "As it was intended."

Gawan grabbed Tristan's forearm in a fierce shake—one of their old ways. "I thank you for your aid, truly."

Tristan returned the show of brotherhood with a fierce shake of his own. "Aye, and 'tis given without a single thought. You'd do the same for me, Conwyk, and I bloody well know it."

Dreadmoor was indeed right. Gawan thought of their unusual friendship, of how he'd already garnered Angel status by the time he first encountered the fierce knight Dragonhawk and his garrison. A mighty lot of lads, to be sure. And it had pained him to know he couldn't interfere when their murder occurred.

" 'Twas nothing you could have done, Conwyk," Tristan said. "Aye, I can read your thoughts just by looking at that somber expression on your face. Don't you see, man? 'Twas my lot in life to endure centuries of roaming, and I vow, I'd do it again. I wouldn't have my Andrea, had it gone differently." He grinned. "I am rather thankful for your friendship over the years, given my mood wasn't always sweet."

Gawan raised a brow. "I've seen very little of you for the past fifty years due to your foul humor. Fair drove me away, last time I recall."

Tristan laughed. "Aye, I did, and I'm truly sorry for it."

Stepping back, Gawan regarded his old friend. "I swear, this woman of yours has done you good. 'Tis a fine change in you, methinks."

"The power of true love, methinks," Tristan said.

As they quit the Brooding Chamber, Gawan gave it another glance. "You know, Dreadmoor, I believe I fancy this chamber of yours enough to duplicate it at Grimm. What say you?"

"I say 'tis a fine fancy you have, and you may speak with that young pup Jason about the matter. 'Twas he who came up with the design, after all. A smart lad, that one."

"Indeed," Gawan said. "I'll keep him in mind."

With that, they quit Tristan's Brooding Chamber and made their way to the great hall.

Musty. Sweet. Clovery, maybe? Dark, too. *Veeery* dark. And the scent of dank, wet stone . . .

Where was she? Gosh! If there was ever a *worse* time to vanish into thin air, she didn't know of it. Right smack in the middle of the Number One, *Numero Uno,* Top kiss of the Best Kiss Known to Man in the history of the world, and with her Intended, no less. Why did she have the distinct feeling that was just the way her luck usually ran?

Hot. She was very, very hot. She tried to open her eyes, but they felt glued together. When she tried to lift her hand, or a foot, they, too, felt as heavy as a cement block. Yet her mind raced like the wind, taking in smells and temperatures and . . .

. . . voices. Muffled, maybe far off, but yes! Voices. A man's and a woman's. Ellie couldn't make out the words, but by the rise and fall in pitch and tone, it didn't sound like a very happy conversation.

It sounded more like an argument.

Doing her best to clear her mind of that blazing-hot kiss she and Gawan had shared—not to mention the feel of his hands against her skin, which she swore she could still feel, nor the overwhelming sensation of feeling in her heart from the mere thought of him—she took a deep, cleansing breath and strained her ears, hoping to catch anything of the conversation.

Then, blessedly, she did.

The voices grew closer, still muffled, as if they were talking into a tin can, but Ellie was able to make out some, if not all, words.

"American . . . damnit, woman . . . bobby . . . look . . . shoulder . . . dead . . . Jaysus—"

"More time . . . looks better . . . dunno be . . . fool . . . more time . . . jail . . ."

And then the voices were snuffed out, and shards of light began piercing Ellie's eyes. She struggled to remember every word she could make out, the smells—she thought she'd even heard a cow moo.

Before she could brace herself, she was lunging head-first into a tunnel. A tight, dark tunnel, with a teensy spot of light that grew larger and larger at the end. Where the *bleep* were the brakes?

Eighteen

Gawan stared at the photograph with utter amazement.

'Twas Ellie. *His* Ellie. Caught completely unawares by the photographer as she stood at the back of Tristan's holiday cottage, facing the North Sea as the sky's dramatic clouds formed overhead, her back straight with arms wrapped tightly about herself, that wild, riotous hair whipping about her and, had she been wearing a swath of roughened wool draped about her, and mayhap a pair of high-laced boots, a splash of indigo across her cheeks, and a dagger or two stuffed into her belt, she'd look just like a Welsh warrior maiden, in truth.

His Ellie, he'd thought.

He glanced around, without moving his head, to see if by chance he'd said it aloud.

Nay, he hadn't, he realized as he watched the men in their various chairs, reading whatever book they'd filched from the library. And certainly, if he had said it aloud, he would have heard about it by now. The Dreadmoor knights were, if anything, merciless.

"The fax is in, Conwyk," Tristan called from the library.

Indeed, just as Gawan rose from his stool by the hearth, the fax machine began a series of *beeps* as it chugged out whatever papers Tristan's solicitor had managed to send.

As he crossed to the library, the knights behind him

rose, as well, and followed him into the massive reading room.

Gawan went straight to the fax machine, perched upon a heavy, solid oak desk. The first page came out, and Tristan immediately handed it over to Gawan.

The lady Dreadmoor, who leaned against the desk beside her husband, walked over to Gawan and read the paper in silence with him.

"Does it have anything of import, sir?" Jason asked.

"Aye, like mayhap her name?" Sir Christopher, who had moved closer, said. "Or mayhap an address, even."

Gawan scanned the first page. " 'Tis a questionnaire of sorts, and aye"—he felt a slight ding of excitement—"it has a name and address." He peered at the typed-in answers. "It says *Nunya Bizz* for the name." He glanced at Andi. "Nunya Bizz? What sort of a name is that?" Ellie, for some odd reason, did not look like a *Nunya Bizz* to him.

"Oh, geez," Andi said, then pointed to the address. "The whole thing is a fake. Look," she said, dragging her finger beneath the address. "One Mainstreet, Mayberry, PoDunk, USA."

"What does that mean?" Jason asked, although Gawan already had a feeling he knew what. "PoDunk? 'Tis a strange-sounding village, to be sure."

"Nunya Bizz, I'm guessing, is slang for None of Your Business. And this address? Mayberry? PoDunk? Those are all names used in reference to the South." She rubbed her head. "Although she was accurate in the USA part."

Gawan scrubbed his jaw. "Now *that* sounds just like something she'd do." He glanced at Andi. "But why? I wonder."

"Colonists. They do the most damnable things, in truth," Tristan said. "I did warn you, lad, about American maids, although I'll have to speak to my solicitor about being more cautious with these questionnaires. Po-

Dunk, indeed—wait, here's another page coming through." He handed it to Gawan.

After glancing over it, Gawan read the information out loud. "Mayhap this one is correct. Name: Mary Bailey. Address: Thirteen Bedford Falls."

Andi sighed and placed a hand on Gawan's arm. "I'm afraid it's a fake, too." She pointed at the name and address he'd just read. "See here? Mary Bailey? Bedford Falls?"

Gawan gave her a blank look.

She reached out and gave her husband a punch in the arm. "Tristan, doesn't that ring a bell with you?"

At first, Tristan's face was as blank as Gawan's felt; then recognition flashed in his eyes. "Damn me, but it does now."

"Aye, 'tis that black-and-white Christmas movie the lady's made us watch a thousand times over the past two weeks," Kail said with a grumble. "I vow, if I have to watch it again, I shall hang myself."

The knights grumbled in agreement.

"I think it's a wondrous movie," Jason said, although his brow furrowed. "*It's a Wonderful Life.* But I don't understand why your solicitor didn't catch on, Sir Tristan."

Gawan stared down at the information required to let a holiday cottage from Dreadmoor Estates. "Indeed, man, your solicitor has allowed a very slippery fish to shimmy by." And he wondered, not for the first time, what would make Ellie give false information. It didn't make a bloody ounce of sense.

"Wait," Andi said, who'd taken the fax from Gawan. "There is a phone number here. An emergency contact number." She glanced at Gawan. "It's a long shot, but maybe she left a legitimate number, just in case something happened to her. She'd have been crazy to come to a foreign country and not have an emergency contact available."

"Indeed, but I am beginning to believe that, aye, Ellie is more addled than by what caused her near-demise." He inclined his head to the phone beside Tristan. "Do you mind?"

"Aye, man, call the number." He counted on his fingers. " 'Tis but four o'clock in the afternoon there. Surely, someone will answer."

A number of ayes sounded from the knights, who'd stood close by watching with interest. *A fine lot of men,* he thought. *Loyal. More like family.*

"Here's the country code for the US," Andi said, and handed him a slip of paper with the number on it.

"Aye, thank you," Gawan said, then punched in the country code, then the area code, then the number *Mary Bailey* had left in case of an emergency.

Oy, when Ellie reappeared again, he'd have to resist the urge to wring her scrawny little neck.

Someone on the other end picked up, and Gawan held up a hand. Everyone grew silent.

"Hello?" the voice said.

A voice that sounded *exactly* like Ellie's.

"Right, this is—"

"Ha-ha, I'm not really home, silly. And this is an unlisted number, so this has to either be Dad, Kyle, Kelly, or Bailey. Or I've gotten my bleeping self in trouble over in England, which, if that's the case, I'm up bleep creek without a bleeping paddle. Leave a message, will ya? Someone's bound to check my voice mail sooner or later, I hope."

A long *beep,* followed by silence, which, Gawan took the message leaver's advice and left a short message.

"I have reason to believe your sister is in danger. Call me here, in England, at this number. As soon as possible." He left his name and number, then clicked the OFF button on the cordless.

"Gawan, what's wrong?" Andi said. "You look like you've seen a ghost."

"Or heard one," said Tristan. "What did they say, man?"

"Aye, Conwyk, you're killin' me with all this waitin'," Kail said.

Gawan rubbed his brow. "Damn me, but 'twas her. 'Twas her own bloody phone." He began to pace, and hardly noticed that the knights who happened to be in his path moved out of his way. "Before I thought her quirkiness was rather charming, endearing, mayhap." He turned and faced Tristan. "But now I want nothing more than to strangle her."

"Oh, that's because you're in love with her, sir," Jason said, and he was rather proud of himself if the way he stood so cocksure meant anything. "Or else you wouldn't give a bloody fig, aye? And I must say, I've noticed it's made you rather stodgy, of late. 'Tis what love does, I assume, since Sir Tristan became just as stodgy when he first fell in love with Lady Andi."

The other knights chuckled.

Andi grinned and twirled a hank of Tristan's hair between her fingers. "Were you stodgy, my lord?"

With a swift move, Tristan pulled his wife onto his lap, and was rewarded with a squeal. "I'm passing stodgy now, and you'll humor me if you know what's good for you, wench."

The Dragonhawk knights whistled, cawed, and laughed at their leader's prowess to hush the lady Dreadmoor.

Gawan took a short moment to regard the two. Stodgy or not, the Scourge of England wore every ounce of love he felt for his lady on his tunic sleeve for everyone to see.

Damn, lucky whoreson.

"If I might intrude upon this vastly amusing revelry, I may be able to offer a bit of aid."

Gawan, like the rest of the occupants of the library, turned to the doorway, where Jameson, that stealthy

Dreadmoor steward, stood ramrod rigid, his black suit as crisp as the moment he'd put it on earlier that morning, and not a bloody gray hair out of place.

Gawan wondered how he managed the like.

"Aye, Jameson," Gawan said, shoving his hands in his pockets. "Any aid is welcome, as we've come to yet another dead end."

Jameson gave a slight nod. "Mayhap you could leave multiple messages on the voice mail, and leave various numbers, just in case you cannot be reached."

Gawan nodded. "Good thinking, man. I'll do it."

"And," Jameson continued, "mayhap the constable could trace the address of that number?"

"Aye," Tristan agreed, "and I daresay Hurley can be trusted. He helped settle some rather unsavory affairs before that blasted curse was broken, in truth."

Gawan nodded. His stupid self should have thought of that first. "Aye. Fine idea, that."

Tristan grinned, leaned over the legs of his wife, who was still sprawled across his lap, and gave Gawan a slap on the arm. " 'Tis the way of it, man, when your woman is at stake. The brain sort of turns to gruel."

Gawan frowned. "Gruel, indeed. Methinks it's beyond gruel. More like old, watery broth."

Several knightly chuckles filled the room.

"So, Sir Gawan," Jason said, coming to stand before him, arms crossed over his chest, and, Gawan noticed, nearly as tall as himself, "I've been giving much thought to the events of this afternoon—you know, between Lady Ellie and you."

More irritating, wolfish noises sounded from the knights.

"And," Jason continued, ignoring his mates, "well, beg pardon, sir, but methinks 'twould be justly right to accompany you back to Grimm."

Gawan studied the lad's face, ever so serious, all but for that mischievous twinkle in his eye. "And why, pray tell, do you think that, Jason?"

The young knight palmed his sword hilt and held Gawan's gaze with a most serious one, indeed. "To guard your lady's honor, of course."

Gawan narrowed his eyes. "Against *whom*?"

A smile tugged at Jason's mouth, but he held his gaze steady. "Why, against you, of course."

Through the muck of ayes and arghs and oys that spread about the room, Gawan knew right then he'd never leave Dreadmoor without the lad.

And mayhap, he thought, remembering his last encounter with Ellie, Jason had it aright.

"It is a fine idea," Jameson said, his stoic features not changing once. "That poor girl should not be left unattended whilst lingering at Castle Grimm, no less."

Gawan gave Jameson a scowl. *And well deserved,* he thought.

The old steward's mouth twitched.

A rarity.

A quick glance at Tristan proved he wholeheartedly agreed. His wife, on the other hand, had a dreamy look about her that indeed reminded Gawan of Ellie.

"Jason's a wonderful guardsman, Gawan," Andi said. "Very dependable."

Jason gave Tristan's wife a nod. "Many thanks, my lady." He turned that blasted twinkling mischievous pair of eyes toward Gawan. "I'll be ready whenever you are, sir." Then he winked.

Gawan almost used his I'm-a-Bloody-Angel card, but knew 'twould be useless, especially considering that each of the Dreadmoor knights had heard Ellie and him inside the bloody Brooding Chamber.

With a frown, Gawan gave Jason a short nod. "Very well, pup. You shall be here and forever Ellie's personal guard." That stuck in his gorge, for some reason. "Against *me*."

That stuck in his gorge even more.

Someone snickered.

"But," Gawan said, just as Jason puffed up like the

cocksure peahen he was, "let us get one thing affixed. And this goes for all of you," he said, glaring at every soul in the library. "There's been no mention of l—well, lo—er." Damn, he felt flustered all of a sudden. "Just because we're each other's Intended does not mean we've exchanged vows of lo—"

"Damnation, Conwyk," Tristan said, barking out a laugh. "I vow, 'tis a new side of you, seeing you stutter about so. Can you not even say the bloody word?"

More laughs.

Except from Tristan, who gave an airy *whumph,* once his lady sunk her wee elbow into his ribs.

"Aye, Grimm," said Kail, "we won't tell." He crossed his heart with his big, thick finger. "Promise."

Gawan watched all the occupants of Dreadmoor, including that wily steward, Jameson, have a good jest on him. When they were finished, and he did indeed allow them to finish, he scratched his ear and, God forbid, fought a grin himself. Instead, though, he cleared his throat and met their watery, mirth-filled gazes. "I vow this to each of you: I won't say the bloody word to you fools until it's been said to her first. And"—ignoring several head tosses, pointings of fingers, and why, by the saints, did Tristan have his forefinger across his lips, trying to shush him?—"just because I've kissed the maid doesn't mean I've vowed to l—er, love her. There! I've said the . . . bloody . . . word. . . ."

Everyone's gaze, for some eerie reason or another, rested *behind* him. Tristan pinched the bridge of his nose and shook his head. The lady Dragonhawk, by the by, had a look about her that damn near scared him.

Everyone else frowned.

And Gawan knew, just then, that he'd shown a weakness he hadn't even realized he'd had.

Until now.

With a gusty sigh, Gawan closed his eyes and, like Tristan, pinched the bridge of his nose. Hard. "She's right behind me, aye?"

Seventeen ayes crowded the library at once.

And then slowly, he, the biggest horse's arse in all of England, turned around. He opened his eyes. Peeked, rather, through tiny slits, hoping that would make the impact of seeing what he knew he would see seem not so mighty.

One could hope.

There stood Ellie, only not wounded by his idiot words.

A wide smile split her charming face. "I *remember*."

Nineteen

Oh, what she'd have given for a digital camera. Or a Polaroid. Either would have done. Whichever, she thought, would be faster at capturing the look on Gawan of Conwyk's gorgeous face. The look that said *Open mouth. Insert foot* or, better yet, *Look at me! I'm an idiot!*

Really, she had to concentrate not to look at him and laugh.

Even now, she noticed with an extreme, possibly a sick, unhealthy satisfaction, that his expression screamed *Thank the bloody saints, she didn't hear what I bloody said.* Only, she had heard. Heard, she noted, with more clarity than even she thought possible.

He *loved* her. He might have said just the opposite, but one thing she knew—rather, *felt* she knew about herself—was that she knew *people.* And she knew men. She had a father, two brothers and a sister and yes! She remembered them! And one thing she *vastly* recalled was the way her big, gruff, father—his name was Rick—tripped over his own tongue when trying to say the *l word.*

Just like Gawan had.

Now, *how* he knew he loved her, and in such a short time—and why on Earth did she feel as though she just might love him back, with or without that wacky Welsh mark at the corner of her mouth—she couldn't be sure.

Although, being an Angel, he perhaps had the skinny from someone more higher up than himself.

"Lady? What do you remember?" Gawan asked.

Ellie focused, slowly, though, as she came out of her weird internal conversation with herself, only to stare into the most beautiful, trusting eyes she'd ever seen.

Gosh, she didn't know if her real, fully alive self had this much confidence, but she certainly hoped so.

She smiled at Gawan. "Well," she said, as she allowed him to guide and then ease her onto a leather stool by the hearth. "I not only remember having a father, two brothers, and a sister, but this time, when I disappeared"— she looked up at him—"I heard voices. And I remember smells, as well."

Gawan crouched down in front of her, his dark brows pulled into a semifrown, that sexy hair loose from the queue, and those broad shoulders pulling the material of that ivory shirt taut. Good *Lord*, how was she supposed to concentrate?

"What did the voices say?" he asked. He didn't touch her, though.

Behind him, all of the Dreadmoor knights looked on. Anxious. Waiting.

She closed her eyes for a second, and recalled the disjointed voices, and then stood and paced in front of the fire. "There were two voices, male and female. The words came out choppy, so they don't really make a whole lot of sense."

"They might make sense to us, girl," Gawan said, rising and crossing his arms over his chest.

Ellie nodded. "That's what I'm hoping. Anyway." She glanced down at herself, straightened her sweater, and then continued. "The male voice spoke first, and he said, 'American. Damn it, woman. Bobby. Look. Shoulder. Dead. Jaysus.' And he said it just like that: *Jay-sus*. Heavy on the *jaaay*."

Gawan scratched his chin. "Sounds like an Irishman."

"American—that must mean you, lady," Jason said. "But who's Bobby?"

"Mayhap 'tis the speaker's name?" Kail said.

"Nay," answered Sir Richard, who came to keep in pace with Ellie. "He wouldn't have said his own name like that."

Kail scratched his ear. "Hmm. Quite right."

"What about *shoulder*?" said Gawan, staring at her shoulder. "Are you injured there?"

Ellie rotated her shoulder a time or two. "It doesn't hurt. But then, nothing really hurts, although something has to be wrong if I'm slipping in and out of consciousness."

"Okay, let's hear what the female voice said," Andi said. She'd climbed off Tristan's lap and now perched on the corner of his desk.

Ellie nodded. "Okay. She said, 'More time. Looks better. Dunno be. Fool. You'll see. Jail.' "

Gawan raked a hand through his hair, rubbed his jaw, then shoved his hands into his pockets. Ellie could tell by the strained look on his face how aggravated he was getting. "What else do you remember, girl? You mentioned smells?"

Ellie breathed in slowly, as if that alone could help recall the odors. But really, she didn't need it. She remembered with a striking brightness. "It smelled musty, like dampened stone, and supersweet, sort of . . . clovery, I guess. Earthy." She snapped her fingers. "And hay. I could smell hay this time, I think."

"Indeed, it sounds as though she could be anywhere along the coast," Tristan said.

Gawan mumbled a Welsh curse. Gosh, and the power she'd felt just before he'd kissed her—rather, before she'd kissed him—seeped out of him again.

Only this time, the power was fueled not by passion, but by fury.

"Blasted snow," he said, then cursed again. "It never

snows this early here." He once again scraped his knuckles over his eyes, then drew a deep breath, trying, Ellie noticed, to calm himself. It worked a *little*. " 'Twill be ceased by the morn, hopefully. Tristan, I'll be off first thing to your cottage. Then to have a word with the constable."

Tristan nodded. "Aye, and I'll go with you."

"What about the voice mail?" Andi said. "Maybe if she listens to it, another part of her memory might return."

"There's a voice mail?" Ellie asked.

A few snickers went through the knights like the wave through a stadium.

"Oy, girl, there's a voice mail. And there're these." Gawan slipped some papers from Tristan's desk and handed them to her. "Read these first and tell me if anything strikes you."

Ellie looked around, and then glanced at the papers Gawan had handed her.

At first, the papers made no sense at all. The first was a questionnaire of some sort, obviously filled out by . . . a . . . prankster.

Electricity zapped through her as she read both pages.

"Nunya Bizz? PoDunk? Bedford Falls? Good Lord, I can't believe that guy didn't even question me!" She waved the papers at Gawan. "That's *me*. I wrote all that when I rented the cottage. I've done it a gazillion times." She glanced at Tristan. "Sorry about that, Tris." She smiled, although it was a bit sheepish. "But your guy totally fell for it."

"Aye," Tristan said, a slight scowl fixed to his face, which she was awfully glad not to have directed at her. "My solicitor was apparently so charmed by you that he allowed his better judgment to stand down."

Gawan then gently tugged on the papers in her hand, and slipped something else in their place. A picture.

Ellie stared. And stared some more.

She looked up, her eyes met Gawan's. "That's *me.*"

"Aye, so it is." His eyes softened as they stared at her, and everyone else in the room ceased to exist.

"Voice mail?" Andi said.

Soundly bringing *everyone* back into the room at top speed.

"See you that number, girl?" Gawan said, pointing to a telephone number on one of the forms. "I called it. 'Tis you on the voice mail."

"Gawan, the phone," Tristan said.

Turning, he took the cordless from Tristan, punched in the numbers, and then gave the phone to Ellie. "Don't speak. Just listen."

And she did.

"I"—she shook her head—"always do that thing . . . with the . . . making people think I'm home. Ugh!" She handed the phone back to Gawan. "I'm starting to think my real, very much alive self is an annoying, bleeping lunatic."

The knights, as usual, were easy to amuse. They all chuckled.

Jameson—gosh, she didn't realize a guy could stand still for so long—finally moved. "If you heathens are quite finished with the lady, mayhap she'd like to retire to her own chamber for a bit of peace this eve?"

"I'll have a word with her first, Jameson." Gawan pierced Jason, of all people, with a dark scowl. "Alone."

Jason, who Ellie thought was such a cute, sweet guy, pointedly ignored that mean look on Gawan's face and smiled at her. "My lady, I've been awarded the fine duty of being your guardsman, not only for the remainder of your stay here, at Dreadmoor, but whilst at Grimm, as well." He gave her a bow, and how many girls get *those* these days? And what a cute accent.

"Um, thanks, Jason. That'll be great." Ellie wasn't sure exactly why she needed a guardsman, but since he was offering, why not?

"So if you'd rather not have speech"—he dared a

brave glance at Gawan—"alone"—he moved his considerably softened gaze back to hers—"then I shall accompany you thusly to your chamber." He gave her that charming smile he had. "Whatever your wish."

The knights roared.

"By the saints, Jason, you've been practicing, aye?" said Sir Robert. "Damn me, but it sounds quite grand."

Ellie looked first at Jason, then at Gawan, then at Jason again.

What was going on between those two?

It was Tristan, though, who enlightened her. Being that it was his castle, he probably felt the need to do the enlightening himself.

He rose from his desk, strode toward her, and then guided her into the corner, where he semisheltered her from the others. "Lady, forgive these witless oafs their jesting. They mean no insult, I assure you."

Ellie smiled. "None taken. Really."

Tristan nodded, his sapphire eyes glittering. "Excellent. But"—he scratched his brow—"you see, a while ago, in the Brooding Chamber, just before you vanished—"

"You guys all saw?" she asked, her face already heating up. "Me and Gawan—"

"Nay, girl, we did not. But we're a witty lot, us medievals." His grin was infectious, even though she was totally mortified. "And we know yon grumpy Angel, who of late has become quite the foul sort, indeed." His grin widened. "Usually rather easy of character, even though he did make a living hacking off heads at one point. Still, he's become—" He waved a hand in the air as he tried to think of a word.

"Stodgy," Jason offered.

"Aye, so right, Jason. Stodgy. All in all, lady"—Tristan's face grew a bit sterner—"you are in a castle filled with vow-driven medieval knights—your Intended, who pledged those vows before any of us, included. And whilst his judgment of propriety may be a bit clouded by his affections for you, ours shall remain ever so sharp." He gave her a wink. "In other words, lady, this young pup Jason here is going to make sure your honor is guarded. At all times."

Ellie smiled, although she'd have given anything to see around the big knight. No doubt Gawan's face was pulled into a cranky frown, but Tristan completely blocked her view. "Yes. Well. That's great," she said, giving Tristan a pat on the shoulder. "Swell. I've never had my own guardsman before. I don't think, anyway."

Andi laughed. "Tristan, leave her alone, you big hypocrite." She winked at Ellie. "Remind me to tell you of the night before our wedding. And no, Ellie, I can almost guarantee you've never had a guardsman like Jason before." She walked over and pulled her big husband away from Ellie. "He's the best, I swear."

Ellie looked at Jason, who simply winked.

She noticed, not for the first time, that a lot of winking went on at Dreadmoor Castle.

"But she can certainly have one little conversation with Gawan." Andi gave Jason and her husband a glare. "Alone."

Gawan, true to Ellie's thinking, had a majorly grumpy look on his handsome face, which softened when he glanced at Andi. "Thank you, Lady Dreadmoor. 'Tis wondrous to know at least *you* remain trustful of my lecherous self."

Andi smiled. "No problem." She gave a glare and a wave to everyone in the room. "Clear out, guys, and no hanging out at the door to listen this time."

The Dreadmoor knights all groaned as they headed to the door.

Andi looked at Jason. "You can stay relatively close to the door, but no pressing the ear against the wood, and I mean it."

Jason gave her a nod. "I wouldn't think of it, my sweet lady."

Several of the guys laughed, made a few bawdy noises,

and pushed Jason out the door. Ellie could have sworn she heard one of them call him a suck-up.

The youngest Dragonhawk knight, completely unaffected by the fun being poked at him, was the last to leave. He turned in the doorway, his hand on the handle. "I shall be"—he inclined his head to a place behind him—"just there, by the hearth, lady, should you need me. You've only to call my name." He winked, wagged his brows at Gawan, and closed the door.

Leaving her perfectly and completely alone with the most breathtaking, thousand-year-old medieval knight-turned-Angel she'd ever in her life laid eyes on.

Her *Intended,* for crying out loud.

And she had a mark in the corner of her mouth to prove it.

"Ellie?"

That sexy voice, soft, a bit raspy, and good Lord, the accent, rushed through her. With a clever, inconspicuous calming deep breath, she turned around. Even gave him an easy smile, as if she wasn't close to being as affected by his presence as she really and truly was. Calm. Cool. Collected. Totally pulled together and confident. Boy, she was proud of herself.

"Yes?" she said, the word coming out on a dopey, idiotic squeak.

"About what you overheard me saying. Earlier." He rubbed a brow. "Before, I mean."

"It's okay. Really." She smiled wider, wondering if he could see all of her teeth. She shrugged. "I know you didn't mean it anyway." *Yes! There's that confidence.* "I can't remember everything about myself, or my family—*yet*—but I get a strong sense that I know people pretty darn well." She poked him in that rock-hard chest of his. "And you like me. Really like me." She decided to join the fun at Dreadmoor and gave him a wink. "A lot."

Gawan's eyes turned more chocolate, and his mouth twitched at the corner. "Is that so?"

She gave a firm nod. "Yep." She tapped the *special* corner of her mouth. "I've got this—don't forget."

"I shall endeavor never to forget, lady. Trust me."

Those seductive words sent a shiver down her spine, and she had to make herself take the next breath.

He took a step closer, flexed his fingers, shoved his hands in his pockets, and leaned toward her. "We'll decipher this mystery, Ellie of Aquitaine." His eyes searched hers, and for a moment, she thought she recognized a brief flash of sadness in those tumultuous brown depths. It was quickly replaced by determination. "No matter the cost, you'll get your life back. I *vow* it."

For a moment, Ellie envisioned Gawan as his previous self. His live medieval self. Big. Seasoned. Rough. Wild. Fierce.

When he gave a vow, he meant it.

Ellie bravely, to her notion, met his intense gaze with one of her own. She studied every sun and laugh line around the corners of his eyes, the fullness of his strong lips, the muscle flinching in his beard-stubbled jaw, and the sincerity of those deep brown pools that he stared so hard at her with.

Ellie grabbed the sides of his face, pulled him down to her, and kissed him quick and thoroughly on the mouth. Then she let go and stepped back, out of his reach. "I believe you," she said, a little breathily even to her own ears, before she turned and left the room.

Twenty

Somewhere in time, high in a blanket of darkness, three stars furiously blinked. . . .

"The girl's life force is beginning to fade faster than suspected," Elgan said. "Our young Conwyk is running short on time."

"Och, bloody hell," Fergus said. "Och."

"Och, indeed." Elgan drifted closer. "'Tis maddening."

"Nay, 'tis *mad,*" Aizeene said furiously, an arc of star shine spattering about. "We know where her live self is. We must intervene!"

"We cannot, and you well know it." Elgan heaved a heavy sigh. "We must have faith in our young warrior. Besides, 'tis the final word of the Order: no intervention."

"You asked, then?" Fergus said.

"Of course I did." Elgan drifted closer still. "The girl Ellie grows weaker, but her will, like Gawan's, is fierce. There's still hope, although I fear hope may not be enough." Silence, then: "I fear that whilst our warrior may save the girl's life, he may in turn fail his deadline."

"Nay!" Aizeene's and Fergus' starlight both feathered about in unison. Fergus, though, cleared his throat. "What I mean, er, 'twill interfere with our promotion, aye?"

Elgan's own star shine dimmed. "For all your bluster,

Fergus, I daresay you are the most softhearted thug of a Scot I've ever encountered." He sighed. "And the biggest liar. Nay, 'twill not interfere with our promotion. But, I fear, 'twill most certainly interfere with young Conwyk's."

Fergus' starshine began to fade. "Then let us be about the business of watching our warrior and the girl with a steady eye."

"And with a vast amount of hope," Aizeene said, following suit.

"Aye." Elgan, too, faded. "Hope. And prayer."

*In the early hours of a Midwinter's morn
Present Day, Dreadmoor Castle*

Gawan stared, as he had for the past score of hours, at the pattern stitched into the bed curtains above his head. More likely than not sewn that way apurpose, to have something to look at, for those weary souls who could not gain an easy spot of rest between sunset and dawn.

Much like himself.

And much, he thought, to the thanks of one Ellie of Aquitaine.

Saints, she'd invaded his bloody mind and would not leave it, even for a solid second.

How his *grandmothair* would cackle at him now, as 'twas she who passed on that bloody Welsh belief of finding one's Intended by way of an exquisitely charming mark on one's mouth. He'd not believed her, at first. It hadn't taken him long, though, and he'd been naught but a scrappy young lad of seven.

By the saints, he certainly had no doubts about it now.

Now that he'd not only seen the bloody mark on Ellie's luscious mouth, but had *taken* it. With that first kiss, on the wall walk at Grimm.

And he'd done it purposely.

Oy, somewhere in the Heavens, his *grandmothair* was giving him a blistering he was powerfully glad not to be present for.

Starting at the beginning of the long, winding vine of English ivy stitched with the tiniest of stitches in the curtains above him, he began, once more, to count the leaves. *One. Two. Three. Four . . . Twelve . . . Twenty-seven . . . Ninety-two . . .*

With a stream of his favorite Welsh curses, and a good punch to the useless pillow beneath his head, he stopped counting those ridiculous leaves and glared at them instead.

The feel of Ellie's soft skin would not leave his hands, nor would the taste of her lips leave his mouth, nor would the feel of her supple body pressed against his disappear. Her scent—Christ, even now, 'twas deep inside his senses, with each bloody breath he took, and he knew that for now, it would not go away. Not to mention the sly minx had fair left a scorch mark on his stomach where she'd sneaked inside his tunic.

Worse than all of that combined was that Ellie *herself* wouldn't leave his mind. The things that made her special, the quirky things that made her *Ellie,* all of which he feared he'd soon be living without. Like her confidence, her sharp wit, her sweetness, and of course, that peculiar, desirable charm she had about her. All of those things drove him mad with wanting to keep her, protect her, *forever.*

And 'twas the one thing that could never be.

He sighed and draped an arm over his eyes. Aye, he'd left out a most important detail when telling Ellie they were each other's Intended. He'd meant to tell her, by Christ's blood. He had, truly.

Then she'd risen up on her booted little toes and kissed him soundly and good.

And he'd been lost.

Not that he faulted her. Nay, not by any sort of means. 'Twas obvious she felt it, too, the pulling of Intended souls. She'd kissed him, firstly, with a vast amount of bravery, for no way in bloody hell had she known just what she was doing to him. That, followed by a passion so powerful, he all but fell over with the strength of it.

Aye, he'd keep such thoughts of love and fervor to himself, for if any of the lads in Tristan's blasted hall heard him utter even the slightest of confessions, they'd be merciless.

In truth, he just might resort to his centuries-old employment and lop off a head or two.

Or, he thought with some mild satisfaction, fifteen.

I believe you. . . .

Bleeding priests, her words, those fierce, trusting words, sealed with a sweet kiss would no doubt haunt him for the rest of his pitiful existence. He was, after all, a knight before anything else. Sworn to uphold vows he'd made without hesitancy, and without selfishness. As an Angel, aye, he'd had centuries of experience and knowledge. His bloody skills had been of little use, since the trail she'd left behind was nigh onto inexistent. But again, he was born a warrior, had lived as a knight, and had died a knight. His vows came from the core of his soul. When he made one, he kept it. Unconditionally.

Ellie would get her life back.

And he'd make sure of it, no matter what the cost to his heart.

"*I'mmm* Henry the Eighth I am, Henry the Eighth I am, I am. I've—"

"Lady!"

Ellie jumped at the sound of Jason's voice, muffled behind the door. "What is it, Jason?"

"Pardon me, lady, but you're driving me daft. You've been singing that verse now nigh onto the whole of the night."

Ellie turned back to the window and stared out into the darkness. The moon had drifted, or the Earth had drifted—either way, the shadows had elongated, making the outside of the castle look spooky. "Sorry. I can't sleep. I think it has something to do with the whole In Betwinxt–Intended thing."

"I'll come in, then, if you please, and we'll pass the rest of the morn *not* singing that irritating verse. Aye?"

Ellie laughed. "Aye, it's a deal. I'm bored silly. Come on in."

Jason slipped inside and then quietly closed the door behind him. He crossed the floor, to where Ellie sat in the alcove, and she had to bite back a grin. He still wore his sweater and jeans from earlier, but he now had his sword strapped to his hip.

"When you offered to be my guardsman, Jason, I had no idea that meant you'd be keeping post outside my door." She pointed. "With a sword."

As he dragged a straight chair up to the alcove, he straddled it backward and gave her a boyish grin. "When I was alive—the first time—and during the centuries I spent as a spirit, my blade was ever at the ready"—he patted the hilt—"on my person. Besides"—he gave her a sincere look—"when one pledges to be a lady's guardsman, one should never be without the proper gear."

Ellie smiled. "Gotcha. Well, I feel a lot safer with you around—that's for sure."

"No doubt."

She studied him. Lanky, but still strapped with youthful muscles that were bound to get bigger, if his height had anything to do with it. Dark auburn hair pulled back into a queue—he was such a cute guy. Sweet, too. Sweet and fearless.

"So tell me, Jason," she asked, pulling her knees up and resting her chin upon them, "what makes Gawan so special? As an Angel, I mean? He moves and behaves just like the rest of you."

Jason thought a minute, then rubbed his chin and regarded her. " 'Tisn't very knightly to gossip, but I suppose I could tell you what I admire about him."

"Let's hear it, then," she said. "Tell me."

"Very well." He leaned forward, arms resting on the back of the chair. "Once, when he was first awarded his title, he was your typical Angel." He flapped his arms like wings. "You know, like you'd see on the telly."

"He could *fly*?"

Jason nodded. "Oh, aye, for a certainty. He's a big lad anyway, but with that wingspan, by St. Peter's toes, he was enormous."

Wow. She scooted closer. "What else."

With a chuckle, Jason continued. "'Twasn't long after we, the Dragonhawk knights, in our ghostly forms, mind you, met Sir Gawan, that he accepted another position. Where as before, only the unliving could see him, as was the course, his new position afforded him a mortal body in which to live in here, on Earth."

"That's amazing." She tucked her hair behind her ear. "Go on. This is great stuff."

"Great stuff, indeed," Jason said, then continued. "When he took the position, he had to give up several of his skills in order to live an Earthbound life. One being, of course, the ability to fly. Another being the ability to cross centuries. Oy, that indeed was quite a fetching skill, no doubt."

"So you're telling me he could jump from century to century? Go back and forth?"

"Aye. Invisible to the mortal world, as well. Only us spirits could see and interact with him."

Ellie whistled low. "Amazing."

"In truth."

She looked at him. "So why didn't he just pop back to the time just before you were killed to warn all of you?"

A grave smile, even in the half shadows that covered his face, changed his expression. "Because, my lady, we were not his charges." He glanced out the window, the waning moonlight streaking his face. "You see, we weren't simply killed, or even simply murdered. We were *cursed*." He shrugged. "As much as Sir Gawan wanted to help us, he could not."

"I see." She thought she did, anyhow, and she reached out and patted his elbow. "I'm glad the curse is broken now. You guys—knights, rather—are the most amazing men I've ever known."

Even in the shadowy room, Ellie could see Jason blush. "Many thanks, lady. I take that as the highest of compliments."

She gave a short nod, mimicked from watching the other medievals. "As you should."

Jason chuckled.

"So tell me," Ellie continued, "what *skills* does Gawan have left?"

Jason cocked a brow and smiled. "Grand ones, still, although he only uses them in utmost emergencies. For one, he can bend another's will with his mind. 'Tis how he learned you weren't at any of the local infirmaries."

Ellie blinked. "You're kidding me?"

"Nay, I am not. 'Tis probably his most fascinating skill. Although the ability to read one's mind is a powerful gift, indeed."

Ellie gasped. "He can do *what*?"

Oblivious to her shock, Jason grinned wider. "Oh, aye, although he has quite a strong will about himself, you know, not to just plunder one's thoughts at random. For if it were I, there's countless maids' minds I'd be taking a peek into."

Unbending her knees, Ellie leaned forward and grabbed Jason's arm. "Do you think he's . . . um"—she tapped the side of her head with her forefinger—"been in my thoughts? Much? Lately?"

Realization set in, and Jason cleared his throat and patted Ellie on the shoulder. "Oh, nay, lady, I daresay, 'twould be most unchivalrous to do such."

Ellie sighed with relief, remembering some of the thoughts she'd recently had about Gawan. "Good."

"Unless"—Jason pulled his ear—"of course, he had to do it—just a wee peek, at best. You know, to aid your matter."

Ellie closed her eyes and thought over all her ponderings while in Gawan's presence. Several came to mind.

Maybe that was why he was always smothering a grin with his hand, or those sexy lips were constantly twitching.

She collapsed her head into her hands. "Oh, gosh. I'm in Mortification Land."

Jason tapped her on the shoulder, and she ignored him. Then he crooked a knuckle beneath her chin and raised her face away from her hands.

"Lady, open your eyes."

With a gusty sigh, she did.

Jason gave her that adorable quirky grin. "I daresay those thoughts of yours can't be all too dreadful, aye?"

Ellie counted back to all the lusty thoughts she'd had about Gawan of Conwyk. "Ooh, Jason, I think I'm too embarrassed to even tell."

He stared a minute, then barked out a laugh. He stood. "Well, then, fair maiden, it seems to have helped your cause, rather than hindered it—if yesterday's Brooding Chamber incident tells the true tale of it."

"Oh!" She swatted at him, but he darted out of the way. "You are too cute to be so evil."

He gave her a slight nod as he reached the door. "Guilty. Although," he said, rubbing his jaw with a knuckle, "if you really want to know if he's sneaking into your thoughts, then ask him directly."

Ellie blinked. "Really?"

Jason smiled, just as he stepped through the door. "A knight's first sworn vow: *never lie*." He winked and closed the door silently.

A grin pulled at Ellie's mouth until she gave in and allowed a full-blown smile—teeth and all.

Maybe she'd give that medieval warrior a few thoughts to ponder after all.

Twenty-one

By the time the storm had slowed enough to safely drive, 'twas just at eleven thirty. Whilst the snow had stopped falling, the roads were slick, slushy, and iced in parts. Gawan had said his farewells to the Dreadmoor knights and Jameson, and now presently followed Lord and Lady Dreadmoor in a Rover not unlike Gawan's own. They headed into Northumbria to pay a visit to the constable's office before making their way out to the cottage Ellie had rented.

Gawan eased a glance toward her. She simply sat, staring out the window. Earlier, he'd caught her slipping casual looks toward him, but then she'd settled into the drive and had remained silent. He wondered briefly if his imagination played tricks upon him or if she was looking a bit paler than usual. Mayhap 'twas the cold.

"Do you feel ill?" he asked, keeping his eyes on the slick road ahead.

"You mean, other than mostly dead?" She took a deep breath. "I think I feel okay. Why?"

Jason, her newly appointed personal guardsman occupying the rear seat, spoke up. "Aye, lady, you do look a bit more ashen than usual this morn."

"Gee, thanks. You guys do a lot for a girl's ego."

Gawan glanced at her. "No jesting, Ell. Is there aught amiss?"

She turned, making her hair, which she'd pulled into a horse's tail, swish, and gave him one of those charming smiles. "I promise, nothing is amiss. You'll be the first one to know, if something does go amiss." She patted his shoulder. "Okay?"

Gawan gave a short nod. "Aye. Okay."

With that, she turned back to the scenery flashing by.

After leaving several contact numbers on Ellie's voice mail, they had then spent the rest of the morning digging their way out of the snow and applying chains to the Rover tires. Will then lowered the drawbridge, and they left for what Gawan prayed would be a successful visit to the constable's.

Still, his thoughts of the night before weighed heavily on his mind, and whilst he did indeed take into consideration Christian of Arrick-by-the-Sea's advice to enjoy what small amount of time he could have with Ellie, he thought 'twould be better to allow her to make that final decision. In fact, just sitting beside her, with her not vanishing, was a gift. It gnawed at him, though, to think she could fade away with the next breath.

He cast a quick glance her way. Aye, still there.

He feared that even that might be taken away, and far sooner than either would wish.

Earlier, it'd been chaos leaving the keep, what with the men bustling about. 'Twas a miracle, in truth, that the entire garrison hadn't accompanied them. They were all vastly concerned about Ellie and wanted nothing more than to help, no matter how much they jested and poked fun at him. *A good-natured lot of lads,* he thought. *Not a better garrison in all of England.*

Past or present.

Finally, they reached the small township, and drove directly to the constable's office, which was located on a corner, next to a bakery and, beside that, a chippy. 'Twas a slight force of officers, in truth, but Tristan had said Constable Hurley could indeed be trusted.

When they entered through the narrow red doors marking the constable's quarters, a middle-aged man took one look at Tristan and paled. He sat behind a desk covered by various papers in disarray, a computer, a picture of a teenage boy and girl, and a telephone.

With a manly cough and an even manlier clearing of throat, the constable recovered and stood. A small bit of his color even returned. He held out a hand to Tristan.

"Aye, Dreadmoor, how are you this morn?" He gave a nod to Andi. "Lady Dreadmoor, you're looking well."

Andi gave him a smile. "Thanks. So are you."

Ellie, Gawan noticed, hung back a bit, close behind him, and didn't say a word.

Tristan, on the other hand, wasted no time in getting to the matter.

"Constable Hurley, this is Gawan of Cowyk, from Castle Grimm, just up the way," Tristan said. He inclined his head. "You remember Jason."

Hurley gave Jason a quick nod.

"A rather similar situation at Grimm as the one in which you so graciously offered aid for me at Dreadmoor needs your attention, if you've the stomach for it."

Hurley, Gawan noticed, paled again. But he did hold his stomach, in truth. He turned his gaze to Gawan. "How can I be of service, Lord Grimm?"

Gawan stepped away from Ellie, and noticed the constable hadn't so much as given her a single glance. He'd hoped that since Hurley had been able to see Tristan whilst he was still a spirit, he'd somehow have the capability of seeing Ellie, as well. Mayhap being In Betwinxt prevented it.

Gawan gave Hurley a stern look. "I've a missing person, of a sort, who needs help. She's been in an accident, she's lost her memory, and we're working against a time limit, Constable." He pulled out a copy of the photo of Ellie. "We've only this picture to go on, I'm afraid. And a phone number." Gawan handed Hurley a slip of paper with Ellie's number written on it. "She's an American."

"The girl rented one of my holiday cottages, which is

where that photo was taken," Tristan said. "The storm kept us from visiting the cottage yestereve, but we're headed there now."

Constable Hurley sat down.

"Here are copies of the information my solicitor took from the girl, before letting her the cottage," Tristan said. "As you can see, she gave false information, other than the phone number."

Gawan walked closer to the desk, unbuttoned his wool coat, and shoved his hands in his pockets. "I called that number, and 'tis the same girl, but she leaves no name on the voice mail. We've left several contact numbers in hopes that someone—mayhap a family member—will return the call. No one, so far, has."

Everyone watched Constable Hurley, who finally drew a deep breath, mopped a hand over his brow, and met Gawan's gaze. "Forgive me. I fear I'll later kick myself in the arse for asking this, but how do you know it's the same girl on the voice mail?"

Gawan grinned. "I know her voice. 'Tis the same."

Hurley scratched his cheek as he pondered that. "You know the voice, but not her real identity, and she's injured, you say."

The lady Dreadmoor then walked up and patted the constable on the shoulder. "Okay, it's like this. She's almost a ghost—floating between a mortal life and the spirit one. We can see her, touch her, but then she disappears"—Andi snapped her fingers, and the constable jumped—"just like that. She doesn't remember who she is, and we can't find her live body. Gawan's checked all the hospitals." She turned and pointed directly at Ellie. "She's standing right there, behind Gawan."

Hurley shifted a watery gaze in the direction of Andi's finger, where Ellie stood, swallowed a few times, then nodded. "I see." He heaved a sigh. "Unfortunately, so. Rather, I don't see *her,* but I understand. Please give the, er, girl my regards."

Gawan nodded, and glanced at Ellie.

"Tell him I said thank you," she said.

"We call her Ellie, and she gives her thanks for your kind help on the matter," Gawan said.

"Right." Constable Hurley stood. "I'll make some calls and see what I can come up with." He extended a hand to Gawan. "I'll be in touch, my lord." He glanced at Tristan and Andi. "Lord and Lady Dreadmoor, a pleasure, as always." He gave a nod in Jason's direction. "Lad, good to see you in, er, such fine health, as well."

Jason nodded in return. "Aye, thank you."

"Constable," Gawan said, "I would appreciate your utmost confidentiality whilst dealing with this delicate matter. Dreadmoor swears you're the best and can be completely trusted."

Constable Hurley gave a curt nod. "As always, sir. You can trust me, for a certainty, because I can promise you, no one else would bloody believe any of this." He gave a sheepish grin. "I'll be in touch."

With that, they all left and made their way down the winding North Sea coastline, toward Tristan's holiday cottage.

Ellie turned sideways in her seat. "I think I'm nervous."

Gawan gave her a quick glance and resisted the urge to touch her anywhere, to give comfort. The blunt way she confessed her feelings truly charmed him. "Why is that, girl?"

She shrugged. "I guess because of what we might find at the cottage. Or what we *won't* find."

Jason leaned forward from the back seat. "Do not fear, lady. If Sir Gawan tells you 'twill be all right, you can believe it, in truth."

Gawan lost his resistance and found her hand upon her knee, and threaded his fingers through her slim, powerfully cold ones. "We will manage that course once we're there, aye?"

She tightened her fingers around his and smiled. "Okay. Aye." Turning her head, she glanced out the window. "What if I left stuff all over the place? What if I was"—she shrugged—"a major slob. There could be panties hanging from the shower rod, for all I know."

Jason chuckled.

Gawan grinned and squeezed her hand. "If you've drawers hanging high and low from yon garderobe, I'll hasten in there and yank them down for you straight-away. Aye?"

"No!" she said, and laughed. "I can yank my own drawers down." She turned her head and rested it against the back of the seat, staring at him. "But thanks for the offer."

Gawan gave a short nod, his heart truly melting at the soft look in her eyes. He hoped his words didn't stumble over his tongue when he spoke. "My pleasure, as always."

It wasn't long before Tristan turned in to a small, family-run chippy situated near the sea road. It had been hours since they'd eaten, and damnation, Gawan's belly growled as soon as they walked inside and the aroma hit his nose. His appetite lessened, though, when Ellie refused to eat anything.

Something was changing with her, and it bothered Gawan to the core. He ate a little, and then had the fishmonger bag the remainder of his fried cod and chips. The others, too, wordlessly followed suit. Gawan met Tristan's eyes, and knew his friend understood. They continued on their way.

After a while, the cottages that dotted the coastline became fewer and fewer, with wide stretches of craggy meadows covered with snow-laden clumps of brown heather and rock. Sheep, here and there, grazed on hidden bits of grass buried beneath the frost.

"It's quite beautiful here," Ellie said, echoing Gawan's own thoughts. "I don't remember ever smelling such fresh, sweet air." She stared, her gaze fixed on some spot far off. "Or having such an intense sense of . . . I don't know"—she looked at him—"the past. Of course, that might be due to the fact that everyone I presently know, with the exception of Andi, Will, and Jameson, is so old." She smiled and turned back to the scenery flashing by. "I like it."

Oy, Gawan thought. Not nearly as much as he.

Saints, if but things could be changed.

"Well, lady," said Jason, "while Sir Gawan may be considerably, er, old, I am still quite youthful, in truth, in case you find old no longer suiting you."

"Mind yourself, pup," Gawan said, then noticed Tristan had pulled onto a single lane track. Beyond, on a hilltop and overlooking the sea, sat a lone whitewashed cottage. "That must be your rental there, Ellie." He pointed to the small white building ahead. "Quite secluded, and Grimm is at least twenty-two kilometers away."

"I wonder why you were on Grimm's land?" Jason asked, leaning forward in his seat. "By the saints, 'tis a lonely little croft, aye?"

"I wonder how the heck I got out here. I don't see a rental car," she said. "And if the completely alive version of me is anything like the me now, I'd probably have been afraid to drive over here." She glanced at Gawan. "The roads are too narrow and you drive on the wrong, well, left side of the road instead of the right."

He grinned. "I know. And I find it hard to believe you're afraid of anything."

She smiled.

Good, Gawan thought. He wanted Ellie's nerves to ease a bit before they entered that cottage. In truth, he'd be going in before her, anyway, because more than once since finding out about the cottage, Gawan feared what he'd find inside. Nay, he knew Ellie was for a certainty still alive, else her body would no longer remain solid. In truth, his gut—along with the voices Ellie had remembered when last she vanished—told him she was being tended elsewhere.

By the saints, he prayed they tended her well.

They pulled in behind Tristan and got out. Tristan immediately made his way to Gawan.

"I hadn't thought of it before, but mayhap you and I should investigate the cottage first."

"Aye," Gawan said, interrupting. "I've just thought the same thing." He glanced at Tristan's wife. "Lady, would you mind keeping Ellie company whilst we go in first? She's a bit jittery about the whole thing, as it is."

Andi smiled, the fierce wind whipping her hair about her face, her wee nose already red from the cold. "Absolutely." She turned and walked toward Gawan's Rover, the gravel of the drive crunching under her booted feet.

Jason joined them once Andi had replaced his company. "I would like to go in, too, sirs, if it's all the same to you?"

With a nod, Gawan said, "Aye, then. Let's be done with it."

Tristan pulled a key from his coat pocket, and as they managed the front walkway, the three were silent while he placed the key in the door and turned the lock. With an easy push, the door swung open.

Gawan stepped in behind Tristan, then Jason behind him. All three stood in the small foyer of the cottage and stared.

It was completely empty.

"Damnation," Tristan said.

With a pang of unease, Gawan moved around Tristan and hurried through every room, searching every closet, pantry, and the lone garderobe.

"Anything?" Tristan called out from another room of the cottage.

"Nay," Gawan said, just before all three met back at the foyer.

Gawan pushed a hand through his hair. "Bleedin' priests, man. It doesn't look as though she's even stepped foot in the place."

"Shall I go retrieve her and Lady Andi?" Jason asked.

Both Gawan and Tristan answered together: "Aye."

Dragging a hand over his jaw, Gawan stepped into the small larder and opened the refrigerator. " 'Tis empty, and clean as a whistle." He closed the small white door. "The bedchamber is the same, as well. Everything's as though not a soul has stayed here."

Just then, Ellie and Andi, with Jason in the rear, came through the doorway. Jason closed the door behind them.

Ellie simply stood, at first, looking around. Then, without a word, she moved from room to room, until she reappeared in the living area.

She scratched her chin. "Well. This was highly anticlimactic." She looked at Gawan. "I have a pretty good feeling that the real, very much alive me isn't quite this neat."

Andi went to the hearth and sat down on the stone ledge. "When did Ellie sign the rental release?"

"Just under a fortnight ago," Tristan said. "Yet the release has her letting the cottage for another two weeks."

"Maybe she"—Ellie closed her eyes and pinched the bridge of her nose—"maybe I had finished whatever it was I came here for and had already packed everything up?"

Gawan moved toward her then, and took her by both arms. "I want you to search each room carefully, girl. Think." He tapped the side of her head. "Remember how you found your ear bauble beneath the rock on the beach?"

She nodded. "You're right." She paced for a moment, and everyone remained quiet, and then Ellie started in the larder. She went straight to the refrigerator and opened it, as Gawan had.

She stared for a moment, as though trying to decide what sort of snack to choose, and then she closed the door. Opening the freezer, she quickly inspected it and closed it, as well.

Next, the pantry, a small walk-in with just enough

space for one person to step inside. She stepped inside, looked around, then came out.

The whole while she studied the rooms thoroughly, everyone else remained in the living area, quiet.

Several minutes later, Ellie walked back to join them, her face pulled into heavy concentration. She stood, her lips moving silently as she worked to decipher something in her head.

Then a spark snapped in her lovely blue-green eyes, and she went to the refrigerator and opened the door. Gawan and the others followed her.

On her hands and knees, Ellie removed the bottom drawer of the refrigerator—the one Nicklesby always filled with vegetables and such—and poked her hand in. There was a little sticky, ripping noise just before she withdrew her arm.

Holding up her hand, she gave Gawan a wide grin. "Wow."

Pinched between Ellie's two fingers was a blasted key.

Twenty-two

"How did you know to look there?" Andi asked. Ellie stood, closed the door to the fridge and shrugged. "It just sort of came to me." She looked at the key. "I guess I must hide things in weird places."

"Mayhap you suspected someone might try to find it?" Tristan said.

"Well, according to my voice mail, I did." She studied the key closely. "It's small, like it goes to a locker, or something."

"Might I?" said Gawan, who'd come to stand close to her.

She handed the key to him. "What do you think?"

Gawan nodded. "Mayhap a safe-deposit box or a locker at the airport." He glanced at Tristan.

Tristan took a turn looking at the key. " 'Twould do us little good, though, as we've no name to go along with the key."

Gawan rubbed his jaw. "Aye, but see you here," he said, and pointed to a series of numbers imprinted on the key. "These may be logged into their system. Mayhap, with a bit of persuasion, the key master might look into matters for us."

It amazed Ellie, still, as she looked at Gawan and remembered he had the ability to *coerce*.

"Mayhap 'tis a postal key?" Jason said as he leaned over Gawan's shoulder and inspected it.

Andi glanced at her watch. "We won't know until tomorrow, I'm afraid." She tapped the face. "It's almost four o'clock. Closing time for everyone."

"Bloody right," Tristan said.

Andi moved closer to her husband and linked her arm through his. "I've got a doctor's appointment tomorrow," she said, then looked up at Tristan. "I can go by myself if—"

"Nay," Gawan said. "Forgive me, lady. It's not that I don't appreciate Tristan's aid." He scratched his brow. "But there's no way in bloody hell I'd ask Dreadmoor to miss his unborn's first appointment." He clapped Tristan on the shoulder. "I'll ring your mobile with any news."

Tristan gave a short nod. " 'Tis agreed, then. I confess I feel the need to make sure the man responsible for bringing my babe into this world—and seeing to my bride in the meanwhile—is not a brainless twit."

Ellie watched the exchange between Tristan and Andi and felt a pang of envy at their obvious love.

"Ellie?" Gawan said.

Good Lord, she'd gone mushy.

Then it hit her again.

Again.

She walked back to the fridge, opened the door, and got back onto her knees. Pulling out the opposite drawer to the one on which she'd found the key, she felt with her hand, on the underside of the lid.

Just like the key, another treasure had been stashed, held in place with a piece of tape. Working it loose, she pulled it free.

"What is it, girl?" Gawan said, right beside her, where he'd come to crouch.

She pulled out a small rectangle of paper, maybe two inches by one inch. It had a name.

" 'Langston,' " she read.

Gawan leaned closer. "That's it?"

Ellie turned the paper over. "Yep, that's it."

"Damnation, lady, but you have the oddest of hiding places," Tristan said. "Clever girl."

"So your name may very well be Langston?" Jason asked, leaning against the honey-stained oak counters.

"There's the Langston estate up the way," Gawan said, rising and pulling Ellie with him. "Passing odd."

"Aye, but he's just an old croaker, last I heard," Jason said. "Caused quite a stir in the old day, though."

"Rather, his ancestors," Tristan said. "But that was centuries ago."

"It obviously means something, though," Andi said.

Ellie dug and dug inside what memory she had. *Langston, Langston, Langston.* Didn't stir up even a single dust mite of a memory.

"I'll ring Constable Hurley with these new finds this eve," Gawan said. He moved a hand to Ellie's elbow, which immediately sent tingles up her arm. "Tristan, Andi, thank you for your aid," he said, and with his other hand, he gripped Tristan's in a firm shake. "And for the services of your finest young Dragonhawk knight." He leaned over and placed a kiss on Andi's cheek. " 'Tis wondrous, the change you've stirred in this big oaf. I daresay none other could have succeeded at the like."

Andi, Ellie noticed, blushed clear to her toes, but she gave Gawan a big smile. "Strange, I guess, how things that were meant to be just work out when you least expect them to." She looked at Ellie, leaned forward, and whispered, "Everything will be okay. I know it." She took her hand and squeezed it. "See you soon."

Ellie smiled, although the first thought that popped into her head was *God, I hope you're right.* "Thanks. For everything."

Tristan placed a hand on Ellie's shoulder. "Lass, I leave you in capable hands, in truth. But should you need anything else, you have Nicklesby ring me straightaway." He leaned over and kissed her cheek. " 'Twill all work out." He glanced at Gawan. "Saints, you've a bloody Angel beside you," he said, then gave her a solemn smile. "And the best pair of warriors I know. How could it not work out?"

Somehow, Ellie thought as they made their way back to Castle Grimm, she really hoped things would work out for the best a little bit quicker. No way would she tell Gawan that she had started feeling different. *Yeah,* she thought, taking in a deep breath, *maybe just different.* She didn't feel like running a marathon, for sure, but overall, not too bad.

Different.

And then she threw a prayer Heavenward that *different* didn't necessarily mean *dead.*

As she watched the blustery northern English seascape flash by through the window of the Rover, Ellie let her thoughts drift, allowed them to wander, to make up a bunch of what-ifs—almost like a roadtrip game.

What if, say, the whole mystery of Who Is Ellie was solved? *What if* Gawan rescued her, from wherever she presently was. He'd meet his Angel retirement requirements, she'd be completely and wholly *alive*—always a plus in her book—and they'd be free to . . . what? Date? Well *duh,* of course, they'd date. They were each other's bloody Intendeds! Of course they'd date.

A sound pulled Ellie from her what-if game, and she glanced to her right, from where the sound originated.

Gawan's gaze focused straight ahead.

Obviously not him, so she turned in her seat and peeked at Jason.

His head was tilted backward, and his eyes were closed.

Sleeping. Some guardsman you are, cutie. . . .

Gawan covered his mouth, coughed, and cleared his throat.

It was only then that Ellie recalled the juicy info Jason had revealed the night before.

She narrowed her eyes and stared at Gawan, who continued to face forward.

She smiled, and knew if she could have seen that smile in a mirror, she'd have described it as *evil*.

Oh, gosh, Gawan is so hot. She watched him. Not even a muscle flinched.

Mmm, his hair is so sexy. Wild, loose, looong curls that feel so soft. And his eyes—wow. A girl could get lost while gazing into them.

Gawan shifted in his seat but his eyes stayed glued to the road.

And the way his hands feel, mmm, nice and rough, like a man's hands should feel. And good Lord Almighty, the way he kisses—the way his tongue feels. God, just thinking about his body pressed against mine almost makes me—

"Come now, Ell," Gawan said, squeakier than what he probably would have preferred, all while shifting again in his seat. He patted her awkwardly on the knee. "Wake up, girl. We're almost at the gatehouse."

Ellie laughed out loud. "Ha! You are a naughty Angel, Conwyk." She turned to him, and stared until he glanced at her. "You were reading my thoughts, weren't you?"

He said nothing, just stared at the road.

"Knights don't lie, so don't even think about it."

A slow smile lifted the corner of his delicious mouth. " 'Twas only a peek, girl, and you'd been so silent, I was worried." He brushed a knuckle across her jaw. "Truly. And 'twas you being the naughty one, aye? Saying things that nigh onto made me swerve the Rover into a pile of snow."

Jason let out a snore.

"He had a rough night last night," Ellie said, inclining her head toward her zonked-out guardsman. "He stayed up with me quite a while." She cocked her brow and studied Gawan's handsome yet haggard features. "Didn't get much rest either?"

Although the glance he gave her was a quickie, because the roads were slippery with ice and snow, it still gave Ellie a clear picture of how little sleep Gawan actually had. Without a word, he slid a hand over to hers, linked his big, rough fingers between her own, and gave a slight squeeze.

"Naught that I cannot manage," he said in that sexy voice of his. And then he was quiet.

And until they turned onto the lane that took them through the gatehouse, and to the great double oak doors of Castle Grimm, so was Ellie.

Somehow, having her hand held by a medieval warlord gave her a warm, comforting feeling that reached way beyond her bones and muscles.

It reached clear to her soul.

The Rover hadn't even pulled to a stop before the doors to Grimm were thrown open, and Nicklesby, God bless him, hurried out, his gangly arms and legs adorably rushing down the steps to greet them.

"Young Conwyk! Lady Ellie! By the crow's tail, do hurry and come in out of this bluster!" he said, coming straight for Ellie and helping her out of the Rover. "Jason of Dreadmoor, is that you, lad? Unfold yourself and climb from the Rover thusly."

"Nicklesby, man, settle yourself down," Gawan said with a chuckle. "We've only been gone for two nights." He walked around to the back of the Rover to help Jason with his belongings.

Nicklesby, meanwhile, hurried Ellie up the steps. "Aye, well, there's been a bit of a—oh, dear. Just hurry inside and see for yourself."

As Ellie stepped into the great hall, she grabbed Nicklesby's skinny yet sturdy arm to keep herself from tripping out of sheer surprise. "What the—"

"Bloody hell is going on here?" Gawan finished, stepping in behind her. He set Jason's bag down, and Jason, who'd walked in behind him, closed the door and whistled.

"By the saints," Jason said, shifting the bag he had strapped over one shoulder. " 'Tis more spirits than I've seen in me whole life."

Ellie scanned the room with disbelief. Not because of the ghosts that filled the great hall. That had somehow stopped being startling. More so because of the many new ones that had come in, all in the short while they'd been at Tristan's.

And they were all looking *dead* at her.

Sir Godfrey bustled through the crowd of ghosts. "By the by, boy," he said to Gawan, " 'tis bloody well time you came home. What with Arrick gone back to his own pile of leaking rocks, 'tis been naught but myself and yon Nicklesby there to keep this mob settled!" He gave a nod to Ellie. "Lady, I'm afeared you're the cause of the fuss."

"Me?" she asked. "Why am I the cause?" She glanced at the assembled ghosts. They all seemed to be staring directly at her.

"They've come to see your mark," Sir Godrey said, pointing to that same place on his mouth where Gawan said Ellie had a mark.

Gawan took Ellie by the hand, pulled her away from Nicklesby's grasp, and led her across the hall. "You good folks, move there, and allow the lady to have a bit of reprieve before you stare her down."

All at once, the ghosts scattered, leaving a wide path for Gawan to drag Ellie up the stairway.

"Oh, I think I see it!" exclaimed one lady ghost, her hair piled high. She was holding a pair of opera glasses up to her face.

" 'Tis wondrous, my good lord Grimm!" shouted another, who reminded Ellie a lot of Mary Poppins. "Might I have a moment with you?"

Gawan stopped halfway up the stairwell and turned to face the crowd of spirits who'd gathered at the bottom. "I do thank you all for your interest. You're more than welcome to take your reprieve at Castle Grimm."

He pulled Ellie close to him. "But the girl's had a taxing day and needs her rest."

Several ghostly groans filled the hall.

Gawan held up a hand. "In truth, she'll be more than happy to regale you of our meeting later this eve. But until then, she needs her rest."

"I will?" Ellie whispered, and Gawan squeezed her hand, then inclined his head toward Jason. "Now, standing at yon doorway, looking rather befuddled, is one of the finest knights in all the land. One of the Dragonhawk's knights."

Several oohs and ahhhs erupted from the crowd as the spirits turned their attention to poor Jason.

Jason gave Gawan a look of despair.

"Sir," Nicklesby said, at the foot of the steps, "shall I bring you tea?"

"Aye, Nicklesby." Gawan glanced at Ellie, and the heat in his eyes made her shiver. "But later."

Nicklesby, that old Nickle, gave a lopsided grin and a quick nod. "As you wish."

Again, Ellie found herself all but dragged up the steps. They'd almost made it to Gawan's chamber when a small figure burst through the stone wall. Young Davy skidded to a halt.

"Blimey, I'm ever so glad you've returned!" he said, looking first at Gawan, then at Ellie. "All these ladies runnin' about, makin' a fuss an' pinchin' me cheeks," he said, rubbing those accosted cheeks. He looked at Ellie. "Will you play me a game later?" He smiled a conniving gap-toothed grin. "No one plays me near as good as you do, lady."

What a con. Sweet, but definitely a con.

Ellie gave him a grin. "Of course I'll play you. Let me catch my breath for a little while and talk with Gawan, then I'll meet you later." She looked around, then leaned over and whispered, "You'll have to find a good place to go, as the hall looks a bit crowded these days."

He grinned back. "For a certainty."

And with that, he scampered down the passageway and disappeared.

"That boy has taken a liking to you that he's not taken with another," Gawan said. He pulled her onward. "Come on, whilst the others are occupied with Jason."

"That was really rotten, throwing Jason to the ghostly wolves, by the way," Ellie said, chugging up the stairs behind him.

He gave her a grin. "I know. 'Twill keep his chivalrous arse out of my way for a spell."

Ellie gulped at the thought of Gawan wanting to keep her personal guardsman *out of the way*.

They rounded the bend in the passageway, Gawan threw open the door to his chamber, yanked Ellie inside, and then kicked the door shut with his booted foot. He wasted no time throwing the lock, either.

They stared at each other, both breathing a bit hard from the exerted dash from the great hall, Ellie with expectancy, and Gawan with something else entirely. A while ago, in the Rover, he'd hardly said a word. Now he was all of a sudden in a gigantic hurry to get her alone, yet just standing there.

And Ellie noticed, as Gawan scratched his chin, rubbed his eyes, then tugged on his ear, that he looked *nervous*.

"Gawan, what?"

"Saints, girl," he said, then started to pace, at the same time unbuttoning his black wool coat and tossing it across the foot of his bed. "I've something to tell you," he said. "I should have told you sooner."

Ellie's heart plummeted to her stomach. Later, she'd remember that there wasn't a whole lot of stuff you could tell a woman who was already mostly dead, her live body lost, and her memory a collage of naughty adolescent experiences and head thumpings in church that would really, reeeally upset her.

But for now, a ton of scary thoughts—none making a lick of sense—ran through her head.

"What is it?" she managed, peeling out of her own coat.

Rubbing a hand over his jaw—a habit Gawan had that Ellie found extremely sexy—he stopped, took in a deep breath, and just stared.

"Bleedin' priests," he said, his accent thicker than usual. "I'd rather be facin' a half dozen berserkers in battle with me bare hands than to have to stand here and tell you this."

Now she wanted to throw up, and she wasn't even sure what a berserker was.

"*What*?" she asked, and slid down into the straight-backed chair near the wall.

He raked a hand through that boyish long hair, closed his eyes, and then opened them. He drew in a long breath, exhaled. "I stole your mark."

The pounding of her heart felt like a drum against her rib cage. Ellie blinked. "Excuse me?"

He began to pace again, and he waved his hand in the air as he attempted to explain. "Your Intended's mark, in the corner of your mouth—I stole it."

It took everything Ellie had not to snort out loud. Obviously, it was something that stressed Gawan out big-time. But she didn't quite get it. She stood, and walked toward him.

"Gawan, I don't—" She grabbed his arm. "Would you stop pacing and stand still for a minute?" He did, but did not turn to face her.

The feel of his muscles flinching beneath her touch only made her want to touch him even more. She did, too. Sliding her fingers through his, she tugged on him. "If you don't kiss me right now, Gawan of Conwyk, I'm going to scream."

With a fierceness she didn't expect, that was exactly what Gawan of Conwyk did—kiss her.

And, she noted, kissed her good and truly well.

Twenty-three

At first, they just *breathed*. He studied her, slowly and intently, and not just that crazy mark on her mouth, either, nor with just his eyes. In the funniest of places, he touched her—the bones in her wrists, the shell of her ear, the scar under her bottom lip. Ellie all but squirmed while he fascinated over every little thing, until she thought she would melt straight into a big, gooey puddle.

And then, thank God, he lowered his head. Expecting a forceful pillaging of the mouth, she almost fainted at the sensation of Gawan's lips simply settling over hers. He didn't cup her face, or the back of her head, or anything. He just *leaned* into her. But she could feel his body almost shaking, as if it took every ounce of strength he had *not* to go crazy on her.

One hand, finally, slid around her waist and pulled her gently but tightly against him, his hips pressing into her, her thighs pressing against him, and then his other hand moved to her jaw, his knuckles scraping across the tender skin of her throat, and then to gently touch that special corner of her mouth she never even knew she had.

And then he urged her mouth open with his, and as they tasted each other—the slowest, most erotic, sensual tasting she'd ever experienced—Ellie wound her fingers through his long curls and held on. It could have lasted an hour, or a minute. She couldn't tell. All she knew was that she didn't want it to stop.

Everything, to her dismay, did exactly that. It suddenly stopped.

Including Gawan's exploration of her mouth.

With a soft peck to her lips, he rested his forehead against hers and held her close. "Ell," he said, his already raspy voice heavy, his accent thick, "I've got to finish telling you"—he pulled back and looked her in the eye—"and if you disappear on me, girl, I vow, 'twill be my end."

She gave him a smile that felt drunken. "You expect me to comprehend anything you say after a kiss like that?" The way he called her *gel* was just too darn sexy.

A solemn smile tipped the corner of his mouth up. "Aye, I do, and I hope to the saints above I won't trip over me bloody tongue saying it. And I pray you won't hate me after the telling of it."

Oops, there went her stomach again.

His mouth opened to, of course, speak and spill the dreaded Telling of Whatever, and Ellie pressed two fingers over his lips, shushing him. "Do not tell me to sit, because I won't. And stop beating around the bush, Gawan, and spit out whatever it is you want to say." She smiled. "Besides, I couldn't hate you if I wanted to, so don't ever say that again."

Gawan met her gaze with those sinful chocolate eyes, drew a deep breath, and then proceeded to *spit it out.*

"We will not remember each other, Ell," he said quietly, and then stayed quiet.

She cocked her head and resisted the urge to clean out her ear with a finger. "What do you mean, we won't remember each other?" She couldn't help it this time—she snorted. "That's ridiculous. As *if* I could forget you."

His steady gaze held hers. "Aye, you will. Because you are my charge, in truth. And I vowed to get your life back." He took another deep breath, as though he wasn't entirely satisfied by how his words were coming out. "Once I've completed a mission with a charge, both of our memories are stricken." He moved away from her. " 'Tis the Order's way, and has been for centuries. I don't recall any of my charges." He turned and stood, hands in pockets, looking at her with that painfully honest look. "I won't recall you, Ell. Nor will you recall me. Ever."

A ton of bricks dropped on her head wouldn't have hit her any harder than that tidbit. "What about Nicklesby, Sir Godfrey, or the ladies?"

"Nay, Ellie. They're not *my charges*." He rubbed the spot between his eyes, pushed the bed curtains back, and sat on the end of the bed. "But *you are*." He looked up. "There's more."

Her legs wobbled, and she thought it'd be nice if the chair she'd slinked into earlier was right behind her. Instead, she stiffened and braced herself. "Tell me."

"Once your life has been restored," he said, and Ellie loved his confidence that her life would in fact be restored, "you will not recall any of this." He pinned her with a stare that wasn't all too gentle. Quite ferocious, actually. "Nor will you recall any of *us*. 'Twill be something akin to déjà vu, or a nagging thought, mayhap, a twinge of something familiar, but no full memory." He sighed, a heavy, heavy sigh. " 'Twill all be lost."

Now Ellie *did* find that chair. She backed up, toward the wall, until her knees caught the back of the seat; then she lowered herself.

It seemed weird to her that any of this would matter after so short a time. But it did. Probably had something to do with that whole Intended business. She wasn't Welsh. Why did it matter so much to her?

Just then Gawan, who'd moved so quietly that she hadn't heard him, squatted down beside her and took her hand. "I'm sorry," he said, his voice low. "Were I able to change things, Christ knows I would."

"Can I have a little time by myself?" she said. Really, she felt like crying, even though she thought tears weren't a cheap commodity in her real, truly alive self's armory. And when she looked at Gawan's face, especially now, after the asking for time alone, crying seemed more and more like a good thing to do. Perfect, even.

And she'd do it alone.

She stood, hands still linked. "I just . . . I'll be back in a little bit."

And with Gawan still crouching, he let her hand slide out of his as she walked to the door.

And left.

A knock sounded against the door Ellie had just closed. Rising from his crouched position, a loud popping noise coming from his knees, he shoved his hand into his hair. "Aye. 'Tis open."

Jason walked through, closing the door behind him.

He simply stood there.

Wiping his face with his hand, Gawan moved to the massive window across the chamber and looked into the darkness. "Aye, pup, what is it?"

"She won't remember any of us, sir?"

Over his shoulder, Gawan skewed the young knight with a glare. "You were listening?"

Jason, damn his overconfident self, moved closer. "Aye, of course I was. I'm her guardsman, after all."

"Hmm." Gawan turned and sat on the sill. "Why aren't you trailing her now, then?"

With a forefinger, the lad scratched his head. "She begged me to let her take her leave, just for a while."

"Couldn't say her nay, aye?"

"Not when she has her mind set, nay," Jason said. "Would you care for a go at the blades, then? Mayhap 'twill remove that foul look from upon your face?"

"Aye," Gawan said, thinking that the best thing he could do presently would be to work off some of the anger and frustration he had building. "Meet me in the lists in fifteen minutes."

"What about Lady Ellie?" Jason asked from the doorway.

"When she's ready, she'll come to me. Now off with you, and don't be late."

Jason disappeared into the passageway.

And Gawan could only pray Ellie would indeed come to him. He'd give her just so much alone time before he went in search of her.

With that, he walked to the wardrobe, flung open the door, and pulled out his sword.

Less than a bloody fortnight before either Ellie or he would have even a glimmer of a memory of each other. And only that amount of time if he didn't find her live self before then.

A fierce energy, a power of sorts built inside him— one akin to the feeling that used to come over him just before battle.

He hoped mightily young Jason of Dreadmoor could withstand the burden of his fury.

"By the saints!" Jason ground out, deflecting a hearty swing Gawan had just taken at his head. Jason, ever the fighter, no matter how sweet the maids all thought he was, came back at Gawan full force.

The steel of their swords echoed through the bailey.

Gawan relished the struggle. Relished the burn in his muscles, the icy-cold wind blasting across his sweat-soaked tunic—relished anything that gave him some measure of pain.

No pain even came close to that of not remembering Ellie.

Thrusting hard, he gave Jason all he thought the boy could handle, until finally, after nearly two hours, the lad waved off.

"Enough!" Jason cried and stumbled backward at the last hacking swing Gawan took at him, which caused the boy's blade to go flying. "I yield!"

Gawan shoved the tip of his blade into the dirt and leaned on the hilt, breathing hard, and watched Jason throw himself to the ground beside his sword and sprawl out. The outdoor floodlights caused shadows to streak across his lanky form.

"The legends are bloody true," Jason said, then picked his head up from the dirt and looked at Gawan. "You do fight like a caged animal."

Wiping his brow with the back of his arm, Gawan nodded at the boy. "Sorry, mate."

"Lord Grimm, we find your skill with your rather *large* sword exhilarating. In fact, could you promise another showing for us, say, on the morrow?"

Gawan cocked his head and stared at the dozen or so ghostly maids of all ages and centuries perched high upon the wall walk overlooking the bailey. Lady Beauchamp waved a lacy something toward him. "What say you?" she asked.

A dozen or more *please*s sounded from the other ladies.

"Mayhap, then," he said. "On the morrow."

They all giggled and disappeared, chatting noisily.

Jason sat up, tore off his gloves, and rested his forearms on his bent knees. The light was to his back, casting his face into shadows. "Whatever are you going to do, my lord?"

Gawan pierced him with a look. "About?"

"Lady Ellie." Jason picked up a stone and tossed it. "It cannot end the way you say."

Sheathing his sword, Gawan walked over and gave Jason a hand up. "Aye, boy, I fear it does. 'Tis the way of things."

Jason, too, sheathed his blade, and looked at Gawan. "I know this sounds powerfully selfish, but it pains me to know she won't remember me, either. I've grown rather fond of her."

Gawan knew the feeling well. "I know, lad." And he truly didn't know what else to say about it. It was written in the laws of all law, from the Higher-Ups of the Order. He couldn't change things, not at all, and it bloody well killed him to admit it. Even to himself.

He inclined his head toward the hall. "Let's get inside before we turn to icicles, aye?"

With a solemn expression, young Jason of Dreadmoor gave a nod. "Aye, then." He looked at Gawan. "You are, by far, the fiercest warrior I've ever seen. But please refrain from telling Sir Tristan. He'd never let me hear the end of it." He worked his arm, at the socket, a time or two. "I know my poor limbs will ache this eve."

"As will mine. You're a strong knight, boy, and a fine swordsman, in truth." He clapped Jason's back. "Tristan has trained you well."

"Thank you, sir."

As they entered the great hall, Jason stopped so suddenly, Gawan plowed into the back of him.

The great hall was filled with countless ladies and lords of yesteryear. They lined the walls, they sat in chairs, they crowded the staircase, and in the center of the room, they danced. *Waltzed.* The chattering was so loud, 'twas nigh onto deafening. Somewhere in the corner, a spirited gentleman with a top hat pounded a frolicking tune on a piano Gawan knew wasn't there earlier. Torches that hadn't been lit for years were flickering. A massive fire blazed in the hearth.

And then the crowd of ghostly revelers parted, ever so slowly, and the music came to a halt. In the center of the hall, looking a bit more solid than everyone else, thank the saints, was Ellie of Aquitaine.

And Gawan's mouth went dry as a bone.

Dressed in a long black gown that clung to her very shapely curves, her beautiful mass of hair swept up, she was truly the most breathtaking woman he'd ever laid eyes on.

Across the hall, their gazes met, melded, held steady. And then she smiled.

"By the saints," said Jason, mostly under his breath.

"Aye," Gawan managed, although not knowing how.

Just as he began to move, Nicklesby hurried from the crowd, and rushed up to Gawan. "My good sir, as you can see, the lady has something special planned for you, and I vow 'twouldn't seem right to attend said something"—he leaned his skinny self forward and sniffed—"smelling like that." He waved a hand. "Do hurry, for you know how the girl vanishes without warning."

So Gawan did what any sane man would do. He hurried.

Twenty-four

As Gawan rushed through a shower, a thousand thoughts crossed his mind. What, by the saints, was that girl up to? And mainly, where had she acquired such a gown? Since Nicklesby was the only mortal in the castle, besides himself and Jason, he could only guess that the wiry man was behind it.

He'd thank Nicklesby graciously later.

After rinsing the suds from his hair, he stepped out, dripping wet, and ran the towel about him as fast as possible. He tied the cloth about his hips, then brushed his teeth, combed his hair, ran a razor over his stubble, and made plenty of passes to the pits of both arms with the deodorant stick. That done, he moved to his chambers.

Someone had laid out one of his black suits. Certainly, he didn't need to truss up thusly?

"Aye, boy, put the bloody thing on and be done wi' it!" Godfrey said, materializing through the wall. "In case ye didn't notice, yer Intended has on a fine silk gown, indeed. You'd look plum dim-witted in yon denim breeches."

"What's going on, Godfrey?" Gawan said, dropping the towel and pulling on his boxers. "And of course I noticed she was wearing a bloody gown."

"Well, then, chop chop! Ye don't want to keep the lass waitin'! She could bloody well disappear at any time."

With deft fingers, for he'd had to wear such suits countless times whilst on a mission, Gawan threw on his trousers and tunic, pulled on socks and black shoes, cinched his belt, tied his tie, and pulled on his jacket.

"There! Aye, boy, ye look halfway decent, I'd say!" Sir Godfrey cocked his head, that ridiculous plume atop his hat all but impaling Gawan's eye. "Too bad ye don't have a bit of lace to go just here." He pointed a long finger at Gawan's neck.

"Will you cease?" Gawan said. He cleared his throat. "How do I look? In truth."

Sir Godfrey walked a slow circle around Gawan—irritatingly slow. Finally, he nodded. "Well done. Except why don't you squirt a bit of that perfume on yourself?"

"Good idea." Gawan stepped into the garderobe, sprayed one squirt of cologne, then looked in the mirror. "Damnation, what about my blasted hair? 'Tis damp."

"Me hears the ladies talk, and wind is the lass fancies your hair pulled back, just so she can free it from yon garter," Godfrey said, pointing to the leather thong on the sink.

Gawan banked *that* to memory, tied his damp hair back, and left the chamber.

Down the passageway he strode, not knowing what he was about to walk into. With Ellie involved, one could never predict.

As he managed the staircase, he found the hall completely dimmed and empty of the spirit folk who'd occupied it earlier. Godfrey had disappeared behind him. Jason was nowhere to be seen, nor was Nicklesby.

Candles lit every surface of the great hall, and the hearth's blaze had burned down but not out, giving an orange glow to the place. He blinked. A Yuletide tree, nearly reaching the rafters, sat in one corner, tiny candles lighting the piney branches. Where had that come from? As he took each step, he looked for Ellie, but it wasn't until he got a few steps from the bottom that he saw her. When he realized what she was doing, he froze, wishing mightily that he could keep this particular memory of her, if any at all, long into forever.

She'd kicked off whatever footwear she'd worn and was standing barefoot on a chair near the hall entrance, staring into a large oval mirror. With the hem of her dress held tightly in one hand, she had the other probing at the corner of her mouth as she stared at herself. With a slight clearing of throat, she lifted her chin, met her own gaze, and then, by all of the saints in satin robes, she spoke.

To the mirror.

Barely more than a whisper, yet Gawan heard the words as though they'd been shouted into his ear and traveled straight to his heart. He stood there, mesmerized by the quirky, intimate charm of hearing his Intended lady practice three little words.

"I love you," she said, pulling herself closer to the mirror. "I *looove* you. In truth," she said, with a decidedly mocked medieval accent. "Oy, I love ye." She giggled at herself and then cleared her throat once more, as though trying to force herself to be serious. "Saint's toes, I love you." She snorted. "Okay, okay." She took a deep breath, and Gawan dared not move for this was the grandest experience he'd ever experienced in nearly a thousand years. Her expression turned seductive, with one brow raised high, her lush lips puckered. "I want you. Now." This time, she laughed, slapped a hand over her mouth, then straightened, and let out a hearty sigh. She shrugged her shoulders, worked her head side to side a time or two, inhaled and exhaled, and then stared at the mirror, long and hard. "God I love you, Gawan of Con . . . wyk. . . ."

Then their eyes met in the mirror.

And they stared.

Please, Lord Almighty, keep me from falling off the back of this chair. Ellie thought, dropping her hem and bracing herself with a hand to the wall. She closed her eyes, which probably wasn't the best thing to do to keep her balance, but at least it helped lower her mortification factor.

Which was relatively high at the moment.

Gawan had caught her practicing *I love you*s in the bloody mirror!

"Ell, open your eyes."

That sexy, raspy voice washed over her, close—as in right behind her—and sent a shiver down her spine. "I'd rather keep them closed for now, if you don't mind," she said, keeping her eyes closed. "I'm not finished being mortified."

Gawan chuckled, and the next thing she knew his hands were around her waist, and her feet left the chair as he picked her up and set her on the floor in front of him, her back to his front. She kept her eyes closed, yet the heat from his body crowding hers all but made her feel like a drunken, dopey fool. With one of his hands on her hip, and the other splayed against her flat stomach, she nearly teetered, and with the scent of his freshly bathed self and the dampness of his hair closing in on her, she thought if he hadn't kept a solid hold on her, she'd have keeled right over.

He was *that* intoxicating.

She lifted her hands and set them on his. As she stood there, with him behind her, and her eyes squeezed shut, her breathing became difficult, and her heart pounded against her chest, fast. For once, and she knew it had to be a milestone for her, she couldn't say a single word.

Why bother with a single one, she thought, since she'd already said three of them. And he'd *caught* her.

Then his chin nudged her neck, and his warm, sensual lips found a spot close to her earlobe only an Intended could possibly know about. Not quite a kiss, but something more erotic. It caused goose bumps when the words, spoken in a raspy medieval whisper rushed against her skin.

"*Cara 'ch,*" he said, and then kissed the place he'd

just whispered against. His mouth lingered there, barely moving yet tasting at the same time, and the intimacy of it was almost more than she could stand. She didn't even know what the words meant, yet they touched somewhere deep inside that Ellie felt fairly sure hadn't been touched before.

"What does that mean?" she asked, surprised her tongue could form words at all. "Car, er." She sighed as he kissed her jaw. *"Cara 'ch,"* she imitated. Barely.

He turned her around, and kept one hand resting against her hip. The other one skimmed her bare arm—God, he loved the dress she had on, low, scooped back and thin straps at the shoulders—until his knuckle brushed her jaw, then lifted her chin. "Saints, girl, open your eyes now," he said. "I want you looking at me when I tell you."

She gulped. And then she did slowly open her eyes.

And stared into the ancient eyes of a once-medieval Welsh warlord turned Guardian Angel. Her Guardian Angel.

" 'Tis an endearment from the old language," Gawan said, grazing her lower lip with his thumb. He stared at her for what seemed like forever, and then his face grew serious, the muscles in his jaws tensed, and his brows pulled forward. "It means *I love you*, girl," he said, his voice decidedly much more raspier. "And by God's teeth, I do," he said, just as his mouth brushed across hers, a breath of a kiss that sent her knees to wobbling. "Say it," he said, the words coming out in a rush against her lips. "No' in the mirror this time, girl." He pulled back, his dark brown eyes searching hers. "To me." He touched both of her eyelids. "And wi' your eyes full open."

How it had happened, she couldn't quite understand. Or why, for that matter. *Now,* even. Now that she knew they'd neither one remember the other? And under such weird conditions, with her being In Betwinxt and all. How unfair was all that? But, she said to her self, drawing in a breath for her knees' sake, she'd made the decision not to dwell on *that,* once she'd decided to tell Gawan what she was about to tell him. Face-to-face. In person.

Not to a mirror.

As she looked into his eyes—those dreamy, seductive brown pools—a calmness stole over her. She couldn't explain it, exactly, and wouldn't give it a second thought until much, much later, but either way, she *felt* it. *And it felt right.* And so, she said it.

"*Cara 'ch,*" she said, mimicking his ancient language, then, "I love you, Gawan of Conwyk," in her own. She smiled. "In truth."

It was fun, really, to see the stern, intense look from his handsome features ease into such a different expression. Almost like pulling the shades down in slow motion. His brows lifted, slowly, and the muscles stopped ticking in his jaw. His mouth—God, what a great mouth—softened and lifted at the corners into a roguish grin, until that grin became a full-blown, *beautiful* smile—with teeth.

And in the next breath, that beautiful smile crashed down on hers, and Gawan kissed her with a fervor that made her heart sing, made her insides tingle.

And oooh, yeah, baby—she kissed him back.

What normal, sane girl wouldn't?

Well, she thought, as his arm pulled her closer, his hand pressing her lower back against him, his other cupping the back of her head while he kissed the daylights out of her, she wouldn't call herself *normal,* exactly.

All Ellie could think of was Gawan's hands sliding over her, nothing between his skin and hers except a very thin piece of silky material, his muscles bunching beneath her touch, the way his dampened curls, which she'd worked loose from that leather thing he wore, felt between her fingers, and his mouth moving hungrily over hers. He held her jaw just so, tilting her mouth to fit

the slant of his, and God, his tongue sent shivers all
over her.

The loud clearing of a throat slowed them down.
Didn't stop them, but slowed them down.

Before they both wound up nekkid on the great hall
floor.

"This is daft," Gawan said, his breathing ragged
against her neck. "What are you doing to me, girl?" His
hands moved over her bare back, he crowded her with
his big body, and she bit back a squeal.

*Come on, girl, make it last! Stop acting like you're
going to a fire!* an inner voice said. She was pretty sure
it was her voice, but even more sure her dad had been
the one to say it to her. A lot.

"Whoa, there big fella," she managed, gasping for air
and untangling her fingers from Gawan's hair and placing her palms flat against his chest. "We've got—well,
there are things I want to accomplish tonight."

His eyes darkened. "Aye, me, too."

Gulp.

He pulled her tightly and lowered his head to nibble
the tender skin on her neck, his still-damp locks falling
against her cheek.

"Um, wow," she mumbled, then cleared her throat
and pushed him back again. "Is that your sword or are
you happy to see me?" she snorted. "Just kidding. Don't
answer that—Gawan!"

He lifted his head, a wolfish grin on his face. "Aye?"

She glared at him. The best she could, anyway.

He cleared his throat and loosened his hold on her,
just a bit. "Aye, love, what is it?"

Love? Oh, yeah, she could hear that come from those
gorgeous lips all day long and not get tired of it. "Well,
I didn't get all dressed up just for you to grope me and
make out with me."

He quirked a brow. "You didn't?"

She slapped his arm. "No, I didn't." She raised one

brow. "Well, not *only* that." She smiled. "I want to talk. To you." She inclined her head to the corner. "Over there."

Gawan followed her inclining head gesture to the corner, although he kept a fierce hold on her. "Where did you get that Yuletide tree, girl?"

Ellie smiled, and pulled him in that direction. "It's a fake—and not as in artificial fake, as in *not really there* fake. Lady Follywolle and a few of her friends conjured it up for us. Cool, huh?"

He stopped her, his fingers sliding between hers. "You are the most charming girl I've ever encountered, Ellie of Aquitaine."

Ellie grinned. "Well, coming from someone who actually *knew* the real Ellie of Aquitaine, that's really something." She glanced behind her, to the tree, then back up at Gawan. "I don't know how much longer I have with you," she said, trying her very best not to tear up, because she *swore* to herself she wouldn't cry, "and I can't remember everything about myself, but for some reason, I feel Christmas—Yuletide—is important to me. It makes me happy." She lifted her hand and touched the very sexy bottom lip of Gawan of Conwyk. "And I want to spend my first and last one with you now, in case I don't—"

Gawan's mouth stopped the rest of the words from escaping. His kiss was strong, intense—almost desperate— and when he lifted his head and Ellie looked into his moist eyes, she knew, then, that she didn't need to explain another thing to him.

With his mouth against hers, he whispered, " 'Twill be a wondrous Yuletide, then," he said, and kissed her deeply.

"I love you," Ellie mumbled, between gasping breaths, against his mouth. "I won't forget you. Never."

" *'M aggre ydy eiddo, 'n dragwyddol 'n ddarpar,*" he whispered back, fiercely, and then kissed her long. He lifted his head and stared straight into her soul. *"Blyth 'n ddarpar."*

Just as Ellie was about to ask what the heck those delicious-sounding medieval words meant, Nicklesby popped his head out of the larder where, apparently, *everyone*—spirits included—was hiding.

"Sorry, sir, a phone call," Nicklesby said.

Gawan didn't even break eye contact with Ellie. "Take a message."

"Er, sir," Nicklesby said, clearing his throat, "You'll want to take this. 'Tis a Rick Morgan. An American. He claims you have information he wants and later just won't do."

Gawan's body stiffened, and Ellie's skin tingled. They both stared at each other, and while Gawan acknowledged Nicklesby, he didn't let Ellie go.

"I'll take it in the library, Nicklesby," Gawan said.

And he pulled Ellie along, barefoot, wearing a long black dress, and still quaking from his last kiss.

Holy bleeping saints in robes—or whatever it was that Gawan said.

It was her father.

Twenty-five

"I'll put him on speakerphone," Gawan said. "Here."
He dragged a chair close to the desk. "Sit down,
and"—he dropped a kiss across her brow—"don't shout
out. More likely than not, he won't be able to hear you."

"Okay," Ellie said. She eased into the chair and
waited.

Gawan met her gaze. 'Twas that of anticipation and,
more likely than not, fear. He couldn't blame her, by
any such means.

Moving around to his chair, he pushed the ALL SPEAK
button. "Conwyk here."

A male voice, deep, gruff, and American, sounded on
the other end of the line. "Rick Morgan. You left about
a dozen messages on my daughter's voice mail. If I
hadn't stopped by, I would've never heard any of them.
What's going on?"

"That's my dad," Ellie whispered, and Gawan could
see the excitement in her face. She gripped the edge of
his desk and leaned forward. "I know him."

"Aye, Mr. Morgan, 'twas I who left the messages. I
hoped someone would happen by there, as I've not had
any other contacts for her."

"Where's my daughter?" Rick Morgan said. "Everything else can wait. Is she alive?"

Gawan knew what he had to say would sound more
than absurd to Rick Morgan. The man's voice shook
with fear—Gawen could hear it. He wasn't a father, but

by the saints, he could well imagine what it would be
like, thinking the worse.

"She's missing," Gawan said, knowing he could not lie.
"But I have a fair assumption that, aye, she is still alive."

"Jesus Christ," Rick Morgan said, and his voice fal-
tered. "Who the hell are you? A cop?"

"Nay, I am not," Gawan said. He glanced at Ellie,
whose lovely face was drawn into a look of despair.
Bleeding saints, her eyes had filled with tears, and he
could see the strained pull of her mouth. "But I've the
constable here looking into matters. Your daughter
leased a holiday cottage from a friend of mine, and I'm
afraid she did not give her true identity on the lease,
else I would have contacted you immediately." Gawan
continued when Ellie's father remained silent. "She left
only the number I called."

A heavy sigh sounded from Rick Morgan. "Hardheaded girl. I told her I didn't like the idea of her going
over there alone. She wouldn't listen."

"Daddy," Ellie said, "can you hear me?"

Rick Morgan remained silent.

Gawan pried Ellie's fingers from the desk's edge and
threaded them through his. They were cold, and her
hand shook.

And the whole bloody mess was killing him.

"Why was she here?" Gawan asked.

Another sigh, mayhap a curse, and then Rick Morgan
cleared his throat. "She'd been doing some personal research on her mom's side of the family. That's what she
does, you know—genealogy research." He swore under
his breath. "No, I guess you didn't know. Christ, I didn't
want her to go there. *Damn* hard-ass head."

Gawan moved his gaze to Ellie's, and she gave a slight
shrug. So that was what his girl was: a damn hard-ass-
head family researcher, for the saint's sake. She was
nosy, opinionated—aye, it suited her.

"Mr. Morgan, can you tell me a few more things?"
Gawan asked.

"What else do you need to know?"

Gawan kept his eyes on Ellie. "Her name, for one."

A shuddering breath preceded his answer. "Eleanor Jane Morgan. We call her—well, we call her several things: Janie, Nor-Jane. Mostly just Nor."

Gawan blinked and so did Ellie. Her name was really Eleanor.

"Her mother? Siblings?"

"Her mother passed away several years ago. Car accident. She's got two brothers and a sister. And excuse me for being blunt, but how's this helping you find her?"

Ellie's tears fell freely now, and silently, blessedly, for Gawan knew he couldn't bear hearing her sob out loud.

" 'Tis useful, believe me," Gawan assured Rick Morgan as he looked into the man's daughter's face. "Sir, when could you and your lads and daughter leave?"

The line was quiet a moment before Rick Morgan spoke. "It'll take a day at least to settle with clients," he said. "We own a family business—contracting—and my younger daughter is in school. I'll have to get her home. Me and my older son are the only ones with passports, though."

"Can you get the others expedited?"

"If I can't, then it'll just be me and Kyle." With a deep breath, Rick Morgan's gruff voice broke. "Am I coming to plan my baby's funeral?"

The question shook Gawan clear to the bone, and Ellie's face had gone so ashen that he tightened his grip on her hand. Or mayhap he'd tightened it just to try to anchor her where she was, which was with *him*. "Not if I can help it."

Silence again.

Gawan cleared his throat. "I'll arrange your flights—"

"We can arrange them. Just tell me which airport."

Gawan clearly saw where Ellie acquired her tenacity. "London-Heathrow. Ring me with the flight information and a helicopter will be there waiting to bring you here."

"Will do. And thank you. For your help."

And then they disconnected.

Gawan let Ellie alone for a few seconds to gather her thoughts—or memories. Then he lifted her chin with a forefinger. "What's going on in that head of yours?" He could look himself, but he wanted her to tell him.

She stared at their linked hands, and with one slim finger from her other hand, she touched Gawan's knuckles. "It's weird. Sort of like talking about two different people. The me *now* and"—she drew a deep breath and looked at him—"*their* me." She went back to drawing circles over his hand. "I remember them. My dad, my sister, Bailey, and my brothers, Kyle and Kelly." She shook her head and smiled. "I remember my mom. Anna. She was a great mom."

Gawan studied every line and every curve of Ellie of Aquitaine's sweet face. And aye, no matter that he knew her full true name now, she'd always be Ellie of Aquitaine to him.

As he watched her tumble memories about, he simply settled on staring. He knew that, be it God and the saints' will that her family find her, her memories of her time spent with him and the others would indeed vanish. 'Twas why she felt so disjointed. 'Twould all balance out, in truth.

All, he knew, except for *them:* Ellie and him.

And once more he was reminded of how they could never be.

Right then he gave thanks for that, for the grief of remembering her yet not having her threatened to choke him.

"I still don't know why I came here, though," Ellie said, breaking into his gloomy thoughts. "Not details, anyway. I remember so much other stuff—even clients I've had recently." She shook her head. "Just not *this.*"

Gawan pasted on an encouraging smile. " 'Twill come to you, girl. Do not doubt that. And your family will be here soon. Tomorrow morn, we're off to see what that cleverly hidden key of yours opens." He pulled her up and wrapped his arms about her, resting his chin on the top of her head. "Until then, though, we've a Yuletide to enjoy." He looked down at her. "Aye?"

Her eyes smiled. "Definitely, aye." She cocked her head. "I can't believe my name is Eleanor Jane Morgan. Isn't that a funny coincidence?"

Gawan looked into his Intended's wide blue-green eyes. Eyes that, for now, looked into his own, trusting and full of newfound love. He thought of Queen Eleanor—of her boldness and fearlessness, not to mention her hardheadedness, along with her enormous heart—and he dropped a kiss on *his* Eleanor's nose. "Nay, girl. 'Tisn't a coincidence at all."

A sniffle sounded at the door, and Gawan and Ellie both looked at the same time.

"Oh, dear!" said Lady Follywolle, who, amongst several other hankie-waving lady spirits, stood just outside the library doorway. " 'Tis the most *romantic* thing I've ever in my days seen!" She blew into her lace hankie, the swan on her head bobbing to and fro. "Oh, dear!"

"Oy, Millicent," said Sir Godfrey, taking his own bit of lace and dabbing at her eyes. "Cease all that blubbering and dry up. 'Twill make all the other eyes in this womanly hall begin leaking."

Young Davy, who'd wormed his way between all the ladies' skirts, stood grinning as he peeped around one very drenched Bella Beauchamp. "Lady Ellie! I hope it's all right, but Sir Jason has been playing me a fine game of knucklebones. He said he'd play in your stead, whilst you and Sir Gawan had your dance"—his little face screwed up—"whatever that means. We've both won a game each!"

Ellie gave a wide smile to that young spirit, who, like everyone else, had fallen daft by her charm. "I'll let it slide this once, but I want to play you both in just a little while," she said. "Meanwhile"—leaning back against Gawan, and setting off an echo of audible sighs amongst the lady ghosts—"I've a dance to collect."

Gawan tightened his arms around his lady, then lowered his lips to her ear. "And you shall have it," he whispered, and felt her shiver. "You shall have it, and more."

"Move along, you men and ladies there," Jason said from somewhere beyond the library entrance. "Give yon lovebirds a spot of breathing room. Hurry along, then."

It was then that Gawan knew he was rather fond of Jason of Dreadmoor, for he wanted nothing more than to have some time alone with Ellie.

"Ta for now, loves," a sopping wet Lady Beauchamp said with a dramatic wave of her hankie. "We shall most assuredly see you later." With a wink, she, along with the others, vanished.

Jason, with Nicklesby just behind him, poked a head in the doorway. He pointedly looked directly at Gawan. "Beg pardon, sir, but 'tis just a reminder that I leave with you." He grinned. "I am now, and forever, the lady Ellie's personal guardsman. Her honor means much to me, and whilst I will indeed grant you a bit of privacy with her, I shall be ever so close, just there"—he inclined his head—"in the larder with young Davy and Nicklesby. Should her honor be compromised in any way, sir, forgive me, but I will not hesitate to use my sword." He gave a low bow. "Until." He winked at Ellie.

Then he left, that wiry Nicklesby grinning as he followed.

It was then, Gawan realized, just how much he loathed Jason of Dreadmoor.

"That mouthy, arrogant pup," Gawan said, and frowned. A good warrior's frown, he thought.

"I think he's sweet," Ellie said. "Cute and sweet."

Gawan turned her around to face him, but kept his arms about her. "That sweet lad has skewered many an enemy with his blade, lady."

She raised an eyebrow. "That's a little hard to believe, Conwyk. Anyway," she said, and leaned up on her bare tiptoes, her lush mouth hovering powerfully close to his, "are we going to spend our time talking about Jason and his skewering skills?"

Gawan nudged her mouth with his, and swept her with a good, solid kiss until he felt her sigh against his lips. "What think you?" He fingered the narrow strip of black silk at her bare shoulders, and by the devil's pointed tail, he couldn't stop himself from skimming the soft skin on her exposed back. "Wherever did Nicklesby get such a gown?" he asked, and it came out a growl. " 'Tis enough to tempt a bloody eunuch."

Ellie chuckled, the sound intoxicating. "Well, then, you ol' eunuch, we'd better think of something else to do than gaze into each other's eyes and make out." She pressed against him.

Gawan narrowed his eyes. "You are a wicked wench." He lifted a brow. "What have you in mind?"

A smile lifted her sweet mouth. "Now I know why all of this"—she waved a hand around the room—"you, the castle—all of it interests me so much. I'm a researcher. I love history." She cocked a brow. "Know what I want?"

Gawan could think of one thing in particular he wanted, but blast that damn knight in his larder for putting a stop to it. "What, Ellie of Aquitaine? What is it you want?"

"First," she said, "I want you to take me up to that armory upstairs. That armor—all of it. They're yours, aren't they? And I don't mean yours as in they're yours in your castle. I mean, they're *yours*. You wore them."

A pride he'd not expected filled him, just at the sight of her amazement. "Aye. 'Tis so."

She looked at him, lifted a finger to trace his jaw. "That's the most amazing thing. Besides you, of course."

Gawan found he had a rather difficult time swallowing. "And after that?"

She rose back on her toes and pressed a kiss to his mouth. "Well, then I want that dance. And while we're dancing, I want you to tell me everything about yourself—any- and everything." She kissed him longer this time, and he felt his own body shake with pent-up energy as her tongue boldly swept his. "And then," she said, breathless, "I want you to take me to the best place you've got to hide from my sweet and very cute personal guardsman."

Just then the grandfather clock in the great hall chimed ten. He glanced down at the woman in his arms, who was the only person he knew who could smile sweetly and wickedly at the same time.

"I feel like Cinderella before midnight, only I'm not sure how much time we have."

"Then let's hurry and find your shoes," Gawan said and tucked her hand into the crook of his arm.

And they did.

Twenty-six

'Twas twenty past ten when Ellie vanished.

Gawan knew that, since he'd just glanced at the wall clock in the armory. When he turned back round to where Ellie had been standing in utter amazement touching ever so gently something no one had touched in centuries—his twelfth-century gear and sword—he blinked. And she was gone.

And his stomach plummeted. He knew when she disappeared 'twas naught more than her live body regaining enough consciousness to pull her from In Betwinxt, and he hated himself for wanting to keep her, as she was, just for the sake of his own selfish benefit.

Saints, but he couldn't help it. Just like he couldn't help the gnawing ache that gouged his heart, knowing that they had not much time together, not at all.

He had to find her. With or without the constable's cooperation, he'd search every single house and barn within a hundred kilometers of Grimm. 'Twas his bloody vow, and by all of the blessed bleeding priests, he'd uphold it.

Then, just as quickly as she'd vanished, she reappeared.

Ellie—and even though she now recalled all the nicknames and pet names her family called her, she thought of herself as nothing other than Ellie—pressed the heel of her palm to her forehead to try to slow down the spinning. "Oops." She gave Gawan a smile. "Sorry about that."

The look on his face was a combination of relief and something else. Frustration? "Hey," she said, and squirmed up next to him. "I'm not finished with you yet, mister."

He put a hand on either shoulder and looked at her, his dark brows furrowed. "Ellie."

"No take backs."

He quirked a brow. "Say again?"

"I said, no take backs." She smiled and wrapped her arms around his waist, even though her head pounded like a Muther. "That means, you can't take back, you know, from before. In other words"—she squeezed him—"I refuse to allow you to foul up this night. Yeah, yeah, I know we have to find me." She shook her head. "That sounds crazy. Anyway." She pinned him with a mock frown. "But we can't very well do much of anything tonight—except have one night of togetherness." She grinned. "And get your mind out of the gutter, Conwyk. Even if you are my Intended, I'm not having sex with you—especially with mean old Jason lurking around every corner. Besides, even if we were married, it wouldn't really count, would it—the marriage, I mean . . . well, the sex, too—since I'm In Betwinxt? I mean, could you imagine, well, if I disappeared, right in the middle of—" She rubbed her temples. "Oy, me head aches with such notions."

Gawan chuckled, not a hearty rumble, but an I'm-in-church-so-stop-making-me-laugh chuckle, low, hardly even noticeable. "Indeed, girl, the notions make my own head pound. Come, and have mercy on me, aye? Quit all this talk of sex and wedlock, before you make me fast forget I swore knightly vows at all." His brown eyes darkened. "We shall make the most of this night, in the most honorable of ways I can manage, which is nigh

onto impossible, what with you in that fetching gown."
He stared at her then, long, and hard, with pure, raw
male desire.

She knew then just how powerful Gawan of Conwyk
truly was.

Then he drew a deep breath. " 'Tis far too late this
eve to worry about the matter further. Tomorrow we'll
return to the constable with your key and new information, and then begin our search in the daylight hours."

Ellie grinned. "In other words, no take backs."

The corners of Gawan's sexy mouth tipped up. Not a
smile, really, nor a smirk. And it was awfully cute. "Aye,
indeed. No take backs."

And so for hours into the night, they walked through
the castle, fingers linked, and Ellie drank in every ounce
of information Gawan gave her. While walking every
faintly lit passageway, she learned how he'd been trained
as what she referred to as a *junior warlord,* which had
made Gawan roar with laughter. She'd learned how he'd
lost his virginity at the tender age of thirteen, and with
a maid named Gwynedth, no less, and she'd called him
a big fat fibber, but he'd sworn it was the truth. Pinky
promised, even.

She told him about her first crush in kindergarten.
Dewey Devvons. "Golly, he had the cutest little
cowlick"—she tapped Gawan's forehead—"right here."
That had awarded her with a frown.

"Bloody saints, wench, how could you go witless over
a lad who'd allowed a cow to lick him thusly?" he'd said.

Ellie had laughed.

And so it went, the two of them trading stories of their
childhood both had probably long forgotten. Until now.

Stories of their parents, their siblings, their lives. Ellie
heard Gawan's knightly tales of the Crusades, cleaned
up and a lot less gory, of course, and before that, he'd
told her how he'd almost convinced a young Christian
de Gaultiers of Arrick-by-the-Sea that his horse was
his Intended.

"See you, Chris?" Gawan said, recalling the memory. " 'Tis the mark, just there." He laughed, and pulled Ellie into a shadowy alcove in the passageway. "I dared him to kiss it and see what would happen."

With a laugh, Ellie leaned against the wall and looked up. "Did he? Please, tell me he did."

"Indeed, he thought about it. But nay." His eyes, barely a flash of liquid brown in the stream of faint moonlight coming in through one of the hallway windows, looked down at her, and he moved closer.

And then they stood, neither speaking, only breathing. And, sweet God have mercy, *feeling.*

Ellie's heart raced, and heat spread through her body like melting wax, slowly moving over every part of her as Gawan pressed against her, her hips trapped within his muscular thighs. Just his closeness, the smell of him, the knowing of what he truly wanted to do with her yet refused to because of a vow he'd made nearly a thousand years before made her knees shake. His ragged breathing in the shadows was more of a turn-on than . . . well, almost anything, she thought.

Until he touched her.

And it was in the most unlikely of places where he touched her that made her heart slam against her ribs: her hair. With one hand braced against the wall, on the other side of her head, Gawan used his free hand to loosen the mass of hair she'd wound up and poked with a comb, just a simple updo. Deft fingers loosened that comb and her hair tumbled down. The comb clinked as it hit the stone flooring of the alcove.

He let her hair sift through his fingers, and he leaned forward to bring it to his nose, where he inhaled, and his warm breath on her bare neck and shoulders as he exhaled made her head feel heavy, so thank God he'd gently worked his hand through that mass of hair to cup the back of her head.

Just before he angled her jaw, just so, leaned in, and kissed her.

All sense of rational thought left her at that moment. Well, no, it'd pretty much left her a while back and nothing, not her mostly deadness, her family, the research she was doing—nothing mattered except this man's mouth against hers. It was way more than sexual attraction, although there certainly was plenty of that. It was *soul* attraction. The kiss between Intendeds, she'd later find out. Two people designed for each other, who matched perfectly in every way, even though one had been born in the twelfth century, the other in the twentieth. Who would have ever thought?

Later, she'd think about how unfair the whole thing was, but for now she'd concentrate on the way Gawan of Conwyk's body crowded against hers, seeking hers, the way the tendons in his neck stood taut as she grazed the skin there, fingering his Adam's apple as he kissed, threading her fingers through his hair. The way he savored her lips, her tongue, in a slow, sensual melding of mouths, and how his other hand left the wall beside her head and moved to her hip, where it lingered for a moment before it slipped upward, brushing first her ribs, then the outside of her breast, which, God help her, made her moan against his mouth—

"Ahem."

Yep, they were truly Intended. They kept right on kissing.

Ellie wished with all her might that it was more. A lot more.

"Go away, Jason," Ellie heard herself say in a mumble, just before Gawan captured her lips with his.

"Beg pardon, lady, but nay, I won't. But I'll be just there, up the hall, *with my sword,* should things in this alcove become any—"

"Go away, Jason," Ellie and Gawan said in unison.

"Boy, don't you think I'd have more chivalry than to take my Intended against a bloody wall?" Gawan ground out, his breathing ragged.

"A wall's fine with me," Ellie whispered, and Gawan covered her mouth with his hand.

"Aye, sir, I should hope so. But I'll be just over there, by the by."

Jason, bless his knightly, vow-swearing soul, walked off, to *just over there*, which wasn't very far at all.

Gawan removed his hand from Ellie's mouth, and traced the lips he'd just hungrily kissed. "I vow, woman, you've no propriety." He kissed her neck, just below her ear. "Fine, fetching quality you have, methinks."

Ellie squirmed, giggled, and then bent her neck to the side for Gawan to claim. He did claim it, and claimed it good, and she wondered if a thousand-year-old Angel would know how to give a hickey. God knew she hadn't had one in years.

Not for the first time since they'd been in their Alcove of Passion, Gawan's . . . um . . . *joy* in touching her pressed heavily against her hip. The thought of just how well endowed a twelfth-century warlord could be made her light-headed. She tried to angle away from the waist down, not that she succeeded, but she should get points for trying.

Gawan moved his hands back to the wall, one on either side of Ellie's head, and he nudged her mouth open with his and whispered those same ancient Welsh words from before, and then he kissed her.

"Have mercy upon me, girl," he said finally, his medieval accent thicker than ever, "and let's be away from this seductive place before you well and truly get your wall wish." He gave her mouth a quick assault, quick yet extremely effective, she noted. Then he grabbed her by the hand and pulled. "Come."

She fanned herself because she almost *had*.

When they reached the great hall, they found the candles were still lit, the hearth stoked to a roaring blaze, and the wall sconces glimmered. The ceiling-high Victorian-style Christmas tree twinkled with hundreds of tiny candles, bows, and glass ornaments, and somewhere a tinny old-fashioned melody played. And there, into the wee hours of the night, with a ghostly audience, Gawan pulled Ellie close, and held her tight.

And they danced.

Twenty-seven

Gawan didn't yet open his eyes, because he knew when he did, the night would be over. So he kept his eyes shut, and his breathing as regular as could be managed.

His head rested upon the most comfortable pillow, and that pillow had a hand with fingers, and those fingers were gently stroking his hairline.

He accidentally sighed.

"I know you're awake, Conwyk," the pillow said. "I've been watching your eyelids move."

"Damn," he said, cracked open one eye, then the other, and grinned. "Are you sure you're not a constable instead of a researcher? You're a rather shrewd wench."

Ellie giggled. "Shrewd. Hmm." She flicked his ear. "I like the sound of that." She stroked his temple, and then slid her fingers through his hair.

"So you've sat here since I nodded off, keeping watch over my sleeping self all night?" he asked, wishing like hell he hadn't fallen asleep, but 'twas one of the conditions of an Earthbound Angel: live like a mortal.

"Don't be so conceited, Gawan of Conwyk," she said with a grin, and he knew this because she'd leaned way over and looked at him. "I was thinking, too, you know. Not just gazing at your beauty."

He chuckled. "Ah, but you did do at least some gazing, aye?"

She traced his nose. "Of course, silly."

It could have been a dream, but Gawan then thought he'd remembered Ellie whispering to him, whilst he wasn't quite asleep nor awake. "Did I fall asleep when you were talking?"

"No." She took his jaw and lifted it, forcing him to look at her. "What were those words you whispered to me? Last night?"

He hadn't thought she'd noticed overmuch. "Words of endearment, love," he said, taking her hand in his. "Why?"

"Just wondering, is all." She squeezed her fingers around his.

"Methinks 'twould be a fine gesture, indeed, if you took the lady to the tower and watched the sunrise. 'Tis clear enough this morn."

Both Gawan and Ellie jumped as Sir Godfrey appeared through the wall. He grinned and gave a bow. "A fine morn to you, lady."

"Thanks, Sir Godfrey," Ellie said.

Gawan rose and pulled Ellie up with him. "Aye, Godfrey, a fine idea, that."

It was then that Ellie's fingers grew light within his. She kept her eyes trained on him, and she gave a slight yet reluctant smile, just as she disappeared.

Gawan watched the remnants of her solid self vanish, and he swore.

And then he stood still, in the hopes that she'd come right back, as she had the night before.

"Boy, I fear 'tis time," Sir Godfrey said.

The larder door swung open, and across the great hall walked Nicklesby, followed closely by Jason and Davy.

"Has she gone again, sir?" Jason asked, looking around.

"Aye." Gawan swiped a hand over his jaw, then looked at Jason. "I'll be ready in fifteen minutes, lad."

Jason gave a nod and headed for the stairs.

"Nicklesby," Gawan said, following Jason, "Mr. Morgan may call whilst I'm out. You realize I've not told him everything."

"Most certainly, sir," Nicklesby said, tightening the sash on his robe. "Shall I go with you?"

Gawan stopped at the stairs. "I can use your skills best here, my friend."

"And mine, too?" asked Davy. The curious lad stood wide-eyed, his soft hat cocked over one brow, as always.

"Aye, boy. Yours, too."

"Breakfast at all?" Nicklesby asked.

"Nay." Gawan took the stairs by two. "If the constable rings, tell him I'm on my way."

'Twas nearly two hours later, when Gawan and Jason, accompanied by Constable Hurley, stood before the man in charge of safe-deposit boxes at the bank.

Mr. Delwaney—so said a name tag pinned to the front of his too tight jacket—a plump, bespectacled balding man of average height rose from his chair behind the desk. He gave a short glance to Hurley, then turned to Gawan. "Name?"

"Eleanor Morgan," Gawan said.

Mr. Delwaney asked, "And you are?"

"We're in Ms. Morgan's stead, Stanley. Can you tell us if she has a box leased?" Hurley asked.

Stanley Delwaney shook his head. "You know better than that, Constable. Unless you have a warrant?"

Damnation, Gawan didn't have time for this. As much as he wished things could be different for him and Ellie, they simply could not be. But by the bleeding priests and saints above, he would make sure Ellie didn't suffer for it.

He leaned forward, looked down at Stanley Delwaney, and pinned him with a glare. "We need no warrant." Then, with his mind, he spoke clearly to Delwaney. *Does Eleanor Jane Morgan have a safe-deposit box here, and if so, get it. Now.*

Wordlessly, Stanley turned to his computer, typed in Ellie's name, and pulled up her information. He went to a large steel door in the back, next to the safe, opened the door and retrieved a thin metal box. He handed it to Gawan through the sliding bulletproof window.

"What the bloody hell?" whispered Hurley. Then he looked at Gawan and wiped a brow. "I won't even ask."

Withdrawing the key from his pocket, Gawan opened the box. Inside was an old leather-bound ledger. "Ellie mentioned a ledger in one of her visions," he said. Turning to Stanely, who stood completely still, he handed him the empty box and key. *Put this away, and delete all information regarding Eleanor Jane Morgan from your files. You won't remember our visit here, nor will you recall Eleanor Jane Morgan.* "Good morn," Gawan said out loud, and then they left.

"What did you do?" Hurley said as they stepped out into the biting cold. "Bloody brainwash him?"

Gawan stared at the ledger. "Something like that." He turned the pages and skimmed the old faded words penned against parchment now yellow with age.

"What do you make of it?" Jason asked, leaning forward and reading alongside Gawan.

"I'm not certain," he said. " 'Tis more personal notes—findings of a sort, dates." He shook his head. "Maybe Ellie will know. She obviously thought it important enough to place it under lock and key." He turned to Hurley. "Constable, have you come up with anything regarding the fingerprints at the Dreadmoor rental?"

"Nothing for certain, as there seem to be several sets of prints about the place. You say her father and siblings are flying over from America?" He took a small pad of paper and a pen from his pocket. "Their names?"

Gawan gave him Ellie's father's full name.

"So you've discovered why she was here, then?" Hurley asked.

"Somewhat vaguely, aye. Her father claims she's a

family researcher—a genealogist—and supposedly, she came here on personal business."

Hurley pulled his overcoat collar up and turned his back against the chilled wind. "He has no idea who, in particular, she was researching?"

"Her mother's family," Gawan said, and then a thought struck him at the same time. "By the saints, she didn't tell me her mother's maiden name."

"Addler." Ellie appeared at Gawan's side and leaned over the ledger. "Oh my God, that's the ledger from my vision—only it really happened, I think." She blinked, looking all too confused and pale. "It's my great-grandfather's—my mom's grandfather. Grandpa Phin. I found it in an old bureau that belonged to him." She looked up at Gawan. "His family changed their name to Addler when they came to America."

"Saints," Jason said. "Then what brought you here?"

"I obviously found the familial link." She looked up. "But I don't remember what it is. I sort of remember the research—just not the link."

Constable Hurley paled. "She's here now, isn't she? Your Ellie?"

Gawan glanced at *his* Ellie, who was not looking at all as vibrant as she had earlier that morn. "Aye, and she gives her regards and begs you to lose that pasty complexion. She doesn't bloody bite."

Hurley looked around, then gave a nod and a sigh. "Aye. Sorry, then."

Gawan rubbed his chin. "Knowing why Ellie was here—better yet, the link she found—would certainly help matters." He glanced at his Intended, who gave him a wan smile. "But we've not the time for it." He looked at Hurley. "If you could make a few phone calls, mayhap someone could look into a database of sorts to see about a family changing their name to Addler and leaving for the Americas at the turn of the century. Meanwhile"—he glanced at Jason—"we need to find her." He'd had a building of anxiety about that, well, ever since he'd met her, but especially since this morning, when she'd disappeared and reappeared so quickly. And now she looked so fragile. Standing in that fetching black gown, looking so bloody fragile. *By the saints* . . .

"Gawan, don't," Ellie said, her cool fingers slipping through his. "I'm fine."

He squeezed her hand, wishing he could bind her to him forever. . . .

A brisk sea wind whistled through the buildings, and the clouds overhead swirled gray. "I've already contacted Dreadmoor and his men. They'll be here any moment, but a few more could only speed matters along, if you have any to spare, Constable."

Hurley nodded. "I'll make some calls. But I can't gather any warrants to search homes or establishments. Not without just cause. Location?"

Gawan gave him a thirty-kilometer radius in all directions from Tristan's cottage. "I don't even bloody know what it is we're searching for. She's heard a male voice and a female voice speak over her, and she's smelled wet stone, hay, and clover. Otherwise, 'tis been nothing but darkness."

"Damn," Hurley said, scratching his head. "She could be in a field or a cave for all we bloody well know."

Gawan nodded. "Aye. I do know, not to mention the farmsteads and crofters stretched about the coastline. The more men we have searching, the better." He pressed his eyes with his knuckles.

"Here's Sir Tristan now," Jason said.

"Damn me, it looks like a bloody circus," Hurley said. "Are you positive you need my men?"

Gawan wondered, indeed, as four vehichles and two motorbikes pulled up the the street walk. Andi drove one vehicle, holding three knights. Tristan drove another, also with three knights. Kail, Tristan's captain, drove yet another, with four knights, and two more were on their motorbikes.

A circus, indeed. And one Gawan was ever so grateful for.

Tristan unfolded himself from his car and walked straight over to Ellie. "How do you feel, lady?" he asked.

She smiled and leaned into Gawan. "Super, thanks. Are you here to search for *me*?"

He gave her a short nod. "In truth, while it sounds passing odd, I can assure you, I've seen odder." He slapped Gawan on the arm. "Finally, this uncanny snow and mist have lifted, although it's bloody freezing out here. I don't much recall it being this cold in our day."

"You've just gone soft, my lord," Jameson said, stepping up to the group. "I daresay the weather is quite suitable." He nodded at Gawan, then at Ellie. "Good day to you both. Young Jason, to you as well."

Constable Hurley glanced at the old steward. "You can see her?"

Jameson, without changing his expression, winked at Ellie. "For a certainty, Constable. You cannot? More the pity. A lovely girl, indeed."

Gawan completely agreed.

Andi and the others joined them, and after greetings were passed all round, Gawan stood at the head of the search group. "Tristan, men"—he smiled at Andi— "lady, thank you for helping. I vow I couldn't be armed with a better garrison than this one."

And then he proceeded to give out directions, coordinates, and markers for their search. "We'll meet back here, since this appears to be the center of our grid."

Everyone said their ayes and started in their given direction. Before Tristan left, he stood, gripped Gawan by the shoulder, and squeezed. "We'll search until we find her," he said, and Gawan could see the fierceness of the infamous Dragonhawk just beneath the man's calm exterior. "We'll not stop until we do."

And Gawan prayed 'twas soon.

Twenty-eight

After nearly a week of searching, they'd found naught.

Gawan had spoken to a dozen crofters, and had gone into each one of their heads, only to find them speaking the bloody truth: they'd not seen anything suspicious— certainly no fetching American lass like the one in his photo.

He'd hoped that, with Ellie along for most of his searches, mayhap she'd recognize a voice. But nay, she had not.

And bleeding priests, every hour that passed, she seemed fainter than the last. It was killing him.

Tristan's men had even gone into the Borders, and so far, they'd encountered nothing. Naught by the roadside, nor in the fields or farmer's crofts—nothing.

And yet the Dragonhawk and his knights—and his lady, not to mention that old wiry steward Jameson— had only stopped to eat, then rest during the night. Before dawn broke, they were back at it, searching in different directions.

A fine lot, the Dreadmoors.

Now Ellie sat, as she had almost every eve, close to Gawan on the sofa before the hearth, only this time, they waited for her father and siblings to arrive. Jason, fine lad that he was, had given them a brief bit of privacy.

"It's only three days before Christmas Eve," she said,

moving her fingers gently over his knuckles. "Your retirement."

He wanted to touch her so badly, it pained him. But he dared not. He'd battled every selfish demon within to keep his hands from her. Worse still, she felt it, too— 'twas blatantly obvious. Not just because he could see how stormy her sea-colored eyes would turn after a kiss, but because he'd sneaked into her mind a time or two. Shameless, he knew, but he'd not been able to help it. And after seeing the depth of love she truly felt for him, he almost wish he'd stayed out.

Instead of ravishing her, though, he held her hand as gently as he could. "Aye, girl. I know."

"What's going to happen?" she asked.

Gawan didn't want to think about it. He wondered what could be worse: having a loved one taken from you unexpectedly, as in dying from an accident, or knowing it was coming. And not merely knowing it, but knowing when, to the minute, every last memory of the person you love is wiped clean, never to return. Either way, 'twas a pain he'd not wish on his worst bloody enemy.

Aye. The very last thing he wanted Ellie to do was worry about it. So instead, he leaned forward, brushed a soft kiss across her lips, and smiled. "We'll see."

Ellie marveled at how difficult it was for Gawan to hold her hand gently. So difficult, in fact, that his hand shook. As big and strong as he was, it made it all the more of a marvel that he had so much control. She could only imagine what he'd been like in his head-lopping days.

They had less three days together, and they'd be spending that little scrap of time looking for her stupid, injured, half-dead self. And then *whack!*—come midnight on Christmas Eve, the memory of the gorgeous, sweet, powerful, sexy man who'd touched her more deeply than anyone could ever hope to reach would be gone.

She blew a strand of hair from her eyes and turned to him. He stared at their hands, fingers entwined. "We'll see?" she repeated in a quiet voice, and then he lifted his eyes and met her gaze. "Have I told you lately how much I dislike these dopey rules?" She frowned and fought back tears. No matter how hard she tried, she could only think of losing him in seventy-two. "Seriously dopey."

"Ell," Gawan said, his raspy voice steady.

With a burst of frustration, she stood up and started to pace. "No, Gawan, I mean it. Why does it have to be this way?" Hooking her thumbs into into her jean pockets. "Can't They bend the rules? Just this once?"

Sliding forward on the sofa, Gawan rested his forearms on his knees, which were splayed out in the way guys casually sit. He stared at his feet. " 'Twould follow that a bloody Angel would have a bit more power, aye?"

Ellie stopped and looked at him. "No offense here, Conwyk, but while it's pretty cool that you're older than *dirt,* and have a very naughty, if not phenomenal, ability to bend people's will and read their thoughts, you're an *Earthbound* Angel. Not a magical Angel—Earthbound." She marched over to him and stood, giving his boot toe a small kick with her own. She tugged on his hair. "And you've been amazing. The most incredible—amazing— no . . ." She scratched her chin. "Help me here, Conwyk."

"I fancy *phenomenal,*" he said without looking up.

Taking both of Gawan's hands in her own, she tugged and, with very little resistance, pulled him up. She wrapped her arms around his waist and leaned her head back to look at him. She gave him a smile. "Wanna hear something funny?"

Gawan stared down at her, steady, intense, as though memorizing every single line in her face. "I vow if something humorous could be found in this situation, you'd be the one to find it." He lifted a hand and lightly traced her lip. "Tell me what's funny, Ellie of Aquitaine."

"Well," she said, trying really hard to concentrate since his touch was the most intimate of touches, "before we found out who I really was, I kinda had thoughts that maybe I'd be something really fantastic, like, I don't know, a detective or an FBI agent or something." She smiled, his eyes still trained on her. "Funny, huh?"

"I find your line of work exceptionally interesting. But I've not yet found out how or where you learned your warrior skills. I daresay Tristan is still nursing a few tender body parts from your assault that day in his rental."

Ellie laughed. "Brothers, Conwyk. I've got older brothers."

Gawan nodded. "I'll be sure to thank them." He studied her for a moment, then pulled her close and tucked her head beneath his chin. "I vow you're paler than before." She felt his deep breath as his chest rose against hers, and she squeezed her eyes shut because the thought of never feeling him or smelling his skin ever again threatened to overwhelm her, no matter how many pep talks about *not thinking about it anymore* she gave herself.

"Blimey, Sir Gawan, don't squeeze her so hard. You'll make her go all the *way* away. And, lady, why are your eyes squeezed so tight? Are you sleepy?"

Ellie opened her eyes and met the wide gaze of young Davy. He wiped his nose on the back of his billowy white sleeve. "I guess I am a little tired. Where's Cotswald?"

Davy shrugged. "Sometimes he runs off and comes back days later. Methinks he likes to go to other castles, where he might find a cat or two to chase." He cocked his head. "Your face looks sad. Don't be." He shoved his hands into his trouser pockets. "If Sir Gawan 'ere can't find ye, and you, well, you know, you could always come here and live wi' us."

Sir Godfrey, accompanied by the ladies Follywolle and Beauchamp, wandered in. "Aye, girl," Sir Godfrey said, his voice gruff, "yer always welcome here amongst us ghosties. But dunno worry overmuch. Things have a way o' working themselves out, most times."

As Lady Follywolle nodded her agreement, her big white coiffed bird bobbled its long neck. " 'Tis so, sweetling. Most assuredly, you are always most welcome here at Grimm."

Gawan's embrace grew tighter and he cleared his throat. "You are a fine family, indeed."

Just then Nicklesby rushed in from the larder, Jason on his heels.

"The helicopter is just five minutes out," Nicklesby said; then he looked at Ellie and paled. "Oh, my dear, mayhap you should rest a bit."

"Aye," Jason said, coming to stand beside her. "I vow, my lady, you're looking quite worn."

Ellie smiled at everyone. "You guys are all so great." She reached out and grabbed Jason's hand. "*You* are a big worrywart." She grinned. "And I think it's cute. But I'm fine." When she looked at all the unconvinced expressions, she laughed. "Honestly, guys, I'm fine. Really." And when her gaze met Davy's, he blushed clear up to his soft hat. "And you have got to be the sweetest guy. Thank you very much for inviting me to stay with you, if, well, you know."

He smiled and gave a nod.

"Now," Nicklesby said, running his skinny self all around, "you folks must go for now! You must remember what Sir Gawan has told you. Only appear whenst he calls for you." Nickelsby gave each one a pointed look. "Aye?"

"Don't get your shirttails in a tussle, Nicklesby," said Sir Godfrey. "We won't do nothin' until called upon." He turned to his companions. "Come on then, ladies and young Davy. Let's find us a good watchin' spot for that helicopter."

They moved off—all except Davy. He glanced up at

Ellie, still snuggled in Gawan's embrace. "You'll still be here come the morn, aye?" he asked.

Ellie pulled free of Gawan's grip, which was quite tight, she thought, and bent over at the waist, eye level with Davy. "I've drawn the conclusion that whatever happens is meant to be." She smiled and hoped he understood her. "But if I am here, you owe me another chance at knucklebones, you little swindler."

Davy gave her a solemn smile, and a nod. "Aye, the chance will be yours for the takin', then," he said. "See ya."

And with that, he vanished with the others.

She moved back into Gawan's arms for a quick fix, a fast hug, and found herself not wanting to budge an inch as his warmth somehow managed to seep into her ever-growing cold skin.

"*Cara 'ch,* Eleanor Jane Morgan," he whispered against her ear. His mouth moved from her ear to her lips, where he gently nudged them open for the sweetest of kisses. The heat in his eyes all but scorched her when he finished. "Damn but I love you, wench," he said. "Forever."

And Ellie thought she just might give in and cry.

"Yeah, well," she said, with a slow kiss of her own, "I love you, Gawan of Conwyk"—she copied his movement and traced his very sexy bottom lip—"for *infinity.*"

And Ellie stood right within the strong arms of her Intended until Nicklesby hurried to the great hall doors.

"They're landing," he said.

Ellie whispered as she stepped out of the comfort of Gawan's arms, "Good luck."

Somehow, she thought they'd both need it.

Gawan gave her a final kiss to the nose, thought better of it, and brought his mouth down to cover Ellie's. Lips that once felt warm now felt cool; he feared each kiss would be his last and so he kept taking them. A small groan from Ellie, not to mention her fingers tugging at his hair, encouraged him thusly, until Nicklesby made in his throat a rather fearful noise that Gawan didn't fancy in the least. He drew back from Ellie, moved her near the hearth to sit in a straight-backed chair he'd placed there for that very reason, grabbed his wool coat from the closet, and left Nicklesby at the door whilst he went to the chopper pad in the east bailey.

Moments later, Gawan awaited as Ellie's sire stepped down from the helicopter. The Morgans had encountered a few problems getting the two passports expedited for Ellie's brother and sister. Then the plane had experienced problems before takeoff from the States, and they'd had another delay. Finally, they'd arrived at Heathrow.

The exaggerated wind from the chopper's blades made it seem as though a cyclone had touched down in the bailey. Rick Morgan emerged first, duffel bag thrown over one shoulder—and aye, Gawan knew it to be Ellie's sire right away—ducking as he moved under the whirring blades toward Gawan. He shoved a gloved hand toward Gawan, who took it.

"Mr. Morgan," Gawan said with a nod and a firm shake.

The first thing Gawan noticed were the worry lines etched around the man's eyes. Damnation, he probably hadn't slept a bloody wink. Gawan couldn't blame him.

Two more lads followed out of the craft, both as big as their sire. Ellie's sister stepped out last. Shorter than Ellie, and petite, she wore a dark cap stretched over her head and a big scarf wrapped about her neck. Like the others, she had but one duffel thrown over her shoulder.

"Aye, Morgans," Gawan said, stepping up beside Ellie's sire. "Follow me."

Around the side of the east wall, Gawan led the Morgan family up the steps and through the double doors of Castle Grimm.

He briefly noticed it'd begun to snow once again.

After a hearty stomping of boots at the entrance, the Morgan family stepped into the great hall.

Gawan's gaze shot straight over to Ellie, who, as he'd suspected, was no longer in her seat. Instead, she paced before the hearth, and at the sound of the crowd walking through the door, she started to bolt toward them. Then, blessedly, stopped.

Their eyes met, and he gave what he hoped was a comforting, if somewhat slight, smile. Then he turned his attention to her family.

"Mr. Morgan," he said, "this is Nicklesby. He'll show you to your chambers, where you can set your belongings down and freshen up before we begin."

"Have you had any more news?" he said, and Gawan noticed how bleak the man's eyes—blue-green, just like Ellie's—were. The man, who was just an inch or two shorter than Gawan, and strongly built, ran a hand through a head of thick dark hair tinged with a bit of gray at the temples. "Since yesterday?"

Four pairs of eyes waited, hoped for some morsel of news, and Gawan had none. "Nay, nothing new." He extended a hand to each of Ellie's brothers, who each in turn did accept and shake with strength.

One, the older lad, Kyle, was the spitting image of his father. Kelly, Gawan noticed, had small variances in features, but no doubt shared the same sire as the others. The lass, though. Bailey, who did indeed extend her hand, as well, had surprisingly fair-colored hair, cut to the shoulders, with a slender nose and high cheekbones. Like the others, Ellie's blue-green eyes stared back wide, expecting.

"Do you know my sister well?" she asked, her voice strong yet feminine.

All four waited for an answer. Briefly, Gawan looked Ellie's way. She had come closer and, damnation, had tears in her eyes.

"Aye"—he could answer in no other way—"I feel I truly do."

Nicklesby—and Gawan would remind himself later to give the scrawny man a fierce hug—hurried the Morgans up the steps to the upper chambers. "Come along, let's get you settled, then," he said. "Here, young lady, shall I take your bag?"

With a smile that reminded him of Ellie's, she shook her head. "Thanks, but I've got it."

Nicklesby, ever so tactful, gave a short nod and rushed ahead of Rick Morgan. "This way, then, as I'm sure you're anxious to have a bite to eat and discuss matters."

Gawan stood and watched them disappear, their heads turning this way and that as they looked at the furnishings of Castle Grimm. He turned to Ellie, who'd crossed the floor to meet him.

"They don't see me," she said, disappointment lacing her face.

"Nay, but we didn't expect them to, love." Gawan dragged a hank of hair from her eyes. "And 'tis a wondrous gift, indeed, that I've been given the ability to do so, for you are quite a sight to behold."

Ellie smiled up at him, although the smile was faint, indeed. "Aww, shucks. You medieval warlords say the darnedest things."

His Ellie. Ever so brave, even whilst facing something no maid should ever face. "Aye, indeed we do, and we say them sincerely, in truth."

She glanced in the direction of the steps, and her face softened. "I haven't seen my dad look so weary since the night my mom was killed." She shook her head. "I hate that he's going through this again."

Gawan nodded, for he could well imagine the agonizing sorrow not only to lose your beloved mate, but to think your child had been taken, as well. The thought was unbearable.

He'd try mightily to put them all at ease.

Within minutes, the Morgans returned to the great hall, and Nicklesby seated them near the hearth on the sofa. Gawan took a chair beside Ellie's. Leaning forward, he placed his forearms on his knees and began.

He looked straight at Rick Morgan. "What I have to say is not going to be an easy bone to swallow. But I vow, 'tis the truth. So bear with me."

All four Morgans stared at him, faces taut, and Gawan knew, indeed, 'twould be a vastly larger bone than he'd suspected.

And then he told them Ellie's story from the moment Gawan came across Ellie in the freezing rain until, just a few minutes before they reentered the great hall. They continued to stare, eyes fixed on Gawan.

Rick Morgan stood up, and, like his daughter, began to pace.

"You're full of sh—" Kyle said.

"Be quiet, Kyle," Rick told his elder lad. "Just be quiet."

"This is stupid, Dad!" the other brother, Kelly, said.

Kyle, whose face flushed with anger, sat back and hushed, and after the look Rick Morgan shot his second son, he, too, was quiet.

Then Rick Morgan stopped in front of the hearth and stared into the fire. "You're telling me my baby girl's sitting"—he glanced at the place Ellie was indeed sitting—"right there?"

Gawan glanced at Ellie, who looked even paler still, and then rubbed his face. "I know it sounds daft, but 'tis true." He moved to Rick Morgan. "And I can prove it."

Twenty-nine

Ellie saw it coming, and she suspected Gawan did, too, long before it even happened.

And, she thought as she peeked through her half-cracked eyelids, that Gawan was indeedy-o one strong warrior to withstand it like he did.

Her dad—big, muscular, and not looking his forty-eight years at all—glanced down at the floor, shook his head, then pulled back one muscular arm and racked Gawan across the chin.

The others shrieked.

"Daddy!" Bailey said, flying off the sofa.

"Jesus, Dad!" Kyle said as he jumped in between the two, pushing his father back. "Lay off, now," he said.

Kelly just stood, looking as if he wouldn't mind getting in a good swat.

Gawan hadn't moved an inch. Not one good solid inch. He cast a quick glance at Ellie, lifted one eyebrow, and rubbed the jaw that Rick Morgan had nearly dislocated.

"Nice job," Ellie said to Gawan. "You've just moved several places up my Holy-Crap-You're-Awesome meter."

Gawan shrugged, then looked at her father. "Mr. Morgan, I—"

Rick Morgan tried to push past Kyle. If Kyle hadn't been careful, he would have gotten a knock, too.

"Daddy, stop it!" Bailey said, almost in tears now.

"Bail, you old Bailer, you," Ellie said softly. She'd give anything to go hug her little sister. "If they only knew Daddy was trying to flatten an Angel."

"My good sir! Me likes a good wrestle in the rushes, just as much as the next lad, but you needs open yer ears, man," said a *very* familiar voice. "The boy's tellin' ye the truth!"

Sir Godfrey stepped through the wall, just on the other side of the hearth. He stood in all his glory, too— all that ruffled lace and velvet. And that big fat ostrich plume boinging around every time he moved his head. "I tell ye, shut yer trap and listen to the lad!"

Bailey—you had to love her—drew in an impossibly long breath that seemed to go on and on.

"Oh, boy. Bailey's gonna blow," Ellie said just as Bailey blew.

The scream, in Ellie's opinion, rivaled any of those B-rated horror scream-fest babes. Bailey had practiced it—had it down to a science. Ellie should know. She'd heard that scream more times than she could count. And the great hall literally shook with it.

Just before the Castle Grimm Fiasco ensued.

For a second, Ellie wished harder than anything that a cinematographer could have captured the whole thing on tape. It was fantastic, and had she been feeling a bit better, she would have enjoyed it immensely.

Jason ran from the library, where he was supposed to be keeping the Grimm spirits busy. Fat chance of that, she could have told him, as they all ran through the wall ahead of the Dreadmoor knight.

Nicklesby ran from, of course, the larder, with a wooden spoon in one hand, and his red-and-black-checked apron swirling around his lanky self like a dressing gown as he frantically waved an oven-mitted hand.

Bailey screamed for a good two mintues, easily, and the only person paying her any attention was Jason, who tried to get her to calm down.

And Ellie's dad . . . well, it was the first time she could

remember someone—or something—actually having the capability of shutting him up. His face had gone white, his eyes were wide like a pair of blue-green fried eggs, and his mouth was open.

Kyle and Kelly just kept turning in circles, staring from one ghost to the other. Cursing.

Finally, the Morgans, minus Ellie, all stood in a circle, nearly back-to-back, and the Grimm inhabitants stood facing them.

Then, finally, everything was silent.

"Did ye tell 'im ye were an Angel, boy?" Godfrey asked.

Still, everything remained silent.

"Er, don't forget to tell him yer an Earthbound Angel."

"Godfrey!" Gawan finally said. Rather, growled.

"Why not show 'em yer"—Godfrey flapped his lace-and-velvet-covered arms like a chicken—"proof?"

Ellie, at that point, could help it no longer. She laughed. It came out as a hiccup, really, which due to the insanity of the whole thing, made her just burst out into laughter. Everyone's eyes, except those of the other Morgans, of course, turned to her.

"Poor lamb," said Lady Follywolle, her swan close to takeoff. "She's going to laugh herself sick."

Staring at that ridiculous swan bobbing its long neck up and down released the rest of Ellie's insanity. She howled with laughter. So much so, she backed up and sat down in the chair. "Oh my *God*! Could this be any crazier?" She glanced at Gawan, who, to his credit, was ferociously fighting a grin.

"This can't be real," Rick Morgan finally said, finding his own seat on the sofa. He rubbed both hands over his face. "This is insane."

"What are those things?" Bailey finally said.

"My dear girl, we're not things at all," said Lady Beauchamp. "Truly, your lovely sister there thinks the world of us." She glanced at Ellie. "Don't you, sweetling?"

Ellie nodded. "Absolutely. By far the nicest bleeping folks I've ever encountered."

Lady Beauchamp turned back to Ellie's sister. "See there, love? She just said we were by far the nicest bleeping folks she'd ever encountered."

Bailey blinked, hiccupped, then sniffed. "Daddy?"

"What, baby?" said her dad, sounding muffled through the hands still covering his face.

"Only me and Nor say *bleeping* in place of a curse word. We made it up when we were little." She glanced at Ellie—rather, where she was sitting. "Ask her who her first boyfriend was. And *not* Gooey Dewey."

Ellie laughed. "Little Joe. One fine Cartright."

Gawan glared at her, and she grinned. "Take it easy there, warlord."

Lady Beauchamp smiled at Bailey. "Little Joe. And she says he was one fine Cart—"

"—right," Bailey finished the word. She smiled and looked around. "She's here."

Whilst Gawan was powerfully glad to get the Castle Grimm Fiasco, which was what Ellie called it, behind him, his fear for Ellie's life grew by the second. She hadn't paled further, and he could still touch her, but by the saints, she didn't have long. He could sense it.

Yet she held her chin high and made the most of it.

Aye. A true descendant of Queen Eleanor if ever he'd seen one. And bloody priests, she was *his*. Even if for only a bit longer. He'd found more happiness with her in such a short time than he had in nearly a thousand years.

After things settled down in the great hall, Ellie's family, who were still dubious of her In-Betwinxt existence but slowly warming to the idea with each question they asked her, had finally been overtaken by jet lag and gone to bed.

Jason, Gawan had noticed, had taken quite a shine to Ellie's little sister. But he'd been a good lad, offering her a walk around the castle to settle her nerves, after, of course, asking permission from her sire. Who had blinked, then agreed.

Before Rick Morgan had retired to his chamber, he'd stopped at the foot of the stairway and turned to Gawan. "I'm sorry for giving you that lick," he said. "I-it's a hard thing to come to grips with, you know?" He shook his head, then looked Gawan square in the eye. "You know when I realized you weren't pulling my leg? When that one sopping-wet ghost lady said my baby was laughing." He gave a wan smile. "That girl, she's tough. Crazy, hardheaded, but tough." He leveled at Gawan the most pleading stare he'd ever witnessed. "Find her."

Gawan nodded, and Rick Morgan walked away.

"Wow," Ellie said, coming to stand beside him. "You just passed Rick Morgan's Are-You-Worthy-Enough Class with flying colors."

"How's that?" Gawan asked, drawing her close now that they were alone.

"Because," Ellie said, threading her fingers through his, "he didn't hit you again."

Gawan stared at her. "He loves you fiercely." Ever so gently, he lowered his head and brushed her lips with his. "I know the feeling." When he pulled back, he smiled. "If you wish to sit and go through your great-grandfather's ledger again, we can."

Ellie tapped a finger to her chin. "Hmm. Go through old ledger, or spend time with a gorgeous warlord with cute accent?" She shook her head. "I just can't decide—oh, wait." She looked at him. "There's been something I've completely missed the *whole* time I've been busy falling in love with you." Her eyes narrowed to slits. "I want to see something, and I want to see it *now*." She stuck out her index finger and poked him in the chest. "And get your head out of the gutter, you naughty boy. Trust me"—her grin was wicked—"if I could do *that,* you'd be in big trouble. But *you* know what I want to see. And I *so* mean it, Gawan of Conwyk, Angel Extraordinaire."

Oy. He knew just what she meant, the wily girl. "You are a shrewd wench, Eleanor Jane Morgan."

"And you like that," she said, nodding.

"Nay. I *adore* that." He felt a pang of emptiness take over him, and the sense of losing her washed over him like a big salty wave from the North Sea. He grabbed the cloak from the hall closet and wrapped her tightly. "If you're going to make a spectacle out of me, I should need a bit of stretching room." He gave her a peck on the nose. "Then I'll sequester you in my chambers for the rest of the eve and force you to tell me every childhood story you can recall." And he'd pray it could last all night.

Ellie knew she was fading. *Knew* it. She didn't yet have that feeling of desperation, like the one a person probably had when drowning. But she knew she didn't have long. And she was going to make sure Gawan did *not* know it. Or at least didn't dwell on it.

He'd given her a gift, one she might not remember later, but by golly, she remembered it now. She had her whole family here, and if something went wrong and she couldn't be found, or if she didn't make it, she'd have had the opportunity to see them one last time because of Gawan. And while they'd not made physical love, he'd not been stingy showing her how much he loved her. It all seemed so surreal, falling for each other that fast. Yet, for her, it felt *right*. Righter than right, even. It felt *perfect*.

Gawan walked close beside her, his arm not too tight around her, and guided her across the glowing, glittery winter wonderland of Castle Grimm. With the tall gray Grimm towers, and that giant mouth of a portcullis, it truly did look like something out of a fairy tale. On they walked to the courtyard, where in the spring dozens of flowers bloomed, Gawan said, and the border bumped straight up to the edge of the cliff. The moon hung over the choppy North Sea, and a light sprinkling of snow fell steadily. Gawan had told her how uncanny it was to get snow—and this much of it—this time of year. *Uncanny,* he'd said.

For Gawan of Conwyk to find *anything* uncanny was, well, uncanny.

"Are you sure you want to see this?" he asked.

Ellie stopped and cocked her head. "Are you kidding? Of course I want to."

Gawan guided her to a stone bench set amidst the rosebushes overlooking the sea. "You sit here. I'll need to stand back a ways." He unbuttoned his coat. "Promise me you won't scream. 'Tis overwhelming, the sight of them."

"I won't scream."

He gave a nod, dropped his coat and shirt, and looked at her, just before he walked off. As the moonlight painted his broad, muscular tattooed chest in a pale glow, and his shoulder-length curls tossed about him in the wind, Ellie thought she'd never seen anything so breathtaking.

Only she hadn't seen a medieval Welsh warlord who had gained Angel status call forth his useless yet magnificent reminders that he'd done something extraordinary, once, several lifetimes ago.

And there, with the tumultuous North Sea roaring behind him and snowflakes falling about, stood Gawan of Conwyk. Born in A.D. 1115, died in A.D. 1145. Honorbound by his knightly vows, awarded in death a pair of Guardian's wings to symbolize his selfless deeds. And as he closed his eyes and said the strange words that carried to Ellie's ears only because of the fierce midwinter's wind blowing directly at her, those wings of Gawan's unfolded from their hiding place within his shoulder blades, spanned nearly twelve feet tip to tip, and they—

he was the most astounding and glorious sight she'd ever beheld.

Not for the first time since meeting the man, Ellie found herself speechless. Humbled.

And within the blink of an eye, he'd retracted those wings and was striding closer to her silently, and when he got to her, she helped him into his shirt and coat, and he embraced her, his mouth buried in her neck.

"I didn't frighten you, did I?" he asked against her skin.

Ellie held on tight. "I'm never scared with you." And she wished she could stay there, enclosed within his arms, forever.

"Even that wouldn't be long enough for me," Gawan whispered in her ear.

"Stay out of my head, Conwyk," she said, and he chuckled.

And she cried.

By the next afternoon, Gawan thought he'd lose his bloody mind. Ellie could recall little about the research that had brought her to England, and by the saints, he'd gone into every single head of every man, woman, and child in the area. And he was still no closer to finding Ellie's live self. They'd searched dozens of caves with no luck. The snowfall had picked up to a steady downfall of white, but it wasn't overbearing. Gawan, Ellie, and the Morgans met Tristan and his men in the village, where they'd passed quick introductions, leaving out that everyone except Jameson and Andi were well over seven hundred years old. They split into groups, a Morgan riding with each group.

Rick Morgan, Nicklesby, and Sir Kail, along with Ellie, rode with Gawan. Since Nicklesby and Kail could see Ellie, they rode in the backseat of the Rover, leaving Ellie to sit by the window, whilst her sire rode up front.

The Dreadmoor knights had decided to drive a bit

farther inland, while Tristan and his group took the coastline north of the village. Gawan took the coastline south. A nagging feeling pitted his gut. He felt Ellie's live self was close to Grimm. Already they'd combed a goodly portion of the beach. Gawan, with Ellie by his side, had just exited a small cave when he scanned the coastline for the hundredth time. Frustrated, he cursed.

"Why in bloody hell can't we find you?" he said, his voice rising above the wind. " 'Tis maddening."

Ellie, who'd been standing beside him, leaned against him and tugged his head down to her lips. "I love you, Sir Gawan."

Gawan's heart stood still as he closed his eyes, taking a calming breath. "And I you, Ellie of Aquitaine." He held her for a moment, then sighed. "I want to revisit that farm up the way again."

"We've been there several times already," she said. "Didn't the constable say he thought they owners left for the winter?"

"Aye. At this point, it wouldn't hurt to have another look. 'Tis one of the closest homesteads to Grimm's land."

Ellie nodded, and together with the rest, they climbed in the Rover and drove a short distance down the coastline, then turned inland and drove several kilometers toward the cluster of stone buildings that made up an old working farm. Gawan had known the previous owners. He'd not yet met the new ones, although they'd searched the buildings high and low.

As they drove into the lane and made their way up to the main house, Gawan spotted the tail end of a truck sticking out of the stable entrance. "That truck wasn't here before. Maybe someone is here." He stopped the Rover, put it in park, and got out. The others followed.

As he inspected the truck, Gawan's insides froze.

Bent side-view mirror. Missing headlamp.

"Christ."

"What is it?" Ellie said.

The others gathered around.

"This truck nearly ran me off the lane the night I found Ellie." He took her by the hand and moved toward the house, giving a quick glance to Rick, Kail, and Jameson as he strode across the gravel lane. "Hold anyone you come across."

They split up, and Gawan and Ellie went to check the house. After several sharp raps, they waited for someone to answer the door. No one did.

"Maybe they've already come and gone," Ellie said. "They may have just left that old truck in the barn."

"Mayhap. But I'm not leaving here until I'm sure." He continued around the house, Ellie close to his side, and checked the windows, even a small garden house just off the back. Nothing.

Until Gawan saw the curtain move.

He froze, squeezed Ellie's hand, and whispered close to her ear. "Stay here. Someone's just there, upstairs. I'll be right back."

"Okay."

Gawan knew he'd have to use coercion to excuse himself from breaking into the house, but he'd not leave until he'd asked a few questions of the person peeking out that window.

The front door was locked, but Gawan wasn't wasting any time. With two hard kicks, the door cracked, and with a final shove, the old door door fell off its hinges.

It was silent within. Silent, with a heavy stale scent of musk and cigarette smoke. Easing across the sparsely furnished room, he took the stairs two by two, not caring how much noise he made doing it. Upstairs there were three doors. One closed, two open.

He went straight to the closed door, flung it open and stepped inside. No bed, no furniture, only a closet door. Closed.

He strode over and flung it open.

Inside, a woman crouched. She jumped up, screamed, and leapt out, sobbing, cursing, arms flailing.

Gawan grabbed her arms and restrained her. She appeared to be in her midfifties, with graying hair pulled back at the nape; the evidence of a harsh life lined her eyes and mouth. With his mind, he commanded her: *Stop flailing about, woman, and calm down. I'll not harm you. Be still, and listen to me.*

She did.

Have you seen a young woman, American, with reddish-brown hair?

The woman, whose wide eyes were staring straight at Gawan, nodded.

Just at that moment, a thundering of footsteps sounded up the staircase. Moments later, Kail came through the door.

"By the saints," Kail said.

"Find anyone else?" Gawan asked.

"Aye. Out in the stables. So far into his cups, he's barely breathing. Rick Morgan is making sure he doesn't die before you question him."

"Ellie?"

"With Jameson."

Do you know where the young American woman is? Gawan said to the woman silently.

Again, she nodded.

Gawan's gut twisted. *Where?*

With a sharp Cockney accent, she answered. "Standing stones, up the way on the cliffs. In the kirk."

You stay here, quiet, with this man, Kail. Sit you downstairs and do not move.

"Yes."

"Bleeding priests," Gawan said. "Kail, stay here with her and the drunkard."

"Where is she?" Kail asked, grasping the woman by her elbow and leading her out.

"Stones of Tenish."

Gawan hurried down the stairs and started to run. Outside, he grabbed Ellie's hand and pulled her along.

"Jameson, go relieve Rick and send him to the Rover."

"Where is she, sir?" Jameson asked.

"Tenish. Hurry."

"What's going on?" Ellie asked breathlessly as she ran alongside him.

"I'm not sure, girl. Just come with me." He didn't want to cause her worry, and by the saints, he wasn't sure just what he'd find.

At the Rover, he and Ellie got in, and Rick, running out of the stables, jumped in the backseat. He didn't say a word.

Blessedly.

It didn't take them long to get to the stones. Gawan's heart was in his bloody throat, and Ellie must have known how worried he was, because she'd slipped her cool fingers between his and squeezed.

Gawan got out, ran to Ellie's side, and brought his mouth down on hers for a fierce kiss. "Wait here, love. I'll be right back."

He didn't wait for an answer. He crossed the lane and ran and didn't turn around; he didn't look over his shoulder. Saints, it'd been before his eyes the whole bloody time, yet he'd been blinded—even with Ellie's subtle clue.

Dark. Hay. Clover. Dampened stone. Earthy.

Over his shoulder, he heard Rick shout, and as Gawan ran up the gentle slope of the frost-covered hill, he thought of nothing, save what he may find.

Patches of ice made his boots slip, and he caught himself more times than he cared to count with the palms of his hands as he scrambled to the top.

At the top, the sea wind furiously whipped stinging snow at his face, but Gawan lowered his head and plowed straight into it, weaved through the ancient standing stones Ellie had so admired weeks ago, and made his way to the dilapidated old kirk, just down the other side of the slope.

Ducking through the doorless archway, Gawan skidded in at a full run, one hand already groping the mobile clipped to his belt. Dread washed over him as he went deeper into the old stone building, and the shafts of dull winter light coming through the hole-filled roof afforded him little vision.

He didn't need it.

Even though he knew Ellie wasn't dead, he—a bloody warrior, for Christ's sake—braced himself for what he'd find. Even that didn't stop his breath from catching in his lungs when he saw two booted feet just inside a small alcove, near the back of the kirk. His throat thickened so he could barely swallow.

His fingers flew over the mobile numbers. Tristan answered. "Tell me."

"Standing Stones of Tenish. Call the medics, but if they're not here by the time I get her down the slope, they'll have to catch me."

Gawan shoved the mobile in his pocket and squeezed into the alcove. 'Twas dark—nigh onto black—but he needed no light. Ellie was going to bloody live and he was going to get her out *now*.

She made no noise at all, not even when he touched her face and called her name. 'Twas then he realized they couldn't both get out of the alcove together. He swore, prayed he wasn't doing more damage, and then squeezed back out of the slight crack in the rock, grasped her ankles, and pulled her straight out. Not even then did she make a single sound. Christ, had she been in this leaky kirk the whole time? Or had that woman kept her in that drafty old homestead?

There, in the disjointed beams of gray light, Gawan quickly took inventory of Ellie, still wrapped in several wool blankets. Just as he'd done when they'd first met, he ran his hands over her limbs, her hips, making sure nothing was broken, and by Christ, nothing seemed to be out of alignment.

What, by the saints, had happened to her?

With no other thought save getting Ellie somewhere warm, he picked her up—by saint's blood, she was light as a feather—and made his way over the rocks and dirt of the kirk floor.

"Cara 'ch, Ellie Morgan of Aquitaine," he said against her cheek as they walked out of the old kirk. "Forever."

When he glanced up, Rick Morgan was rushing toward him.

"Jesus Christ," said Rick, coming up beside yet not blocking Gawan's descent. "Nor."

It was only then that Gawan looked up, then around, and noticed he'd taken something very much for granted.

The In-Betwinxt Ellie—*his* Ellie—was gone.

He'd found her live self, and now the two were one.

Even as he heard the medics' sirens blaring in the distance, his heart ached. He was grateful to have found her, yet inside, a hole was being ripped wide open.

And on that snow-covered hill, amidst thousand-year-old standing stones, a piece of him died.

Thirty

"Gawan, close your eyes for just a minute," Andi said. "I'll wake you up when the doctor comes in."

"Aye," said Tristan, "you can't just sit there, leaning on your knees with your head hanging down. You'll get a bloody crick in your neck."

With a hefty sigh, Gawan leaned back in the chair and rubbed his stubbled jaw. "I'll be fine." He glanced around.

The waiting lobby was full. Nigh onto every soul at both Grimm and Dreadmoor filled the place, not to mention the four Morgans. Some stood against the wall; some sat on the carpeted floor, backs to the wall.

Rick Morgan sat, much as Gawan did, forearms resting on his knees, head bowed. Once, he'd lifted his head and glanced at Gawan. The worry etched into the man's face grew deeper by the second. He'd given Gawan a slight nod, then had gone back to staring at the space between his feet.

Even Nicklesby, Gawan noticed, sat very still in a corner chair, simply staring. Jason sat with Ellie's sister; both were quiet. Everyone looked exhausted.

It had been a night from hell.

After the medics had all but pried Ellie from Gawan's arms, they'd rushed her to the infirmary. After quick X-rays, and CT scans of Ellie's head and body, they'd rushed her into emergency surgery. While her arms and legs were uninjured, and her head, surprisingly, hadn't suffered any mishap, she had acquired multiple internal injuries, which, had she not been found when she had, would surely have taken her life.

The constable had arrived and taken the woman at the farm and her drunken husband into custody. While the man had still been unconscious with drink, the woman confessed everything.

Her husband had struck Ellie with his truck that night Gawan had found her. Fearful of being sent to jail for drunk driving or, worse, vehicular homicide, he brought Ellie to his wife and forced the woman to take care of Ellie. They'd moved her back and forth from the farm to the kirk, afraid of their secret being found out. Ellie could not have lasted on her own, without food, water, warmth. So for that, Gawan was eternally grateful to the woman.

Still, they had no idea why Ellie had been on Grimm's lane. That the man had nearly run Gawan off the road while carrying an unconscious Ellie in the back of his truck made Gawan's stomach ache.

And now she fought for her very life.

All those concerned about Ellie had been directed to wait in the intensive care waiting lobby until her surgery was completed. Which, thought Gawan, was taking bloody forever. The medics had taken her at close to five the evening before, and now 'twas nearly four in the morning.

For the hundredth time, he rose and began to pace. Shoving a hand through his knotted hair, he rubbed his eyes and walked to the window. In twenty hours, his retirement would take effect. And while he knew he wouldn't remember later, he wanted to know now that Ellie would be well and healthy. 'Twas making him daft, the waiting, and the *click click click* of the minute hand on the clunky old wall clock echoed so loudly in the lobby, he forced himself not to yank it from the wall and break it.

"Mr. Morgan?"

Everyone sitting stood up.

Rick Morgan crossed the floor, and as he passed Gawan, he inclined his head. "Come on."

Appreciation swept over Gawan, for the man certainly didn't have to allow Gawan to listen in on a personal family matter. Out in the hallway, the doctor waited. He looked weary, Gawan noted. And before Gawan could hop into the other man's head, he spoke.

"Your daughter is in critical condition, Mr. Morgan," he said, meeting Rick Morgan's eyes with a steady, forthright gaze through a pair of spectacles. "I don't know how she bloody made it as long as she did. Her lung was punctured by a fractured rib, and her spleen had ruptured. And the drastic shock she was in—well"— he glanced at Gawan—"it's a miracle she made it."

Rick Morgan held his younger daughter close. "Is she going to continue to make it?"

The doctor placed a hand on Rick Morgan's shoulder. "This is a critical time for her, I'm afraid. She's young, and prior to this, she was healthy, so her chances are good. She's stable right now. But given what she's been through—" He squeezed Rick's shoulder. "We'll see."

Once the physician left, a nurse dressed in blue trousers and tunic walked up and smiled. "Are you the Morgan family?"

Rick Morgan nodded.

"Two can come back," she said.

"Just two?" Ellie's brother Kyle said.

"I'm afraid so. ICU regulations." She glanced around. "Which two? You can follow me."

Gawan locked eyes with the nusre. *Five can come in and stay at all times, even during nonvisitors' hours, if they wish. Let your coworkers know the physician says it's all right.*

"Okay," she said, eyes wide. "You can all follow me."

Rick Morgan looked at Gawan, and then silently followed the wide-eyed nurse. As they passed the small nurses' station in the center of the ward, Gawan willed them each to let the Morgans and him stay on in Ellie's room, just for good measure.

Gawan was in no way prepared to see his Intended the way he now saw her: tubes, beeping machines, her face pale, and a ventilator doing Ellie's breathing for her. Aye, he knew the names of such machines, and he hated seeing them strapped to her.

Ellie's sister cried and held her hand.

Her brothers, flanking Ellie's sides, just stood there, silent, their hands resting on the covers beside her.

Rick Morgan's face had blanched, and as big as the man was, Gawan noticed the trembling in his hands as he swiped back a bit of Ellie's hair. "Christ, girl," he said, his voice cracking. "Christ."

Gawan stood back, near the foot of the bed, and watched Ellie's chest rise and fall with each horrible click of that machine. He watched for as long as he could stand it, before he simply closed his eyes.

And so it went on like that, all day long. The Morgan siblings went in and out, graciously allowing others to replace them. Only Rick Morgan and Gawan remained constantly. The Dreadmoor knights took their turns coming to see Ellie, but none of them stayed long. Only Jason, who by the bloody saints looked as pale as Ellie, lingered a while, whispered something in her ear, and then left.

Hours passed by, and Gawan didn't sit—not one minute of them. He could do nothing, save stand beside Ellie, hold her hand, and pray she'd make it. Once, when Rick Morgan stepped into the garderobe, and no others were about, Gawan whispered into Ellie's ear, *"I mewn hon buchedd a I mewn I 'r 'n gyfnesaf, Adduneda 'm cara atat forever 'n ddarpar."* 'Twas a heartfelt verse in his native tongue, and he prayed that, even though she was deep in slumber, she might hear it. He supposed he'd never know.

'Twas hours later when Nicklesby touched his arm. "Sir, are you aware of the time?"

Gawan glanced at the clock. Nearly six p.m. "Nay, not until just now."

"You've only a few more hours remaining," Nicklesby said, his voice quiet. "I know this is passing sorrowful, Sir Gawan."

"I know what needs to be done, my friend," Gawan said, grasping Nicklesby's bony shoulder and giving a thankful squeeze. "Not yet, though."

"Poor lamb," he said, casting a glance at Ellie. "I'll be just outside, if you need me." Then he left.

By the next hour, everything changed drastically.

'Twas Rick Morgan, Andi, Tristan, and Gawan in Ellie's room when her body jerked. That blasted intubator began to shriek, and within the next second, the monitor indicating her heartbeat let out a long, solid scream. Gawan knew well and good what that meant. He and Rick Morgan yelled, "Nurse!" at the same time.

The nurse ran in, took one look at Ellie, pushed past Gawan, and slammed her fist against a round silver button on the wall, sending off an alarm overhead.

A code was called.

Gawan was losing Ellie.

The curtain to Ellie's room was yanked, and in a matter of seconds, the room was filled with all sorts of hospital staff, squeezing past one another to get to her. A doctor—not the one who had performed the surgery—ran in and yelled, "Someone get these people out of here!"

And then what his Ellie would have termed a Fiasco ensued. Again.

Because by the bloody saints above, Gawan wasn't going anywhere.

While he didn't want to interfere with Ellie's care, Gawan knew he could not leave. Not for one bloody second. He willed the doctor and other staff to ignore everyone else and simply do their jobs, which they did.

Meanwhile, everyone from the waiting lobby poured

out to stand in wait by Ellie's room. Even the Grimm ghosts had shown up.

Gawan paced, glanced over shoulders, and swore. Everything was chaotic, Bailey was crying, Andi was crying, and the men were cursing in various languages.

Gawan lurked into the physician's mind.

She's gone.

"Nay!" Gawan yelled at the doctor. "Stay your course—do you hear? Keep to your bloody task!" Fury rolled inside him like a great North Sea wave, his insides burned with it, and as he watched the lifeless body of his truly Intended lay there, unresponsive, Gawan let out a battle cry he'd not released in centuries.

And as all eyes turned to him, everything, everyone in Ellie's room grew completely silent. No beeping machines, no curses, no commands from the doctor, no weeping. Silence.

With his eyes locked on Ellie's face, he released something else. An ancient Welsh verse. Rather, a plea. A *barter*.

His life force for Ellie's.

And just that fast, without hesitation, it was done.

A white light boomed into the room, and silently, everyone squinted against its brightness. The stillness was deafening.

Like a bolt of lightning, the memories Gawan had shared with Ellie of Aquitaine flashed through his mind at top speed, yet he saw each one with perfect clarity. And just at that last second, that last breath of a heartbeat, just before Gawan of Conwyk vanished into thin air before the entire ICU, Ellie opened her eyes, and their gazes locked.

And then Gawan disappeared.

Ellie blinked and looked around. After several more blinks, her vision cleared, somewhat, and she wondered where she was and why so many people she didn't even know were standing around, staring at her.

All at once, as if she'd been in a soundproof room and someone had flung open the door, disjointed, loud noise crowded in, and before she let her eyes drift shut, she met the gaze of her dad, who gave her a smile, although she thought he looked as if he'd been through absolute hell.

She sincerely hoped she hadn't caused that look.

Before she could investigate that notion, a heaviness fell over her, and she drifted off into a hard, fast sleep.

Thirty-one

Northeastern England
A Midsummer's Eve
Six months later

"**B**y the by, sir," Nicklesby said, running this way and that, and straightening Gawan's already-straightened tunic, "you always want to present your very best in *any* given situation, aye?"

Gawan frowned at Nicklesby. "Will you cease with your bothersome nagging? I'm just going to the bloody bookstore." Gawan pushed the wiry man away and headed across the hall. "Bleeding priests," he muttered.

"Forgive my boldness, sir, but ever since your retirement, you've been passing cranky," Nicklesby said with a sniff.

"Stodgy is more like it," said Sir Godfrey, sifting through the stone wall. "I daresay you're more than difficult to live with of late."

Gawan grunted, ignored the frilly spirit and strode toward the front door. "Mayhap it has to do with the lot of whiny whelps I've been forced to babysit these past few months."

As he neared the entrance, he passed the large oval mirror hanging just near the doorway, stopped, and backed up. First, he glanced at his visage, then tilted the mirror away from the wall, just a bit, and peered behind it. With a shrug, he moved on. "I'll return shortly."

With that, he left.

Nicklesby let out an enormous sigh and stared at the doorway. "Godfrey, 'tis far more difficult to manage than I thought 'twould be. 'Tis a miracle, his return. But he's not himself."

"Aye," Godfrey said. "Passing odd, to think he recalls centuries of things, even being a bloody Angel."

"Just not his charges," Lady Follywolle said. " 'Tis breaking my heart, in truth." She sniffed and dabbed her eye with a lace square. "I can barely take it another moment!"

"Here, now, Millicent," Godfrey said, patting her shoulder. "We're lucky to have him back at all. If it weren't for all of that bloody chivalry, he'd have remained"—he jabbed his finger Heavenward—"up *there.*"

Nicklesby shook his head and *tsk*ed. "So right, Godfrey. 'Tis frightfully quiet round here of late, though." He inclined his head. "Look at young Davy there. He just sits by yon window and peers out. He barely even plays with Cotswald."

"The lass fares well, though, aye?" Godfrey asked.

Nicklesby nodded. "Indeed, she does. A full recovery. And as we'd hoped, she's following her previous footsteps."

"Only Sir Tristan has the matter under control, aye?" Lady Follywolle said. "Lady Ellie certainly suspected something, or someone, before. Her getting hit by that truck may have been an accident, but she didn't willingly take a midwinter's swim in the North Sea."

"Aye, in truth, the entire garrison has been on guard, including young Jason and another, standing sentry at her cottage," Nicklesby said. "A fine lot of lads, those."

"Indeed," Godfrey said. "What if neither Ellie nor Gawan remembers?"

Nicklesby frowned. "Godfrey, you old poop. 'Tis naught but our high hopes that she and Sir Gawan will even notice each another." He *tsk*ed again. "It goes completely against the Order's rules, in truth."

"And her family?" Lady Beauchamp said. "They don't remember any of us either?"

"Nay," Nicklesby said. "An odd set of laws, yet laws just the same. I imagine 'twould be difficult for so many to assume no memory of us, versus *having* no memory of us, aye?"

"And you're sure Elgan, Fergus, and Aizeene know what to do?" Godfrey said.

"Aye, they know," Nicklesby said. He sighed again. "They've yet another meeting planned tonight with the Order. I mean, the boy gave his life force, for pity's sake. Still, we can only hope." He looked at them. "Nothing is guaranteed, and you know how stodgy the board members can be."

They all sighed at once, as though agreeing, and then Lady Follywolle cocked her head, her coiffed swan giving a nod. "Have any of you noticed Sir Gawan's obsession over the hall mirror of late?" She shook her head. " 'Tis strange, in truth, the way he looks it over."

"Aye," Godfrey said, "I've seen him do it more than once meself."

" 'Tis many a thing I've noticed," Nicklesby said, "that nags him, yet he has no true memory of." He turned and headed back to the larder. "Although I can't imagine what it is with the mirror." He shook his head. "Passing odd, indeed."

Eleanor Morgan took a long, deep breath of crisp air, smiled, and then turned and jogged up the walkway. She could hardly believe it—she was in the northeast of England! And, to her dad's dismay, she was there alone.

She snorted. And under the name of Mary Hatch.

She was so—what was the word she was looking for? *Shrewd.*

Yep. Definitely that. And in her line of work, you had to be. Especially when dealing with criminals—even if they were almost a hundred years old.

Not that a genealogist came across many criminals. But she had. And it was *personal*.

As she ran, she glanced over at the sea, just beyond the buildings of the village. *Wild*, she thought, *untamed*. The North Sea. Even the name sounded lethal. *Beautiful*.

She slowed to a walk, regulating her breathing. She couldn't believe how good she felt after having been in the hospital for so long. So much of what had happened was missing, which the doctor told her was quite normal. One day, she'd just awakened in the hospital. They'd told her she'd been out for a run, and a car had swerved too close. Maybe it was a good thing she remembered zilch about it.

The bookstore's bell tinkled when she pushed the door opened and entered the cool, darkened interior. Mahogany wood and wall-to-wall books, with an antique lamp here and there, made the place warm and inviting. Three men stood behind the podium, poring over an old tome. They looked up when she walked in.

"Aye, good eve to ye, girl," one said. "Can we help ye?"

She thought the *ye* was adorable. "Yes. I'm Mary Hatch. You called and said I had a book in?" She felt guilty giving a fake name to the man's face, but if her great-grandfather's notes meant anything, the Langstons weren't people to play around with. The less everyone else knew about her, the less *they'd* know.

"Aye, sweet maid," the second man said, giving her a big white smile. He was tall, very dark-complected, bald, with a slim goatee. She thought his accent was just *it*. "Have a look round whilst we get it for ye."

"Och, aye," said the third man, who grinned a split-toothed grin. "Have a look round. And do take your time."

"Thanks." Eleanor unzipped her running jacket and

started to browse. Tons of old volumes filled the store, and she thought she might just want to get a cot and stay the night. Turning down one aisle, she looked through the local history section, breathing in the delicious smell of old leather and aging pages.

At the front of the store, a bell tinkled, announcing the arrival of another customer. She leaned back on the heels of her sneakers and peeked around the end of the aisle, but all she caught were the long, jean-clad legs of some guy.

She went back to browsing.

But what could she say? She was nosy. So she listened.

"Good eve to ye, Lord Grimm. How fare ye?" one of the book guys said.

"Passing fair."

Lord Grimm? Funny name. Cute accent, though.

She went back to browsing.

"Err, Mary Hatch? Your book?"

Eleanor lifted a volume from the shelf. "Thanks, guys. I'll get it in just a sec." She looked at the old leather-bound in her hand. *Naughty Ladies of the 1680s.* She opened the page. *Ooh, interesting.*

"Just a minute, Lord Grimm. Don't you wish to browse?" said one of the booksellers. "I've a few new selections on medieval armor and weaponry."

"Mary Hatch! Please, come retrieve your book!" one of the others said.

"Posthaste!" the third said.

Sheesh. Talk about pushy salespeople. "Okay, okay. Hold your bleeping oysters, fellas. I'm coming." Putting the book beneath her arm, Eleanor walked toward the front of the bookstore, just as the bell tinkled again.

When she got to the end of the aisle, *Lord Grimm's* heels were just turning the corner outside.

With a smile, she turned to the book guys. "Sorry. Here's one more, okay?" She handed them the *Naughty Ladies* book, pulled the money out of her running pants, and paid for her purchase. She couldn't help but notice the solemn look on their faces. She wondered what Lord Grimm had done to tick them off.

"And a nice eve to ye, lass," the bald guy said. "Er, see ye later." He handed her the two books.

Eleanor grinned and took them. "Not if I see you first." She turned and walked toward the door.

And just as she pushed, someone from the other side pulled. Eleanor half stumbled out smack into a very large guy. Two strong arms grabbed her by the shoulders and steadied her.

"Beg pardon," he said in a fairly cute, raspy voice.

A shiver coursed down her spine, and by the time Eleanor gained her balance and looked around, all she saw was one boot disappearing into the store, the door closing behind him.

With a shrug, and a slight sense of disappointment that she'd only seen the boot, she made her way to the chip shop up the street before calling a cab to take her back to the cottage.

Nicklesby sighed into the phone's reciever. "Fergus, you poop! They were in the store together and not once did they lay eyes upon each other. I thought you had matters under control."

"Pah!" spat Fergus. "The managing of a hundred charges' 'tis easier than getting those two tae notice on another! By Wallace's sword, 'tis making me daft!"

Nicklesby sighed. "What of Aizeene and Elgan? What were those two oafs doing?"

"Trying their bloody best tae gain the lass' attention." He blew a gusty sigh into the receiver. " 'Twas no use. She had her wee nose stuck in a musty old tome."

"By the crows, very well. I'll ring Lord Dreadmoor and see about our next step."

As Eleanor sat on the deck of the cottage, facing the tumultuous North Sea and eating everything but the thick white wrap paper of her fried cod and chips, the phone rang. Balling up the paper, before she *did* eat it, she went through the back door and lifted the cordless. "Hello?"

"Hi, Eleanor!" a familiar voice said. "It's Andi. Are you busy?"

Eleanor wiped her mouth on a napkin. "Hi. Just finished eating."

It had been like a sign, or something, meeting the Dreadmoors. Andi—who was waddling around almost seven months pregnant—and her extremely handsome hubby, Tristan, happened to send out enough mass advertisement for their holiday rentals that one had ended up in Eleanor's in-box. She and Andi—who was an American, too—had hit it off immediately, and they'd even picked her up at the airport. Not only that, but they were in tight with the local constable, who now had her great-grandfather's ledger and her notes under investigation. And although she'd considered using one of her funny aliases, she thought she'd do better to give her real name. At least, with the Dreadmoors and the constable. Locally, like at the bookstore? Mary Hatch would do just fine.

"Well, do you mind if I drop by?" Andi said. "Tristan has to take care of some business, and I don't want to be bored out of my gourd."

"Far be it from me to want to be responsible for you going out of your gourd," Eleanor laughed. "Come on over."

After they hung up, she thought about Andi's husband, Tristan. A handsome guy—heck, the entire castle was filled with big, handsome guys—yet they all seemed a little odd. Off. Cute, very polite, but a bit off.

She couldn't quite put a finger on it.

Half an hour later, Tristan dropped Andi off. With a wave and a *How fare thee?* out of the window, he drove off.

She smiled at Andi as they walked through the house and onto the deck. "You know that thing about pregnant women glowing?"

Andi laughed. "Am I blinding you with it?"

Eleanor leaned against the wooden rail and smiled. "Yep. H-A-P-P-Y is written right across your forehead." And how could anyone blame her?

Andi patted her tummy, or bump, as the Brits called it, and moved to stand next to Eleanor. "I think I'm growing a whale." She pushed her hair behind her ears and grinned. "Listen. I don't have any female friends around here, and I want you to do something for me. Huge favor."

Eleanor lifted a brow. "What?"

The smile Andi gave her split her pretty face in two. "We've been invited to a party at a castle just north a ways, and I'd really like you to come."

Eleanor tapped her chin with a forefinger. "Hmm. When is it? I may not be here."

"Ha-ha, you wily girl. You'll be here." Andi cleared her throat. "It's tomorrow night. Please?"

Eleanor shoved her hands into her running jacket pockets. "I don't have anything to wear, except a business casual."

Andi patted her shoulder. "Well, it's slightly formal, but not to worry." She winked. "I've got something that'll look fantastic on you."

Blowing out an exaggerated breath, Eleanor agreed. "Oh-kay. You talked me into it."

"Great!" Andi said. "We'll pick you up around six thirty, and I'll bring the dress and shoes." She turned and gazed out over the sea. "It's different here." She looked at Eleanor. "From back home."

Scanning the seascape, taking in the briny scents, the gulls screaming overhead, the wildness of it—Eleanor nodded. "It really is." She looked at Andi. "Funny. Sometimes I think I must have dreamed about this place. England." She sighed and glanced back over the water, and watched a bird dive straight into a wave. "It's new and exciting, yet weirdly familiar."

Andi put an arm around her shoulders. "Yep, I get that feeling all the time."

The next night, Eleanor rode in the backseat of Tristan's Rover. She knew Andi and he were loaded, living in a castle and all—but sheesh! One could never tell it. Andi and Tristan—actually, their entire castle of guys— were all humble and supernice. Especially the one sitting beside her. Jason, he'd said his name was.

Out of the corner of her eye, she noticed he kept looking at her.

Cute, but way too young. Dressed in a formal black tux, he was rather handsome. *Bailey would probably drool on sight.*

As Tristan maneuvered the car up the winding coastline, Eleanor marveled at the information the police had come up with that afternoon. Constable Hurley, a local cop, had stopped by and confirmed Eleanor's leads on her great-grandfather's family, who'd left England in 1912 to come to the Americas only after changing their last name. It hadn't been easy, but after finding the marriage certificate of her grandpa Phineas' parents, woven into the leather binding of his ledger, she'd been able to uncover several things—her mother's true surname, included.

"My lady," Jason said, startling her from her thoughts, "is aught amiss?"

Is aught amiss?

Talk about déjà vu.

She gave the guy beside her a smile, thinking how handsome he looked in his suit, with his longish hair pulled back. "I'm fine, thanks. Just thinking."

He smiled and gave a short nod.

Moments later, the car began to climb the sloping lane leading toward their friend's castle. With a quick glance down at herself—golly, she hoped this black dress Andi let her borrow didn't look too *revealing*. She secured the light, gauzy black wrap about her bare shoulders and uncrossed her legs.

"You look rather fetching in that gown," Jason said, giving her a smile. "In truth."

The way he spoke just cracked her up—and every time he did speak, she had the strangest feeling come over her, gnaw at her insides.

Familiarity.

Yet she knew she'd have remembered a cutie like Jason. "Thank you," she answered with a smile of her own. "You look pretty darn good yourself."

His cheeks turned pink.

As the castle came into view, Eleanor all but gasped. "Wow."

Tall gray towers on all sides hurtled toward the sky as the ancient twelfth-century towers rose from the rock. A wall encircled it, and Eleanor could barely wait to get inside.

Lately, she'd grown a fascination for castles.

Through an enormous *gatehouse* they drove, then over a drawbridge, the sound of the wood rumbling beneath the tires of the Rover. At the end of the drawbridge, a *portcullis*, which as they drove beneath, Eleanor looked up at, awed at the large, jagged steel teeth.

Beyond that, the castle. Rather, the *keep*.

It took her breath away.

And, as she stepped out onto the gravel close to the entrance, where several other vehicles, and a few motorcycles, stood parked, another wash of déjà vu came over her.

Thirty-two

"Shall I take your wrap, my dear?"

Eleanor smiled at the sweet-looking, tall, skinny man standing just inside the entrance of the keep. Funny. With a proper black suit and bow tie, with his hair combed back neatly, his large ears poking out, and his rather long pointy nose, he reminded her of . . . of . . .

Ichabod Crane.

Taken aback by her inner thought, Eleanor handed the man her gauzy wrap. "Yes, thank you."

He gave a short nod and draped her wrap over a forearm. "I'm Nicklesby, lady, and if you find yourself needing aught, I shall be ever at the ready. You've nothing to do but ask."

Nicklesby. Perfect. "Thanks, Nicklesby."

"Come on," Andi said, pulling Eleanor's arm.

Jason was one step behind her.

As they entered the hall, the tinny sound of some old-fashioned musical instrument played a light, merry tune that for some reason reminded her of Christmas. A Victorian Christmas, maybe, like something straight out of a Charles Dickens novel.

Eleanor looked around as Andi pulled her along. High ceilings were crisscrossed with dark wooden rafters, and old-fashioned sconces decorated the stone walls. Within the mammoth stone hearth blazed two long rows of pillared candles set in black iron; they cast off the fragrant scent of vanilla. Massive tapestries hung here and there,

the stitches revealing medieval scenes that drew Eleanor's attention. She found herself pulling free of Andi.

Weaving through the throng of men from Dreadmoor,
who seemed to watch her every move, she walked up to
the tapestry and stared.

A battle scene, and a fierce one at that. Queen Eleanor
of Aquitaine, astride a powerful horse in the center, was
surrounded by her own band of armored knights and
farmers with pitchforks. One warrior, Eleanor noticed,
wore no armor, and had numerous tattoos across his chest
and back. Her stomach pinged. Wow. He looked . . .

"Eleanor, I'd like you to meet someone," Andi said,
grasping her arm and giving a tug. "Come on, he's
really cute."

Eleanor was so captivated by the tapestry that it was
several seconds before she allowed Andi to pull her away.

"Eleanor, this is—" Andi looked around. "Where'd
he go?"

Eleanor looked around, as well, and really couldn't
see a thing except the enormous guys from Andi's castle,
and that cute butler, Nicklesby, who seemed to be at her
elbow at all times. And Jason, of course, who seemed
to want to go everywhere she did.

Ever at the ready.

She wondered briefly why the guys didn't have dates.

"I'll be right back," Andi said. "Don't wander off.
Tristan!" she called, then eased into the crowd.

Eleanor moved back to the tapestry.

" 'Tis wondrous. Aye?" Jason stepped up beside her.
"Quite fierce, that one," he said, pointing at the one
warrior without armor.

"Either fierce or crazy." But Eleanor thought him
rather fascinating. After a few moments of studying the
tapestry, she clutched her small black purse beneath her
arm, excused herself from Jason's company, and headed
off to find a bathroom. After worrying her lips on the
ride over, she'd eaten off all of her lipstick.

Moving through the crowd, she made her way to the

giant staircase, just off the main entrance. She had to admit, the castle was beyond gorgeous. Modern, yet plainly medieval, its breathtaking interior matched the striking exterior. Before she left, she'd have to catch an outside view of the sea.

As she made her way to the staircase, she passed by a wall mirror, just inside a small alcove by the main entrance. As her foot touched the first step, she froze. Her skin broke out into goose bumps, and as she turned and glanced at her reflection in the mirror, she felt herself turn around and walk over to it.

At first, she just stared. Too short to see into the mirror from the floor, as it was hung a bit higher on the wall, she sat in the straight-backed chair below it. Thinking better of *that,* she turned and, with hardly any thought at all, kicked off her shoes, turned around, and stepped up onto the chair.

Staring at her reflection, she stood there, dumbstruck. What was she doing, standing on someone's chair, looking at herself? Lipstick? That was it. She just wanted to apply a bit more lipstick.

I love you. . . .

Eleanor's skin turned cold. She turned, but no one was behind her. No one seemed to be paying her a bit of attention.

I want you. Now.

This time, she couldn't turn around. Mesmerized by her crazy inner voice, she simply stared into the mirror. She stared for so long, her vision blurred. She blinked to clear it. And when it did clear, she gasped.

In the mirror's reflection, a man stood on the staircase behind her, staring back, their gazes locked.

Gawan stood, frozen to the very last step, and stared at the beauty whose gaze he couldn't tear away from. Their eyes were fastened within the mirror's reflection, and they stayed that way for a score of seconds or minutes. He knew not which.

Suddenly, it hurt to breathe, and every muscle burned as his body tensed. Unable to move, he simply stood. And stared.

Before he knew what was happening, his lips began to move—at first a whisper. A stunned, coarse whisper. The ancient Welsh verse barely reached his own ears.

Not once did his gaze leave hers.

"I mewn hon buchedd a I mewn 'r 'n gyfnesaf—" he began, his voice breaking like that of a lad of sixteen.

"Adduneda 'm cara atat forever 'n ddarpar . . ." she finished on a whisper.

In this life and into the next, I vow my love to you, forever Intended. . . .

Gawan's throat closed, his heart slammed into his ribs, and a tidal wave of memories crashed over him, yet his feet, thank the saints, began to move him closer to the woman standing barefoot upon his straight-backed chair, staring into his oval mirror. *His* woman.

His *Intended.*

It was then he noticed a tear sliding down her cheek, her body trembling. A small black purse she'd been clutching slipped from her fingers and fell to the floor.

When he reached her, he grasped her around the waist and set her on the floor. Slowly, he turned her around.

Her eyes shut tightly, tears trailing out of them and down her cheeks.

With a ragged breath, Gawan lifted her chin and fought the crushing urge to pull her into a ferocious embrace she'd not be able to tear free of. Saints, he wasn't even sure he could manage another bloody word, much less a score of them. *Christ, he remembered.*

"Ellie, open your eyes," he said. "Now."

Her body shook beneath his hands, and he squeezed a bit tighter, just in case she started to slip to the floor. Her breathing, like his own, became labored, as though she'd been running for her very life.

Slowly, her lids cracked open, and the most beautiful,

tear-soaked blue-green eyes stared back at him. Her mouth moved, but no words came out.

Gawan bent his head closer.

And then he quickly realized no words were needed.

Ellie threw her arms around Gawan's neck and pulled his head down. Their lips met, settled, and simply melded.

Wrapping his arms tightly about her, he lifted her off the floor and allowed memory after memory to assail him. He reveled in the familiar feeling of his Intended's lips against his, the taste of her on his tongue, her soft body, made just for him, pressed against him.

Then her mouth began to move against his, and he pulled back, reluctantly so, just to hear her sweet words.

"You found me," she said, in between a series of wet, soppy kisses. "Gawan of Conwyk." She bit his lower lip. "Junior Warlord." She dragged a slow kiss across his mouth. *"Angel Extraordinaire."* After a long, sensual kiss that nearly made him shout, she whispered against his lips, "My *Intended.*"

A thunderous bellow echoed across the great hall, followed by several more, and as Gawan and Ellie turned around, they found the entire Dreadmoor garrison, along with every ghostie within a hundred kilometers, standing behind them, cheering.

Ellie laughed and buried her face in Gawan's neck. He held her close and drew in a long, delicious breath tinged with the scent of her hair, her skin, *her.* "My Ellie of Aquitaine."

And then he had no choice but to let his Intended down, for there was an entire garrison of knights who wished to hug her—the Dragonhawk himself included, not to mention one special young knight in particular.

"Jason!" she exclaimed happily, and launched at the lad with more spirit than a fierce Welsh *Wode* maiden in battle.

To the lad's credit, he apparently had been awaiting

her memory to return from the moment she left England. He caught her in full leap and squeezed her thusly.

"My lady Ellie! I've missed you!" he said, and quickly found he'd have to muse over fond memories at a later date.

Not only was there many a fierce knight about the great hall who stood rather impatiently to welcome Ellie home, but a skittish Nicklesby, who all but hopped about from one foot to the other, anxiously trying to worm his way into the crowd.

She spotted the wiry man and made a beeline for the him. "Nicklesby! Oh, Nicklesby! Can you believe it?" she asked as she all but snapped the skinny man's neck in twain with her fierce hug.

Nicklesby hugged her back, unashamed as tears welled up in his eyes. " 'Tis a wondrous miracle, aye," he said. "I'm powerfully glad to see you home."

"Move there, yon bothersome Grimm steward, and let me 'ave a word with the lass!"

Ellie turned from Nicklesby's embrace and Gawan thought he'd never get used to seeing such a beautiful smile light upon her face. "Sir Godfrey! Ladies!" she said as the three Grimm spirits floated toward her.

"Lady! What about me?"

Through the crowd burst young Davy. To the dismay of several knights, the lad plowed through to get to Ellie. "I'm here!"

Ellie laughed and bent over at the waist. "Are you ready for another game of knucklebones?"

"Most assuredly, aye!" he said, just as a barking Cotswald shoved through the crowd, Nicklesby chasing after him.

Gawan's heart swelled as he watched his people embrace his woman. They'd fast learned to love her as an In-Betwinxt spirit.

They loved her more as a very much alive and breathing woman. *His* woman.

And as Gawan moved through the throng of people, he pushed Jason aside and peeled Ellie from Tristan de Barre's arms. Gawan drew her close, and over the top of her head clashed gazes with three of the most wily beings ever to set foot in his hall.

Elgan, Fergus, and Aizeene gave a short nod, their broad, knowing smiles most satisfying, indeed. They'd acquired their own retirement, after all. He couldn't wait to introduce them properly to Ellie. Indeed, that would wait.

Moving his mouth to Ellie's ear, he first kissed the soft shell, felt her shiver, and then whispered, "Forgive me, girl, but this cannot wait." He kissed her lobe, and then whispered again, "Wed me, Ell. I vow you'll not regret it."

Ellie slowly lifted her head and stared into his eyes.

The entire hall grew deathly silent.

Gawan's heart ceased beating.

Then a wide smile split her face in twain. "Yes!"

As Gawan pressed his mouth against Ellie's, their teeth clacked together as each one smiled. They laughed, but their laughter was quickly drowned out by the raucous cheering of the knights, ex-Angels, and ghosts filling Grimm's great hall.

Overcome with happiness and love, Gawan took his wife-to-be even tighter within his arms and kissed her good, well, and true.

Aye. He'd found her.

He glanced at Elgan, Fergus, and Aizeene, now joined by Nicklesby. They stood, grinning like fools. He owed them much.

With a bit of help, he'd found his Intended.

And bleeding priests and saints above, he'd not let her go again.

Thirty-three

"Eleanor Jane, stop laughing!"

Ellie tried. Honest, she did. After Rick Morgan scolded her for the third time—and they hadn't even walked down the steps yet—she drew in a long, deep breath, let it slowly out through pursed lips, and-

Started shaking again.

Giggling.

Good Lord, she couldn't help her stupid self.

It was her *wedding day.*

It'd taken only a few short weeks to plan it—with Andi's help, that was. Ellie's family had flown from home to join them in England, and while their memories from *before* the accident didn't return, they warmed up quite fast to Gawan and the rest. Rick Morgan and Gawan had discussed at length just what he thought his daughter deserved, and none of it had to do with wealth. Her father was all about propriety when it came to his girls. He'd settle for no less in a son-in-law.

God, she loved her dad.

Bailey and Andi had indeed had a ball planning the Big Day, although Bailey was a little confused as to why Ellie wanted a medieval gown. Bailey supposed, she'd said, it had to do with being in a castle and all.

Ellie smiled and let her baby sister keep on right on thinking it. As chummy as she and Jason had become, Ellie had a feeling Bailey would learn she'd just been married into a rather unusual family.

Ellie glanced down at her gown and smiled. It was the most breathtaking thing she'd ever seen: burgundy silk covered by a fine cream lace overlay, or kirtle, medieval in style, with the front of the lace parted just beneath her breasts to reveal a large flat of burgundy, and a corset beneath the gown that pushed her already-heaving boobs *way* up.

She loved it.

Bailey's and Andi's were similar in style, both a soft blush silk that looked beautiful on them.

"Come on, girl, they're ready," her father whispered. "And for God's sake, stop all that giggling."

Another deep breath, and Ellie was ready.

And down the steps they started.

It was an evening service. Candles lit the entire great hall, lending it a warm glow. Garlands of white roses and pine boughs draped the staircase, the mantel, and every flat surface.

In the corner, a dashing ghost in a top hat played a lovely old Victorian tune.

Ellie's family hadn't regained their previous memories, but they'd made new ones kind of after being reintroduced to Godfrey and the ladies. Not that they weren't still unsettled about it. But what could you do when the proof was right before your very eyes? Once Godfrey had eased his ruffled self in and out of the wall several times, another Grimm Fiasco had occurred. Afterward, the Morgan family had *sort of* accepted the fact that there was a lot more to Castle Grimm than met the eye.

As a burst of nerves hit Ellie once again, another giggle seeped out. Her father didn't say anything this time, but squeezed her arm.

At the bottom of the stairs, just as she took the last step, Ellie caught her reflection in the big oval mirror—

the very one in which she first practiced saying *I love you* to Gawan, and the same mirror that somehow dragged back their memories of one another . . . with the help of a trio of very persistant Higher-Ups. She smiled at herself. How happy Gawan of Conwyk made her.

When she stepped down and turned, her heart stood still. Gawan stood off to the side, at the head of two long lines of guests. Her breath escaped her, and her heart slammed hard against her breastbone.

Her Intended was the most beautiful man she'd ever seen. He was dressed in his original chain mail and battle tunic—black, with a large silver cross stitched into the center—his sword polished, gleaming, and strapped to his side. She all but stopped breathing at the sight of him. While her family thought it was just a medieval theme, Ellie knew differently.

And he was *all* hers.

Tristan, that devil, stood beside him, dressed in his own battle gear—as were every one of the Dreadmoor knights. Christian de Gaultiers stood next to him, and he winked at her. To know who they actually were, and *when* they came from—it astounded her. Humbled her.

Made her tremble, even.

At least I'm not laughing now. . . .

Rick Morgan took Ellie's hand and placed it in Gawan's hand. "My daughter is now yours." Her father said his practiced lines carefully. Then with a wink at Gawan, he whispered, "Good luck."

Ellie resisted the urge to elbow him.

Tristan, on the other side of Gawan, chuckled.

She almost chuckled, too, but then Gawan leaned down, and with his mail creaking, he kissed her lips and whispered against them, "You are the most fetching maid I've laid eyes in my entire thousand years' existence." His eyes darkened as he looked at her, lighting up especially when they clapped onto her heaving bosoms. The smile he gave her barely tipped the corners of his mouth, and it was *wicked*. "Try to cease your laughter, wench, whilst we say our vows, for I promise," he said, pulling her close and brushing another whisper against her ear, "you won't be laughing afterward."

Ellie gulped.

Gawan laughed.

As they walked on a scattering of white rose petals between the two lines of guests, Ellie eyed each guest and gave a smile of gratitude. The ladies Follywolle and Beauchamp, of course, were bawling into their hankies, Bailey was frowning at Ellie for her giggles, and Andi just smiled a knowing smile.

The line of guests trailed out the entrance and across the bailey to the cliffs facing the sea. The last of the guests, six on one side, seven on the other, in full medieval regalia, had their swords drawn and lifted to an arc. Ellie and Gawan walked beneath the blades, and each set of knightly eyes she met winked.

And it was there, standing in the brisk July evening air, facing a sea that had seen many goings-on at Castle Grimm over the last several centuries, where Gawan turned her toward him. And before the priest and Morgans and Dreadmoors and Grimms, and all their inhabitants, worldly or otherworldly, he said the words, first in ancient Welsh, then in English, and in his sexier-than-sexy accent. Ellie would carry them in her heart and memory forever.

"In this life and into the next, I vow my love to you, Eleanor Jane Morgan." His chocolate eyes darkened as he held her gaze. "Forever Intended."

Thank God, the laughing had stopped.

Now she cried.

And in between her tear-cracked words, Ellie repeated the same verse, first in his native medieval Welsh, for she had indeed memorized it when she was In Betwinxt, and then in English. "In this life and into the next, I vow my love to you, Gawan of Conwyk." She gave him a smile. "Forever Intended."

Tristan stepped forward and handed Gawan a beautiful garnet-and-silver ring, which he slipped over Ellie's finger. He brought his lips to hers and whispered, "*Blyth 'n ddarpar,* wife," he said and kissed her. "Eternally Intended."

From her own thumb, she pulled free the ring she'd had made for Gawan. A solid band of silver, and later, she'd show him the inscriptive pair of Angel wings and the words *Blythe 'n ddarpar* on the inside, along with their entwined initials.

As Ellie slipped the band over Gawan's finger, she whispered the same words back to him, against his lips, on an exhaled whisper, "*Blyth 'n ddarpar* to you, too, mister," she said, then felt his mouth smile against hers.

Just as Gawan moved a hand to her jaw, no doubt for a kiss that would knock her medieval slippers off, the priest cleared his throat.

"Sign here, first!" he announced, and produced a legal and very old-looking piece of parchment—their marriage certificate.

Everyone laughed.

Once Gawan signed, then held the paper for Ellie to sign, he handed the legalities back to the priest, who announced, "Now you may kiss her, lad!" And to everyone's delight, he did in fact do just that.

And amidst the hollers and battle cries and whistles that echoed across the bailey and out to the North Sea, Gawan stepped up, slid his hand behind her head, and kissed her *good.*

Epilogue

"**W**hy isn't Davy around?" Ellie asked as she danced with her husband. "I didn't notice him during the ceremony."

Gawan looked down at her, his strong hand firmly pressed against her lower back. He bent his head and whispered in her ear, "I wanted to wait until after the ceremony to tell you."

"Tell me what?"

He smiled down at her. "Come."

Ellie's stomach did a flip-flop as Gawan led her to a window seat in the far corner of the great hall. He gently pushed her to the cushion.

She lifted a brow. "What's going on?"

A smile tipped Gawan's mouth. "I couldn't have told you sooner, love. This occurred just before the ceremony began, and I didn't know myself until after the nuptials." He pulled out a slip of paper from his tux coat pocket. " 'Tis your first surprise, lady."

Ellie blinked, then took the paper and read it.

It was certified, from Tristan's solicitor.

"Read it, love," he said.

It was then she noticed Grimm's hall of guests had

gathered around her. *What is going on?* So she read the letter.

Pertaining to the true Christian surname of Phineas J. Addler, it is hereby found to be on the date of June 28, 1912, Cornelius and Katherine Crispin, along with their young son, Phineas, filed for an official, legitimate name change, to that being of Addler..

Ellie looked up. "Crispin?"

Gawan's gaze was steady. "Read on, love. The next is in narrative, but the official documents are being held by Constable Hurley."

Ellie's heart beat faster as she read. "Oh my God." She cleared her throat.

It has been found to be well and true that one younger offspring of Cornelius and Katherine, sibling to Phineas, had gone missing and was never found. Only after studying in thorough detail the ledger of one Phineas Addler, and the notes of one Eleanor Jane Morgan, that certain leads found by Ms. Morgan were to reveal the name of the younger brother, and his unfortunate demise, as well as name the murderer.

Her heart leapt to her throat.

After thoroughly investigating one Avery Langston, now ninety-nine years of age, it is revealed that due to a family row over titles and monies, the younger Crispin brother, unfortunately, witnessed the death of the older Langston boy by the hand of the younger one, both now deceased—all witnessed by Avery Langston. In turn, the Crispin youth indeed was murdered, his body thrown into the North Sea, to spare the Langston family name. This confession given by one Avery Langston.

Ellie's hands were shaking now, and Gawan took the paper from her, sat beside her and pulled her close. Emotions choked her. "Young Davy?"

"Your great-uncle," Gawan said.

"Holy-moly."

Gawan kissed her temple. "Holy-moly is right."

Rick Morgan moved forward and lifted Ellie's chin with his knuckles. "Your mom would be proud," he said. "A fine bit of research you did, honey. It took guts to come here alone."

Ellie smiled and squeezed his hand. "Thanks, Dad."

Gawan cleared his throat. "Er, wife, there's something else."

Ellie looked at him. "I'm not sure I can handle it."

A round of knightly chuckles went through the hall.

Gawan tapped her nose. "I vow you can." He cleared his throat. "No sooner did the constable call with the news, and the fax came through, than a visitor arrived at our front gates."

"A visitor?"

Gawan nodded. "I had no choice but to say him aye when he asked to come through."

Ellie stared at Gawan. "Have you been drinking?"

A round of laughter filled the hall.

With his hand, Gawan gently grasped Ellie's chin and turned it away from him, toward the crowd of merry wedding guests.

That crowd parted.

Nicklesby stood, along with Elgan, Fergus, and Aizeene. Grinning.

Then *they* parted.

A young boy stood there, hands in pockets. White billowy shirt. Black knickers, black suspenders. Black stockings, scruffy brown ankle boots. Soft hat, cocked to one side.

He broke into a wide, ear-to-ear grin.

Just before he broke into a run.

"Lady!"

Ellie jumped up from her seat and stood, staring at the very real figure running at top speed toward her. Her breath lodged in her throat, so she couldn't speak.

Young Davy Crispin skidded to a halt, just before stumbling into her. He blinked, smiled wider, and then threw his arms around her waist.

Tears streamed down Ellie's eyes as she hugged a very much alive Davy Crispin tightly, and the hall roared with cheers.

"It's all right if I live here, aye?" Davy asked, his voice muffled against Ellie's gown. He lifted his head and looked at her. "Sir Gawan says he didn't think you'd mind overmuch."

Ellie sniffed, glanced at her beaming husband, and kissed Davy on the cheek. "Do you think I'd turn down the chance for a professional knuckleboner to live in my home?" She hugged him. "Not in a million years." She grinned at him. "Don't think for a second that I'm going to call you great-uncle."

"I wouldn't think of it, lady."

Laughter filled the hall, and Davy was pulled from Ellie's embrace and shuffled around amongst the knights.

Ellie glanced at her husband, whose chocolate eyes glinted with mischief. And love.

How many more miracles could she possibly handle in one lifetime?

"They're going to hear the chopper blades," Ellie said, as Gawan held the train of her gown while she climbed into that chopper.

"Aye, but if you think there's any way in bloody hell I'm going to spend my wedding night with a lot of meddlesome medieval ghosties and knights, you're daft." He climbed in beside her and yanked the door closed. "Nosy lot, they are."

Before sitting, he leaned over and whispered to the

pilot, who then nodded and started hitting all sorts of buttons and levers before the blades began to turn.

"Where are we going?" Ellie asked, peering out of the window. "Don't you think it's rude to leave our guests?"

Gawan pulled her to him, lifted her hand, and kissed her fingers. "There's plenty of merriment to be had this eve at my hall." He smiled a slow, sexy smile. "They'll not miss us."

As the chopper lifted, Ellie looked out. "I told you they'd hear. Look at Tristan." She squinted against the waning light. "I think he just flipped us the bird."

Gawan laughed. "If he did, 'tis only because he didn't think of something so witty as whisking away his bride."

Ellie looked at Gawan, who was staring at her with the look of a starved man. She smiled. "We're married."

He did not smile. Just stared, while his eyes smoldered. "Aye, I know that."

And she studied every little detail of his handsome face: the lines at the corners of his eyes, the long lashes any girl would kill to have, and the two nicely formed brows over the sexiest brown eyes she ever looked into. And, God, those lips . . .

Nice teeth, too.

They were out over the sea now, still flying close to the coast, when the helicopter headed toward a very small island off the mainland. On it, a lighthouse; beside it, a white keeper's cottage.

Ellie looked at Gawan, and he merely smiled.

When they landed, and there really wasn't much room for *that*, the chopper lifted and flew off, leaving them on the small lighthouse island, completely alone.

With the wind blowing fiercely, Gawan, who'd shed his chain mail back at Grimm but still wore his knight's tunic and hose, and of course, his sword, led her to the cottage door, where he lifted an arm, reached over the lip of the door, and produced a key. Silently, he opened the door, then swept Ellie into his arms and stepped over the threshold.

He kicked the door shut with a booted foot.

Still in his arms, she looked at him. "You must have pull."

He grinned. "Let's just say I *know* people, and they owed me a favor." Before he set her down, he pulled her closer and kissed her, soft at first, and then his tongue swept over hers and it turned into a long, heated kiss.

He pulled back, and she could feel his heart pounding.

"We've got a bit of climbing to do," he said, and set her down.

As if she could bloody walk *now*.

He took her by the hand and led her across the one-room cottage, to a door on the side. "This way."

Through the door they went, and stepped into the shell of the lighthouse, a long, spiraling black iron stairway leading to the top.

When they did reach the top, Ellie was proud that she didn't keel over from the exertion. All that running after the accident must have done her good.

"That's the one thing I truly miss," Gawan said as he looked down at her. "Reading your thoughts."

Ellie smiled as she took the last step. "Yeah, well, shame on you for doing that, you naughty . . ."

Her words died on her lips as she reached the top and stepped into the lighthouse loft. "Oh my," she said, breathless.

The loft encircled the light tower in the center. The oil-burning lamp and all the gears still intact sat unused, untouched by time.

In the circular room, windows replaced what had once been a wide-open deck that circled the light. Gawan walked over and threw open one of the full-sized windows. Ellie saw nothing but the North Sea, heard nothing but the crashing waves against the base of the island rock, felt nothing but the pounding of her own heart.

"It's beautiful," she said, and when she turned to Gawan, the feral look in his eyes robbed her of breath.

And they stared.

Gawan, she noticed rather fast, had not spared one single detail. He'd known he wanted to take her here, and by golly, he'd done it *right*. On the floor, a big pallet of down coverlets and pillows, surrounded by fat pillared candles, served as their honeymoon suite. Nearby, a bucket of ice and two bottles of *something* inside.

"Don't worry," he said, moving closer. "I've a fridge in yon corner filled with food." He circled behind her, pulled her against him, and moved his warm mouth over her neck. "Because, Eleanor of Conwyk, I vow by the time we come up for air, you'll be vastly starved."

She gulped.

"Of course," he said, biting her earlobe, "you once claimed that *a wall would do*."

"Uh-huh," she said, bending her neck to the right, just a bit, in case he had trouble finding it.

He didn't.

Pulling her earlobe gently between his teeth, he kissed, painfully slow, the sensitive area below it. While his fingers were big, they were far from clumsy as he continued to drag his lips across her neck, and he loosened every satin-covered button on the front of her gown. His hands skimmed the burgundy silk covering her stomach, on either side of her ribs, and the outer curves of her breasts.

He was driving her crazy.

"Help me out of this gear, girl," he said, his accent heavy. " 'Twould take me far longer by myself."

First came his sword and belt, which he propped up against the window. Then the black tunic, which she helped him lift over his head and lay, alongside the sword and belt, on the floor. Next came his hose pants, or leggings, and he kicked off his boots and spurs.

"So," Ellie said, her eyes growing heavy with desire, "*that's* what a knight wears under his mail."

Gawan grinned. "Aye. One doesn't wish for certain parts to be pinched between the steel."

"Ouch," Ellie said, smiling. "Come here, warlord."

And he did, and then all of Ellie's confident humor vanished as Gawan finished removing her burgundy gown. He dropped it to the floor.

He stared at her heaving breasts, which were accentuated by the corset.

With a slowness that made Ellie's breath catch, Gawan traced the silky material just at the swell of her breasts, and then followed the boning to her hips. When he looked up, his eyes all but burned with passion.

He muttered something to her in Welsh, and Ellie had no clue what he'd said. It sounded pretty good.

Reaching behind his head, in a totally male fashion, he pulled his undershirt over and off, and tossed it on the floor.

Loose, long curls fell over his shoulders, swarthy skin covered rock-hard muscles, and those ancient battle markings crossed his chest, down his arms, and, she knew if she looked behind him, down his back. Her fingers itched to touch him.

As her corset came loose, Gawan dropped it to the floor, only to frown when he saw yet more undergarments to rid her of: her bra and panties.

But instead of ridding her of them, he pulled her against him, one hand splayed across her back, the other buried in her hair, and he angled her head just so, traced her bottom lip with his thumb, then replaced it with his mouth.

Fully alive, not In Betwinxt, Ellie's entire body tingled with new sensations, and she threaded her fingers through his soft hair and kissed him back. Although there was a slight scruff to his cheeks, his lips were soft and pliable, and they left nothing of her untasted. When their tongues brushed together and he skimmed her breast with callused hands, she nearly came unglued.

Slowly, they moved backward, and Ellie's fingers

trailed down Gawan's stomach, where she reveled in every muscle etched there, a series of ridges placed there by the vigorous swinging of a heavy sword.

And the farther down her hand trailed over that skin and rock, the more desperate his kisses became.

While still standing, Gawan stopped long enough to shed what Ellie would laughingly later refer to as his *warrior's drawers,* and then pull her down atop him, amidst the soft down blankets and pillows piled high in that antique lighthouse.

Heat shot through Ellie's body as Gawan's hands deftly found, released, and discarded first her bra, then her panties, and his hands left not a single inch of her body unexplored. He kissed her hungrily everywhere, always ending back at her mouth, yet he took an exquisite, lingering taste of her lips, of her tongue, and of that crazy corner of her mouth that had marked her for eternity as his Intended.

No words were needed between them, only their senses, and as he moved over her, he braced himself with one arm, leaving the other to touch her everywhere, and the heat rushing through her made her squirm beneath him, until finally, he lowered his head, took her mouth in a sensual kiss, and entered her in a fierce claim, muscles hard, body taut, deliciously *right.*

For a moment, he held still, fully inside her, looking deep into her eyes. "I saw you, for a split second in the hospital," his voice rasped, heavy with passion. "You looked at me, too, just before . . ."

Ellie wrapped her legs around his waist tightly, Gawan filling her even more, and she dragged a finger across his scruffy cheeks, his chin, and then his lips. She met his steady, darkened gaze. "I saw you, too. And I saw us."

He kissed her then, long, slow. "*Cara 'ch,* my wife." His voice was a hoarse whisper.

And he moved, slow at first, then uncontrolled, starved, and Ellie held on until the climax claimed her, so intense she arched, her fingers buried in Gwan's back.

His release rocked her at the same time, overpowering, and his body shook with it.

Gawan slowed then, his breath as ragged as hers, and as the remnants of their climax eased, he remained inside her, his body braced above her, beautiful brown eyes staring down at her.

"I've waited for you, Ellie of Aquitaine, now of Conwyk, for nigh on a thousand years." He kissed her then, slow, his tongue brushing hers gently. "I'll love you forever."

Wrapping her arms around Gawan of Conwyk, Ellie pulled him back for another kiss. Her very own Junior Warlord. Angel Extraordinaire. Her beloved Intended.

She looked at him, and the love she saw in his eyes made her heart tremble with joy. "I'll love you for Infinity."

And she did.

Spirited Away

Cindy Miles

Knight Tristan de Barre and his men were
murdered in 1292, their souls cursed to
roam Dreadmoor Castle forever.

Forensic archeologist Andi Monroe is
excavating the site and studying the legend
of a medieval knight who disappeared.
But although she's usually rational, Andi
could swear she's met the handsome
knight's ghost.

Until she finds a way to lift the curse,
though, love doesn't stand a ghost
of a chance.

**Available wherever books are sold or at
penguin.com**

HIGHLANDER IN HER BED

Allie Mackay

She's fallen in love with an antique bed.
But the ghostly Highlander it comes with is
more than she bargained for...

Tour guide Mara MacDougall stops at a London
antique shop, and spots perhaps the handsomest bed
ever. Then she bumps into the handsomest man ever.
Soon Mara can't forget the irresistible—if haughty—
Highlander. Not even when she learns that she's
inherited a Scottish castle.

Spectral Sir Alexander Douglas has hated the Clan
MacDougall since he was a medieval knight and they
tricked him into a curse...the curse of forever haunting
the bed (the very one that Mara now owns) that was
once intended for his would-be bride. But Mara makes
him feel what no other MacDougall has—a passion that
he never knew he'd missed.

Also Available
Highlander in Her Dreams

**Available wherever books are sold or at
penguin.com**

Penguin Group (USA) Online

What will you be reading tomorrow?

Tom Clancy, Patricia Cornwell, W.E.B. Griffin,
Nora Roberts, William Gibson, Robin Cook,
Brian Jacques, Catherine Coulter, Stephen King,
Dean Koontz, Ken Follett, Clive Cussler,
Eric Jerome Dickey, John Sandford,
Terry McMillan, Sue Monk Kidd, Amy Tan,
John Berendt...

You'll find them all at
penguin.com

*Read excerpts and newsletters,
find tour schedules and reading group guides,
and enter contests.*

Subscribe to Penguin Group (USA) newsletters
and get an exclusive inside look
at exciting new titles and the authors you love
long before everyone else does.

PENGUIN GROUP (USA)
us.penguingroup.com